D0880378

1

think like a

Dinosaur and other stories

james patrick kelly

WITH A FOREWORD BY JOHN KESSEL

GOLDEN GRYPHON PRESS ✧ 1997

For the editors who helped make these stories
Gardner Dozois, Ed Ferman, John Kessel
Shawna McCarthy, Sheila Williams

PUBLISHER'S CATALOGING-IN-PUBLICATION DATA
Kelly, James P. (James Patrick)
Think like a dinosaur and other stories / James Patrick Kelly ; with a foreword by John Kessel. — 1st ed.
p. cm.
ISBN 0-9655901-9-4 (hardcover : alk. paper)
1. Fantastic fiction, American. I. Title.
813'.54—dc20 1997 97-71966

ISBN 1-930846-20-7

First Softcover Edition 2003.

Contents

Foreword

Prince Wen Hui's cook
Was cutting up an ox.
Out went a hand,
Down went a shoulder,
He planted a foot,
He pressed with a knee,
The ox fell apart
With a whisper,
The bright cleaver murmured
Like a gentle wind.

One thing I like about Jim Kelly's stories is that when I read them I forget what I know about writing. He catches me up. To make a comparison that Space from "The First Law of Thermodynamics" might appreciate, like Eric Clapton's guitar solo on the live version of *Crossroads,* each successive moment in a Kelly story seems exactly right as it happens, but is unpredictable until it happens.

Kelly's prose is clean as a well-honed blade, his moves as pure as those of Prince Wen Hui's cook as he cuts up that metaphysical ox. The stories look simple, but reveal depths. They surprise me. They show me things I haven't seen before, and remind me of things I have seen but passed over. Like the cook in the poem, Kelly wields his cleaver with humane ruthlessness.

To me, this is the heart of it. Lots of writers are humane. Some are ruthless. Very few are both at once.

For years now I've feared that Kelly might end up as nameless as Prince Wen Hui's cook. Sure, he's often mentioned on lists of prominent SF writers, but never at the top. Part of the problem is that he's not produced a novel that ranks with the best of his short fiction. Or it may be that his novels frequently contain portions that earlier appeared as well-regarded short stories, which makes it hard for some people to read them as novels.

But the short story is not a warm-up for a novel, or a lesser art form. And of my generation of SF writers, no one writes as wide a range of stories, from SF (''Breakaway, Backdown'') to contemporary fantasy (''Dancing with the Chairs'') to grim cautionary tales (''Pogrom'') to satire (''Mr. Boy'') to romance (''Faith'') to horror (''Monsters'') to comedy (''Standing in Line with Mister Jimmy''). In the midst of the cyberpunk-humanist dustup of the mideighties, when the conventional terms of the debate held that no writer could be interested in both traditional fiction of character with the gloss of high art *and* in cutting-edge technology with an anticultural bent, Kelly was the only writer in the humanist camp to be included in *Mirrorshades,* the definitive cyberpunk anthology. He can do hardheaded extrapolation to rival Bruce Sterling, twist a plot as well as Connie Willis, develop characters as convincingly as Kim Stanley Robinson, and fashion a sentence as beautifully as Karen Joy Fowler. It's hard to draw a bead on such a chameleon, especially when he doesn't spend any time shouting from the rooftops what a great writer he is.

There's no flash, no *Sturm und Drang,* no posturing. Like the cook, if you don't pay attention you think he's only doing a job. Making dinner. Writing popular fiction. So beautifully it cuts.

As an example of humane ruthlessness, let's look at the nasty paradoxes of ''Think like a Dinosaur.'' Those of you who have not read this story yet should read it first, lest I spoil your fun.

''Think like a Dinosaur'' examines the moral consequences of a commonplace piece of science-fiction furniture, the teleporter. After an efficient and sexually suggestive frame detailing Kamala Shastri's return from the stars, Kelly flashes back to her departure three years earlier. He rapidly moves into an extended edgy conversation between Kamala and Michael Burr, the human who assists the alien Hanen in preparing migrators for teleportation.

This conversation is Kelly at the top of his form. On the most elementary level, it provides a deft incidental description of the hi-tech space station. It contains such offhand cultural surprises as the mention of married male and female Catholic priests, taken for granted in this future world. It shows Michael manipulating the conversation minute by minute to guide Kamala. Michael is hiding something, distracting her from some truth. Why?

Though we don't realize it at the time, Michael's nonstop banter, his story about Father Tom and Mother Moogoo, also sets up the theme of the story: What happens to people after they die? Are they gone, just pieces of meat? Or is there something that lingers like the spirits in Michael's graveyard anecdote, like the ghost of Mrs. Ase in Kamala's story? To the dinos such beliefs are a sign of our "baby-thinking": superstition we must abandon if we are ever to mature. The Hanen ask, if we honor dead bodies, why we don't erect memorials over our shit. (There's that ruthlessness.)

When we get to the teleportation scene (described with convincing detail, from Planck-Wheeler lengths to nanolenses and "sparkers"), we confront what has been lurking in the subtext since the first paragraph: this transporter works like a fax machine. It sends a description of the migrator that is used to create an identical copy at the destination. But the original person remains at home, and after her description has been transmitted, she is killed.

The realization snaps back through all the details we've seen, giving them new significance. Michael's job is to do the killing. He's the concentration camp guard who dispenses the Zyklon B. Kamala knows this. That's why she is so nervous. His friendly hand on her shoulder a while back?—no wonder her muscles were rigid. But Michael is capable of compassion (which is why he never told the Hanen the end of his story about his night in the graveyard), and this leads to his fatal mistake. When a glitch calls the information transfer into question, he frees Kamala from the marble rather than let her suffer in darkness expecting death any second while the Hanen figure out what went wrong with their transmission.

Then he has to kill Kamala with his own hands. To the Hanen this should make no difference. A person is information, not matter. What remains after transmission has no moral consequence—she's just a dead thing, "a bone or a feather." As long as Michael could dispose of migrators by pushing a button, though he was uncomfortable, he could keep the moral import at bay. But now he must brutally murder a living being.

Or at least it seems that he does. Kelly twists the knife one last time, reinforcing the paradox. Right after showing us Kamala's murder, in graphic detail, he brings her back to life in closing the frame story. Did Michael Burr kill Kamala Shastri, or didn't he? It depends on how you think.

The result is an idea story that pursues its premise to its conclusion with ruthless logic. A gripping horror tale. A story of human characters that raises an ethical question it does not answer.

So what? Such teleporters don't exist, probably never will.

Ah, but we, the habitual readers of science fiction, accustomed to miraculous technology that has no human consequences, are like Michael Burr sitting in front of the control panel's clean white button. SF encourages us to think like dinosaurs. To be proud of it. As David G. Hartwell has pointed out, "Think like a Dinosaur" is in dialogue with Tom Godwin's "The Cold Equations," the touchstone story of Campbell-era science fiction. The SF of Campbell's *Astounding* prided itself on its hardheaded attitude toward conventional pieties, urging us to deal with "reality" and not sentiment. Kelly pokes a little fun at the Campbellian hard-SF writers, those old-fashioned social Darwinist dinosaurs.

But are they extinct, or are they the future? The jury is still out. The exhortation to *think like a dinosaur* is both SF's virtue, and its vice.

The virtue is that we're not used to such ruthlessness. It violates conventional literature's conceptions of what is humane, shows us a view from which our customs look arbitrary. It makes us think the unthinkable.

The vice is the temptation to hubris, to think we are something more, or other, than human. Those who dare to think the unthinkable are at risk of committing atrocities, and justifying them as logical.

"Think like a Dinosaur" doesn't resolve this opposition for us, but it puts it in the strongest possible terms and leaves us to contemplate the consequences. Can we think like Michael

Burr? Is what is gained by such thought worth what is lost? What actions might such thought justify? What is the human cost of "progress"?

A story as brilliantly constructed as "Think like a Dinosaur" may leave you with the impression that the author is some kind of dispassionate technician, rather like the dinos themselves. But Kelly has written that "without doubt, the most exhilarating moment in the creation of any story is when what I see on the screen surprises me. . . . I prefer to send my people out to discover the story. If, on the road to denouement, they chance across a cave that leads to a secret empire, I let them climb down for a look."

"The First Law of Thermodynamics" contains such empires.

First off, it is a devastatingly accurate picture of the generation that came of age in the 1960s, with all its self-indulgence, its confusion, its cross of political idealism and adolescent solipsism. Its heartbreaking naïveté. The story offers nostalgia with a cutting accuracy of vision that keeps it from being indulgent. Lance's raps on drugs and politics, for instance, are painfully funny deflations of the arrogant posing of the sixties generation —and of all twenty-year-olds, for that matter—at the same time they are sad reminders of all the hard lessons Lance is going to have to learn over the next twenty years.

This is a story about pretense. Cassie pretends to be hip and carefree when she is scared by her own irresponsibility. Van pretends to be able to drive when he can't walk. Lance pretends to be profound when he's a clueless adolescent. Space pretends to be Lance.

Roger Maris, the tragic baseball-hero acid-dealing Vietnam-vet farmer, is the story's pivot. As Maris says, "When you're young, there ain't all that much of you, so you pretend there's more." The delicious irony is that this character isn't Roger Maris, it's some anonymity under so many layers of bullshit it's impossible to tell who he "really" is. "Roger Maris" is the apotheosis of someone trying to reinvent himself as superstar. And yet he makes a throw with a stone that only a major-leaguer could expect to make. What does that prove? That you can become what you pretend to be?

But what are you? When, alone in the humanities building, away from the distorting influence of his friends and of what the world thinks, Space gets the chance to make his statement, to change the world, to spray-paint on the wall the secrets of his inmost soul, all he can come up with are inane clichés. (Kelly being ruthless.) The closest Space comes to originality is the "*Maris 61/61*"—a completely apolitical assertion. In the end Space realizes he must choose a direction for his life, and sacrifice possibility in that choice. Otherwise you remain a child, a fantasy, never realized.

I love the last scene of this story, as Space walks through a door into the classroom, sees the man at the front, approaches, and in a single vertiginously beautiful 143-word sentence, falls into him. Space becomes Jack Casten, a middle-aged man with a real life in his wallet—limited, not perfect, not a superstar, but not useless. (Kelly being humane.)

And I especially love the last line, which justifies the title and transforms it, resonating back to the story's beginning, its first sentence ("He . . . had never forgotten his name before"), to Space's "all life vibrated with a common energy" and "remembering the name on his student ID card was about as important as remembering the first law of thermodynamics." The first law of thermodynamics becomes both ruling metaphor and literal truth. There is a mysterious energy—personality? character?—that abides in all life. We don't know where it comes from, where it goes, but however transformed by our decisions, throughout our lives it persists.

Wake up, America! What you hold in your hands is as stunning a collection of SF and fantasy short stories as has ever been produced.

The fact that "Think like a Dinosaur" won the 1996 Hugo Award for best novelette may indicate Kelly is finding the recognition he deserves. But in the end recognition is not the issue. Although we never learn the name of Prince Wen Hui's brilliant cook, the art remains.

Then I withdraw the blade,
I stand still
And let the joy of the work
Sink in.
I clean the blade
And put it away.

—John Kessel
Raleigh, North Carolina
5 February 1997

think like a dinosaur and other stories

think like a dinosaur

Kamala Shastri came back to this world as she had left it—naked. She tottered out of the assembler, trying to balance in Tuulen Station's delicate gravity. I caught her and bundled her into a robe with one motion, then eased her onto the float. Three years on another planet had transformed Kamala. She was leaner, more muscular. Her fingernails were now a couple of centimeters long and there were four parallel scars incised on her left cheek, perhaps some Gendian's idea of beautification. But what struck me most was the darting strangeness in her eyes. This place, so familiar to me, seemed almost to shock her. It was as if she doubted the walls and was skeptical of air. She had learned to think like an alien.

"Welcome back." The float's whisper rose to a *whoosh* as I walked it down the hallway.

She swallowed hard and I thought she might cry. Three

years ago, she would have. Lots of migrators are devastated when they come out of the assembler; it's because there is no transition. A few seconds ago Kamala was on Gend, fourth planet of the star we call Epsilon Leo, and now she was here in lunar orbit. She was almost home; her life's great adventure was over.

"Matthew?" she said.

"Michael." I couldn't help but be pleased that she remembered me. After all, she had changed my life.

I've guided maybe three hundred migrations—comings *and* goings—since I first came to Tuulen to study the dinos. Kamala Shastri's is the only quantum scan I've ever pirated. I doubt that the dinos care; I suspect this is a trespass they occasionally allow themselves. I know more about her—at least, as she was three years ago—than I know about myself. When the dinos sent her to Gend, she massed 50,391.72 grams and her red cell count was 4.81 million per mm^3. She could play the *nagasvaram,* a kind of bamboo flute. Her father came from Thana, near Bombay, and her favorite flavor of chewyfrute was watermelon and she'd had five lovers and when she was eleven she had wanted to be a gymnast but instead she had become a biomaterials engineer who at age twenty-nine had volunteered to go to the stars to learn how to grow artificial eyes. It took her two years to go through migrator training; she knew she could have backed out at any time, right up until the moment Silloin translated her into a superluminal signal. She understood what it meant to balance the equation.

I first met her on June 22, 2069. She shuttled over from Lunex's L1 port and came through our airlock at promptly 10:15, a small roundish woman with black hair parted in the middle and drawn tight against her skull. They had darkened her skin against Epsilon Leo's UV; it was the deep blue-black of twilight. She was wearing a striped clingy and velcro slippers to help her get around for the short time she'd be navigating our .2 micrograv.

"Welcome to Tuulen Station." I smiled and offered my hand. "My name is Michael." We shook. "I'm supposed to be a sapientologist, but I also moonlight as the local guide."

"Guide?" She nodded distractedly. "Okay." She peered past me, as if expecting someone else.

"Oh, don't worry," I said, "the dinos are in their cages."

Her eyes got wide as she let her hand slip from mine. "You call the Hanen dinos?"

"Why not?" I laughed. "They call us babies. The weeps, among other things."

She shook her head in amazement. People who've never met a dino tended to romanticize them: the wise and noble reptiles who had mastered superluminal physics and introduced Earth to the wonders of galactic civilization. I doubt Kamala had ever seen a dino play poker or gobble down a screaming rabbit. And she had never argued with Linna, who still wasn't convinced that humans were psychologically ready to go to the stars.

"Have you eaten?" I gestured down the corridor toward the reception rooms.

"Yes . . . I mean, no." She didn't move. "I am not hungry."

"Let me guess. You're too nervous to eat. You're too nervous to talk, even. You wish I'd just shut up, pop you into the marble, and beam you out. Let's just get this part the hell over with, eh?"

"I don't mind the conversation, actually."

"There you go. Well, Kamala, it is my solemn duty to advise you that there are no peanut butter and jelly sandwiches on Gend. And no chicken vindaloo. What's my name again?"

"Michael?"

"See, you're not *that* nervous. Not one taco, or a single slice of eggplant pizza. This is your last chance to eat like a human."

"Okay." She did not actually smile—she was too busy being brave—but a corner of her mouth twitched. "Actually, I would not mind a cup of tea."

"Now, tea they've got." She let me guide her toward Reception D; her slippers *snicked* at the velcro carpet. "Of course, they brew it from lawn clippings."

"The Gendians don't keep lawns. They live underground."

"Refresh my memory." I kept my hand on her shoulder; beneath the clingy, her muscles were rigid. "Are they the ferrets or the things with the orange bumps?"

"They look nothing like ferrets."

We popped through the door bubble into Reception D, a compact rectangular space with a scatter of low unthreatening furniture. There was a kitchen station at one end, a closet with a vacuum toilet at the other. The ceiling was blue sky; the long wall showed a live view of the Charles River and the Boston skyline, baking in the late June sun. Kamala had just finished her doctorate at M.I.T.

I opaqued the door. She perched on the edge of a couch like a wren, ready to flit away.

While I was making her tea, my fingernail screen flashed. I

answered it, and a tiny Silloin came up in discreet mode. She didn't look at me; she was too busy watching arrays in the control room. =A problem,= her voice buzzed in my earstone, =most negligible, really. But we will have to void the last two from today's schedule. Save them at Lunex until first shift tomorrow. Can this one be kept for an hour?=

"Sure," I said. "Kamala, would you like to meet a Hanen?" I transferred Silloin to a dino-sized window on the wall. "Silloin, this is Kamala Shastri. Silloin is the one who actually runs things. I'm just the doorman."

Silloin looked through the window with her near eye, then swung around and peered at Kamala with her other. She was short for a dino, just over a meter tall, but she had an enormous head that teetered on her neck like a watermelon balancing on a grapefruit. She must have just oiled herself because her silver scales shone. =Kamala, you will accept my happiest intentions for you?= She raised her left hand, spreading the skinny digits to expose dark crescents of vestigial webbing.

"Of course, I . . ."

=And you will permit us to render you this translation?=

She straightened. "Yes."

=Have you questions?=

I'm sure she had several hundred, but at this point was probably too scared to ask. While she hesitated, I broke in. "Which came first, the lizard or the egg?"

Silloin ignored me. =It will be excellent for you to begin when?=

"She's just having a little tea," I said, handing her the cup. "I'll bring her along when she's done. Say, an hour?"

Kamala squirmed on the couch. "No, really, it will not take me. . . ."

Silloin showed us her teeth, several of which were as long as piano keys. =That would be most appropriate, Michael.= She closed; a gull flew through the space where her window had been.

"Why did you do that?" Kamala's voice was sharp.

"Because it says here that you have to wait your turn. You're not the only migrator we're sending this morning." This was a lie, of course; we had had to cut the schedule because Jodi Latchaw, the other sapientologist assigned to Tuulen, was at the University of Hipparchus presenting our paper on the Hanen concept of identity. "Don't worry, I'll make the time fly."

For a moment, we looked at each other. I could have laid

down an hour's worth of patter; I'd done that often enough. Or I could have drawn her out on why she was going: no doubt she had a blind grandma or second cousin just waiting for her to bring home those artificial eyes, not to mention potential spin-offs that could well end tuberculosis, famine, and premature ejaculation, *blah, blah, blah*. Or I could have just left her alone in the room to read the wall. The trick was guessing how spooked she really was.

"Tell me a secret," I said.

"What?"

"A secret, you know, something no one else knows."

She stared as if I'd just fallen off Mars.

"Look, in a little while you're going some place that's what . . . three hundred and ten light-years away? You're scheduled to stay for three years. By the time you come back, I could easily be rich, famous, and elsewhere; we'll probably never see each other again. So what have you got to lose? I promise not to tell."

She leaned back on the couch, and settled the cup in her lap. "This is another test, right? After everything they have put me through, they still have not decided whether to send me."

"Oh no, in a couple of hours you'll be cracking nuts with ferrets in some dark Gendian burrow. This is just me, talking."

"You are crazy."

"Actually, I believe the technical term is logomaniac. It's from the Greek: *logos* meaning word, *mania* meaning two bits short of a byte. I just love to chat is all. Tell you what, I'll go first. If my secret isn't juicy enough, you don't have to tell me anything."

Her eyes were slits as she sipped her tea. I was fairly sure that whatever she was worrying about at the moment, it wasn't being swallowed by the big blue marble.

"I was brought up Catholic," I said, settling onto a chair in front of her. "I'm not anymore, but that's not the secret. My parents sent me to Mary, Mother of God High School; we called it Moogoo. It was run by a couple of old priests, Father Thomas and his wife, Mother Jennifer. Father Tom taught physics, which I got a D in, mostly because he talked like he had walnuts in his mouth. Mother Jennifer taught theology and had all the warmth of a marble pew; her nickname was Mama Moogoo.

"One night, just two weeks before my graduation, Father Tom and Mama Moogoo went out in their Chevy Minimus for ice cream. On the way home, Mama Moogoo pushed a yellow light and got broadsided by an ambulance. Like I said, she was old, a hundred and twenty something; they should've lifted her license back in the fifties. She was killed instantly. Father Tom died in the hospital.

"Of course, we were all supposed to feel sorry for them and I guess I did a little, but I never really liked either of them and I resented the way their deaths had screwed things up for my class. So I was more annoyed than sorry, but then I also had this edge of guilt for being so uncharitable. Maybe you'd have to grow up Catholic to understand that. Anyway, the day after it happened they called an assembly in the gym and we were all there squirming on the bleachers and the cardinal himself telepresented a sermon. He kept trying to comfort us, like it had been our *parents* that had died. When I made a joke about it to the kid next to me, I got caught and spent the last week of my senior year with an in-school suspension."

Kamala had finished her tea. She slid the empty cup into one of the holders built into the table.

"Want some more?" I said.

She stirred restlessly. "Why are you telling me this?"

"It's part of the secret." I leaned forward in my chair. "See, my family lived down the street from Holy Spirit Cemetery and in order to get to the carryvan line on McKinley Ave., I had to cut through. Now this happened a couple of days after I got in trouble at the assembly. It was around midnight and I was coming home from a graduation party where I had taken a couple of pokes of insight, so I was feeling sly as a philosopher-king. As I walked through the cemetery, I stumbled across two dirt mounds right next to each other. At first I thought they were flower beds, then I saw the wooden crosses. Fresh graves: here lies Father Tom and Mama Moogoo. There wasn't much to the crosses: they were basically just stakes with crosspieces, painted white and hammered into the ground. The names were hand-printed on them. The way I figured it, they were there to mark the graves until the stones got delivered. I didn't need any insight to recognize a once-in-a-lifetime opportunity. If I switched them, what were the chances anyone was going to notice? It was no problem sliding them out of their holes. I smoothed the dirt with my hands and then ran like hell."

Until that moment, she'd seemed bemused by my story and slightly condescending toward me. Now there was a glint of alarm in her eyes. "That was a terrible thing to do," she said.

"Absolutely," I said, "although the dinos think that the whole idea of planting bodies in graveyards and marking them with carved rocks is weepy. They say there is no identity in dead meat, so why get so sentimental about it? Linna keeps asking how come we don't put markers over our shit. But that's not the secret. See, it'd been a warmish night in the middle of June, only as I ran, the air turned cold. Freezing, I could see my breath. And my shoes got heavier and heavier, like they had turned to stone. As I got closer to the back gate, it felt like I was fighting a strong wind, except my clothes weren't flapping. I slowed to a walk. I know I could have pushed through, but my heart was thumping and then I heard this whispery seashell noise and I panicked. So the secret is, I'm a coward. I switched the crosses back, and I never went near that cemetery again. As a matter of fact,'' I nodded at the walls of Reception D on Tuulen Station, ''when I grew up, I got about as far away from it as I could.''

She stared as I settled back in my chair. ''True story,'' I said, and raised my right hand. She seemed so astonished that I started laughing. A smile bloomed on her dark face, and suddenly she was giggling too. It was a soft liquid sound, like a brook bubbling over smooth stones; it made me laugh even harder. Her lips were full and her teeth were very white.

''Your turn,'' I said, finally.

''Oh no, I could not.'' She waved me off. ''I don't have anything so good. . . .'' She paused, then frowned. ''You have told that before?''

''Once,'' I said. ''To the Hanen, during the psych screening for this job. Only I didn't tell them the last part. I know how dinos think, so I ended it when I switched the crosses. The rest is baby stuff.'' I waggled a finger at her. ''Don't forget, you promised to keep my secret.''

''Did I?''

''Tell me about when you were young. Where did you grow up?''

''Toronto.'' She glanced at me, appraisingly. ''There *was* something, but not funny. Sad.''

I nodded encouragement and changed the wall to Toronto's skyline dominated by the CN Tower, Toronto-Dominion Centre, Commerce Court, and the King's Needle.

She twisted to take in the view and spoke over her shoulder. ''When I was ten we moved to an apartment, right downtown on Bloor Street so my mother could be close to work.'' She pointed at the wall and turned back to face me. ''She is an accountant, my father wrote wallpaper for Imagineering. It was a huge building; it seemed as if we were always getting into the elevator with ten neighbors we never knew we had. I was coming home from school one day when an old woman stopped me in the lobby. 'Little girl,' she said, 'how would you like to earn ten dollars?' My parents had warned me not to talk to strangers, but she obviously was a resident. Besides, she had an ancient pair of exolegs strapped on, so I knew I could outrun her if I needed to. She asked me to go to the store for her, handed me a grocery list and a cash card, and said I should bring everything up to her apartment, 10W. I should have been more suspicious because all the downtown groceries deliver, but as I soon found out, all she really wanted was someone to talk to her. And she was willing to pay for it, usually five or ten dollars, depending on how long I stayed. Before long I was stopping by almost every day after school. I think my parents would have made me stop if they had known; they were very strict. They would not have liked me taking her money. But neither of them got home until after six, so it was my secret to keep."

"Who was she?" I said. "What did you talk about?"

"Her name was Margaret Ase. She was ninety-seven years old, and I think she had been some kind of counselor. Her husband and her daughter had both died and she was alone. I didn't find out much about her; she made me do most of the talking. She asked me about my friends and what I was learning in school and my family. Things like that. . . ."

Her voice trailed off as my fingernail started to flash. I answered it.

=Michael, I am pleased to call you to here.= Silloin buzzed in my ear. She was almost twenty minutes ahead of schedule.

"See, I told you we'd make the time fly." I stood; Kamala's eyes got very wide. "I'm ready if you are."

I offered her my hand. She took it and let me help her up. She wavered for a moment, and I sensed just how fragile her resolve was. I put my hand around her waist and steered her into the corridor. In the micrograv of Tuulen Station, she already felt as insubstantial as a memory. "So tell me, what happened that was so sad?"

At first I thought she hadn't heard. She shuffled along, said nothing.

"Hey, don't keep me in suspense here, Kamala," I said. "You have to finish the story."

"No," she said. "I don't think I do."

I didn't take this personally. My only real interest in the conversation had been to distract her. If she refused to be distracted, that was her choice. Some migrators kept talking right up to the moment they slid into the big blue marble, but lots of them went quiet just before. They turned inward. Maybe in her mind she was already on Gend, blinking in the hard white light.

We arrived at the scan center, the largest space on Tuulen Station. Immediately in front of us was the marble, containment for the quantum nondemolition sensor array—QNSA for the acronymically inclined. It was the milky blue of glacial ice and big as two elephants. The upper hemisphere was raised, and the scanning table protruded like a shiny gray tongue. Kamala approached the marble and touched her reflection, which writhed across its polished surface. To the right was a padded bench, the fogger, and a toilet. I looked left, through the control room window. Silloin stood watching us, her impossible head cocked to one side.

=She is docile?= She buzzed in my earstone.

I held up crossed fingers.

=Welcome, Kamala Shastri.= Silloin's voice came over the speakers with a soothing hush. =You are ready to open your translation?=

Kamala bowed to the window. "This is where I take my clothes off?"

=If you would be so convenient.=

She brushed past me to the bench. Apparently I had ceased to exist; this was between her and the dino now. She undressed quickly, folding her clingy into a neat bundle, tucking her slippers beneath the bench. Out of the corner of my eye, I could see tiny feet, heavy thighs, and the beautiful dark smooth skin of her back. She stepped into the fogger and closed the door.

"Ready," she called.

From the control room, Silloin closed circuits, which filled the fogger with a dense cloud of nanolenses. The nano stuck to Kamala and deployed, coating the surface of her body. As she breathed them, they passed from her lungs into her bloodstream. She only coughed twice; she had been well trained. When the eight minutes were up, Silloin cleared the air in the fogger and she emerged. Still ignoring me, she again faced the control room.

=Now you must arrange yourself on the scanning table,= said Silloin, =and enable Michael to fix you.=

She crossed to the marble without hesitation, climbed the gantry beside it, eased onto the table, and lay back.

I followed her up. "Sure you won't tell me the rest of the secret?"

She stared at the ceiling, unblinking.

"Okay, then." I took the canister and a sparker out of my hip pouch. "This is going to happen just like you've practiced it." I used the canister to respray the bottoms of her feet with nano. I watched her belly rise and fall, rise and fall. She was deep into her breathing exercise. "Remember, no skipping rope or whistling while you're in the scanner."

She did not answer. "Deep breath now," I said, and touched a sparker to her big toe. There was a brief crackle as the nano on her skin wove into a net and stiffened, locking her in place. "Bark at the ferrets for me." I picked up my equipment, climbed down the gantry, and wheeled it back to the wall.

With a low whine, the big blue marble retracted its tongue. I watched the upper hemisphere close, swallowing Kamala Shastri, then joined Silloin in the control room.

I'm not of the school who think the dinos stink, another reason I got assigned to study them up close. Parikkal, for example, has no smell at all that I can tell. Normally Silloin had the faint but not unpleasant smell of stale wine. When she was under stress, however, her scent became vinegary and biting. It must have been a wild morning for her. Breathing through my mouth, I settled onto the stool at my station.

She was working quickly, now that the marble was sealed. Even with all their training, migrators tend to get claustrophobic fast. After all, they're lying in the dark, in nanobondage, waiting to be translated. Waiting. The simulator at the Singapore training center makes a noise while it's emulating a scan. Most compare it to a light rain pattering against the marble; for some, it's low-volume radio static. As long as they hear the patter, the migrators think they're safe. We reproduce it for them while they're in our marble, even though scanning takes about three seconds and is utterly silent. From my vantage I could see that the sagittal, axial, and coronal windows had stopped blinking, indicating full data capture. Silloin was skirring busily to herself; her comm didn't bother to interpret. Wasn't saying anything baby Michael needed to know, obviously. Her head bobbed as she monitored the enormous spread of readouts; her claws clicked against touch screens that glowed orange and yellow.

At my station, there was only a migration status screen—and a white button.

I wasn't lying when I said I was just the doorman. My field

is sapientology, not quantum physics. Whatever went wrong with Kamala's migration that morning, there was nothing *I* could have done. The dinos tell me that the quantum non-demolition sensor array is able to circumvent Heisenberg's Uncertainty Principle by measuring spacetime's most crog-glingly small quantities without collapsing the wave/particle duality. How small? They say that no one can ever "see" anything that's only 1.62×10^{-33} centimeters long, because at that size, space and time come apart. Time ceases to exist and space becomes a random probablistic foam, sort of like quantum spit. We humans call this the Planck-Wheeler length. There's a Planck-Wheeler time, too: 10^{-45} of a second. If something happens and something else happens and the two events are separated by an interval of a mere 10^{-45} of a second, it is impossible to say which came first. It was all dino to me—and that's just the scanning. The Hanen use different tech to create artificial wormholes, hold them open with electromagnetic vacuum fluctuations, pass the superluminal signal through, and then assemble the migrator from elementary particles at the destination.

On my status screen I could see that the signal that mapped Kamala Shastri had already been compressed and burst through the wormhole. All that we had to wait for was for Gend to confirm acquisition. Once they officially told us that they had her, it would be my job to balance the equation.

Pitter-patter, pitter-pat.

Some Hanen technologies are so powerful that they can alter reality itself. Wormholes could be used by some time-traveling fanatic to corrupt history; the scanner/assembler could be used to create a billion Silloins—or Michael Burrs. Pristine reality, unpolluted by such anomalies, has what the dinos call harmony. Before any sapients get to join the galactic club, they must prove total commitment to preserving harmony.

Since I had come to Tuulen to study the dinos, I had pressed the white button maybe three hundred times. It was what I had to do in order to keep my assignment. Pressing it sent a killing pulse of ionizing radiation through the cerebral cortex of the migrator's duplicated, and therefore unnecessary, body. No brain, no pain; death followed within seconds. Yes, the first few times I'd balanced the equation had been traumatic. It was still . . . unpleasant. But this was the price of a ticket to the stars. If certain unusual people like Kamala Shastri had decided that price was reasonable, it was their choice, not mine.

=This is not a happy result, Michael.= Silloin spoke to me

for the first time since I'd entered the control room. =Discrepancies are unfolding.= On my status screen I watched as the error-checking routines started turning up hits.

"Is the problem here?" I felt a knot twist suddenly inside me. "Or there?" If our original scan checked out, then all Silloin would have to do is send it to Gend again.

There was a long infuriating silence. Silloin concentrated on part of her board as if it showed her firstborn hatchling chipping out of its egg. The respirator between her shoulders had ballooned to twice its normal size. My screen showed that Kamala had been in the marble for four minutes plus.

=It may be fortunate to recalibrate the scanner and begin over.=

"*Shit.*" I slammed my hand against the wall, felt the pain tingle to my elbow. "I thought you had it fixed." When error-checking turned up problems, the solution was almost always to retransmit. "You're sure, Silloin? Because this one was right on the edge when I tucked her in."

Silloin gave me a dismissive sneeze and slapped at the error readouts with her bony little hand, as if to knock them back to normal. Like Linna and the other dinos, she had little patience with what she regarded as our weepy fears of migration. Unlike Linna, however, she was convinced that someday, after we had used Hanen technologies long enough, we would learn to think like dinos. Maybe she's right. Maybe when we've been squirting through wormholes for hundreds of years, we'll cheerfully discard our redundant bodies. When the dinos and other sapients migrate, the redundants zap themselves—very harmonious. They tried it with humans, but it didn't always work. That's why I'm here. =The need is most clear. It will prolong about thirty minutes,= she said.

Kamala had been alone in the dark for almost six minutes, longer than any migrator I'd ever guided. "Let me hear what's going on in the marble."

The control room filled with the sound of Kamala screaming. It didn't sound human to me—more like the shriek of tires skidding toward a crash.

"We've got to get her out of there," I said.

=That is baby-thinking, Michael.=

"So she's a baby, damn it." I knew that bringing migrators out of the marble was big trouble. I could have asked Silloin to turn the speakers off and sat there while Kamala suffered. It was my decision.

"Don't open the marble until I get the gantry in place." I ran for the door. "And keep the sound effects going."

At the first crack of light, she howled. The upper hemisphere seemed to lift in slow motion; inside the marble she bucked against the nano. Just when I was sure it was impossible that she couldn't scream any louder, she did. We had accomplished something extraordinary, Silloin and I; we had stripped the brave biomaterials engineer away completely, leaving in her place a terrified animal.

"Kamala, it's me. Michael."

Her frantic screams cohered into words. "Stop . . . *don't* . . . oh, my god, someone *help!*" If I could have, I would've jumped into the marble to release her, but the sensor array is fragile and I wasn't going to risk causing any more problems with it. We both had to wait until the upper hemisphere swung fully open and the scanning table offered poor Kamala to me.

"It's okay. Nothing's going to happen, all right? We're bringing you out, that's all. Everything's all right."

When I released her with the sparker, she flew at me. We pitched back and almost toppled down the steps. Her grip was so tight I couldn't breathe.

"Don't *kill* me, don't, *please,* don't."

I rolled on top of her. "Kamala!" I wriggled one arm free and used it to pry myself from her. I scrabbled sideways to the top step. She lurched clumsily in the microgravity and swung at me; her fingernails raked across the back of my hand, leaving bloody welts. "Kamala, stop!" It was all I could do not to strike back at her. I retreated down the steps.

"You bastard. What are you assholes trying to do to me?" She drew several deep shuddering breaths and began to sob.

"The scan got corrupted somehow. Silloin is working on it."

=The difficulty is obscure,= said Silloin from the control room.

"But that's not your problem." I backed toward the bench.

"They lied," she mumbled and seemed to fold in upon herself as if she were just skin, no flesh or bones. "They said I wouldn't feel anything and here . . . do you know what it's like . . . it's. . . ."

I reached for her clingy. "Look, here are your clothes. Why don't you get dressed? We'll get you out of here."

"You bastard," she repeated, but her voice was empty.

She let me coax her down off the gantry. I counted nubs on the wall while she fumbled back into her clingy. They were the size of the old dimes my grandfather used to hoard, and they glowed with a soft golden bioluminescence. I was up to forty-seven before she was dressed and ready to return to Reception D.

Where before she had perched expectantly at the edge of the couch, now she slumped back against it. "So what do I do?" she said.

"I don't know." I went to the kitchen station and took the carafe from the distiller. "What now, Silloin?" I poured water over the back of my hand to wash the blood off. It stung. My earstone was silent. "I guess we wait," I said finally.

"For what?"

"For her to fix . . ."

"I'm not going back in there."

I decided to let that pass. It was probably too soon to argue with her about it, although once Silloin recalibrated the scanner, she'd have very little time to change her mind. "You want something from the kitchen? Another cup of tea, maybe?"

"How about a gin and tonic—hold the tonic?" She rubbed beneath her eyes. "Or a couple of hundred milliliters of Serentol?"

I tried to pretend she'd made a joke. "You know the dinos won't let us open the bar for migrators. The scanner might misread your brain chemistry, and your visit to Gend would be nothing but a three-year drunk."

"Don't you under*stand?*" She was right back at the edge of hysteria. "I am not *going!*" I didn't really blame her for the way she was acting, but at that moment, all I wanted was to get rid of Kamala Shastri. I didn't care if she went on to Gend or back to Lunex or over the rainbow to Oz, just as long as I didn't have to be in the same room with this miserable creature who was trying to make me feel guilty about an accident I had nothing to do with.

"I thought I could do it." She clamped hands to her ears as if to keep from hearing her own despair. "I wasted the last two years convincing myself that I could just lie there and not think and then suddenly I'd be far away. I was going someplace wonderful and strange." She made a strangled sound and let her hands drop into her lap. "I was going to help people see."

"You did it, Kamala. You did everything we asked."

She shook her head. "I couldn't *not* think. That was the problem. And then there she was, trying to touch me. In the dark. I had not thought of her since. . . ." She shivered. "It's your fault for reminding me."

"Your secret friend," I said.

"Friend?" Kamala seemed puzzled by the word. "No, I wouldn't say she was a friend. I was always a little bit scared of her, because I was never quite sure what she wanted from me." She paused. "One day I went up to 10W after school. She was in her chair, staring down at Bloor Street. Her back was to me. I said, 'Hi, Ms. Ase.' I was going to show her a genie I had written, only she didn't say anything. I came around. Her skin was the color of ashes. I took her hand. It was like picking up something plastic. She was stiff, hard—not a person anymore. She had become a thing, like a feather or a bone. I ran; I had to get out of there. I went up to our apartment and I hid from her."

She squinted, as if observing—judging—her younger self through the lens of time. "I think I understand now what she wanted. I think she knew she was dying; she probably wanted me there with her at the end, or at least to find her body afterward and report it. Only I could *not.* If I told anyone she was dead, my parents would find out about us. Maybe people would suspect me of doing something to her—I don't know. I could have called security, but I was only ten; I was afraid somehow they might trace me. A couple of weeks went by and still nobody had found her. By then it was too late to say anything. Everyone would have blamed me for keeping quiet for so long. At night I imagined her turning black and rotting into her chair like a banana. It made me sick; I couldn't sleep or eat. They had to put me in the hospital, because I had touched her. Touched *death.*"

=Michael,= Silloin whispered, without any warning flash. =An impossibility has formed.=

"As soon as I was out of that building, I started to get better. Then they found her. After I came home, I worked hard to forget Ms. Ase. And I did, almost." Kamala wrapped her arms around herself. "But just now she was with me again, inside the marble . . . I couldn't see her, but somehow I knew she was reaching for me."

=Michael, Parikkal is here with Linna.=

"Don't you see?" She gave a bitter laugh. "How can I go to Gend? I'm *hallucinating.*"

=It has broken the harmony. Join us alone.=

I was tempted to swat at the annoying buzz in my ear.

"You know, I've never told anyone about her before."

"Well, maybe some good has come of this after all." I patted her on the knee. "Excuse me for a minute?" She seemed surprised that I would leave. I slipped into the hall and hardened the door bubble, sealing her in.

"What impossibility?" I said, heading for the control room.

=She is pleased to reopen the scanner?=

"Not pleased at all. More like scared shitless."

=This is Parikkal.= My earstone translated his skirring with a sizzling edge, like bacon frying. =The confusion was made elsewhere. No mishap can be connected to our station.=

I pushed through the bubble into the scan center. I could see the three dinos through the control window. Their heads were bobbing furiously. "Tell me," I said.

=Our communications with Gend were marred by a transient falsehood,= said Silloin. =Kamala Shastri has been received there and reconstructed.=

"She migrated?" I felt the deck shifting beneath my feet. "What about the one we've got here?"

=The simplicity is to load the redundant into the scanner and finalize. . . .=

"I've got news for you. She's not going anywhere near that marble."

=Her equation is not in balance.= This was Linna, speaking for the first time. Linna was not exactly in charge of Tuulen Station; she was more like a senior partner. Parikkal and Silloin had overruled her before—at least I thought they had.

"What do you expect me to do? Wring her neck?"

There was a moment's silence—which was not as unnerving as watching them eye me through the window, their heads now perfectly still.

"No," I said.

The dinos were skirring at each other; their heads wove and dipped. At first they cut me cold and the comm was silent, but suddenly their debate crackled through my earstone.

=This is just as I have been telling,= said Linna. =These beings have no realization of harmony. It is wrongful to further unleash them on the many worlds.=

=You may have reason,= said Parikkal. =But that is a later discussion. The need is for the equation to be balanced.=

=There is no time. We will have to discard the redundant ourselves.= Silloin bared her long brown teeth. It would take her maybe five seconds to rip Kamala's throat out. And even though Silloin was the dino most sympathetic to us, I had no doubt she would enjoy the kill.

=I will argue that we adjourn human migration until this world has been rethought,= said Linna.

This was typical dino condescension. Even though they appeared to be arguing with each other, they were actually speaking to me, laying the situation out so that even the baby sapient would understand. They were informing me that I was jeopardizing the future of humanity in space. That the Kamala in Reception D was dead whether I quit or not. That the equation had to be balanced and it had to be now.

"Wait," I said. "Maybe I can coax her back into the scanner." I had to get away from them. I pulled my earstone out and slid it into my pocket. I was in such a hurry to escape that I stumbled as I left the scan center and had to catch myself in the hallway. I stood there for a second, staring at the hand pressed against the bulkhead. I seemed to see the splayed fingers through the wrong end of a telescope. I was far away from myself.

She had curled into herself on the couch, arms clutching knees to her chest, as if trying to shrink so that nobody would notice her.

"We're all set," I said briskly. "You'll be in the marble for less than a minute, guaranteed."

"*No,* Michael."

I could actually feel myself receding from Tuulen Station. "Kamala, you're throwing away a huge part of your life."

"It is my right." Her eyes were shiny.

No, it wasn't. She was redundant; she had no rights. What had she said about the dead old lady? She had become a thing, like a bone.

"Okay, then," I jabbed at her shoulder with a stiff forefinger. "Let's go."

She recoiled. "Go where?"

"Back to Lunex. I'm holding the shuttle for you. It just dropped off my afternoon list; I should be helping them settle in, instead of having to deal with you."

She unfolded herself slowly.

"Come on." I jerked her roughly to her feet. "The dinos want you off Tuulen as soon as possible, and so do I." I was so distant, I couldn't see Kamala Shastri anymore.

She nodded and let me march her to the bubble door.

"And if we meet anyone in the hall, keep your mouth shut."

"You're being so mean." Her whisper was thick.

"You're being such a baby."

When the inner door glided open, she realized immediately that there was no umbilical to the shuttle. She tried to twist out of my grip but I put my shoulder into her, hard. She flew across the airlock, slammed against the outer door, and caromed onto her back. As I punched at the switch to close the inner door, I came back to myself. *I* was doing this terrible thing—me, Michael Burr. I couldn't help myself: I giggled. When I last saw her, Kamala was scrabbling across the deck toward me but she was too late. I was surprised that she wasn't screaming again; all I heard was her ferocious breathing.

As soon as the inner door sealed, I opened the outer door. After all, how many ways are there to kill someone on a space station? There were no guns. Maybe someone else could have stabbed or strangled her, but not me. Poison how? Besides, I wasn't thinking, I had been trying desperately not to think of what I was doing. I was a sapientologist, not a doctor. I always thought that exposure to space meant instantaneous death. Explosive decompression or something like. I didn't want her to suffer. I was trying to make it quick. Painless.

I heard the *whoosh* of escaping air and thought that was it; the body had been ejected into space. I had actually turned away when thumping started, frantic, like the beat of a racing heart. She must have found something to hold on to. *Thump, thump, thump!* It was too much. I sagged against the inner door—*thump, thump*—slid down it, laughing. Turns out that if you empty the lungs, it is possible to survive exposure to space for at least a minute, maybe two. I thought it was funny. *Thump!* Hilarious, actually. I had tried my best for her—risked my career —and this was how she repaid me? As I laid my cheek against the door, the *thumps* started to weaken. There were just a few centimeters between us, the difference between life and death. Now she knew all about balancing the equation. I was laughing so hard I could scarcely breathe. Just like the meat behind the door. Die already, you weepy bitch!

I don't know how long it took. The *thumping* slowed. Stopped. And then I was a hero. I had preserved harmony, kept our link to the stars open. I chuckled with pride; I could think like a dinosaur.

I popped through the bubble door into Reception D. "It's time to board the shuttle."

Kamala had changed into a clingy and velcro slippers. There were at least ten windows open on the wall; the room filled with the murmur of talking heads. Friends and relatives had to be notified; their hero had returned, safe and sound. "I have to go," she said to the wall. "I will call you all when I land."

She gave me a smile that seemed stiff from disuse. "I want to thank you again, Michael." I wondered how long it took migrators to get used to being human. "You were such a help and I was such a . . . I was not myself." She glanced around the room one last time and then shivered. "I was really scared."

"You were."

She shook her head. "Was it that bad?"

I shrugged and led her out into the hall.

"I feel so silly now. I mean, I was in the marble for less than a minute and then"—she snapped her fingers—"there I was on Gend, just like you said." She brushed up against me as we walked; her body was hard under the clingy. "Anyway, I am glad we got this chance to talk. I really *was* going to look you up when I got back. I certainly did not expect to see you here."

"I decided to stay on." The inner door to the airlock glided open. "It's a job that grows on you." The umbilical shivered as the pressure between Tuulen Station and the shuttle equalized.

"You have got migrators waiting," she said.

"Two."

"I envy them." She turned to me. "Have *you* ever thought about going to the stars?"

"No," I said.

Kamala put her hand to my face . "It changes everything." I could feel the prick of her long nails—claws, really. For a moment I thought she meant to scar my cheek the way she had been scarred.

"I know," I said.

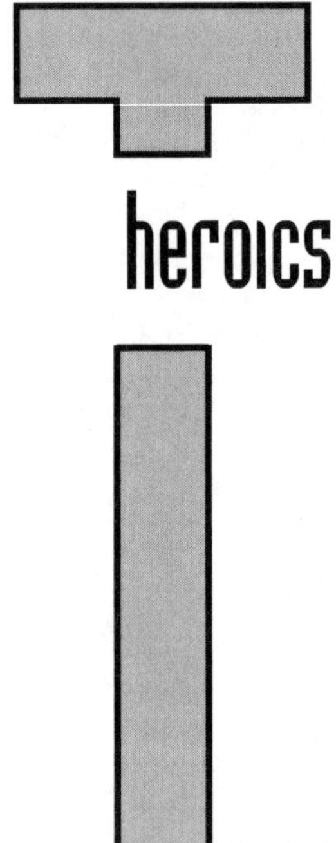

heroics

he kids were screaming. Two had climbed onto the Chris-Craft's foredeck and were doing a kind of panicky dance, as if the fiberglass had turned white-hot beneath their toes. Little kids: six, seven maybe—around Jamie's age. They were wearing the wrong size life preserver; the orange horseshoes came almost to their knees. There was an older boy amidships who didn't have a life preserver; Mike could see his bare back arch as he worked over something in the bottom of the boat. Smoke was billowing from the stern. A smudge on the summer sky.

Then Mike was running down the beach. The sand seemed to clutch at his feet; he wasn't going to get there in time. He had never seen a boat fire before. He didn't know if the thing could explode or not. Sure it could—why didn't they jump? And as soon as he thought it, he heard himself call. "Jump! My God, *jump!"* The wind was swinging the bow away from shore and pushing the boat out toward the middle of the lake. Two old ladies in flowered housedresses ran to the end of the dock and stood by the empty boat hoist, shrieking back at the kids. Their dresses billowed in the wind like the flames that had begun to lick at the black smoke. "Get off the boat." It sounded like someone else shouting; Mike had never heard such power in his voice. He felt distanced from himself, a little crazy. *"Jump now!"* The big kid finally stood up and staggered back against the wheel, holding his forearm to his head to shield himself. The fire reared up suddenly, huge as an angry man. The flames snapped like a flag in the wind.

As Mike bounded from the beach onto the dock, his foot went through a gray plank. He sprawled headlong; it felt like someone had taken a hammer to his shin. He got up immediately, but the pain stayed with him — brought him back to himself. "Damn, damn, damn." He spoke the words as a kind of incantation against the pain as he hobbled down the dock toward the old ladies. He had an image of himself sprinting down the dock and diving off the end without breaking stride. He was not a big man, but he was in superb shape. He told himself he could still do it even as he slowed to a walk. He could smell the fire now, the bitter perfume of spilled gasoline. The old ladies were wailing like ghosts. *Save them, save them, save them.* The air at the end of the dock seemed to shimmer. He would have to burst through to get to the lake. He wasn't sure anymore. His leg stung. He looked down and saw that he was bleeding on a pair of brand-new Nikes. Not the cheap models he usually settled for but the top-of-the-line air-cushioned racing shoes he had always wanted. *Save them, save them.* He sat down to take the Nikes off. One of the little kids toppled into the water. Mike knew he wasn't going to do anything. He hadn't expected to be afraid. He nodded at the frantic ghosts in their burning-plaid housedresses and heard himself say, "Call the fire department."

He woke up. The bedroom was very still, as if someone had just stopped screaming. The bottom sheet on his side was damp with his sweat. Peg had rolled over to her side of the bed and taken the top sheet with her. He listened to her breathe for a while and then propped himself up on an elbow. The luminescent blue readout on the clock radio said 2:26 A.M. In the next room Jamie whimpered in his sleep. Mike rolled out of bed to get his son a drink of water.

The clock read 5:33 when he finally decided that it was useless trying to sleep anymore that night. He got up and put on a white shirt, jeans, white socks, and his gray $39.95 Nikes. He stuffed one of the ridiculous black bow ties into his shirt pocket and went down to make breakfast.

"You're up early this morning." Peg came up behind him while he was reading the baseball scores.

"Couldn't sleep."

"It's that spicy food." She poured herself a cup of coffee and sat down across the kitchen table from him. "I told you not to put too much red pepper in the chili." She picked up the comics section.

Mike grunted unhappily. Upstairs he could hear Jamie talking to himself about superheroes in imitation adult voices.

"Want to hear your horoscope?"

He didn't answer.

" 'Remember that the way to achieve your secret ambitions is by planning. Start tonight. A relative has a message for you.' "

"Would you stop already?" He pushed away from the table. "It's goddamn voodoo. I don't want Jamie hearing that crap."

"You had a bad night, huh?" She was sympathetic now—too late to do him any good.

"Have to go." He clipped the bow tie to his collar. "See you tonight." They kissed.

"I love you, grouch," she said.

Secret ambitions. He had given up secret ambitions; he was thirty-nine years old and knew better. Mike was a high-school biology teacher with a master's degree in education from State. He was at the top of the wage scale and, through creative scrimping, had never missed a mortgage payment or a VISA installment. He loved his wife, and his kid was happy, and they lived year-round on a lake that tourists drove hours to visit. He had locked himself in and thrown away the key. Not that he didn't have ambitions, but they were modest and not at all secret. He wanted to win the masters' division in a 10K race someday and hoped to be able to afford a boat trip through the Grand Canyon before he died. He wanted Jamie to go to M.I.T. and maybe go into research, but he was realistic about what parents could expect from their children.

Duffy was the one with ambitions. He seethed with ambition. He read too many books and wanted it understood that he had no intention of spending the rest of his life as manager of the four-aisle grocery his grandfather had founded. He was always telling Mike that they were living lives of quiet desperation, the two of them. Mike was always reminding Duffy that Thoreau was a troublemaking asshole who couldn't hold a steady job.

It was Duffy who had given him the summer job at Wilson's. Mike mostly worked the little grocery's meat and produce counters and stocked shelves, but he didn't mind bagging when things got hectic up front. It wasn't a bad way to spend the summer, although Peg said his hands smelled like chicken parts and he didn't much care for cleaning under the freezers or smiling at idiot customers and wise-ass kids. Still, he averaged around four thousand dollars for three months' work, and that was the difference between living right on the lake and suffering back in the hills with the mosquitoes. If he had to listen to old Mrs. Matijczyk complain about teachers' salaries, he also got to be with Duffy. Even though Duffy was wrong at least half the time, he was Mike's best friend and had been since they had run together on the mile relay team that still held the state schoolboy record.

While they were in the back room, stripping the gummy outer leaves from a case of iceberg lettuce that had sat too long in the cooler, Mike told Duffy about the dream. He hadn't intended to mention the dream to anyone, but the memory of it had become an itch that he had to scratch. Better to tell Duffy than Peg, who would refer the case either to a gypsy or Ann Landers.

Duffy considered. "How much you have to drink last night anyway?"

"Come on, Duff. Peg thinks it's pepper; you blame it on Schlitz. And what does that explain anyway?"

"I don't know what you want me to say."

Mike didn't know either. "Yeah, well, forget it then." He didn't know why he expected Duffy to understand when he didn't understand himself.

"Sometimes I feel guilty about not fighting in 'Nam." Duffy flicked some green off his shirtsleeve. "You know, like we never got to test our courage under fire?"

"Naah." Mike had reduced a rotting head to a worthless yellow heart the size of a tennis ball. He tossed it into the garbage and shrugged. "Sounds like warmed-over Hemingway to me."

For a while there was no sound except the soft squeak of lettuce being pulled apart.

"So maybe you're just a little afraid that you're a coward," Duffy said. "You've never been in serious danger, have you?"

"There was the time I spun out the Camaro."

"I mean, there's nothing wrong with it. You can't know these things ahead of time. It just happens and you react. It's okay to wonder, I guess, but it's not worth an ulcer."

"I feel strange." Mike shook his head and then rummaged through the compost in the bottom of the soggy cardboard case. The speaker above them crackled and they heard Marge the cashier say, "Tom Duffy to the front, please. Tom."

Mike shrugged. "I think we got them all."

"Okay. Wrap them and get them out there before they start to stink again. Thirty-nine a head."

"You going to testify at my commitment hearing?"

"Tell you what." Duffy patted him on the shoulder. "I've got a twenty in my wallet that says you'll be a hero someday. I still remember that time you got tripped in the eight-eighty and you got up and won the goddamn race. That took guts. So if you want to bet against yourself, I'll take your money." He reached for his back pocket. "Standing bet, what do you say?"

Mike smiled. He hadn't thought about that race in a long time. The State meet—as he closed on the tape it had been like the headlong, triumphant, heart-bursting finale of a symphony. "Get out of here," he said, giving Duffy a friendly shove, "or I'll report you to the commissioner. There are laws about corrupting young athletes."

"You haven't been young since the Eisenhower administration," said Duffy as he pushed through the swinging doors.

That evening as Mike jogged, the race kept flashing at him like a beacon. He remembered all the little details, like the loose, crazy feeling he had when he'd gotten up, as if nothing mattered anymore. He saw the torn lining in Coach's sport coat, flapping as the old man jumped up and down like a freshman. There was Duffy running on the grass alongside the track, screaming at him. "Move on him! He's dead! Put out!" The rictus on Sanchez's face when he looked over his shoulder to see Mike behind him. The way he could feel his own eyes bulge, as if they might explode. He remembered thinking that he wasn't running anymore, he was falling inevitably toward the finish line like a suicide plunging toward the pavement. The tape was like a knife across his chest as he won and he doubled over, gaping at the bloody cinders stuck to the scrape on his knee. The cheers had straightened him up. Strangers had cheered for him; people were standing up. It had never happened before. Or since.

Mike had put Beethoven's Fifth in the Walkman. Flying with the music and his memory, he did his 10K course in 40:49:15, a personal best. The exhaustion afterward was sweet and clean, as if he had sweated out all the poisons that had accumulated within him that day. He felt so good that he took Jamie for a sunset swim. Peg watched from the porch. As he floated beside his son, he could feel the last vestige of doubt washing away. The water was warm; the sun was huge and red. A man would be a fool to expect more than this. The dream had relaxed its painful grip on his imagination. If it snuck up on him again, he was certain that he could run away from it.

There was nothing on TV but reruns, so after they put Jamie to bed for the night Peg asked Mike to make love. Even that was good, perhaps because each wanted to make up for the morning spat. It would have been the perfect ending to the day had not Peg wanted to talk afterward. It was only 9:15, she said. Too early to sleep.

She asked him how his day had been, and he said fine. She said he had looked tired at breakfast and why hadn't he slept well, and he said he was a little tired then and more tired now but he was fine. Fine. He thought she might take the hint, but she didn't; he had to admit they really hadn't had a chance to talk in a while. She ran her hand up his belly and sifted his chest hair through her fingers and asked why was he so tired and did it have anything to do with her, and he said no, it was only a nightmare he'd had and he didn't want to talk about it just now but maybe some other time. He kissed her then and meant it, too. There was a long silence. He lay on his back with his head sunk deep into his favorite down pillow and his other foam pillow under his bad back and tried to remember their last serious conversation. All that came to mind was TV and school and softball and jogging and the League of Women Voters and aerobics class and Jamie's swim team practice. So he told her he loved her and she said she knew it, and he asked her how her day had been.

"Betty and I went into town," Peg said. "She had to get her car inspected, and rather than have her sit all afternoon looking at old motorcycle magazines in the office at Bub's Shell, I said she could come with me down to the Sears to shop for new towels."

"What's wrong with the towels we have?"

"We got them from your sister as a wedding present, Mike. They're thirteen years old and they smell like sweat socks when they get wet, and two of them still have brown stains from the time you creosoted the porch. But I didn't see a set that I liked that we could afford. Anyway, when we got done at Sears we called Bub, and he said another hour. We were going to hit Dunkin' Donuts, but then Betty remembered that there's a palm reader just opened up in the trailer park, so she wanted to check that out."

Mike groaned, pulled the foam pillow from under his back, and covered his ears. Peg tickled him, and when he protected himself she pulled the pillow away.

"It was very interesting and you have to listen."

"How much did it cost?"

"Five. Betty paid."

Mike scowled at the thought of wasted money, even if it was Betty's. And he didn't much care to hear Peg talking about fortune-telling or astrology or any of that other nonsense; it bothered him that he could not tell how much of it she really believed.

"Well, she said that since I wouldn't take gas money and we weren't going to have time for donuts, she would treat. Anyway, it was very interesting and don't be such a poop. She said I had a very long lifeline."

"Betty or the gypsy?"

"She was from California. She said I would have three kids and two long and happy marriages." She chuckled.

"Two?"

"She said I would never be rich, but that I would never have to worry about money."

"What do you mean two? How do you think that makes me feel?"

"She said that someone we knew was sick but wasn't telling, and that this little split line here means a funeral before the end of the year. We thought it might be Rose Concack; she's been looking a little gray lately."

"I'm either divorced or dead — and you're happy? For Christ's sake, Peg." He pulled at the blanket that they had kicked off while they were making love; he was chilled. "Sometimes I think you do these things just to annoy me."

"I'm sorry, Mikey. I thought it might make you laugh."

"Ha-ha. See you at the funeral." He moved to his side of the bed and turned his back to her. "Good night."

The explosion was louder than a starter's pistol, more like a shotgun going off in a living room. Something broke loose inside of Mike at the sound: he went a little crazy as he watched the kids clamber onto the foredeck. Their whimpers carried to him across the mirror-flat lake. Then he was down on the beach, trying to launch the eighteen-foot fossil skiff he had bought at a junkyard for twenty-three dollars. It had sat in the sand all summer, waiting for a motor that Mike couldn't afford, sat so long that the old lapstrake pine had sent roots down into the sand and now would not be moved. When he felt his back pop, Mike knew it was too late. The little kids were screaming, and the big kid was struggling in the bottom of the burning Chris-Craft. Whatever the big kid was trying to do, he wasn't strong enough for it; he had a runner's upside-down build. "Forget it," Mike shouted. "*Jump.*" But although he could hear everything—the frantic drumming of tiny feet on the fiberglass deck, the big kid's panicky groans, even the hiss of melting plastic—they paid no attention to him. He was not that important. He had to run.

He flew down the beach; his feet never touched the ground. It was like falling. There was no choice. At any second a fireball could bloom on the stalk of smoke. Just like in a cop show, except that it wouldn't be stuntmen in flame suits faking agony. It would be those damned kids. About Jamie's age. "*Get off!*"

Rose Concack was already at the end of her dock, weeping and looking even more gray than usual. There was another woman with her whom Mike didn't recognize. They were wearing brightly flowered tents, and he could see the varicose veins, dark as walnuts, bulging from their thick legs. They clutched at each other, weeping, scarcely able to stand upright; they were as heavy and old and useless as the skiff. Only Mike could save the kids. He stepped carefully from the beach onto the dock, but that was a mistake. The momentum was gone, the crazy looseness. The warm air shimmered and congealed around him, and he had to push through it. "*Save them, save them.*" Every time the women shrieked, it seemed to get thicker until at last it was as if the dock was underwater. Except that he could still see the lake's mirror surface, stained with gasoline rainbows and the burning Chris-Craft and his own reflection. He looked at himself and wondered what he was waiting for. What did he want?

Jamie was reading the back of a box of G.I. Joe Action Stars and spooning up a second helping of the cereal. Mike was scanning the want ads for used outboard motors. He was hoping to find an old Merc for under thirty dollars, something he could maintain himself. Peg hadn't gotten out of bed yet, which meant that she was tired or still miffed about last night. Either way, her problem.

"Who do you think is stronger, Dad: Spider-Man or Superman?"

"I have no idea."

Jamie chewed for a moment. As usual, nobody was selling what Mike wanted to buy. "Remember that part in the movie," Jamie said, "when he caught the jet before it crashed?"

He refolded the paper. "Who?"

"Superman. That's why I think that he must be stronger. But I still like Spidey better."

"Yeah?" Mike clipped on his bow tie. He hated bow ties; only clowns and grocery-store workers wore bow ties.

"Yeah, he's braver. Because like if a bad guy shoots him, he really bleeds. But nothing can hurt Superman except Kryptonite and there isn't that much of it, except in space."

Mike stared at him, and Jamie shrank back in his chair. Jamie had a milk mustache, and there was no trace of guile in his widening eyes. There was no way his son could know about the dream or understand why his casual observation had exploded Mike's comfortable early-morning muddle. Mike wasn't sure himself; all he knew was that he didn't want to think about the qualities of courage anymore. "Yeah, well, I guess you're right." Mike's voice felt strange in his throat. "I've got to go to work now," he said, even though it wasn't really time. He felt shaky, and he didn't want to scare the boy. "Tell Mom I'll be home at five." He kissed his son quickly.

"But I think *you're* bravest of all." Jamie seemed to sense that he had said something wrong; he was only trying to make up. "Because you don't have superpowers."

"Gotta go, Jamie." Mike stuck a trembling hand in his pocket, pretending to look for his keys. "I love you," he said, and rushed out the door.

He parked the car in the empty parking lot of the public beach, and sat watching waves lap against the diving dock. He had always believed the world was rational; he had always thought himself the sanest man in it. Now he wasn't so sure about either. It took him a long time to reconstruct his composure, and even then it was a rickety and uncertain job. He told himself that his problem was nine-tenths exhaustion and one-tenth imagination. Too much thinking, not enough sleep. Duffy didn't say anything when he showed up for work half an hour late.

Duffy didn't say much to him all that day, and Mike had the impression his friend was avoiding him. But at 4:30 he came out of his tiny office as Mike was punching out. Duffy pulled his own card from the rack and stuck it into the time clock.

"Knocking off early?" said Mike.

He put a hand on Mike's shoulder. "Let me buy you a brew."

"What the hell for?" Mike wondered how mad Peg would get.

"I ain't telling." Duffy aimed him at the door. "Yet."

They settled into a window booth at the Swan Dive across Summer Street from Wilson's. Duffy ordered a pitcher of Schlitz, and Mike made a crack about their beer bellies. Duffy just smiled as if he had a winning lottery ticket in his pocket. He had long since stopped working out and drank more than was good for a man going to fat. He wouldn't say anything until Marcie brought the pitcher, then he filled each of their glasses and held his up, saluting Wilson's through the glass. "Good-bye and good riddance," he said. "I'm moving to New Hampshire, Mike. To seek my fortune."

"Shit," Mike said. Then he forced a smile.

They touched glasses and then chugged their beers; Mike poured refills. "New *Hampshire?"*

"They got what they call the Golden Triangle there, fastest growing area in the country. Population's going to double in the next twenty years, easy. You remember my cousin Ed was out here last spring? He has three convenience stores near Nashua. Calls them ShortStops. Basically all they carry is dairy, bread, beer, soda, smokes. He does a huge volume, and he's talking six new locations by next year. I get three."

"Your own little chain."

"Yep. Ed's going to give me the crash course, and then we're going to be partners. He says he wanted someone he could trust. Of course I've got to put up some serious money of my own. But, hey, it's like Coach always used to say: No guts, no glory."

They drank to Coach and his philosophy. Mike drained his glass and poured another.

Duffy leaned across the table and lowered his voice. "Truth is, it's past time for me to leave. Wilson's is hurting; everybody shops at the new IGA out by Sears, and I don't blame them. You can park there and the produce doesn't smell. I've found a buyer who thinks he can make a go of it, and good luck to him. I've got his promise to keep everyone on. You especially."

Mike sighed and stared at the golden bubbles bursting in his beer.

"Hey, Mike, it's not like I've been keeping it a secret. I've been looking ever since the divorce, you know that. What do I need to stay around here for? I mean you, you've got a family, a good job. You're happy."

Silence.

"I haven't told anyone yet. Keep my secret until tomorrow?"

Mike nodded. Duffy emptied the pitcher. "Aren't you going to congratulate me?"

Mike extended a hand across the table and they shook. "I'm going to miss you, you son of a bitch." He didn't feel the tear until it dribbled down his cheek.

Duffy's eyes were watery too. "Truth is, Mike, you're about the only thing I'm going to miss in this town."

They sat for a while not looking at each other. Mike read the sale posters on Wilson's windows as if they might explain it all. "Diet Coke 6/$1.99. Eggs Ex. Large $1.15." Not much of a sale, which was why Peg mostly shopped at the IGA. Both men seemed a little embarrassed at how easily their emotions had surfaced. They finished their beers. Duffy wouldn't let Mike pay. They went home.

Peg was grim when Mike walked in the door. He was an hour and a half late for dinner, and he felt as brittle as stale bread.

"Didn't you tell Jamie five?" She sounded like a divorce lawyer.

"I'm sorry." A fight was the last thing he needed. "Duffy's moving to New Hampshire."

The hard stare softened. "Oh, Mike." Then she hugged him and Mike let himself sag in her embrace. He was surprised at how quickly she understood, and he was grateful. But then she always seemed to get stronger when he was at his weakest.

"He's going to manage convenience stores. He's happy." Peg's hair was damp; it smelled like lavender. Mike ran his fingers through it, remembering how smooth it had been when they were first married. ''I guess it's bad news for me, though.''

''For us.''

He nodded.

''What are you going to do?''

He kissed her. ''Is it okay if I run?''

She smiled. ''Sure, go ahead. It's only stew; I turned it down an hour ago.''

He was pulling on his Nikes when the Concacks' boat exploded. It was an impossible sound: a window-rattling thunderclap on a clear day. The sound of a nightmare. He bounded out to the porch and saw it all. The yellow Chris-Craft skewed slowly off course like a bird wounded in flight. A thin plume of gray smoke thickened and turned oily black. The fiberglass engine cowling had been blown out of the boat by the force of the explosion and was floating toward shore. Two kids in orange life vests climbed onto the foredeck. Mike froze, trying to will the cowling back over the inboard-outboard, the boat back on course. The kids started to scream.

There were a couple of inches of brown water in the bottom of the skiff. Mike got behind it and pushed. His feet dug into the sand; it was like trying to move a dead horse. The old wooden boat scraped painfully across the beach. He felt the sand suck one of his Nikes off, and the bow broke the mirror surface of the lake. He sprawled headlong as the skiff shot ahead, floating free. As he picked himself up, he had the crazy feeling that he could do anything. He splashed alongside, heaved himself aboard, and fitted the oars into the oarlocks. He pulled for the burning boat, craning over his shoulder to see the first flames climbing the column of smoke.

''*Jump. It's gonna blow!*'' He was close now, close enough to smell the gasoline rainbows that stained his beautiful lake. The little kids held out their arms, as if they wanted to hug him. The big kid looked up as the skiff thumped against the port side of the Chris-Craft. The fire was all the colors of sunset. There was a man lying facedown in the bottom of the burning boat, a bald old man with a bloody scrape on the side of his head. The big kid whimpered as he tried to sit the old man up. ''Come on, Grandpa, you gotta, you gotta.'' Grandpa was blue-white and limp as a dissection frog.

''Can you swim, kid?'' Mike stood up on the midships seat of the skiff and grabbed the Chris-Craft's gunwale.

''He's hurt.'' The big kid looked about thirteen. Scrawny,

but with the long thighs of a sprinter. He had the same home-made crewcut that Mike's dad used to give him in the summertime.

"Get the kids ashore. Understand?" Mike straddled the two boats. The big kid hesitated, and all Mike could see in his eyes was white. "I'll take care of him." Mike lowered his voice, trying to make him believe that they were two of a kind—if Mike could do it, then the kid could too. "I've got him; you take them. Okay?" He made it sound like a locker-room dare. The big kid nodded and backed away, shielding his eyes from the flames. He clambered up next to the little kids, and they stopped screaming as he took their hands. They all jumped and Mike stood — one foot on each boat, holding them together — and watched until they surfaced. The big kid grabbed the little ones by the life vests and began to tow them toward the dock. It was less than fifty yards; they'd make it. No problem. Mike was so loose he felt like laughing. He could hear the hiss of melting plastic as he stepped over to the Chris-Craft; the fire burned his face like a fever.

He grabbed the old man under the armpits and dragged him to the port side. The skiff was drifting away, and he had to drape the body over the rail while he hung himself overboard and stretched his stockinged foot out. His toes curled over a cleat, and he pulled the skiff back toward them. As he picked Grandpa up, the old man opened his eyes and moaned, "No insurance."

He did laugh then. "Me neither," he said as he lifted the old man over the side and lowered him into the skiff. Mike had to drop him the last few inches, and he slumped to the bottom. The skiff slued away.

Mike stood high on the Chris-Craft's gunwale and poised himself to jump into the water. He could see Peg at the end of Concack's dock pulling the little kids out of the lake. He could see the big kid — brave kid — churning through the water back toward the boats. He could see two old ladies capering on the dock, cheering for him. He was standing at the top of a mountain of adrenaline and thought he could see everything. He didn't ever want to come down.

"Now, Mister." The big kid was below him, treading water. *"Jump."*

Mike did not move. The kid heaved himself up onto the gunwale and grabbed at Mike's ankle. The boat shuddered; Mike twisted, losing his balance. He saw a ball of flame boiling out of the ruined engine, and then he was falling. The water slapped him out of his nightmare. As he came up for air, his chest was tight with fear; he thought he might vomit. He had been crazy to take such a risk. Crazy. But he was all right now. It was over. He had proved whatever there was to prove.

His foot nudged something, and he turned to see the big kid's back break surface. A stain was spreading slowly across the lake.

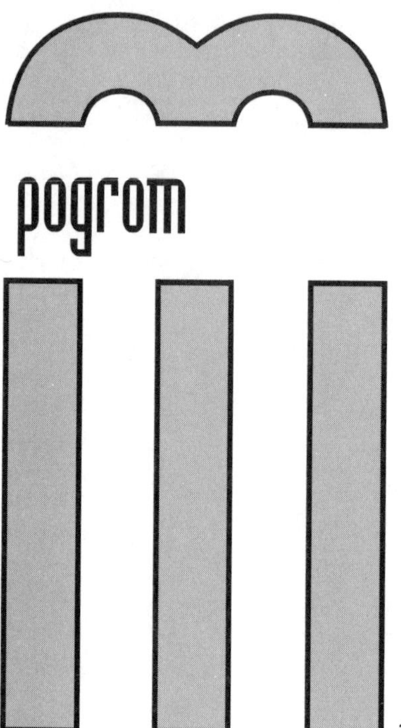

3 pogrom

Matt was napping when Ruth looked in on him. He had sprawled across the bedspread with his clothes on, shoes off. His right sock was worn to gauze at the heel. The pillow had crimped his gray hair at an odd angle. She had never seen him so peaceful before, but then she had never seen him asleep. She had the eye zoom for a close-up. His mouth was slack, and sleep had softened the wrinkles on his brow. Ruth had always thought him handsome but forbidding, like the cliffs up in Crawford Notch. Now that he was dead to the world, she could almost imagine him smiling. She wondered if there were anything she could say to make him smile. He worried too much, that man. He blamed himself for things he had not done.

She increased the volume of her wall. His breathing was scratchy but regular. They had promised to watch out for one another; there were not many of them left in Durham. Matt had given Ruth a password for his homebrain when they had released him from the hospital. He seemed fine for now. She turned out the lights he had left on, but there was nothing else she could see to do for him. She did not, however, close the electronic window that opened from her apartment on Church Hill onto his house across town. It had been years since she had heard the sounds of a man sleeping. If she shut her eyes, it was almost as if he were next to her. His gentle snoring made a much more soothing background than the gurgle of the mountain cascade she usually kept on the wall. She was not really intruding, she told herself. He had asked her to check up on him.

Ruth picked up the mystery she had been reading but did not open it. She studied his image as if it might be a clue to something she had been trying to remember. Matt moaned, and his fingers tightened around the cast that ran from his right hand to his elbow. She thought he must have started dreaming, because his face closed like a door. He rolled toward the eye and she could see the bruise on his cheek, blood-blue shading to brown.

"Someone is approaching," said Ruth's homebrain.

"The groceries?"

"The visitor is not on file."

"Show me," Ruth said.

The homebrain split Matt's window and gave her a view of the front porch. A girl she had never seen before, holding two brown paper Shop 'n' Save sacks, pressed the doorbell with her elbow.

She was about thirteen and underfed, which meant she was probably a drood. She had long glitter hair and the peeling red skin of someone who did not pay enough attention to the UV forecasts. Her arms were decorated with blue stripes of warpaint. Or maybe they were tattoos. She was wearing sneakers, no socks, jeans, and a T-shirt with a picture of Jesus Hitler that said FOR A NICKEL I WILL.

"Hello?" said Ruth. "Do I know you?"

"Your stuff." She shifted the sacks in her arms as if she were about to drop them.

"Where's Jud? He usually delivers for me."

"C'mon, lady! Not arguin' with no fuckin' door." She kicked at it. "Hot as nukes out here."

"I don't know who you are."

"See these sacks? Costin' you twenty-one fifty-three."

"Please show me your ID."

"Shit, lady." She plunked the sacks down on the porch, brushed sweat from her face, pulled a card from her pocket, and thrust it toward the eye in the door. The homebrain scanned and verified it. But it did not belong to her.

"That Jud's card," said Ruth.

"He busy, you know, so he must give it to me." One of the sacks fell over. The girl nudged a box of dishwasher soap with her sneaker. "You want this or not?" She knelt, reached into the sack, and tossed a bag of onion bagels, a bottle of liquid Pep, a frozen whitefish, two rolls of toilet paper, and a bunch of carrots into a pile on the middle of the porch.

"Stop that!" Ruth imagined the neighbors were watching her groceries being abused. "Wait there."

The girl waggled a package of Daffy Toes at the eye. "Gimme cookie for my tip?"

Ruth hesitated before she pressed her thumb against the printreader built into the steel door. What was the point in having all these security systems if she was going to open up for strangers? This was exactly the way people like her got hurt. But it *was* Ruth's order, and the girl looked too frail to be any trouble.

She smelled of incense. A suspicion of sweet ropy smoke clung to her clothes and hair. Ruth was tempted to ask what it was, but realized that she probably did not want to know. The latest in teen depravity, no doubt. The smell reminded her of when she was in college back in the sixties and she used to burn incense to cover the stink of pot. Skinny black cylinders of charcoal that smeared her fingers and smelled like a Christmas tree on fire. Ruth followed the girl into the kitchen, trying to remember the last time she had smoked pot.

The girl set the bags out on the counter and then sighed with pleasure. "Been wantin' all day to get into some A/C." She surveyed the kitchen as if she were hoping for an invitation to dinner. "Name's Chaz." She waited in vain for Ruth to introduce herself. "So, want me to unpack?"

"No." Ruth took her wallet out of her purse.

"Lots of 'em ask me to. They too old, or too lazy—hey, real costin' *wine.*" She pulled a Medoc from the rack mounted under the china cabinet and ran her finger along the stubby shoulder. "In glass bottles. You rich or what?"

Ruth held out her cash card, but Chaz ignored it.

"Bet you think I lie. You 'fraid I come here to do your

bones?'' She hefted the bottle of Bordeaux by the neck, like a club.

Alarmed, Ruth clutched at her chest and squeezed the security pager that hung on a silver chain under her blouse. ''Put that down.'' The eye on the kitchen ceiling started broadcasting live to the private cops she subscribed to. Last time, they had taken twenty minutes to come.

''Don't worry.'' Chaz grinned. ''I deliver plenty stuff before. In Portsmouth. Then we lose our house, got move to Durham. Nice town you got here.'' She set the bottle back on the counter. ''But you can't hear nothin' I say, right? You scared 'cause kids hate you but I ain't breaking your head, am I? Not today, anyway. Just wanna earn my fuckin' nickel, lady.''

''I'm trying to pay you.'' Ruth pushed the card at her.

She took it. ''Place full of costin' shit like this.'' She shook her head in wonder at Ruth's wealth. ''You lucky, you know.'' She rubbed the card against the port of Jud Gazzara's Shop 'n' Save ID to deduct $21.53. ''Yeah, this is great, compare to dorms. You ever see dorms inside?''

''No.''

''You oughta. Compare to dorms, this is heaven.'' Chaz handed the card back. ''No, better than heaven, 'cause you can buy this, but you gotta die to get heaven. Gimme my cookie?'' she said.

''Take it and leave.''

Chaz paused on the way out and peeked into the living room. ''This walter what you do for fun, lady?'' Matt was still asleep on the wall. ''Jeez, you pigs good as dead already.''

''Would you please go?''

''Wake up, walter!'' She yelled at the screen. *''Hustle or die!''*

''Huh!'' Matt jerked as if he had been shot. ''What?'' He curled into a ball, protecting his face with the cast.

''Give nasty, you get nasty.'' Chaz winked at Ruth. ''See you next week, lady.''

''Greta, is that you?''

Ruth could hear Matt calling to his dead wife as she shouldered the door shut. She braced her back against it until she felt the homebrain click the bolts into place.

''Greta?''

''It's me,'' she called. ''Ruth.'' She squeezed the security pager again to call the private cops off. At least she could avoid the charge for a house call. Her heart hammered against her chest.

"Ruth?"

She knew the girl was out there laughing at her. It made Ruth angry, the way these kids made a game of terrorizing people. "Turn your wall on, Matt." It was not fair; she was no pig.

By the time Ruth got into the living room, Matt was sitting on the edge of his bed. He seemed dazed, as if he had woken up to find himself still in the nightmare.

"You asked me to check in on you," she said. "Remember? Sorry if I disturbed you." She decided not to tell him—or anyone—about Chaz. Nothing had happened, really. So the world was full of ignorant little bigots, so what? She could hardly report a case of rudeness to the Durham cops; they thought people like her complained too much as it was. "Did you have a nice nap?" Ruth was not admitting to anyone that she was afraid of trash like Chaz.

"I was having a dream about Greta," said Matt. "She gave me a birthday cake on a train. We were going to some city, New York or Boston. Then she wanted to get off, but I hadn't finished the cake. It was big as a suitcase."

Ruth had never understood why people wanted to tell her their dreams. Most of the ones she had heard were dumb. She could not help but be embarrassed when otherwise reasonable adults prattled on about their nighttime lunacies. "How are you feeling?" She nestled into her favorite corner of the couch. "Do you need anything?"

"What was funny was that Greta wouldn't help me." He had not noticed how he was annoying her. "I mean, I told her to have some cake, but she wouldn't. She screamed at me to hurry up or I'd die. Then I woke up."

What had Chaz called him? A walter. Ruth had never heard that one before. "Sorry," she said. "I really didn't mean to intrude. I should let you get back to sleep."

"No, don't go." He slid his feet into the slippers next to the bed. "I'd like some company. I just lay down because there was nothing else to do." He grunted as he stood, then glanced in the mirror and combed hair back over his bald spot with his fingers. "See, I'm up."

He turned away and waved for her to follow. The eye tracked along the ceiling after him as he hobbled down the hall to his office, a dark shabby room decorated with books and diplomas. He lived in only three rooms: office, bedroom, and kitchen. The rest of his house was closed down.

"I'm pretty useless these days." He eased behind the antique steel desk he had brought home from his office when they closed the university. "No typing with this damn cast on. Not for six, maybe seven weeks." He picked up a manuscript, read the title, dropped it back on a six-inch stack next to the computer. "Nothing to do."

Next he would get melancholy, if she let him. "So dictate."

"I'm too old to think anymore without my fingers on a keyboard and a screen to remind me what I just wrote." He snorted in disgust. "But you didn't call to hear me complain. You've been so good, Ruth. To pay so much attention and everything. I don't know why you do it."

"Must be your sunny personality, Matt." Ruth hated the way he had been acting since they released him from the hospital. So predictable. So sad. "I'm cooking my mom's famous gefilte fish. Maybe I'll bring some over later? And a bottle of wine?"

"That's sweet, but no. No, you know how upset you get when you go out." He grinned. "You just stay safe where you are."

"This is my town, too. And yours. I've lived here thirty-two years. I'm not about to let them take it away from me now."

"We lost it long ago, Ruth. Maybe it's time we acknowledged that."

"Really? Can I stop paying property taxes?"

"You know, I understand the way they feel." He tapped the keyboard at random with his good hand. "The world's a mess; it's not their fault that they're homeless. They watch the walls in the dorms and they see all the problems and they need someone to blame. So they call us pigs and we call them droods. Much simpler that way."

"So what are you going to do? Send them a thank-you note for crippling you? Breaking your arm? Wake up and listen to yourself, Matt. You shouldn't have to hide in your house like a criminal. You didn't do anything."

"Yes, that's it exactly. I didn't do anything. Maybe it's time."

"Damn it, don't start *that* again! You're a teacher, you worked hard." Ruth grabbed a pillow she had embroidered. She wanted to hurl it right through the wall and knock some sense into the foolish old man. "God, I don't know why I bother." Instead she hugged it to her chest. "Sometimes you make me mad, Matt. I mean really angry."

"I'm sorry, Ruth. I'm just in one of my moods. Maybe I should call you back when I'm better company?"

"All right," she said without enthusiasm. "I'll talk to you later then."

"Don't give up on me, Ruth."

She wiped him off the wall. He was replaced by Silver Cascade Brook up in Crawford Notch. She had reprocessed the loop from video she had shot years ago, before she had had to stop traveling. Water burbled, leaves rustled, birds sang. "Chirp, chirp," she said sourly and zapped it. Afloat on the Öschinensee in the Alps. *Zap.* Coral gardens off the Caribbean coast of St. Lucia. *Zap.* Exotic birds of the Everglades. *Zap.* She flipped restlessly through her favorite vacations; nothing pleased her. Finally she settled on a vista of Mill Pond across the street. The town swans cut slow V's across the placid surface. In the old days, when she used to sit on the porch, she could hear frogs in the summertime. She was tempted to drag her rocker out there right now. Then she would call Matt, just to show him it could still be done.

Instead she went into the kitchen to unpack the groceries. She put the dishwasher soap under the sink and the cookies in the bread drawer. Matt was a crotchety old man, ridden with guilt, but he and she were just about the last ones left. She picked up the whitefish, opened the freezer, then changed her mind. When was the last time she had seen Margie or Stanley What's-His-Name, who lived just two doors down? Ruth closed the door again, stripped the shrink-wrap from the fish, and popped it into the microwave to defrost. If she were afraid to show him, Matt would end up like all the others. He would stop calling or move or die, and then Ruth would be a stranger in her own hometown. When the whitefish thawed she whacked off the head, skinned and boned it. She put the head, skin, and bones in a pot, covered them with water, cut in some carrots and onion, and set it on the stove to boil. She was not going to let anyone make her a prisoner in her own kitchen. She ground the cleaned fish and some onions together, then beat in matzo meal, water, and a cup of ovobinder. Her mom's recipe called for eggs, but uncontaminated eggs were hard to find. She formed the fish mixture into balls and bravely dropped them into the boiling stock. Ruth was going visiting, and no one was going to stop her.

After she called the minibus, she packed the cooled gefilte fish into one Tupperware, poured the lukewarm sauce into another, and tucked them both into her tote bag beside the Medoc. Then she reached to the cabinet above the refrigerator, took down her blowcuffs, and velcroed one to each wrist. In the bedroom she opened the top drawer of her dresser and rooted through the underwear until she found two flat clips of riot gas, two inches by three. The slogan on the side read: "With Knockdown, they *go* down and *stay* down." The clips hissed as she fitted them into the cuffs. Outside, a minibus pulled into the parking lot of the Church Hill Apartments and honked.

"Damn!" There must have been one in the neighborhood; service was never this prompt. She pulled on a baggy long-sleeved shirtwaist to hide the cuffs and grabbed her tote.

As soon as Ruth opened the front door, she realized she had forgotten to put sunblock on. Too late now. The light needled her unprotected skin as she hurried down the walk. There was one other rider on the mini, a leathery man in a stiff brown suit. He perched at the edge of his seat with an aluminum briefcase between his legs. The man glanced at her and then went back to studying the gum spots on the floor. The carbrain asked where she was going.

"Fourteen Hampshire Road." Ruth brushed her cash card across its port.

"The fare is one-thirty-five including the senior citizen discount," said the carbrain. "Please take your seat."

She picked a spot on the bench across from the door. The air blowing out of the vents was hot, which was why all the windows were open. She brushed the hair out of her eyes as the mini rumbled around Mill Pond and onto Oyster River Road.

The mini was strewn with debris; wrappers, squashed beer boxes, dirty receipts. Someone had left a paper bag on the bench next to her. Just more garbage, she thought—until it jumped. It was a muddy Shop 'n' Save sack with the top crumpled down to form a seal. As she watched, it moved again.

She knew better than to talk to people on the minibus, but Ruth could not help herself. "Is this yours?"

The man's expression hardened to cement. He shook his head and then touched the eye clipped to the neckband of his shirt and started recording her.

"Sorry." She scooted down the bench and opened the bag. A bullfrog the size of her fist rose up on its hind legs, scrabbled weakly toward her, and then sank back. At first she thought it was a toy with a run-down battery. Then she realized that some brain-dead kid had probably caught it down at the pond and then left it behind. Although she had not seen a frog up close in years, she thought this one looked wrong somehow. Dried out. They breathed through their skins, didn't they? She considered getting off the mini and taking it back to the water herself. But then she would be on foot in the open, an easy target. Ruth felt sorry for the poor thing, yes, but she was not risking her life for a frog. She closed the bag so she would not have to watch it suffer.

The mini stopped at an apartment on Mill Road and honked. When no one came out, it continued toward the center of town, passed another minibus going in the opposite direction, and then pulled into the crumbling lot in front of the Shop 'n' Save plaza. There were about a dozen bicycles in the racks next to the store and four electric cars parked out front, their skinny fiberglass bodies blanching in the afternoon sun. A deliveryman was unloading beer boxes from a truck onto a dolly. The mini pulled up behind the truck and shut itself off. The door opened and the clock above it started a countdown: *10:00 . . . 09:59 . . . 09:58.* The man with the aluminum suitcase got off, strode down the plaza, and knocked at the door of what had once been the hardware store. He watched Ruth watching him until the door opened and he went in.

The empty lot shimmered like a blacktopped desert, and the heat of the day closed around her. To escape it, she tried filling the space with ghost cars: Fords and Chryslers and Toyotas. She imagined there was no place to park, just like when they still pumped gas, before they closed the university. *06:22 . . . 06:21 . . . 06:20.* But the sun was stronger than her memory. It was the sun, the goddamned sun, that was driving the world crazy. She could even hear it: the mini's metal roof clicked in its harsh light like a bomb. Who could think in heat like this?

The bag twitched again, and Ruth realized she could get water from the store and pour it over the frog. She glanced at the clock. *02:13 . . . 02:12 . . .* Too late now.

The carbrain honked and started the engine when the clock reached *00:30.* Three kids trudged out of the store. Two were lugging sacks filled with groceries; the third was Chaz, who was empty-handed. Ruth shifted her tote bag onto her lap, got a firm grip on the handle, and tried to make herself as small as possible.

"Destination, please?" said the carbrain.

"One Simons." A fat kid clumped up the step well and saw her. "Someone on already." He brushed his card across the pay port. "Lady, where you goin', lady?"

Ruth fixed her gaze on the buttons of his blue-striped Shop 'n' Save shirt; one had come undone. She avoided eye contact so he would not see how tense she was. She said nothing.

The second one bumped into the fat kid. "Move, sweatlips!" He was wearing the uniform shirt tucked into red shorts. He had shaved legs. She did not look at his face either.

"Please take your seat," said the carbrain. "Current stops are Fourteen Hampshire Road and One Simons Lane. Destination, please?"

"Stoke Hall," said Chaz.

"Hey, Hampshire's the wrong way, lady. Get off, would ya?"

"Yeah, make yourself useful for a change." Red Shorts plopped his groceries onto the bench opposite Ruth and sprawled next to them. Ruth said nothing; she saw Chaz paying the carbrain.

"Wanna throw her off?"

Ruth clenched her fists and touched the triggers of her cuffs.

"Just leave her and stretch the ride." Chaz settled beside the others. " 'Less you *wanna* get back to work."

The fat kid grunted, and the logic of sloth carried the day. Ruth eased off the triggers as the mini jolted through the potholes in the lot and turned back onto Mill Road. The boys started joking about a war they had seen on the wall. Even though they seemed to have forgotten her, the side of Ruth's neck prickled as if someone were still staring. When she finally dared peek, she saw Chaz grinning slyly at her, like she expected a tip. It made Ruth angry. She wanted to slap the girl.

They looped around downtown past the post office, St. Thomas More Church, and the droods' mall. The mall was actually a flea market that had accreted over the years in the parking lot off Pettee Brook Lane: salvaged lumber and old car parts and plastic sheeting over chicken wire had been cobbled together to make about thirty stalls. It was where people who lived in the dorms went. When the hawkers saw the mini coming, they swarmed into the street to slow it down. Ruth saw teens waving hand-lettered signs advertising rugs, government surplus cheese, bicycles, plumbing supplies stripped from abandoned houses, cookies, obsolete computers. A man in a tank top wearing at least twenty watches on each arm gestured frantically at her to get off the mini. They said you could also buy drugs and meat and guns at the mall, and what they did not have, they could steal to order. Ruth, of course, had never gone there herself, but she had heard all about it. Everyone had. The cops raided the mall regularly, but no one dared close it down for good.

The fat kid reached across the aisle and snatched the abandoned paper sack. "This yours, lady?" He jiggled it, then unrolled the top. "Oh, shit." He took the frog out, holding it by the legs so that its stomach bulged at the sides. "Oh, shit, gonna kill the bastard did this."

"Sweet," said Red Shorts. "Someone left us a present."

"It's suffocatin'." The fat kid stood, swayed against the momentum of the mini, and lurched toward Ruth. "They need water to breathe, same as we need air." When he thrust it at her, the frog's eyes bulged as if they might pop. "And you just sit here, doin' *nothing.*" Rage twisted his face.

"I-I didn't know," said Ruth. The frog was so close that she thought he meant to shove it down her throat. "I swear, I never looked inside."

"So it's dyin'," said Red Shorts. "So let's stomp it. Come on, put it out of misery." He winked at Chaz. "Grandma here wants to see guts squirt out its mouth."

"I'll do your bones, you touch this frog." The fat kid stormed down the aisle to the door. "Stop here," he said. "Let me out."

The mini pulled over. Red Shorts called to him. "Hey, sweatlips, who's gonna help me deliver groceries?"

"Fuck you." Ruth could not tell whether he was cursing Red Shorts, her, or the world in general.

The door opened. The fat kid got off, cut in front of the mini, and headed across town toward Mill Pond. Red Shorts turned to Chaz. "Likes frogs." He was still smirking as they drove off. "Thinks he's a Green."

She was not amused. "You leave it for him to find?"

"Maybe."

The mini had by now entered the old UNH campus. On-line university had killed most residential colleges; the climate shift had triggered the depression that had finished the rest. But the buildings had not stood empty for long. People lost jobs, then houses; when they got hungry enough, they came looking for help. The campuses were converted into emergency refugee centers for families with dependent children. Eight years later, temporary housing had become permanent droodtowns. Nobody knew why the refugees were called droods. Some said the word came from the now-famous song, others claimed that the

Droods had been a real homeless family. The mini passed several of the smaller dorms and then turned off Main Street onto Garrison Avenue. Ahead to the left was Stoke Hall. Red Shorts whispered something to Chaz, who frowned. It was getting harder and harder to ignore them; she could tell they were plotting something.

Nine stories tall, Stoke was the biggest dorm on campus. When Ruth had gone to UNH, it had housed about sixteen hundred students. She had heard that there were at least four thousand droods there now, most of them kids, almost all of them under thirty. Stoke was a Y-shaped brick monster; two huge jaws gaped at the street. Its foundation was decorated with trash dropped from windows. The packed-dirt basketball court, dug into the sloping front courtyard, was empty. The players loitered in the middle of the street, watching a wrecker hitch a tow to a stalled water truck. The mini slowed to squeeze by, and Chaz slid onto the bench beside Ruth.

"Wanna get off and look?" She nodded at the dorm.

"Huh?" Red Shorts had a mouth full of celery he had stolen from one of the bags. "Talkin' to me?"

"Up there." As she leaned over to point at the upper floors, Chaz actually brushed against Ruth. "Two down, three left. Where I live."

The girl's sweaty skin caught at the fabric of Ruth's sleeve. Ruth did not like being touched. Over the years, she had gotten used to meeting people electronically, through the walls. Those few she did choose to see were the kind of people who bathed and wore clean shirts. People who took care of themselves. Chaz was so close that Ruth felt sick. It was as if the girl's smokey stink were curdling in the back of her throat. She needed to get away, but there was nowhere to go. She fought the impulse to blow Chaz a face full of Knockdown, because then she would have to gas Red Shorts, too. And what if one of them managed to call for help? She imagined the mob of basketball players stopping the mini and pulling her off. She would be lucky if all they did was beat her, the way they had beaten Matt. More likely she would be raped, killed, they were *animals,* she could *smell* them.

"C'mon," said Chaz. "You show your place. I show mine."

Ruth's voice caught in her throat like a bone. The mini cleared the water truck and pulled up in front of the dorm. "Stoke Hall," said the carbrain. It opened the door.

"What you say, lady?" Chaz stood. "Won't hurt."

"Much." Red Shorts snickered.

"You shut up," said Chaz.

Ruth stared at the words on her T-shirt, FOR A NICKEL I WILL. She felt for the triggers and shook her head.

"How come I gotta play lick ass?" Chaz squatted so that her face was level with Ruth's; she forced eye contact. "Just wanna talk." The girl feigned sincerity so well that Ruth wavered momentarily.

"Yeah," said Red Shorts, "like 'bout how you pigs ate the world."

Ruth started to shake. "Leave me alone." It was all happening too fast.

"Stoke Hall," repeated the carbrain.

"Okay, okay." Chaz rose up, disgusted. "So forget it. You don't gotta say nothing to droods. You happy, you rich, so fuck me." She turned and walked away.

Ruth had not expected Chaz to be wounded, and suddenly she was furious with the foolish girl. Her invitation was a bad joke. A woman like Ruth could not take three steps into that place before someone would hit her over the head and drag her into a room. Chaz wanted to make *friends* after everything that had happened? It was too late, way too late.

She was already halfway down the step well when Red Shorts leaned toward Ruth. "You old bitch pig." His face was slick with greasy sweat; these droods had no right to talk to her that way. Without thinking, she thrust her fist at him and emptied a clip of Knockdown into his eyes.

He screamed and lurched backward against the grocery sacks, which tipped off the bench and spilled. He bounced and pitched facedown on the floor, thrashing in the litter of noodle soup, bulbs, and bright packages of candy. Ruth had never used riot gas before, and she was stunned at its potency. Truth in advertising, she thought, and almost laughed out loud. Chaz came down the aisle.

"Get off." Ruth raised her other fist. "Get the hell off. *Now!*"

Chaz backed away, still gaping at the boy, whose spasms had subsided to twitching. Then she clattered down the steps and ran up the street toward the basketball players. Ruth knew at that moment she was doomed, but the carbrain closed the door and the mini pulled away from the curb, and she realized that she had gotten away with it. She *did* laugh then; the sound seemed to come to her from a great distance.

Suddenly she was shivering in the afternoon heat. She had to do something, so she grabbed Red Shorts by the shoulders and muscled him back onto a bench. She had not meant to hurt anyone. It was an accident, not her fault. She felt better as she picked up the spilled groceries, repacked them, and arranged the sacks neatly beside him. He didn't look so bad, she thought. He was napping; it would not be the first time someone had fallen asleep on the minibus. She retrieved an apple from under the bench.

She got so involved pretending that nothing was wrong that she was surprised when the mini stopped.

"Fourteen Hampshire," said the carbrain.

Ruth regarded her victim one last time. Since she had tried her best to put things back the way they were supposed to be, she decided to forgive herself. She grabbed her tote bag, stepped off, and hurried to the front door of Matt's decaying colonial. By the time the mini rumbled off, she had pushed the unpleasantness from her mind. She owed it to him to be cheerful.

Ruth had not been out to Matt's house since last fall; usually he visited her. It was worse than she remembered. He could not keep the place up on his pension. Paint had chipped off the shingles, exposing gray wood. Some of them had curled in the sun. A rain gutter was pulling away from the roof. Poor Matt couldn't afford to stay, but he couldn't afford to sell, either. No one was buying real estate in Durham. She heard him unlocking the door and made herself smile.

"*Ruth!* I thought I told you to stay home."

"Mr. Watson? Mr. Matthew Watson of Fourteen Hampshire Road?" She consulted an imaginary clipboard. "Are you the gentleman who ordered the surprise party?"

"I can't believe you did this." He tugged her inside and shut the door. "Do you have any idea how dangerous it is out there?"

She shrugged. "So, are you glad to see me?" She put down her tote and opened her arms to him.

"Yes, of course, but . . ." He leaned forward and gave her a stony peck on the cheek. "This is serious, Ruth."

"That's right. I seriously missed you."

"Don't make jokes. You don't understand these people. You could've been hurt." He softened then and hugged her. She stayed in his embrace longer than he wanted—she could tell—but that was all right. His arms shut the world out; his strength stopped time. Nothing had happened, nothing could happen. She had not realized how lonesome she had been. She did not even mind his cast jabbing her.

"Are you okay, Ruth?" he murmured. "Is everything all right?"

"Fine." Eventually she had to let him go. "Fine."

"It's good to see you," he said, and gave her an embarrassed smile. "Even if you are crazy. Come into the kitchen."

Matt poured the Medoc into coffee cups, and they toasted their friendship. "Here's to twenty-six years." Actually, she had been friends with Greta before she knew Matt. Ruth set the Tupperware on the counter. "What should I serve the fish on?" She opened the china cabinet and frowned. Matt was such a typical bachelor: he had none of the right dishes.

"I'm glad you came over," he said. "I've been wanting to talk to you. I suppose I could tell you through the wall, but. . . ."

"Tell me?" She dusted a cracked bowl with the edge of her sleeve.

He ran his finger around the rim of the cup and shrugged uncomfortably. "You know how lonely I've been since the . . . since I broke my hip. I think that's my biggest problem. I can't go out anymore, and I can't live here by myself."

For a few thrilling seconds, Ruth misunderstood. "Oh?" She thought he was going to ask her to live with him. It was something she had often fantasized about.

"Anyway, I've been talking to people at Human Services and I've decided to take in some boarders."

"Boarders?" She still did not understand. *"Droods?"*

"Refugees. I know how you feel, but they're people just like us, and the state will pay me to house them. I have more room than I need, and I can use the money."

Her hands felt numb. "I don't believe this. Really, Matt, haven't you learned anything?" She had to put the bowl down before she dropped it. "You go to the dorms to tutor, and they beat you up. They crippled you. So now you're going to bring the animals right into your own house?"

"They're not animals. I know several families who would jump at the chance to leave the dorms. Kids, Ruth. Babies."

"Look, if it's only money, let me help. Please."

"No, that's not it. You said something this morning. I'm a teacher all right, except I have no one to teach. That's why I feel so useless. I need to—"

A window shattered in the bedroom.

"What was that?" Matt bolted from his chair, knocking his wine over.

"There are many people on the street," announced the homebrain. "They are destroying property."

Ruth heard several angry *thwocks* against the side of the house and then more glass broke. She felt as if a shard had lodged in her chest. Someone outside was shouting. Wine pooled on the floor like blood.

"Call the police." Matt could not afford private security.

"The line is busy."

"Keep trying, damn it!"

He limped to the bedroom, the only room with a window wall; Ruth followed. There was a stone the size of a heart on the bed, glass scattered across the rug.

"Show," said Matt.

The wall revealed a mob of at least a hundred droods. Basketball players, hawkers from the mall, kids from Stoke. And Chaz. Ruth was squeezing her security pager so hard that her hand hurt.

"Hey, walter, send the bitch out!"

She had been so stupid. Of course Chaz had heard the carbrain repeat Matt's address.

"Boomers. *Fuckin' oldies.*"

She had never understood why they were all so eager to hate people like her and Matt. It was not fair to punish an entire generation.

"Burn 'em. Send the pigs to hell!"

The politicians were to blame, the corporations. They were the ones responsible. It was not *her* fault; she was just one person. "Go ahead, Matt," she said bitterly. "Teach them about us." Ruth pressed herself into the corner of his bedroom. "Maybe we should invite them in for a nice glass of wine?"

"What is this, Ruth?" Matt grabbed her by the shoulders and shook her. "What did you do?"

She shook her head. "Nothing," she said.

faith

Faith was about to cross Congress Street with an armload of overdue library books when she was run over by a divorce. There was no mistaking Chuck's cranberry BMW 325is idling at the light—except that Chuck was supposed to be in Hartford. The woman next to him had enough blonde hair to stuff a pillow. The light changed, and the BMW accelerated through the intersection. Chuck was crazy if he thought he could get away with hit-and-run. The blonde looked suddenly ill; she folded down in her seat like a Barbie doll in a microwave. Without thinking, Faith hurled the top bock in her stack. *Whump!* It was the first time she had ever appreciated Stephen King's wordiness; *The Tommyknockers* bounced off the passenger door, denting it nicely. Chuck raced up Islington and out of her life. The book lay open next to the curb. Its pages fluttered in the wind, waving good-bye to fifteen years of marriage.

She had a long convalescence, during which Kleenex sales reached an all-time high. Chuck got the Beemer, the bimbo, and the freedom to be himself—poor bastard. She got the cape on Moffat Street and their teenager, Flip. By the time the divorce was final, she had lost her illusions about love, half of her friends, and twenty-three pounds.

She realized she was healing one day during her lunch hour. She was in a dressing room at Marshalls and had just wriggled into a size-ten bikini.

"Maybe I should write a book," she said. In the next stall her best friend Betty grunted in frustration. "*The Divorce Diet*, what do you think?" Faith spread her fingers across her tummy. Her mother's bulge had receded until it no longer resembled the front bumper of a pickup. "You too can cry those extra pounds off." She turned and eyed her backside in the mirror. "Stress: the key to tighter buns."

"Hell of a way to lose weight." Betty remained behind the curtain; she usually avoided mirrors like a vampire. "Liposuction is cheaper. Jesus, my thighs look like water balloons." She stuck her head out to admire Faith in the bikini. "You look great, Faith, you really do. When are you going to do something about it?"

The question nagged at Faith. What was she waiting for? Women were supposed to take what they wanted these days, not wait for men to offer it. At least, that was what the cigarette ads said. All her friends wanted to fix her up—Betty, in particular. Betty was hungry for vicarious thrills; she was married to Dave, who spent too much time on the road selling excavation equipment. As Faith rebuttoned her blouse, she wondered if she was ready now to go out.

But not with friends of friends. Not yet. Better to start with something she could abandon, if necessary, without making too much of a mess. She had been following the personals in *Portsmouth Magazine;* she thought she might run an ad.

She wrote it that afternoon at work, where it was easier to see herself objectively. After all, writing ad copy was her business. DWF. Faith hated that acronym. In her mind she could not help but hear DWF as dwarf. Who wanted to go out with Sneezy? Or Dopey? DWF 35. Now she needed some adjectives. Attractive professional. Okay, but there should be more. Attractive, slender, witty, secure professional. No, no, overkill. Delete slender. Now she needed something about her interests. What were her interests? Napping came immediately to mind. After working all day at the agency and then coming home to cook and clean and vacuum and do laundry and scrub toilets, she did not exactly have the energy to train for the decathlon or plow through *The New York Review of Books*. She made herself concentrate; there had to be something. My favorites: the flowers at Prescott Park, jazz, the beach in the winter, candlelit dinners anywhere. Yes, she liked that; it reeked of romance. Last came specifications for her ideal date. The problem was that she was not exactly sure what she wanted. Chuck's shabby betrayal had left her utterly confused about men. Seeking an intellectual and emotional equal. No, too pretentious. She was looking for some guy to split a pizza with, not applying to the University of New Hampshire. She scanned some other ads; what were her fellow dwarfs searching for? Compassionate, warm, honest, gentle, nondrinking life partners to share soft music, moonlit walks, and a lasting friendship. She was horror-struck: these women all wanted to spend the night with Mr. Rogers! That decided her. She batted out a last line. Two deft keystrokes brought the brochure copy for Seacoast Cruises onto the computer screen, and Faith was back in business. She pushed the ad out of her mind until just before quitting time, when she printed it without looking at it, wrote a check for a two-week run, and mailed it.

DWF 35, attractive, witty, secure professional. My favorites: the flowers at Prescott Park, jazz, the beach in the winter, candlelit dinners anywhere. Looking for someone completely different. A little generic, perhaps, but it would do for starters.

When she got home, Flip, also known as The Creature From The Eighth Grade, was conducting SDI research in the backyard. He was directing photons at a nest of communist tent caterpillars with a magnifying glass he had borrowed from Faith's *Oxford English Dictionary*.

"Flip, I'm home. Please don't do that; it's gross."

"Ma, I'm zapping them before they go into launch mode."

"Forget it."

"Can I set them on fire with lighter fluid then?"

"*No*. Was there any mail today?"

"You got a check from Dad. No note, though."

"Flip, I've told you before. Don't open my mail."

"He's my father, you know."

"Yes, I know." She bit back an insult and confiscated the magnifying glass instead. "Look, I'm expecting some letters soon, okay? Addressed to me. Faith Pettingell. Open my mail again, sucker, and I'm taking a hammer to your TV."

"What's the matter, Ma, you got a boyfriend or something? About time you started going out."

Sometimes Flip had all the charm of a housefly. Actually, Faith loved her son dearly and would not have hesitated to rush into a burning building after him, although then they would probably both die of smoke inhalation. Betty, who substituted at the middle school, liked to say that there was really no such thing as a thirteen-year-old, that inside every eighth grader were a ten-year-old and a sixteen-year-old locked in mortal combat. Given enough time, the big kid would win and ask to borrow the car. Meanwhile, according to Betty, the best Faith could do was to silently chant the mother's mantra: "It's only a phase, it's only a phase."

It would have been easier if only Flip did not remind her so much of Chuck.

She got seven replies to her ad. Two she tossed immediately. One guy had handwriting like a lie detector chart; she was not even sure what language he had responded in. The other was only marginally literate. Faith considered herself a tolerant woman, but she simply could not see herself with a man who could not get his subjects and verbs to agree.

She also heard from two lawyers, a plumbing contractor, and a computer programmer. Both of the lawyers played tennis; one had a sailboat. The programmer claimed to have eaten at every restaurant in Portsmouth. The plumber seemed to have had the most interesting life; he was a skydiver and had once lived in Thailand. Everyone but the programmer had been married before; the plumber was in the middle of divorce number two. They all seemed harmless enough, which left her at once pleased and vaguely disappointed. She felt like a little girl on Christmas morning just after she had opened the last present.

There was one other—strange—reply. It came from a man named Gardiner Allan. He did not offer a chatty autobiography or, indeed, any information about himself at all, other than a post-office box number in Barrington. Instead he sent poetry.

Somewhere a stranger
is sleeping alone,
dreaming of gardens.
Roses breathe poems,
sweet sonnets of scent.
Leaves stir like green hearts.

The sun's caresses
inflame her bare skin.
But the cruel breeze sighs,
it isn't enough.
Where is the lover,
tender of flowers?
Then she spots someone
drowsing in shadow,
reaches to rouse him
and uproots herself.
Your dreams can't come true
Until you wake up.

Faith was intrigued. After all, she had advertised for someone completely different. But all this stuff about inflaming caresses and bare skin and lovers. Faith had steeled herself for many things; love was not one of them. She no longer believed in love. And what kind of name was Gardiner Allan anyway? It sounded like an alias—maybe he was an escaped pervert. He had not even given a phone number. Still, no one had ever written her a poem before.

She ended up sending a postcard she had bought at the Museum of Fine Arts in Boston. On the front was a reproduction of Mary Cassatt's painting, *The Letter.* On the back she wrote:

Dear Mr. Allan,
I enjoyed your poem. Is there more to you?

She signed it "Faith" but gave no last name or return address. Let him get in touch with her through *Portsmouth Magazine.* If mysterious and artsy was his game, she could play too.

She began conducting what she described to Betty as experiments in dating. The results were inconclusive. She saw the lawyer with the sailboat just the once, for lunch. He was five feet one. They had not said three words to each other when he started making announcements.

"I should tell you up front that I can't stand people who smoke."

Faith smiled politely. "That's okay, I don't."

"And I don't drink either."

Her smile shrank like cheap jeans. "Oh?"

"And I don't eat red meat or refined sugar."

"You do breathe?"

"Breathe? Breathe? Everyone breathes."

She liked the other lawyer better. He had a voice like an announcer on National Public Radio. He was also a great kisser; he could do things with his lower lip that were probably against the law in Alabama. He stopped calling, though, after she beat him in straight sets: 6–4, 6–2. The programmer wore plastic shoes. He took her to dinner at the Seventy-Two but then ordered for both of them without asking her first. In a moment of weakness, she went out with him once more. This time they went to Luka's. They danced after dinner, but he never made eye contact while they were on the floor. He was too busy shopping the meat market around the bar. On the drive home he took off his shoes. His feet smelled like low tide.

The plumber was gorgeous; the only problem was that he knew it. He had a lion's mane of tawny hair and biceps the size of a meat loaf; he looked and acted at least fifteen years younger than he really was. Faith knew it was shallow of her, but she could not help herself; the closer she stood to him, the tighter her underwear felt. He seemed to have been everywhere and tried everything. On one date they stood outside of Rosa's for almost an hour waiting to get in, but she hardly noticed because he was telling her how he had once had a mystical experience while on psilocybin at the Temple of Dawn in Bangkok. By the time they had reached the door, most of the women in line behind them were eavesdropping shamelessly. Faith glanced back at them in amazement; the competition was ogling her date. She kept fantasizing that Chuck would drive by and see them there.

But somehow their relationship never got out of the shallows. The more Faith did with him, the more she realized that, with this guy, what you saw was *all* you got. He could tell some wonderful stories, yet he seemed not to have learned anything from them. And his boyishness got old fast. Not only did he know the lyrics to "Teenager in Love," but he sang them with conviction. He did not have much use for Flip; she suspected it was because her son made him feel his true age. What ended their affair, though, was his explanation of the Zen of seduction.

"Yeah, I learned it from this cartoonist I used to know in Singapore. The trick is not to want anything." He traced the line of her jaw as he spoke. "Empty the mind of all desire. If you absolutely don't care what happens, it drives them wild. They start throwing themselves at you."

"Is that what happened with us?" Faith propped herself up on her elbow.

"Maybe."

"And you don't want anything from me?"

He grinned then and kissed her. It was a perfectly good kiss, but it left a bad taste in her mouth afterward. She started using her answering machine to screen his calls, which she never returned. Eventually he got the message.

By summer, the experiments were completed. Faith had begun with low expectations, and they had been met exactly. At least she had proved to herself that she could date without getting involved. Now she was going to give men a rest. The weeds were choking her garden and the house needed cleaning and she had been neglecting her son.

She worried that Flip was lonely now that school was out. Usually he would bike over to swim team practice in the morning and then maybe visit his best friend Jerry, but Jerry's family went to their place on Lake Winnisquam in July. She had put Flip on a television diet of three hours a day, so he spent most afternoons either doing chores or fooling around with his computer or reading an endless stream of comics and trashy science fiction. She left work early a few days so that they could go to the beach, but that was very hard for Faith. Flip kept staring at girls' breasts like they were cupcakes and he wanted to lick the frosting off. He's perfectly normal, she told herself as she ground her teeth. She had always assumed that Chuck would provide the necessary parental guidance about sex once Flip reached puberty. Chuck, however, was hardly a role model.

She decided it was better they should go someplace where people wore clothes. "Hey, Flip," she said one night, gallantly trying to compete with *Star Trek;* Captain Kirk was smirking at some space bimbo dressed in high heels and aluminum foil. "I just got the schedule for the Arts Festival at Prescott Park. Guy Van Duser and Billy Novick are on next Friday. How about we fry up some chicken and check them out? We could stay for the play."

"*Bor*ing." At the commercial he ran for the bathroom.

"Come on." She pulled the schedule from her purse. "I thought you'd like the play. *Little Shop of Horrors.*"

"Saw the movie," Flip called. "Both movies."

"How about this? Mondays they're having a science-fiction film festival at the library. *When Worlds Collide.*" She read from the schedule. "*Invasion of the Body Snatchers, Plan 9 from Outer Space.*"

"*Plan 9?* Jerry says that's the worst movie ever made. I heard it's awesome. I could see that. Yeah!"

Flip had been a science-fiction fan since the third grade, a vice he had picked up from Chuck. Betty had been telling Faith for years not to worry. She claimed that science fiction was only another phase.

"Well, his father never grew out of it," Faith said.

"Live with it," said Betty. "It's better than girls, believe me. You can't catch a disease from science fiction."

"It's easy for you to say." Faith twirled the phone cord impatiently. "He's not dragging you to *Plan 9 from Outer Space.* Say, what are you doing Monday? Isn't Dave in Worcester?"

"Yes, but really, there's this Newhart rerun. . . ."

"Come on, I'll take you for ice cream afterward."

About a dozen people turned out on a hot Monday night to see the worst movie ever made. It was about stodgy aliens in silver tights who zoomed around in an Art Deco frisbee raising the dead. The only actor she recognized was Bela Lugosi, who looked as if he had just been raised from the dead. Betty wanted to go after the first reel, but Flip was staying. While the librarian changed reels, Flip struck up a conversation with a friendly man who explained that the reason Bela looked so feeble was that he had died two days after shooting started. The director had then enlisted his wife's hairdresser as a stand-in. While her son listened, Faith idly sized the stranger up as a potential date. She had been doing that a lot lately; she was still trying to figure out her type. This one was tall, skinny, and thirtyish, and he had very blue eyes. Handsome but not tastelessly so—too bad she did not trust men with glasses. Betty caught her looking and raised an inquiring eyebrow. Faith pursed her lips slyly and scooted around to face the screen. No way a Bela Lugosi fan could be her type.

After the movie, they window-shopped up Congress Street and down Market Square. When they got to Annabelle's, Faith was surprised to see the stranger already there, working on a sandwich and a bowl of soup. He grinned at her. "We've got to stop meeting like this."

Faith smiled back. "Small town, isn't it?" It was an absurdly trite comeback, but he did not seem to mind.

She was not quite sure why, but the smile stayed on her face. It felt comfortable there. She ordered a small crunchy chocolate cone while Flip and Betty settled at a table. They left her the chair facing the affable stranger.

"What did you get, Faith?" Betty nudged her. *"Faith?"*

The stranger made eye contact.

"Uh, fine." Faith's cheeks were warm. "Lovely." It was eerie, but she *knew* he would get up. She *knew* he was going to come over to talk to her. The surprise was that she wanted him to do it.

"Excuse me for eavesdropping," he said, "but is your name Faith?"

"Yes," she said.

"I think we may have corresponded." He extended his hand. "I'm Gardiner Allan."

"Uh, Gardiner Allan, right. The poet. You never wrote back."

"But I did. You never answered my second letter."

"I never got it."

He grimaced and made a crack about raccoons running the post office. She wanted to say something clever, but *Plan 9* had turned her brain to cottage cheese. Meanwhile, Betty was practically twitching with curiosity.

"Why don't you pull up a chair, Gardiner?" said Flip.

He glanced at Faith. "I wouldn't want to intrude. . . ."

"Yes, please sit." She scooted her chair to make room. "It's no fun eating alone. I know. This is my friend, Betty Corriveau. My son, Flip."

Betty shook his hand; Flip waved. Faith could not think of anything to say, so she licked her crunchy chocolate ice cream, which was already melting. Gardiner spooned up some soup. The silence stretched. Faith realized the man was probably thinking about all those damned adjectives: *witty, secure professional.* So much for truth in advertising.

"Well, this is a coincidence." Betty to the rescue. "So you're a poet, Gardiner?"

"It's a hobby, actually. Nobody earns a living from poetry—unless they work at Hallmark."

"And what do you do when you're not writing?"

"I breed plants."

"Are you with the university?" said Faith.

"No, I'm not affiliated with anyone. I guess you'd call me a freelancer."

"That must be interesting." Betty sounded skeptical. "What kind of plants do you breed?"

"Oh, different kinds." He shrugged. "I've just developed a tetraploid hemerocallis I'm pretty fond of."

"Hemerocallis," Faith said. "Daylily, right?"

"That's it." He nodded approvingly. "Tets have twice the number of chromosomes, you know. Gives them vigor, clearer colors, better substance. But they don't breed true, so you have to propagate them by division, which is slow, or tissue culture, which is expensive."

"What's that you're eating?" Flip had a low tolerance for adult chitchat. "Looks pretty nasty."

"Tomato dill soup and a vegetarian sandwich."

"Oh, are you a vegetarian?" Betty was grilling him as if she were doing an FBI background check.

"No, I just have to watch my diet." He waved his spoon vaguely. "So, Flip, what did you think of the movie?"

They soon got to comparing favorites. Gardiner kept mentioning films that even Flip had never heard of.

"I just don't understand the attraction," Betty interrupted. "Sci-fi . . . it's just too weird for me."

"Weird, right," said Gardiner. "You know, *weird* comes from the Saxon: *wyrd.* Means fate or 'what is to come.' That's why people like science fiction, I think—kids especially. Their fate matters to them. They're still interested in what's coming. Other people bury their heads in the here and now, as if it was the only reality. Change spooks them and the future scares them silly. Since they don't understand it, they refuse to believe in it. But it's just plain wrong to pretend that 2001 is some impossible fairyland like Oz. Weird or not, it's coming."

Betty was momentarily speechless.

"I didn't know anyone took science fiction so seriously," Faith said.

"Not just science fiction. Fantasy, horror—I don't know. I'm strange, I guess. Different, anyway. Some people are afraid of that." He chuckled. "Hey, Flip, how about *Forbidden Planet?*"

"Is that the one with the robot?"

"Yeah. Did you know it's a remake of Shakespeare's *The Tempest?* Robby is Ariel and Morbius is Prospero. Read *The Tempest?*"

"Shakespeare? You've got to be kidding me. They made us read *Romeo and Juliet* in English, and I just about barfed."

"Flip, you've got to give Will a chance. Great fantasy writer. *The Tempest* has magicians and monsters—it's awesome. Or read some of his horror, *Macbeth* or *Hamlet.*"

Faith liked the way this man's mind worked, but she was not about to let him know that. Not yet anyway. "I'm not sure I see *Macbeth* as a horror story."

"Oh, sure. There's even a curse on it; ask any actor. They're afraid to say the name; they call it 'that Scottish play.' People have died mysteriously. They say Shakespeare used real spells for the witches' dialogue."

Flip gazed at Gardiner as if he were the second coming of Rod Serling. Betty glanced at her watch—he had lost her back at *Forbidden Planet*. Faith wiped drips of crunchy chocolate ice cream from her fingers.

"I'm sorry." Gardiner looked sheepish. "I get carried away sometimes."

"No, no," said Faith. "It's fascinating. Really. Problem is that it's almost ten and I've got to be at work early tomorrow." She pushed her chair back.

"Would you mind if I called you sometime?" The way he said it suggested that he did not expect her to say yes.

"Why not?" She patted his hand. "I'd like that." He had rough skin. "I'm in the book."

"See you, Gardiner," Flip said.

"Nice to meet you."

Faith could not sleep that night. Her bed seemed very big. Very lonely. The way Gardiner had guessed her name bothered her. How many other women named Faith had he accosted? She replayed their conversation in her mind. Something was wrong.

"Damn." She sat up abruptly. *"Damn."* How was he going to get her number when she had never told him her last name?

Flip was upstairs reading and Faith was making dinner. The phone rang. "Flip, can you get that?" She heard him bound across the upstairs hall and held herself poised for a moment, but he did not call, so she went back to her chicken salad. She chopped some leftover white meat, a stalk of celery, a thin slice of Bermuda onion, and a sliver of red pepper. She found the mayonnaise in the refrigerator but did not see the relish.

"Flip, where's the relish?" she shouted.

"I needed it," he shouted back.

"You needed it? A whole jar of relish? What for?"

"Ma, I'm on the phone if you don't mind."

She wiped her hands and picked up on the kitchen extension. "We interrupt this conversation for an important announcement. . . ."

"Ma!"

"Tell your friend you'll get back to him after we settle this relish crisis."

"Ma, I forgot to mention that I ran into—"

"Hello, Faith. This is Gardiner Allan."

"—Gardiner today at the library."

"Gardiner." She felt as if she had just swallowed a brick. "Hi."

"I was going to say something at dinner."

"Flip, hang up." *Click.* "Well, Gardiner, you sure have a knack for surprising people."

"I've had years of practice. I'm sorry, is this a bad time? I could try again later."

"That's okay." She caught the handset between her chin and shoulder as she checked the corn muffins in the oven. "Just puttering around the kitchen. So, how are you?"

He chattered for a while about how Park Seed was interested in exclusive rights to his new daylily for their Wayside Gardens catalog, and then she babbled about the direct mail campaign she was doing for the Fox Run Mall. They complained about the muggy weather. They agreed that Flip was a wonderful kid. She made a comment about how lucky it was that Gardiner had run into him at the library.

"Maybe it wasn't luck," said Gardiner. "Maybe it was fate."

"Weird," she said. It was the first time she had made him laugh.

The preliminaries out of the way, he asked her to dinner. As soon as she said yes, however, they seemed to run out of things to talk about. They agreed on Friday night at six, and then he said he had to go and hung up.

"Flip, let's eat!"

As Faith listened to her son thud downstairs like a bowling ball, she wondered whether she had done a good thing in agreeing to see Gardiner Allan. Flip set the book he had been reading beside his plate.

It was *A Midsummer Night's Dream.*

Gardiner seemed edgy; he walked Faith out to his car like a man on his way to an audit. The backseat of his Ford Escort wagon was covered with a plastic dropcloth. On it squatted an enormous plant with blue-green leaves the size of dinner plates.

"Gardiner, what a beautiful plant!"

"*Hosta seiboldiana.* A new cultivar."

Faith arched an eyebrow. "I've never been out with a perennial before."

"There's a perfectly good reason why I had to bring it, which I'd rather not go into just now." He turned the ignition key; the engine grumbled and caught.

"Does it have a name?" she asked.

"23HS."

"Pleased to meet you, Mr. S." She twisted around in her seat and touched one of the big leaves.

Gardiner said nothing.

"So where are we going for dinner?"

"We've got reservations at Anthony's for six-thirty."

"Great. I love Anthony's." She teased him again. "But I didn't know they served hostas there."

Silence.

"Is something wrong?" she said. "I don't bite, you know. Or at least, not until after dessert."

"Everything's fine; it's my problem."

"I see." She considered. "You know what an oxymoron is, Gardiner? Because what you just said sounded like one."

He pulled off into an empty lot. "Faith, I like you, but there's something I've got to tell you."

She sagged against the passenger door. "Okay, I'm listening." She hated it when men started confessing things on the first date.

"I don't just blurt this out to anyone, you know. People get the wrong idea. But I like you."

"You said that already."

He grasped the steering wheel as if to anchor himself. "I talk to plants."

She waited. "That's all? You mean, you don't deal crack? You're not involved with a sixth-grader?"

"No, listen, I really talk to plants. Hostas, daylilies, hibiscus —you name it. I don't understand myself exactly how I do it. But I'm not crazy, believe me. Just a little different. And I get results: I'm successful at what I do. There aren't that many independent plant breeders left in this country, you know. Most of them work for universities or corporations or else they specialize in just one species. I've registered more than twenty different cultivars in the past ten years. Anyway, sometimes I wait to tell people—women—about this. I wait until they get to know me better. But when they find out, I end up getting hurt."

"Gardiner, I . . ."

"It's all right if you want to go home. I understand; it's happened before. Sometimes I don't even know why I bother. Look, I don't . . . I certainly don't expect you to talk to plants. I'd be pretty surprised if you did. You can think whatever you want—but just don't humor me. Okay? Because first they always say, 'Oh, isn't that cute, he talks to plants,' and then it's 'Poor guy, maybe he's been alone too long,' and the next step is 'Gardiner, have you ever thought about getting counseling?' I don't need counseling! I just need someone to trust me for a change."

Faith hesitated, then reached over and gently squeezed his arm. The muscle was knotted beneath his sleeve, as if he were ready to hit someone. But she knew, somehow, that she was not the one he was angry at. It was the same spooky way she had known at Annabelle's that he was going to introduce himself. Maybe it was body language or the crack in his voice, but she had a good feeling about this man, despite his tirade. She could not say why she trusted him, but she did. "I'm sorry I teased you." She let her hand drop and checked her watch. "Did you say our reservations are for six-thirty? Come on, let's go before they give some tourist our table."

He nodded and pulled back onto Islington Street. "I thought about saying that all day."

"I'll bet."

"That wasn't the way I had rehearsed it."

She sensed he was cooling off, so she grinned. "It's all part of the agenda for a first date, you know. You need to figure out whether you're with a human being or a chimpanzee, so you make up these tests—we all do."

"A test? Maybe so." He grinned back. "So what's your test?"

"Oh, I stick to the basics," she said. "Does he show up? Is he wearing shoes? Can he speak Lithuanian?" Once she got him chuckling, she met and held his gaze. "But as long as we're being disgustingly honest . . . I need to tell you something too. I'm glad you like me, Gardiner. But when a man keeps saying things like that, I hear something else."

"Okay." He sighed. "I understand."

By the time they reached Anthony's, the crisis had passed. With the help of a bottle of Valpolicella, they laughed their way through the antipasto. For the main course Faith ordered her favorite, the cunningly spiced fettuccine carbonara. She warned Gardiner that garlic was another test. He had eggplant something. She finally tried asking him about himself over the cappuccino.

"I grew up in Hollis," he said. "Mom taught math at Nashua High and Dad owned an apple orchard. I went to UNH for a couple of years; I was going to major in plant science and help run the orchard. But it was the sixties, you know. I took a detour and never got back to the highway. I inherited some money when Dad died, so I bought the land in Barrington. I wanted to raise pot, but my girlfriend at the time was paranoid, thank goodness. So I tried my hand at growing legal stuff." He lifted his cup. "The rest is horticultural history."

"You're lucky to be doing something you're good at," Faith said. "Then again, you do have the name for it."

"Gardiner was my grandmother's maiden name. Hated it when I was a kid. I thought it a bad joke my parents played on me. Now I see it more as an omen. Turns out lots of people have names that fit. The guy who took my appendix out was Dr. Cutts. The archbishop of Manila, Cardinal Sin. Grace Kelly. We once had a governor named Natt Head."

"George Bush." Faith giggled. "Dan Quayle."

"There you go."

After dinner, they strolled through town. She told him about growing up in Philadelphia. She hated discussing her marriage because of the whine that always crept into her voice, so she told Flip stories instead. Flip and the lost ant colony. Flip meets Governor Sununu. Flip and the barbecued cat food. She talked about the agency and how she was going to ask for a promotion.

"Does *your* work make you happy?" he asked.

"I don't know what happy means anymore. I thought I was happy with Chuck and he was cheating on me. Isn't happy just our capacity for self-deception?"

"That's a dumb question." He took her hand. "As long as we're being brutally honest."

"Oh." She thought about being offended. She thought about letting go of his hand. She decided not to.

They wandered through the park at twilight. Gardiner went straight for the All-America Selection trial garden. "Front row seats for the plant play-offs. Check out the celosias." He knelt to touch some spiky flowers that looked like burned feathers. "You're gorgeous," he said.

She folded her arms. "Well, thanks."

He glanced up at her, his face bright with pleasure. "Yeah, you too," he said.

Faith had long since decided that men were born compliment-impaired. "They smell nice, anyway."

"No, that's nicotiana. The white trumpets. Another old-timer they've overimproved. They bred for more flowers and gave up most of the fragrance. In your grandmother's day you would've been able to smell that bed in Maine." He straightened up. "Ever hear of Luther Burbank?"

"No." She took his hand again.

"He introduced over eight hundred varieties of new plants way before anyone understood genetics. He had an instinct. They say he could walk down a row of seedlings, deciding what to thin at a glance. He knew just which ones would bear the fruit he wanted. How could he do that?"

She shook her head.

"He developed a spineless cactus. Afterward he said, 'I often talked to the plants to create a vibration of love. "You have nothing to fear," I would tell them. "You don't need your defensive thorns. I will protect you." ' That's a direct quote. *'You have nothing to fear.'* Try publishing that in a scientific journal."

"This has something to do with your hosta."

"Here's another celosia," said Gardiner. "Cockscomb."

"Looks like a brain made of red velvet," she said, "and don't change the subject."

He stopped and faced her. "It wasn't only the words that Burbank said. It was his vibration." He looked uncomfortable. "You see, 23HS is forming gametophytes, getting ready for sexual reproduction. I'm telling it that I love it and making a . . . friendly suggestion about the offspring. A matter of a few chromosomes. It doesn't take all that much focus; it's like driving the interstate."

"Telling it? Right now?"

He nodded. His eyes seemed to get bluer, and for a moment she felt that she could see inside of him. He was afraid.

So was she. "Are you saying you're using telepathy? On a hosta?"

"Telepathy? I didn't say anything about telepathy. I said *suggestion,* Faith." He shivered in the gloom. "I hate explaining this. It always comes out wrong. So why am I telling you?"

"I don't know." She squeezed his hand. "Because you want someone to trust you?"

He stared at the lights across the river. "Would you consider coming out to the farm? I could show you there."

"I might." She surprised herself. "I just might. Promise not to sacrifice me to the corn goddess?"

"He's a mad scientist."

"He's not a scientist. He never got his degree."

It was late on a Saturday night. Betty and Faith were at the kitchen table, drinking Carlo Rossi Rhine out of coffee cups. Flip was with his father and Betty's husband Dave was in Toledo. There were only three brownies left in the pan.

"He talks dirty to plants."

"You promised to withhold judgment until I finished the story." Faith wondered if she should have said anything at all to her. "Don't you ever talk to your plants?"

"No."

"Well, I do. Millions of people do. It's perfectly acceptable behavior." Faith was keeping Gardiner's vibrations a secret for now, which was hard because they were what worried her most.

"All right, I'm withholding. He's got wonderful compost. I'm totally impartial."

"So I went up to his place in Barrington. He owns sixty acres off Route Nine. The farmhouse was built in 1834; there's an attached barn, a big greenhouse. And gardens, amazing gardens."

"Is the house nice?"

"He doesn't live in the house. He could, but it's too big for him. He has a trailer, an old-fashioned aluminum Airstream. Sort of retro. When he was a kid, he thought they looked like spaceships and he always wanted to live in one when he grew up."

"When he grew up," Betty repeated, writing on an imaginary notepad.

"I met his staff; he has an older couple, John and Sue, full-time and three kids from UNH for the summer. Everyone was so friendly and enthusiastic—reminded me of summer camp. They whistle a lot. And it's contagious. As we walked the grounds, I felt glad just to be there. Like I wanted to stretch out on the warm grass and make the afternoon last the rest of my life."

Betty refilled Faith's empty cup. "So when he talks to plants, what does he say?"

"He's a shameless flatterer. 'How's my jewel today? You're smothered with buds. And your lines are so graceful. What, are you reblooming already?' He uses Q-Tips to cross-pollinate.

'You'll like this one,' he says, 'he blooms for weeks.' And he stuffs things in his mouth like a toddler. Bits of leaf, blades of grass, thinnings—he ate a flower. Well, so did I: rose petals in the salad. But while we were in the annual garden, he ate a nasturtium. He claims it helps him stay connected. He has this theory that plants like to be consumed. They want us to make better use of them. But the worst was when he ate a Japanese beetle."

"*Ugh*. Kind of scratchy going down."

"He said he didn't do that very often, but that it reassured the plants and discouraged beetles. I think he was showing off."

"Men'll do that—don't ask me why. In college, a rugby player once swallowed a guppy for me." Betty sounded wistful. "His name was Herman."

"Oh, and he named a flower after me."

"What!"

Faith grinned. "He's been working on a new daylily and apparently it's a big deal. He just sold propagation rights to this seed company, and they've been pressing him to name it because their catalog is going to the printer. So now it's going to be called 'Faith.' In the morning it's a dusty salmon but as the blossom catches the sun, it gets brighter and pinker. 'Improves with age,' he says. And fragrant too. I mean, it was so beautiful, I wanted to cry."

"He named a flower after you on the second date! Ferchrissakes, did you go to bed with him?" She said it so that Faith could take it as a joke if she wanted.

Faith's grin stretched to a smile. "After dinner, everyone else went home and we talked for a long time on the porch swing at the house and then he said, 'I'm going to kiss you now unless you stop me.' "

"I take it you didn't."

"Are you kidding? I wanted to applaud." She dissolved into laughter and then pounded her wrists against her forehead. "Betty, I don't want to do this. I can't be falling already. It's too soon . . . I'm still rebounding from Chuck. Aren't I supposed to wait two years or something?"

"Next you'll be drawing up a flowchart! You're allowed to feel whatever you feel."

"Whose side are you on, anyway?"

"Yours."

"I didn't think you liked him after the way you acted at Annabelle's. You couldn't wait to go."

"The only reason I acted any way at all is because I was attracted to him and wished I could do something about it." She snatched up the last brownie and squinted at Faith. "Did I just say what I thought I heard myself say?"

"You don't think he's too strange?"

"Sure he's too strange." She shrugged. "Everybody is. It's a wonder we can stand one another at all, much less fall in love. I think you already know what you want to do, Faith. But if you're asking me, I say good for you."

Faith was at a loss. She had expected Betty to try and talk her out of seeing Gardiner again. Betty's approval only made her feelings for him more credible. And more scary. She wished she could have told Betty about the vibrations—or whatever the hell they were—but that would have been too reckless a violation of Gardiner's trust. Bad enough that she had blabbered as much as she had. So she was left with what seemed to her an intractable dilemma: her new boyfriend was telepathic. How else could he have recognized Faith at Annabelle's? Or found Flip at the library? Or waited until precisely the right moment to kiss her? It was not only plants that he connected to; Faith believed Gardiner had read her mind. She doubted she could be with a man who would always know what she was thinking. How would she be able to tell if she were being manipulated into doing things that she did not really want? Maybe he did not care at all, maybe he was just using his power to seduce her. When they filmed her life, they would have to call it *Passion Slave of the Mutant*. God help me, she thought, deep into yet another sleepless night, I'm sinking to Flip's level. I'm starting to see my life in terms of "B" monster movies.

Flip and Jerry were in the backseat practicing burps. Faith had never understood why rude noises should strike such profound harmonies in the souls of thirteen-year-old boys. Soon they would move on to farts. She pulled into Betty's driveway and parked next to Dave's Taurus. Something was wrong. Betty never went out when her husband was home.

"You okay?" said Faith.

"No." The screen door slammed. "Where's Gardiner?"

"He had to work late; we're meeting him at the park. Look, are you sure you want to come? I'll call him and cancel. We could go to my place and talk."

"I don't want to talk." She marched from her house as if she never intended to return. "I've been talking ever since he came home. I'm sick of hearing myself."

"Problems?"

"No problem. All I have to do is accept the fact that I have a drive-through marriage. Just take me someplace where people are having fun, okay? The more the merrier."

A dense groundcover of blankets and lawn chairs had already spread around the outdoor stage at Prescott Park Arts Festival by the time they arrived. It had been a wet summer, and many of the performances had been rained out. The penultimate show of the season had drawn a big crowd on a warm Friday night. A harpist and a science-fiction writer were the opening acts for *Little Shop of Horrors.*

They spread the blanket on the lawn between the whale sculpture and the stage. Flip and Jerry wandered off to snack, ignoring Faith's protest that the cooler was full of fried chicken and fruit salad. As the crowd filled in around them, Betty steadfastly resisted Faith's efforts to draw her out. She was about as much company as a land mine. "I'm going to stretch my legs," she said finally. "I'll be back."

Faith was sympathetic; however, she could not help but resent Betty's timing. Faith did not need to be worrying about her friend when she had to decide what to say to Gardiner. One reason she had brought Jerry and Flip along was to protect herself from a serious conversation if she lost her nerve. Now she was alone.

"What's with Betty?" He snuck up behind her, stooped, and nuzzled the back of her neck. "I saw her on the way in."

"I don't know exactly." She held out her hands to be helped up. "Funny, I was just thinking of you."

He took her weight effortlessly. "I can't stop thinking of you."

She almost came into his arms but then pushed away. "Let's take a walk." He made her feel too good.

He veered toward the garden, but she maneuvered him around it as she explained that Betty was having trouble with Dave, but was not talking about it. They passed over the bridge and past the parking lots on Pierce Island, strolling in silence while Faith worked up her courage. "What am I thinking right now?" she said. "Take a guess."

He put fingers to temples and affected an air of deep concentration. "You're thinking . . . let's see, you're thinking that if we don't turn around soon, we'll be late for the harpist. No, no, wait—that's what *I'm* thinking."

"Gardiner, what kind of vibrations do you get from me?"

"Good, good, *good,* good vibrations," he sang in a surfer falsetto.

"Be serious. I'm asking if you can read my mind."

He made a rude noise that Flip would have loved. "Everyone asks that, sooner or later. And I always tell the truth. Which is, I don't know."

"How could you not know something like that?"

"I can't tell what you're thinking, what your cat thinks, or what a rose thinks. If anything. Sometimes I sense emotions. Anger, fear, desire; the strong ones. But so what? We all give unconscious cues to one another and it's not that hard to understand them, if you pay attention. Lots of people don't. They're so locked up inside themselves that they never see anyone else. But just because I look people in the eye doesn't mean I know what's in their hearts. I'm a sender, not a receiver."

She slipped an arm around his waist. "What does that mean exactly?"

"I have no secrets because I broadcast what I feel. The stronger the emotion, the broader the cast. If I'm happy, I'm literally the life of the party. When I'm sad, people want to cry. It's a curse, really—which is why I'd rather be with my plants. It's all so much simpler with begonias. I mean, I can't hide it if I don't like someone. And when I love someone. . . ."

"You don't love me."

"No? Think about it, Faith. I'm the one that's naked. When you're close and I brush your face like this. Can't you tell? When I whisper your name? Faith."

Their lips touched.

After a while, he pulled back. "Do you know what a feedback loop is?"

"*Gardiner,* we're *kissing!*"

"When sound from the speaker gets picked up by the microphone, the system howls. It feeds on itself, increasing with every cycle to maximum output." He sifted her hair through his fingers. "Maybe that's what's happening to us. My love is reflected by you back to me, which makes me think you love me, which makes me love you more, and on and on. It's happened before."

"Doesn't leave much room for my feelings, does it?"

"I wish I knew what they were, Faith. Can you tell me?"

"No. I don't know. Now I'm really confused."

"So maybe it *is* feedback. What you need to do is get far away from me so you can decide what you feel without my interference."

"We'd better go back." She poked him in the ribs. "You sure know how to ruin a kiss."

They missed the first few minutes of the harpist, who was very good. The boys were restless, so during the break before the science-fiction writer read, she sent them over to spit off the pier. Gardiner was restless too; he went in a different direction. Faith was afraid she had hurt him.

She knew that was wrong. She was afraid of hurting him. Hurting herself. She was too damn careful; if this kept up she would never be with anyone again. She needed to take some chances. She spotted Gardiner over by the vertical planting of impatiens. He was cruising the wall of bloom like it was the salad bar at Wendy's.

"Faith, he's here," Betty hissed.

As Faith watched, Gardiner picked a flower and then surreptitiously popped it into his mouth. Nobody saw but her. She grinned and shook her head. The man needed someone to watch out for him, or he was going to get in trouble someday. And she wanted him—no question about that! He had brought her back to life; now she was ready to blossom. Why should she care how he had done it?

"And he's with someone new! I can't believe it."

Faith wondered if she were far enough away to be out of Gardiner's feedback loop. Because, from this distance, he looked very much like someone she could love. "What are you mumbling about?" Even if his kissing did need work.

"Chuck."

"Chuck?" Faith was dreaming now. "Chuck who?"

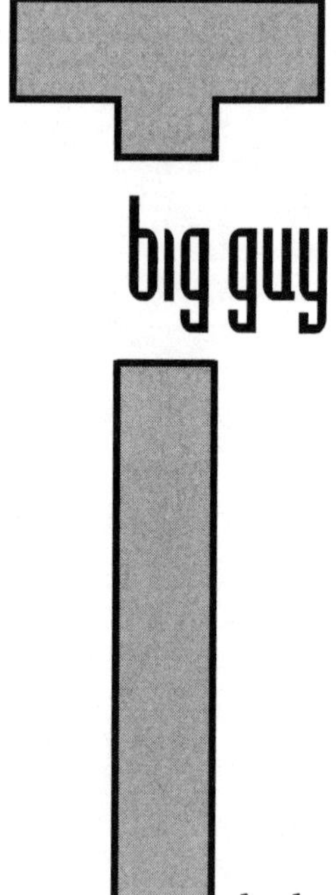

big guy

The last time he linked to Way Out, Murph had deleted his nipples. He was certain Cat had noticed, even though he had kept his shirt on while they were doing it. She *always* kept something on—one of her kinks. He had almost fainted the time with the hat. But Murph was ready for more than just another haunt fuck. He wanted to tell her his name, have her invite him back to her cabin. He imagined himself opening her medicine cabinet, looking under her bed. Had she taken the hint? Could be he'd been too subtle. She hadn't said anything about his edited chest, but of course she wouldn't. Cat loved mystery. To her, it was part of foreplay.

His twenty-seven icon started flashing. Something had set off intrusion detectors in Dr. Bertrand's office. Murph was Bertrand's security op.

"Expand," said Murph. He yawned and tilted his workseat.

The chair's hydraulics sighed under Murph's 278 pounds. The ceiling screen of the cabin showed three views of the psychologist's darkened suite on the quarterdeck. A woman he had never seen before giggled as she entered Bertrand's tiny waiting room. Bertrand reached around her and waved on the lights.

"Hi, Murph." He nodded at the camera. "Couldn't sleep, so I thought I'd get some work done."

The woman stared as if she expected to see someone in the room. Then she spotted the camera and leered. "Gotta pee first." She had a whiskey voice, dark as smoke. Bertrand pointed at the head. She wobbled over, closed the door behind her. Bertrand's wife had left him in January and moved off the ship into town. He'd been up late a lot since then, looking for something to do. Could be he'd found it.

"Hear about Noonan?" Bertrand was pretending there was no woman.

"They say there wasn't a mark on her," Murph said, "but I still don't believe it was suicide. Talked to her Friday and she was as sane as I am."

"Who was supposed to be watching her?"

"Nobody. She dropped Tumey just last week."

The toilet flushed.

"Sorry, Doc, got to go. Off in ten minutes and I'm in the middle of my last round." If Bertrand had been alone, Murph would have given him a few minutes to gripe about his life. Fat men were supposed to be good listeners. "Bumpus is covering my sites after 23:00. Don't forget to reset the system when you leave." He shrank Bertrand's office back to an icon and IDed the woman.

She was Carree Gates, a licensed pro who had commuted all the way from Lawrence. Her most recent gynecologic workup had been just last month. Murph wondered if poor Bertrand had even bothered to check. He could've watched the old guy stretch his safegirl across the couch. Bend her over his desk. Some clients liked it better that way. But it was 22:52 and he was tired of staring through the blue flickering gloom at other people's furniture. Besides, it wasn't his kink. If he had to look at someone having sex, he'd rather watch himself. With Cat.

Could be she lived up near the bow. Or on the boat deck. The thought of hauling himself up five flights of narrow stairs made Murph dizzy. The most exercise he got was eight steps to the door or the head. What if she was one of his clients? He wasn't even sure she was a woman. Once she showed as a thin twentyish man with strong thighs and a relentless appetite. Her true sex was yet another mystery Murph meant to penetrate. He had already decided it didn't make any difference. She was still Cat. A name. An attitude. Black fur. Just so long as she didn't live *too* far away.

Murph had spent the last seven hours watching eighty-six sites—forty-seven of his own clients, thirty-nine of Bumpus's—in order to earn enough free time to link to Way Out. Murph's list alone was heavy enough to mash the average independent op flat against his screens. Eighteen residences, all on the upper decks, nine shops that sold everything from bottle gardens to heroware, five takeouts: pizza, burger, squeeze, krill, and Mexican, four shrinks, three doctors, three app repair services, a lawyer, an acupuncturist, a roomdresser, a dance/defense studio, and a twenty-four-hour daycare. But Murph was no average op. He was a champion. His sites had the lowest incursion rate, real and virtual, of any contract op on the ship. Murph was proud that none of these so-called suicides had turned up on *his* list. He didn't mind what being the best had cost him. Sure, it would be easier working regular eight-hour shifts for some corporate client like the hospital or CDM or Maxit. But then a pushy boss would try to squeeze him into a diet. Drag him to fucking meetings—he'd worked for suits before. Besides, they paid in noodles. What good was free time if he couldn't afford Way Out? Or the kind of custom heroware that impressed a joyride like Cat?

Bumpus checked in at 23:07, filling the entire right screen of Murph's cabin. "Sorry I'm late." Normally he was a twitchy mouse of a man with liquid gray eyes. Tonight he had the faded copy-of-a-copy look of someone who has just jammed a month's worth of living into a couple of hours. Murph knew that look. He'd seen it in his mirror. "Had to clean up." Bumpus opened a window to show Murph his blood workup. The scrubbers had brought his alcohol level down to .02, neocaine to .005. "Any more suicides?"

"Not on our lists." Murph accepted the report. "You owe the government sleep?"

"Not until the weekend, soonest. And I just boosted."

Sleep was pure downtime. All the best ops stayed boosted as much as possible. Ultramen like Murph preferred to pay sleep debt in one lump sum. The minimum daily requirement for a working op was two hours, and Murph was always working. Once a week he had to burn fourteen precious hours of his free time in bed. "Okay," Murph said, "I've got thirty-two active sites on my side. Looking at twenty-nine of yours."

He briefed Bumpus on both lists. It was quieter than usual because a few places had closed for the Labor Day weekend. Some of Murph's residential clients could actually afford to leave the ship. Bumpus had just moved on board a couple of years ago and was still struggling to build his list. So far he had mostly C & D deck types. The only vacations they had time for were virtual. Like Bumpus, who lived down in what used to be the engine room. He was an old forty-six, already vague and a little forgetful. It was what happened when you spent too many years being in too many places at once. Bumpus was fine for the occasional free time or sleep swap, but Murph didn't think he had either the dedication or attention span for independent round-the-clock security anymore. He was nobody's champion.

"Where did you link?" Murph asked.

"The usual." Bumpus eased onto his workseat and lowered the console.

"Like?"

"Like around." Icons began to wink off Murph's screens as Bumpus picked up both lists. "Here and there." He had a high shiny forehead; he rubbed it absently. "Let's see . . . Bliss Market. I peeked at Exit Thirteen." His night out did not seem to have made much of an impression. "And Future Shock, I think that's where I ended up."

"Way Out?"

He yawned. "Your kink, not mine. What's your sixteen site again?"

"Krill Grill on D deck."

"Looks like nobody's—oh, there she is, coming out of the head. Probably bopping her hair." He swiveled to face another wall of screens. "Isn't much action on the haunts these days. Or if there is, I sure as hell can't find it."

"Not like it used to be, eh, Bumpus?"

"Maybe never was." The last icon cleared from Murph's screen. "Think next time I'll just take a walk."

"A walk?"

"Walk. You know, with my feet." He waved randomly at a bulkhead. "Off the ship into town."

"Next you'll be worshiping the sun and eating dirt."

Bumpus's mouth twisted. "When was the last time you left ship?"

"It's Kansas out there, remember?" Murph didn't have time

to wander off. He was carrying a list of forty-seven sites. "See one amber wave of grain, you've seen them all."

"Yeah, but how many bedrooms can you watch before you crack?"

"Your kink, Bumpus. Not mine."

Bumpus grunted and tapped at his console. Murph realized that he'd gotten more reaction out of Bumpus in the last ten seconds than in the previous two years.

"Okay." Bumpus slumped back in his workseat like a balloon with a slow leak. "Your list accepted at 23:17:38. Six hours of free time, starting now. Live fast, fat man." He broke the link.

Bumpus had been Murph's only active screen. When he wiped Murph without warning, the cabin went dark. "Hey!" He had left Murph utterly disconnected from the world. No input, no output. It spooked him. Only two of the six surfaces of Murph's cabin were not screens: the floor and the utility wall. Murph couldn't see anything but the red light of the clock over the sink. 23:17:41, 23:17:42, 23:17:43, seconds of his hard-earned free time dripped like blood into silence and the night. The air seemed to clot with nothingness. He swallowed. The workseat's armrests felt sticky against his wrists. It was like the time he tried to sleep without pills.

"Infoline!" His voice cracked. "Sportsworld! Jabberwock!" On the ceiling, the Captain-Mayor was downplaying the ship's most recent suicide. To his left, the center fielder for the Kansas City Royals loped under a high fly. He flipped his sunglasses and raised his mitt. The woman being interviewed on his right was wearing nothing but a swarm of bees. The busy waiting world gleamed through the walls, reassuring him that he wasn't really alone.

Staples made the catch and headed for the dugout without breaking stride. Two to nothing, Caballeros, top of the fourth. Murph shivered and pushed his anxiety away. No time for it—Cat might be waiting already. He wiped the Captain-Mayor to order a cajun potato squeeze, then called up his heroes on the back wall.

Murph's heroware collection went back eleven years. When he first could afford to link, he had settled for cheap generics. He had a Samson with a cock as thick as a cucumber, a Sir Knight with three add-on armor modules, and a vampire that could change into a bat or a wolf. Later, as he discovered more sophisticated haunts, he had splurged on the limited-edition

Dragon and a *Homo habilis.* Mirrorman, a custom job, had cost him six months' savings.

Eventually he'd realized it was all kids' stuff. High fashion in heroware catered mostly to drones who didn't like being who they were. They were afraid they were too ugly, too boring, too ethnic to attract beautiful, exciting people—and they were right. So they hid in anonymous virtual bodies and played games that kept them from finding out anything important about one another. Fighting games, drug games, sex games.

Once upon a time Murph had been one of them, a miserable slab of fat. He had nothing he was proud of. So he had worked harder than anyone he knew. Now he was a champion and he had Cat. He pointed to the last icon in his collection. Big Guy filled the back wall.

Murph, Cat, and their familiars in Way Out had stopped wasting their free time playing games. Their heroware shredded the mask of virtual fashion, by hinting who they might *actually* be. Cat, for example, claimed she showed furry because she refused to shave her legs or wax her upper lip. Her eyes made it plain that none of her people had come to America on the *Mayflower.* Shortly after he'd found Cat and Way Out, Murph had commissioned Big Guy. Himself, swollen to three times his real weight, a lavish, dripping feast of flesh. Big Guy had six chins, breasts ripe as any marilyn on the Bliss Market, a gut like a bass drum. Had he waddled into one of Bumpus's usual haunts, the drones would have laughed. Or worse, they would have ignored him. Locked him right off their screens as if he didn't exist. In Way Out, no one ever got locked off. People talked before they fucked. Sometimes they even told each other their real names. Invited each other home.

Murph eyed Big Guy, who looked back at him. "Strip." Big Guy was immediately naked. He still had no nipples. Cat had to have seen—his shirt had come completely unsealed last time. Erasing parts was, in Way Out's seduction protocol, a final step in the dance to intimacy. Could be she hadn't said anything because he had only hinted at what he wanted. Less would say more.

"Select." Murph extended his hand toward Big Guy's groin. On the screen, Big Guy reached for him. The cock was the only thing that wasn't outsized. It was Murph's own: wrinkled, circumcised, the color of Cat's lips. He flattened his hand to the screen. "Delete." Where it had been, there was now static.

The door chimed and its icon started flashing. "Expand," he

said. A delivery girl peered into the camera. "Large cajun potato," she said. He hadn't seen this one before. She looked a little like Mandy Moore, whose vid *Not Now* was Murph's favorite. He collected covert pictures of Mandy and taped them to the mirror on the utility wall. Slightly illegal but still a hot barter item. Poor Mandy needed a new security op—a champion like Murph. No one had coverts of *his* clients. The delivery girl had limp hair the color of sand. Brown eyes. A funny little flat spot at the tip of her nose. "Nine-ninety-five," she said. She was maybe thirteen—too young to be making deliveries at 23:25.

"Paying." He authorized a fifteen-dollar debit to Squeeze Pleeze. "You're new," he said while they waited for the transaction to register. "What's your name?"

"Yeah, right." She flipped her hotpak open. A large potato squeeze was the size of Murph's shoe. It came wrapped in crinkled foil. Wisps of steam curled from its crown. Even though he couldn't smell anything through the security door, he could imagine its moist starchy fragrance. Yes, and that edge of garlic and onion and nasty red pepper. He opened the delivery hatch just wide enough for her. The hotpak chimed when it verified his payment.

"Five-buck tip?" She glanced up from the readout suspiciously. "What for?"

"After you give me the squeeze," he said, "keep your hand in the hatch."

Her eyes widened. "They told me about you."

Squeeze Pleeze was on his list. "They tell you I'd bite it off?"

"I'm no joyride, Mister. I'm here. I'm real."

Murph heaved himself off the workseat. "Until I say."

"You won't hurt me." She made it an order.

"No." Dizzy, he was dizzy. Probably because he had been sitting for almost eight hours.

She had to be from town, a commuter. He probably could've IDed her, but why bother? He watched her kneel in front of the door. He turned all the lights in the cabin up. The squeeze came through the hatch. He stooped. When he took it from her, the tips of her fingers curled slightly. The foil was very hot and he dropped it to the floor. The smell was intoxicating.

She was wearing a glove, of course. It came to the folds of her wrist. He tugged at it. She twitched but did not pull away. He uncovered her palm slowly, exposing the ball of the thumb, the head line, a beautiful heart line. She had long, sensual fingers—a woman's fingers already. He brushed their length, lingering over the arches and whorls of her skin. It felt like a dream. When he'd been her age, he'd slept every night. He must've had dreams then. He couldn't remember. When he finished, he crumpled the glove and pushed it back through the hatch.

"Okay." Murph picked up the squeeze, shifting it from hand to hand to keep from burning himself.

She paused uncertainly outside his door for a moment. "Thanks," she said.

"Live fast." As Murph closed the hatch, he realized that she probably couldn't. Her folks would be waiting up for her when she got home. She'd sleep seven, eight hours. Tomorrow she'd ride crowded buses, bump through the halls at school, stare out of windows, and let boredom eat her alive. The weight of all that free time flattened people like her. It cost Murph a lot to live the way he did, but at least he was never bored.

On the back wall, Big Guy was naked. He still had a hole between his legs. Murph copied a patch from the belly. Smooth skin, fine blond hair. 23:30:02. He put Big Guy's clothes back on. Loose blue microseal shirt, black jeans, mesh shoes—what *he* was wearing, only bigger. He had five hours and forty-seven minutes. He picked up his dinner and stuck his tongue through the foil into the warm runny spiced inside. He flopped onto his workseat.

He wondered what would Cat say when she realized that the only way they could do it tonight was in person.

Way Out's welcome screen came up on all three walls and the ceiling. He showed as a huge sleeping black face. He was framed by a tangle of gray hair, sideburns, and a beard.

Murph pressed the last brain tap into place, and the system began sampling activity in his primary sensory cortex. As each sense came on-line, its icon glowed on the console. *Auditory . . . visual . . . olfactory . . .* Direct cerebral I/O cost Murph three years' income. He'd had to take out a loan, but it was worth it. Before, he'd have wasted half an hour wriggling into his reeky joysuit. If he planned a fuck, he'd have to stick his cock into a penile wrap. . . . *somesthetic . . . kinesthetic . . .* The system was already accessing his secondary cortex. When most people linked to the haunts, they were pleasured through their nerve endings. Murph wasn't afraid to invite Cat right into his brain. 23:34:52. He was ready.

"Hi, it's me," he said.

Way Out awoke. "Big Guy!" The corners of his eyes crinkled when he smiled.

"She here?"

"Sure." His voice boomed. "Lots of people here."

"Waiting long?" said Murph.

Way Out yawned. The haunt's breath tickled Murph's face. He lowered the sensory gain. "I've got five hours and forty-two minutes," said Murph.

"Price went up, Big Guy." Way Out's smile shrank to a rueful grin. "Sorry."

"How much?"

"Seven-hundred-thirty an hour." When he shook his head, his hair danced. "Raised my insurance."

A fifty-dollar-an-hour bump. If he linked for the rest of tonight's free time, he'd zero his debit account and activate his line of credit—at 23 percent interest. But that wasn't going to happen. Could be he'd get off in an hour or two, if Cat said yes. "So what?"

"Live fast, Big Guy." He opened his mouth.

"Have to," said Murph.

The jaws spread wider and wider, like a snake's. Murph walked Big Guy in. Way Out's breath was warm and minted to cover a faint whiff of eggs. Murph stepped over the gleaming row of incisors onto the damp nubbly surface of the tongue. The epithelial cells that lined the inside of Way Out's mouth shone with a slick, pink light. Murph ducked under the uvula and entered the hall of faces.

They seemed to stretch to a vanishing point. Way Out had sorted them so that only the first couple were Murph's familiars. To his immediate left, one face morphed from Dead Mike to Plumber to Feelie to Blue to Negro to Dead Mike again. They all called to him in turn to join their party. "Big Guy, right here, right, Big Guy, live fast." Next to them were Jelly Donut and Handgun, both solo, both happy to see him. "Hey, Big Guy!" The Log and Cow Girl were together but weren't looking for company.

He ignored them all. The first face to his right was Cat's. She watched him silently for a moment, her expression unreadable. Then she was replaced by Shiva. "Big Guy," he said, without enthusiasm. Shiva was a pale man with curly red hair and three eyes. He was wearing a necklace of little human skulls. "She's been waiting." He opened his mouth. Murph hadn't liked

Shiva the last time they'd met and had no reason to like him better now. But he was with Cat. Reluctantly, Murph stepped through.

The corn came up to his chest. They must have trampled it down before they spread their blanket in the middle of the vast field. There was a wicker picnic basket next to Cat, who lay on her side, watching him. Beyond her in the distance, he could see the funnels and upper decks of the ship. It rose twelve stories tall on its foundation, anchored forever in a sea of corn. The sky was a flawless nightmare blue. The sun was bright as pain. Way Out was a genius.

"Sit." Shiva was already naked except for the necklace and a dhoti loincloth.

Murph eyed the blanket doubtfully. There wasn't room, not for Big Guy. He stood at the edge, crouched low as he could go, grunted, toppled backward. Cornstalks whipped to the ground under his weight.

"Sorry I'm late," said Murph. The ground was ridged to the corn rows. It smelled of worms. He wiggled his ass, flattening a comfortable spot.

"Shiva was just telling me he lives in Gardner." Cat was wearing a high-necked polka-dot dress that covered her ankles. Her bonnet matched the dress.

"The town?" Not something Murph would have admitted.

"Twenty-one Spring Street," said Shiva. Murph couldn't tell if he was trying to be rude or if he just didn't understand the protocols. "It's a big green Victorian with a porch and a swing. Been in the family nearly two hundred years." He was much too pushy with personal information, even for Way Out. Next he'd be giving them his real name. Murph hadn't even told Cat what deck he lived on yet, much less his cabin number.

"Maybe we should drop by sometime, Cat." Murph shot her a who-is-this-pumpkin look.

"That'd be fine." Shiva laughed easily. "I see a lot of people, but hardly any ship folks."

Had Cat told him already that they lived on the ship? Murph wondered what other secrets they had shared.

"I'm a doctor, you know." He turned to Cat and held out his hand. "Name's John. John Ghatak."

Now Murph *was* shocked. It was as if Shiva . . . Ghatak had crapped on a napkin and held it out for them to admire. Murph fought the impulse to slap at the offending hand. "What the hell are you doing?" Instead he leaned forward and pushed it slowly, firmly back to Ghatak's side.

"Living fast." Ghatak winked his third eye at Cat. "Isn't that the point? This costs seven hundred and thirty dollars an hour."

Cat slid closer to him. "A doctor. Really?" Her head was almost in his lap.

Ghatak rattled his necklace of skulls. "That's why I'm Shiva. Death-bringer and life-giver, god and ghoul." He grasped the string of Cat's bonnet. "Male and female." He pulled it taut. "The lord of sex." The knot under her chin raveled.

"You cut people?" she said.

"Sometimes." Ghatak paused, taken aback. "If necessary."

"Enjoy it?"

"I wouldn't say I enjoyed . . ."

"Stop!" Murph didn't want to waste another second of his life on this. "You can't tell strangers things they don't want to know."

"I was telling *her,* not a stranger." He swept the polka-dot bonnet back and stroked the top of Cat's head. "You were just eavesdropping, Big Guy."

"Funny. Never would've guessed a doctor." She purred and rose to his touch for several strokes. "I'm a biocommodities broker."

Both Ghatak and Murph stared. Cat smiled at them.

"Blood futures mostly. Some kidneys, lungs, the occasional liver." She sat up and settled herself between the two men. "So, a doctor. A broker." She lifted the necklace of skulls over Ghatak's head, dribbled it idly into her open hand, turned to Big Guy. "And you?"

It was all going too fast. Ghatak and Cat weren't strangers. They had been waiting for him. How many times had they been together before? They could afford Way Out better than he could, a rich blood broker and a doctor. Probably doing it while he's watching Squeeze Pleeze and Moon's Noodles and Burger King twenty-four hours a day just to make the monthlies on his brain taps. So he finally frees up enough time to see her and she asks him to spill his real life on some rude asshole who's too cheap to do Way Out right. Who cared what it cost? This was his fucking *life.*

"I protect people." Big Guy's voice was so smooth. Back in his cabin, Murph was shouting.

"What, a cop?" said Ghatak. "A security guard?"

Cat's eyes glittered. He couldn't tell if she was angry or pleased.

Big Guy nodded, definite as a bullet. "Independent op." There were only nine on the ship. He tried to calculate how long it would take her to figure out which one he was.

"I didn't know security guards did that well." Ghatak looked skeptical.

"He's here, isn't he?" said Cat. "Protect me, Big Guy?"

"This is virtuality," Ghatak said. "We don't need protection."

"No?" She smiled, showing Murph her tiny square incisors, the dagger canines that fit into grooves in her gums. Murph had seen that smile before. He peeled the shoe from his right foot.

"So, Doctor"—Cat reached behind her to unseal the dress—"when you cut them open, what exactly do they smell like?"

"What?"

She dipped a shoulder and the dress sagged down to the collarbone, revealed the swell of a breast. "Inside, I mean."

For a second, Dr. John Ghatak of 21 Spring Street, Gardner, Kansas, froze. He looked about as godlike as a rabbit caught in headlights. He tugged abruptly at his dhoti and then popped like a lie. There was a sharp gasp, as air rushed to fill the void he'd left. All that remained was the necklace of skulls.

Cat threw her head back and laughed. "Lacked the courage of his erection." The dress fell to her waist. The fur on her breasts was only as thick as the hair on Murph's arm. "I thought he'd never leave."

He wanted to rub his thumbs across her nipples. "Why were you with him?"

"You were late." She picked up Shiva's necklace. "And he tasted desperate. I liked that." She wrapped it idly around two fingers. "Thought he might try hanging off the edge with me." The skulls clicked. "But he was only pretending not to be afraid."

"So what do I taste like?"

She licked her lips. "Don't know. Yet." She put the necklace on and shed the dress. Her gaze was steady, testing, as she lay across the blanket. She arranged herself languidly, propped on an elbow, hips cocked toward him.

"I'll hang off the edge with you." He reached for her. "I'll even let go." She opened her arms to him. Her mouth. Her tongue was thin and pliant at the edges, but like sandpaper deeper in.

He knelt in front of her. She unsealed his pants, slipped her hand inside. Her palm glided over the curve of his great belly. Lower, *lower*. He watched her, quivering with dread and desire.

Her touch lightened when she realized what he'd done. She glanced up at him. "Why?" She tugged at his pants until they slid down and gathered in great folds at his knees. "You want something different?" But she knew, she had to know.

"To meet you," he said. "Touch your face, see where you live. Everything."

"But you'll lose Cat." She leaned forward. Her tongue scratched at the smooth skin between his legs. "She can be anything, do anything. I'm locked into what I really am."

"I love Cat—and Big Guy. But I'm ready to give them up if you are."

Her breath burned him like steam.

"It's time," he said. "Tell me your name."

"Yes." Her eyes seemed to get very deep. "Oh, yes. But first, I have to taste you."

She stretched as if just waking up. Crouching on all fours, she arched her back, holding the upward thrust at its peak. Then the shape of her body changed. She slid her hands forward and raised her rear end, like she wanted him to take her from behind. Her spine rippled. She seemed to grow larger.

"It'll hurt at first." Her head swayed back and forth hypnotically. "But then I'll close the pain gates in your brain. Afterward will be all pleasure." Her splayed fingers folded and knit themselves into short furry stumps. Her nails flowed like honey, pinched into cruel hooks.

"Hurt?" He saw her muscles bunch as she gathered herself. Everything seemed so slow. Like a dream. He tried to tell her not to. He wanted to hurl himself out of her way, but he was tangled in his own pants. She sprang.

The impact knocked him onto his side. Her claws raked his shoulder, and he almost fainted from the pain. It was as if his nerves had frozen and were shattering into razor shards. Then she was on top of him. She howled in his ear, bit into the side of his neck, shook him. With that first shake, the pain changed. He heard himself scream, but it was the sound of ecstasy. He tried to scrabble away into the corn. Stalks rustled and thrashed at him. Terror was his bliss. She pounced on his back, brought him down, worried at the back of his neck. New wounds spurted like multiple orgasms. He tried to heave her off him and saw the warm soil darken beneath them.

"I'm bleeding," he moaned.

"Good for the corn." She caught him a blow that drove his face into the ground. She put one paw on his head, the other on his back. Her weight caressed the breath from his lungs. "Sleep now, Murph."

She knew just what he needed. He was tired of Way Out, yes. He needed to sleep. Just before she gave him the killing bite, Murph realized that he had never been more alive.

His cabin was dark. He woke to the light of his clock. 03:21:35, 03:21:36. His first thought was that he had one hour and fifty-six minutes left. His next was that he had died. Cat had killed him. He picked at the memory and found it still gave him deep and scary pleasure.

"Messages?" He stripped off a brain tap.

The right wall displayed the mail queue. Ads, bills, Dennis the acupuncturist's August payment, funeral notice for poor Noonan. Nothing. He couldn't stop thinking about Cat. How she'd gotten rid of Ghatak. The way she'd said yes. *Oh, yes.* But how could they meet now? Then he remembered.

She had called him Murph. "Get Bumpus."

Bumpus replaced the queue. He was slumped in the same position he'd been in when he'd wiped Murph. For a moment, Murph thought he had fallen asleep with his eyes open. His face was dead as stone.

"Back already?" said Bumpus.

"No. I want you to watch me. Here, for the rest of my time."

"You?" He yawned. "Why?"

"Could be I'm having a visitor."

"Not a woman?"

"Could be."

"I watch you having sex?"

Murph's door chimed. "Don't know what's going to happen," he said. "Just watch, damn it!"

"It'll cost . . ."

Murph wiped him, yanked off the last tap, got up from his workseat. The darkness seemed to spin as he picked his way to the door. He thought about turning on the hall camera, seeing who it was. But if it was really her, he didn't want his first glimpse to be on a screen.

The door chimed again. Still he hesitated. How had she found out his name so quickly? Where he lived? More mysteries. 03:25:12. He was a champion. 03:25:13. This was a very stupid thing to do, letting a stranger in at 03:25:15. Even if it was Cat—especially if it was. But he wasn't afraid. He had to live fast, or not at all. He opened the door.

dancing with the chairs

Jack stared at the mirror in the men's room of O'Brien's and tried to convince himself he did not look all that bad. He tightened the knot of his Perry Ellis silk tie—the one she had given him for his birthday. He pulled the comb from his back pocket and straightened the part in his hair. Up until a few months ago, he used to pluck out the gray. Now there was too much. Well, he had seen something of life, no doubt about that. A speck of dried blood had crusted over the spot just under his jaw where he had cut himself shaving that morning. He dipped his forefinger under a stream of warm water and washed the scab away. But there was nothing he could do about his eyes.

Someone flushed. In the long mirror, Jack saw a drooping man in a dark suit emerge from one of the stalls. He slouched up to the row of sinks. It was a decent suit, a navy-chalk stripe that hung like worsted wool, but somehow it reminded Jack of a new paint job on a junk car: could be it was the only thing holding the poor slob together. The button just above his belt had popped open. His face was as dreary as a used tea bag. He looked the way Jack felt.

As the guy was soaping his hands, he peered at Jack's reflection and said, "You're in love, aren't you?"

"What?" Jack was startled. "Why do you say that?" It was something he had been wondering about himself.

"You have the look."

"And what's that?"

"Trying to find yourself in mirrors." He unwound a paper towel from the dispenser. "Married, aren't you?"

It wasn't much of a deduction; Jack was wearing his ring. He nodded cautiously.

"But it isn't her."

At that moment, Jack knew what he ought to do was walk. Get the hell out of there. It wasn't his style to put up with this kind of crap. Except that the guy was right. "No," he said. "It isn't." He turned on the hot water and watched himself wash his hands.

The guy didn't say a word until Jack finished. "This woman—she ever make you cry?"

Jack sniffed at the absurdity of it. "No way."

"And when you're in bed with her, do you ever make, like, *sounds?*"

Jack did walk then. He couldn't believe he had stayed as long as he had. Humoring weirdos in the men's room—he shook his head in amazement. A new low.

He crossed the lobby to the heavy oak pedestal that defended the entrance to the dining room. The maître d' was behind it, taking names; O'Brien's was always jammed on Fridays. A handful of people were standing in line. Jack cut around them. The maître d's smile was stretched a little thin as he shrugged and told Jack that he could seat him immediately if necessary but that if he really wanted that table with the view of the harbor, it would be another ten or fifteen minutes. Would he like to wait in the bar? Jack glanced at his watch. She was already late. He tugged his sleeve back into place and said the bar would be fine.

He sat at a table the size of a Cadillac's hubcap, and a waitress came right over. Jack ordered a manhattan for himself. He thought about getting her a margarita but decided to hold off. Susanne was never late; it was one of the things he liked best about her. She was more organized than most men he knew.

She knew exactly what she wanted, and when she wanted something, she didn't hesitate to go out and get it. No wasted motion. Jack had been thrilled when one of the things she had wanted was him. He had told her more than once how it was the thrill of his life.

He wondered what was going on with her. The drink came, and the first thing he did was eat the cherry out of the manhattan. When he went out to eat with the family, he always had to give the cherry to one of the kids. He thought again about leaving the kids. Leaving Anne. Kissing off seventeen years—of what? Pork chops, sitcoms, and bad sex. She had given him the most boring years of her life. Of course, he knew she would make him pay. There would be child support for sure, maybe alimony. He'd lose the house, all that antique furniture that no one could sit on. He sipped his drink. Good fucking riddance. He thought he could do it. If he told Susanne today, they could maybe even be together by that weekend and the week after that and from then on. Happily ever after, world without end, amen. It seemed doable. He took another sip. It seemed very doable.

The man in the blue suit pulled up the chair next to him. "Sorry if I offended you."

Jack gave him an arctic stare. "The seat is taken."

The man sat anyway. "I don't know what's happening to me. Haven't been myself." He laid his head in his hands. "Haven't been *anyone,* really. Look, I'll leave as soon as she comes. Okay? Just let me sit a minute. You don't have to talk, don't even have to listen. It's just. . . . Please."

Jack scooted his chair around and gave the creep his back. Still, he was worried. He had enough troubles, didn't he? And how did the guy know he was waiting for Susanne? Another lucky guess? Maybe ignoring him wasn't enough. Maybe he ought to get someone to throw him out. But Jack didn't want to be in the middle of sorting out this mess when Susanne finally came.

"My wife left me about a month ago. I didn't have a clue ahead of time. She said she'd been seeing someone else and she was in love. Makes you wonder, you know. While she was in love with *him,* what was *I* in? A fantasy world, I guess. The Twilight Zone."

Jack watched the bartender filling beer mugs. He couldn't believe the guy was really going to harass him like this. He didn't need it—not now.

"You probably think I'm a chump. Hey, I *know* it. The thing is, I still can't figure out how it happened." He drew a deep breath. "Name's Frank, by the way."

Silence.

"Yeah, well," said Frank, "I realize this isn't any fun for you, but is there a chance you'd do me a favor? I could really use a scotch on the rocks."

Then it made sense to Jack. He was just a lush hustling free drinks. Probably on a binge—poor son of a bitch had no idea what the hell he was saying or who he was saying it to. Jack turned and was about to cut the guy down when he saw that Frank had pushed a twenty-dollar bill across the little table. Jack could not help but notice the gold Rolex on the man's wrist.

He didn't touch the money. "Why don't you buy it yourself?"

"I can't seem to get anyone's attention." Frank picked up Jack's cocktail napkin. "Maybe if I wave this." He flicked his wrist and the napkin unfolded. "Drinker in distress. Send Johnnie Walker."

Jack raised his forefinger; across the room their waitress veered off course with an answering nod. He couldn't believe that Frank had tried very hard. If anything, they were too fussy at O'Brien's. The staff hovered like servile vultures, filling water glasses, whisking empty plates away, changing silverware. Sometimes you wished they'd let you eat in peace.

The waitress threaded her way to their table. Jack waited for Frank to say something. It was odd; she could see that Jack had a manhattan and Frank was dry, yet she seemed to be expecting Jack to order. Finally Jack said, "Scotch on the rocks—make it a double. And another manhattan." The waitress headed for the bar, and he pushed Frank's twenty back to him.

"Thanks," said Frank. "Lately I've been feeling kind of—I don't know—unreal. Like a ghost. Sometimes I get scared that I'll say something and nobody will notice. You ever feel that way? No, probably not. I used to think I was real. I *was*—I've got twenty-two people working for me. Our group booked nearly three million dollars in '88. I've got a kid, he plays the violin. We started him when he was three. Suzuki method, you know. Last year he went to the National Music Camp out in Michigan. They say he could make Juilliard. And all along the wife was telling me she loved me. Of course, I believed her. Why would she lie about something like that?" He tore the corner off the cocktail napkin, rolled it into a little ball, and tossed it into the ashtray. "But then something like this happens, and you find out that you don't really exist. You're like a cell in *1-2-3*. Someone hits the Delete key and you're gone. The world recalculates around where you used to be like a goddamned spreadsheet."

The round arrived and he stopped ranting. Jack surveyed the bar, wishing that Susanne would come to the rescue.

"Thanks," Frank said to the waitress. There was no way she could ignore him—but she did. An anguished look flickered across his face; Jack could see that he was teetering right on the edge. The waitress laid the check on the table. "I'll take that when you're ready." She smiled at Jack as if she expected a big tip and moved quickly off.

Frank's hand trembled as he brought the glass to his mouth. The liquor seemed to steady him. "Sorry about what I said in the john. About the sounds. It's just, I'm trying to figure things out. I'm trying to find out what's left of me. I used to think I *was* my job, you know? But now I realize that everyone at the office is like . . . parts. Replaceable, just like that." He snapped his fingers. "Maybe if I had friends, they'd miss me. But I don't, not really. I mean, I know lots of people there, but nobody has the faintest idea who I am."

Jack let his hand drop beneath the table and then twisted his wrist so that he could check his watch. He didn't want Frank to know he was looking. He was beginning to feel sorry for the guy; he had to be in a hell of a lot of pain to make a fool of himself like this.

"And I used to think I was my family. But the kid is seventeen, and now he's all wrapped up in the music. Busy becoming himself. And the wife . . ." Frank was filling the ashtray with little napkin balls. "She said something the night we split. About the sounds, I mean. She always used to say I never talked to her when we were in the sack together. That night she said even if I had made *sounds,* that would have been something. It would've shown I was there. Well, where the hell did she think I was? Then I got to thinking: what kind of sounds did she want me to make? Did she want me to growl or what? Yodel?"

Despite himself, Jack smiled.

"It's like I don't exist. I'm forty-four years old, and all of a sudden I realize there's nothing to me."

All across the room people were telling jokes, laughing, gossiping, cutting deals, flirting, planning their weekends. The bar was filled with noise, but somehow all Jack could hear was Frank's awful silence.

"This isn't what men do, is it? Talk, I mean." Frank drained the last of his drink. "Why is that, I wonder?" He eyed his empty glass as if it might be the answer. "I've said too much, I know it. But I've been holding it in ever since. . . ." He shook his head as if to flick away the memory. "So, tell me about her. Your truelove. What's it like when you're with her?"

Maybe it was because the two manhattans had eroded Jack's reserve. Or perhaps it was because Frank had spilled his guts right here on the table in the bar at O'Brien's; Jack was secretly impressed. "She's smart and tough and she's going places. It's the most exciting thing in the world," he said, thinking it might help the poor bastard to hear how good it could be with the right woman. "Nothing else is even close. I never feel so alive as when I'm with her."

Frank wasn't listening. "Julie," he said. "My wife's name is Julie."

Jack resented the interruption; he could have talked about Susanne for hours. Then he spotted her standing at the door and nothing else mattered. He shot out of his chair. "Excuse me, I've got to go." On an impulse, he reached down and shook hands with Frank. "Good luck."

Frank nodded. "Thanks." There was a wet streak down his face. "You too."

Jack bumped through an infestation of drinkers swarming in the aisle by the bar. It seemed like they were blocking his way on purpose. Finally he was hugging her.

"Sorry I'm late," she said.

He could feel the warmth of her cheek on his face; his hand slid naturally to her hip. He was so relieved to see her that he couldn't speak at first.

"Been waiting long?"

Jack hadn't realized how much Frank's story had upset him. "Oh, I don't know," he said. He didn't know why he was whispering. "Met a guy, we were having a drink." He decided then it was best just to forget it. Put it out of his mind. It was Frank's problem. He glanced back at the table; Frank was gone. She patted the small of his back and he let her go. "Let's eat," he said.

The view from O'Brien's best table was sensational. Clouds drifted through a cornflower sky; the marina down the habor was draped with a necklace of pearly yachts. Waves caught the sunlight and scattered it across the water. But Jack wasn't interested in scenery; he was too busy admiring Susanne. She was wearing a beaujolais-colored suit, a white silk blouse with a silver rose clasp at the neck where a man might have worn a tie. Her hair was as dark as coffee. When he had first met her, she had worn it short, but after they had become lovers, she let it grow. For him. It brushed against her shoulders now, and Jack was sure it was the most astonishing hair in the world.

He couldn't help but think of the first time they had eaten at this table, the day after they had first made love. She had told him then that she wanted to get married someday and have a baby and bring her to a place like this where everyone could see. Maybe hold the kid up; she expected applause. Jack intended to remind her of that later.

The waiter stopped by to tell them the specials: lobster kedgeree, fillets of sole amandine, chicken paprika, and spinach quiche. He asked if they wanted drinks, and Jack deferred to Susanne. "I've had enough already." He gave her his best smile; he didn't mean for it to sound like an accusation. She picked up her napkin as if it were made of glass and said nothing. The waiter pointedly took in the view until Jack ended the silence by ordering his usual: steak au poivre, medium. Susanne asked for a large salad as if she were just making polite conversation. The waiter bustled off, and Jack was filled with unexpected dread at the prospect of being left alone with her.

"I've been trying to get in touch with you all week," he said. "Your secretary said you had called in sick."

"No, I'm okay. Played hooky and painted my condo."

"I left messages on your answering machine."

"I know."

He leaned back in his chair. "What's that supposed to mean?"

"I was thinking."

"For three days? About what?"

The waiter interrupted them with a basket of bread and a cheese ball. They concentrated on not looking at each other until he had gone.

"I was just so sick of that eggshell color," she said. "Reminded me of all the beige at the office. I mean, I spend the day at the office, I worry about the office all the way home, and when I get there, what's waiting for me? Sometimes I even sleep with the office." She gave him a crooked smile. "Anyway, I went crazy. The bedroom is peach now, and the living room is this yellowy green, I think it's called meadow brook."

"Susanne, I was worried."

She examined her hands. "I've been thinking about us. About what you said about leaving Anne."

"I'm going to do it. Finally. That's what I wanted to tell you." He reached into the bread basket and rewarded himself with a warm caramel bun. "I was thinking of talking to her today."

"Don't." Susanne kept her face down, as if she were speaking into her soup spoon.

"I have to." Jack was trying to stay calm. "It's time." He wanted her to make eye contact with him. What was she afraid of? "I thought we agreed."

Silence.

"Susanne, what is it?"

She shook her head. "*I* never agreed. That's the problem, Jack. You make things up about us. If I don't say anything, you think I mean yes. If I say no, you hear maybe."

"Susanne, I have to do this if we're going to be together."

She made a sound that might have been a laugh except that she looked at him then and he saw she was crying. He wanted to reach across the table and stop the tears. He didn't want her to cry, not now, not ever. It was important to him.

"I don't know what to say to you, Jack."

He smiled sympathetically. "Just tell me you love me."

"I don't love anybody." She shook her head, and he noticed how strands of her beautiful hair caught on the weave of her wool suit. "I want to love someone." He remembered how her hair looked when it caressed her bare shoulders, the way it spread across a white pillowcase. "But I don't."

He changed his mind; he thought she was very brave to cry in O'Brien's like this. People were noticing, but she didn't care. The tears made her face seem so soft. It made him love her all the more.

"But *I* love *you,*" he said. He reached across the table toward her. She watched his hand but didn't take it. "Right now my love is enough for both of us. I'll wait for you to catch up."

She dabbed her eyes with the napkin and then stared out the window. "A bunch of us used to paint houses when I was at Brandeis. Summer job; I did interiors. I wore these overalls, they looked like an explosion at the Glidden factory. Sometimes I used to paint myself, just for the fun of it. I don't do things like that anymore. I was trimming the bedroom yesterday and wondering why? I felt this urge—I don't know. I painted the window peach, the glass. So no one could see in. I don't like who I am, Jack. I don't think that girl in the spattered overalls wanted to be me when she grew up."

"There's nothing wrong with you. Susanne, you're everything to me."

"I don't want to be everything to you. You ask too much. I'm just one person—and not a very smart one. But you expect me to be the whole world for you. I can't. It's too much, more than anyone can do."

"We can be together. I'm ready now. I thought that was what you wanted."

"I'm so confused, Jack. I know what everyone else wants, but I'm not sure what I want anymore." She covered his hand with hers. "I can't be with you. I'm sorry."

"My God, Susanne, I love you. Doesn't that mean anything? Can't you hear me?"

"You know, they used to call me Susie and I didn't mind it at all." Her face hardened. She pulled away from him. "I can't see you anymore."

"I can't accept that," he said as the waiter brought their lunch. When he set Susanne's salad before her, she got up and walked out.

In front of Jack appeared a steak au poivre, medium. His eyes burned as if they had caught fire. He felt more at that moment than he had in the last ten years. It was very bad—almost more than he could bear. He saved himself by imagining he was down the harbor at the marina, watching himself through binoculars. It was all that kept him from crying. He cut a slice of steak and pushed it to the side of his plate. He was sure everyone would be staring at him, yet when he finally dared a peek, all he saw were people eating lunch, paying him no attention whatsoever. He cut more meat. The waiter glided by, his body cocked against a tray of lobster kedgeree and chicken paprika. He gave no sign of just having witnessed a tragedy.

Relieved, Jack sliced yet another piece of steak. He was very careful: a surgical job of carving. Too bad he wasn't hungry. He was pretty sure that nobody at the office knew about their affair; he had been very careful. Nobody knew anything about him and he hadn't cried. He put his knife down and stared out the window for a while and tried to remember what Susanne had ordered the first time they had gotten that table. The best table in O'Brien's. It wasn't over, he thought. No way; he wasn't giving up yet. She didn't really mean it. She'd been so emotional;

that wasn't like her. She wasn't herself at all. He should have tried to calm her down—what was all that about the paint?

It wasn't until he was cutting the last piece of steak that he noticed the blotches of congealed fat. Jack realized he had lost track of the time, and then looked around O'Brien's in a panic.

Two men in green coveralls were cleaning the empty restaurant. A kid with frizzy blond hair was putting the chairs up on the tables. He was wearing a Walkman, and as he worked, he swiveled his hips and dropped his shoulders to some private melody: a punk Fred Astaire dancing cheek to cheek with wooden Gingers. An older man, about Jack's age, was vacuuming the rug at the far end of the dining room.

"Hey," Jack called. "*Hey.*" He stood. "Where *is* everybody?"

No one paid attention. The kid kept dancing with the chairs.

at had stashed the dust in four plastic capsules and then swallowed them. From the stinging at the base of his ribs, he guessed they were now squeezing into his duodenum. Still plenty of time. The bullet train had been shooting through the vacuum of the TransAtlantic tunnel for almost two hours now; they would arrive at Port Authority/Koch soon. Customs had already been fixed, according to the maréchal. All Rat had to do was to get back to his nest, lock the smart door behind him, and put the word out on his protected nets. He had enough Algerian Yellow to dust at least half the cerebrums on the East Side. If he could turn this deal, he would be rich enough to bathe in Dom Pérignon and dry himself with Gromaire tapestries. Another pang shot down his left flank. Instinctively his hind leg came off the seat and scratched at air.

There was only one problem; Rat had decided to cut the

maréchal out. That meant he had to lose the old man's spook before he got home.

The spook had attached herself to him at Marseilles. She braided her blonde hair in pigtails. She had freckles, wore braces on her teeth. Tiny breasts nudged a modest silk turtleneck. She looked to be between twelve and fourteen. Cute. She had probably looked that way for twenty years, would stay the same another twenty if she did not stop a slug first or get cut in half by some automated security laser that tracked only heat and could not read—or be troubled by—cuteness. Their passports said they were Mr. Sterling Jaynes and daughter Jessalynn, of Forest Hills, New York. She was typing in her notebook, chubby fingers curled over the keys. Homework? A letter to a boyfriend? More likely she was operating on some corporate database with scalpel code of her own devising.

"Ne fais pas semblant d'étudier, ma petite," Rat said. *"Que fais-tu?"*

"Oh, Daddy," she said, pouting, "can't we go back to plain old English? After all, we're almost home." She tilted her notebook so that he could see the display. It read, "Two rows back, second seat from aisle. Fed. If he knew you were carrying, he'd cut the dust out of you and wipe his ass with your pelt." She tapped the Return key, and the message disappeared.

"All right, dear." He arched his back, fighting a surge of adrenaline that made his incisors click. "You know, all of a sudden I feel hungry. Should we do something here on the train or wait until we get to New York?" Only the spook saw him gesture back toward the fed.

"Why don't we wait for the station? More choice there."

"As you wish, dear." He wanted her to take the fed out *now,* but there was nothing more he dared say. He licked his hands nervously and groomed the fur behind his short, thick ears to pass the time.

The International Arrivals Hall at Koch Terminal was unusually quiet for a Thursday night. It smelled to Rat like a setup. The passengers from the bullet shuffled through the echoing marble vastness toward the row of customs stations. Rat was unarmed; if they were going to put up a fight, the spook would have to provide the firepower. But Rat was not a fighter, he was a runner. Their instructions were to pass through Station Number Four. As they waited in line, Rat spotted the federally appointed vigilante behind them. The classic invisible man: neither handsome nor ugly, five-ten, about one-seventy, brown hair, dark suit, white shirt. He looked bored.

"Do you have anything to declare?" The customs agent looked bored too. Everybody looked bored except Rat, who had two million new dollars worth of illegal drugs in his gut and a fed ready to carve them out of him.

"We hold these truths to be self-evident," said Rat, "that all men are created equal." He managed a feeble grin—as if this were a witticism and not the password.

"Daddy, please!" The spook feigned embarrassment. "I'm sorry, ma'am; it's his idea of a joke. It's the Declaration of Independence, you know."

The customs agent smiled as she tousled the spook's hair. "I know that, dear. Please put your luggage on the conveyor." She gave a perfunctory glance at her monitor as their suitcases passed through the scanner, and then nodded at Rat. "Thank you, sir, and have a pleasant . . ." The insincere thought died on her lips as she noticed the fed pushing through the line toward them. Rat saw her spin toward the exit at the same moment that the spook thrust her notebook computer into the scanner. The notebook stretched a blue finger of point discharge toward the magnetic lens just before the overhead lights novaed and went dark. The emergency backup failed as well. Rat's snout filled with the acrid smell of electrical fire. Through the darkness came shouts and screams, thumps and cracks—the crazed pounding of a stampede gathering momentum.

He dropped to all fours and skittered across the floor. Koch Terminal was his territory; he had crisscrossed its many levels with scent trails. Even in total darkness he could find his way. But in his haste he cracked his head against a pair of stockinged knees, and a squawking weight fell across him, crushing the breath from his lungs. He felt an icy stab on his hindquarters and scrabbled at it with his hind leg. His toes came away wet and he squealed. There was an answering scream, and the point of a shoe drove into him, propelling him across the floor. He rolled left and came up running. Up a dead escalator, down a carpeted hall. He stood upright and stretched to his full twenty-six inches, hands scratching until they found the emergency bar across the fire door. He hurled himself at it, a siren shrieked, and with a *whoosh* the door opened, dumping him into an alley. He lay there for a moment, gasping, half in and half out of Koch Terminal. With the certain knowledge that he was bleeding to death, he touched the coldness on his back. A sticky purple substance; he sniffed, then tasted it. Ice cream. Rat threw back his head and laughed. The high squeaky sound echoed in the deserted alley.

But there was no time to waste. He could already hear the buzz of police hovers swooping down from the night sky. The blackout might keep them busy for a while; Rat was more worried about the fed. And the spook. They would be out soon enough, looking for him. Rat scurried down the alley toward the street. He glanced quickly at the terminal, now a black hole in the galaxy of bright holographic sleaze that was Forty-second Street. A few cops with flashlights were trying to fight against the flow of panicky travelers pouring from its open doors. Rat smoothed his ruffled fur and turned away from the disaster, walking crosstown. His instincts said to run, but Rat forced himself to dawdle like a hick shopping for big-city excitement. He grinned at the pimps and window-shopped the hardware stores. He paused in front of a pair of mirror-image sex stops—GIRLS! LIVE! GIRLS! and LIVE! GIRLS! LIVE!—to sniff the pheromone-scented sweat pouring off an androgynous robot shill that was working the sidewalk. The robot obligingly put its hand to Rat's crotch, but he pushed it away with a hiss and continued on. At last, sure that he was not being followed, he powered up his wallet and tapped into the transnet to summon a hovercab. The wallet informed him that the city had cordoned off midtown airspace to facilitate rescue operations at Koch Terminal. It advised trying the subway or a taxi. Since he had no intention of sticking an ID chip—even a false one—into a subway turnstile, he stepped to the curb and began watching the traffic.

The rebuilt Checker that rattled to a stop beside him was a patchwork of orange ABS and stainless-steel armor. "No we leave Manhattan," said a speaker on the roof light. "No we north of a hundred and ten." Rat nodded and the door locks popped. The passenger compartment smelled of chlorobenzylmalononitrile and urine.

"First Avenue Bunker," said Rat, sniffing. "Christ, it stinks back here. Who was your last fare—the circus?"

"Troubleman." The speaker connections were loose, giving a scratchy edge to the cabbie's voice. The locks reengaged as the Checker pulled away from the curb. "Ha-has get a fullsnoot of tear gas in this hack."

Rat had already spotted the pressure vents in the floor. He peered through the gloom at the registration. A slogan had been lased in over it—probably by one of the new Mitsubishi penlights. FREE THE DEAD. Rat smiled: the dead were his customers. People who had chosen the dusty road. Twelve to eighteen months of glorious addiction: synesthetic orgasms, recursive hallucinations, leading to a total sensory overload and an ecstatic death experience. One dose was all it took to start down the dusty road. The feds were trying to cut off the supply—with dire consequences for the dead. They could live a few months longer without dust, but their joyride down the dusty road was transformed into a grueling marathon of withdrawal pangs and madness. Either way, they were dead. Rat settled back onto the seat. The penlight graffito was a good omen. He reached into his pocket and pulled out a leather strip that had been soaked with a private blend of fat-soluble amphetamines and began to gnaw at it.

From time to time he could hear the cabbie monitoring NYPD net for flameouts or wildcat tolls set up by street gangs. They had to detour to heavily guarded Park Avenue all the way uptown to Fifty-ninth before doubling back toward the bunker. Originally built to protect U.N. diplomats from terrorists, the bunker had gone condo after the dissolution of the United Nations. Its hype was that it was the "safest address in the city." Rat knew better, which is why he had had a state-of-the-art smart door installed. Its rep was that most of the owners' association were candidates for either a mindwipe or an extended vacation on a fed punkfarm.

"Hey, Fare," said the cabbie. "Net says the dead be rioting front of your door. Crash through or roll away?"

The fur along Rat's backbone went erect. "Cops?"

"Letting them play for now."

"You've got armor for a crash?"

"Shit, yes. Park this hack to ground zero for the right fare." The cabbie's laugh was static. "Don't worry, bunkerman. Give those deadboys a shot of old CS gas, and they be too busy scratching they eyes out to bother us much."

Rat tried to smooth his fur. He could crash the riot and get stuck. But if he waited, either the spook or the fed would be stepping on his tail before long. Rat had no doubt that both had managed to plant locator bugs on him.

" 'Course, riot crashing don't come cheap," said the cabbie.

"Triple the meter." The fare was already over two hundred dollars for the fifteen-minute ride. "Shoot for Bay Two—the one with the yellow door." He pulled out his wallet and started tapping its luminescent keys. "I'm sending recognition code now."

He heard the cabbie notify the cops that they were coming through. Rat could feel the Checker accelerate as they passed the cordon, and he had a glimpse of strobing lights, cops in blue body armor, a tank studded with water cannons. Suddenly the cabbie braked, and Rat pitched forward against his shoulder harness. The Checker's solid rubber tires squealed, and there was the thump of something bouncing off the hood. They had slowed to a crawl, and the dead closed around them.

Rat could not see out the front because the cabbie was protected from his passengers by steel plate. But the side windows filled with faces streaming with sweat and tears and blood. Twisted faces, screaming faces, faces etched by the agonies of withdrawal. The soundproofing muffled their howls. Fear and exhilaration filled Rat as he watched them pass. If only they knew how close they were to dust, he thought. He imagined the dead faces gnawing through the cab's armor in a frenzy, pausing only to spit out broken teeth. It was wonderful. The riot was proof that the dust market was still white-hot. The dead must be desperate to attack the bunker like this looking for a flash. He decided to bump the price of his dust another 10 percent.

Rat heard a clatter on the roof; then someone began to jump up and down. It was like being inside a kettledrum. Rat sank claws into the seat and arched his back. "What are you waiting for? Gas them, damn it!"

"Hey, Fare. Stuff ain't cheap. We be fine—almost there."

A woman with bloody red hair matted to her head pressed her mouth against the window and screamed. Rat reared up on his hind legs and made biting feints at her. Then he saw the penlight in her hand. At the last moment Rat threw himself backward. The penlight flared, and the passenger compartment filled with the stench of melting plastic. A needle of coherent light singed the fur on Rat's left flank; he squealed and flopped onto the floor, twitching.

The cabbie opened the external gas vents, and abruptly the faces dropped away from the windows. The cab accelerated, bouncing as it ran over the fallen dead. There was a dazzling transition from the darkness of the violent night to the floodlit calm of Bay Number Two. Rat scrambled back onto the seat and looked out the rear window in time to see the hydraulic doors of the outer lock swing shut. Something was caught between them—something that popped and spattered. The inner door rolled down on its track like a curtain descending on a bloody final act.

Rat was almost home. Two security guards in armor approached. The door locks popped, and Rat climbed out of the cab. One of the guards leveled a burster at his head; the other wordlessly offered him a printreader. He thumbed it, and the bunker's computer verified him immediately.

"Good evening, sir," said one of the guards. "Little rough out there tonight. Did you have luggage?"

The front door of the cab opened, and Rat heard the low whine of electric motors as a mechanical arm lowered the cabbie's wheelchair onto the floor of the bay. She was a gray-haired woman with a rheumy stare who looked like she belonged in a rest home in New Jersey. A knitted shawl covered her withered legs. "You said triple." The cab's hoist clicked and released the chair; she rolled toward him. "Six hundred and sixty-nine dollars."

"No luggage, no." Now that he was safe inside the bunker, Rat regretted his panic-stricken generosity. A credit transfer from one of his own accounts was out of the question. He slipped his last thousand-dollar bubble chip into his wallet's cardreader, dumped $331 from it into a Bahamian laundry loop, and then dropped the chip into her outstretched hand. She accepted it dubiously: for a minute he expected her to bite into it like they did sometimes on fossil TV. Old people made him nervous. Instead she inserted the chip into her own cardreader and frowned at him.

"How about a tip?"

Rat sniffed. "Don't pick up strangers."

One of the guards guffawed obligingly. The other pointed, but Rat saw the skunk port in the wheelchair a millisecond too late. With a wet *plop* the chair emitted a gaseous stinkball that bloomed like an evil flower beneath Rat's whiskers. One guard tried to grab at the rear of the chair, but the old cabbie backed suddenly over his foot. The other guard aimed his burster.

The cabbie smiled like a grandmother from hell. "Under the pollution index. No law against sharing a little scent, boys. And you wouldn't want to hurt me anyway. The hack monitors my EEG. I go flat and it goes berserk."

The guard with the bad foot stopped hopping. The guard with the gun shrugged. "It's up to you, sir."

Rat batted the side of his head several times and then buried his snout beneath his armpit. All he could smell was rancid burger topped with sulphur sauce. "Forget it. I haven't got time."

"You know," said the cabbie, "I never get out of the hack, but I just wanted to see what kind of person would live in a place like this." The lifts whined as the arm fitted its fingers into the chair. "And now I know." She cackled as the arm gathered her back into the cab. "I'll park it by the door. The cops say they're ready to sweep the street."

The guards led Rat to the bank of elevators. He entered the one with the open door, thumbed the printreader, and spoke his access code.

"Good evening, sir," said the elevator. "Will you be going straight to your rooms?"

"Yes."

"Very good, sir. Would you like a list of the communal facilities currently open to serve you?"

There was no shutting the sales pitch off, so Rat ignored it and began to lick the stink from his fur.

"The pool is open for lap swimmers only," said the elevator as the doors closed. "All environments except for the weightless room are currently in use. The sensory deprivation tanks will be occupied until eleven. The surrogatorium is temporarily out of female chassis; we apologize for any inconvenience . . ."

The cab moved down two and a half floors and then stopped just above the subbasement. Rat glanced up and saw a dark gap opening in the array of light-diffuser panels. The spook dropped through it.

". . . the holo therapist is off-line until eight tomorrow morning, but the interactive sex booths will stay open until midnight. The drug dispensary . . ."

She looked as if she had been water-skiing through the sewer. Her blonde hair was wet and smeared with dirt; she had lost the ribbons from her pigtails. Her jeans were torn at the knees, and there was an ugly scrape on the side of her face. The silk turtleneck clung wetly to her. Yet despite her dishevelment, the hand that held the penlight was as steady as a jewel cutter's.

"There seems to be a minor problem," said the elevator in a soothing voice. "There is no cause for alarm. This unit is temporarily nonfunctional. Maintenance has been notified and is now working to correct the problem. In case of emergency, please contact Security. We regret this temporary inconvenience."

The spook fired a burst of light at the floor-selector panel; it spat fire at them and went dark. "Where the hell were you?" said the spook. "You said the McDonald's in Times Square if we got separated."

"Where were *you?*" Rat rose up on his hind legs. "When I got there the place was swarming with cops."

He froze as the tip of the penlight flared. The spook traced a rough outline of Rat on the stainless-steel door behind him. "Fuck your lies," she said. The beam came so close that Rat could smell his fur curling away from it. "I want the dust."

"Trespass alert!" screeched the wounded elevator. A note of urgency had crept into its artificial voice. "Security reports unauthorized persons within the complex. Residents are urged to return immediately to their apartments and engage all personal security devices. Do not be alarmed. We regret this temporary inconvenience."

The scales on Rat's tail fluffed. "We have a deal. The maréchal needs my networks to move his product. So let's get out of here before . . ."

"The dust."

Rat sprang at her with a squeal of hatred. His claws caught on her turtleneck and he struck repeatedly at her open collar, gashing her neck with his long red incisors. Taken aback by the swiftness and ferocity of his attack, she dropped the penlight and tried to fling him against the wall. He held fast, worrying at her and chittering rabidly. When she stumbled under the open emergency exit in the ceiling, he leaped again. He cleared the suspended ceiling, caught himself on the inductor, and scrabbled up onto the hoist cables. Light was pouring into the shaft from above; armored guards had forced the door open and were climbing down toward the stalled car. Rat jumped from the cables across five feet of open space to the counterweight and huddled there, trying to use its bulk to shield himself from the spook's fire. Her stand was short and inglorious. She threw a dazzler out of the hatch, hoping to blind the guards, then tried to pull herself through. Rat could hear the shriek of burster fire. He waited until he could smell the aroma of broiling meat and scorched plastic before he emerged from the shadows and signaled to the security team.

A squad of apologetic guards rode the service elevator with Rat down to the storage subbasement where he lived. When he had first looked at the bunker, the broker had been reluctant to rent him the abandoned rooms, insisting that he live aboveground with the other residents. But all of the suites they showed him were unacceptably open, clean, and uncluttered. Rat much preferred his musty dungeon, where odors lingered in the still air. He liked to fall asleep to the booming of the ventilation system on the level above him, and slept easier knowing that he was as far away from the stink of other people as he could get in the city.

The guards escorted him to the gleaming brass smart door and looked away discreetly as he entered his passcode on the keypad. He had ordered it custom-built from Mosler so that it would recognize high-frequency squeals well beyond the range of human hearing. He called to it and then pressed trembling fingers onto the printreader. His bowels had loosened in terror during the firefight, and the capsules had begun to sting terribly. It was all he could do to keep from defecating right there in the hallway. The door sensed the guards and beeped to warn him of their presence. He punched in the override sequence impatiently, and the seals broke with a sigh.

"Have a pleasant evening, sir," said one of the guards as he scurried inside. "And don't worry ab—" The door cut him off as it swung shut.

Against all odds, Rat had made it. For a moment he stood, tail switching against the inside of the door, and let the magnificent chaos of his apartment soothe his jangled nerves. He had earned his reward—the dust was all his now. No one could take it away from him. He saw himself in a shard of mirror propped up against an empty THC aerosol and wriggled in self-congratulation. He was the richest rat on the East Side, perhaps in the entire city.

He picked his way through a maze formed by a jumble of overburdened steel shelving left behind years, perhaps decades, ago. The managers of the bunker had offered to remove them and their contents before he moved in; Rat had insisted that they stay. When the fire inspector had come to approve his newly installed sprinkler system, she had been horrified at the clutter on the shelves and had threatened to condemn the place. It had cost him plenty to buy her off, but it had been worth it. Since then Rat's trove of junk had at least doubled in size. For years no one had seen it but Rat and the occasional cockroach.

Relaxing at last, Rat stopped to pull a mildewed wing tip down from his huge collection of shoes; he loved the bouquet of fine old leather and gnawed it whenever he could. Next to the shoes was a heap of books: his private library. One of Rat's favorite delicacies was the first edition of *Leaves of Grass* that he had pilfered from the rare book collection at the New York

Public Library. To celebrate his safe arrival, he ripped out page 43 for a snack and stuffed it into the wing tip. He dragged the shoe over a pile of broken sheetrock and past shelves filled with scrap electronics: shattered monitors and dead typewriters, microwaves and robot vacuums. He had almost reached his nest when the fed stepped from behind a dirty Hungarian flag that hung from a broken fluorescent light fixture.

Startled, Rat instinctively hurled himself at the crack in the wall where he had built his nest. But the fed was too quick. Rat did not recognize the weapon; all he knew was that when it hissed, Rat lost all feeling in his hindquarters. He landed in a heap but continued to crawl, slowly, painfully.

"You have something I want." The fed kicked him. Rat skidded across the concrete floor toward the crack, leaving a thin gruel of excrement in his wake. Rat continued to crawl until the fed stepped on his tail, pinning him.

"Where's the dust?"

"I . . . I don't . . ."

The fed stepped again; Rat's left fibula snapped like cheap plastic. He felt no pain.

"The dust." The fed's voice quavered strangely.

"Not here. Too dangerous."

"Where?" The fed released him. "Where?"

Rat was surprised to see that the fed's gun hand was shaking. For the first time he looked up at the man's eyes and recognized the telltale yellow tint. Rat realized then how badly he had misinterpreted the fed's expression back at Koch. Not bored. *Empty.* For an instant he could not believe his extraordinary good fortune. Bargain for time, he told himself. There's still a chance. Even though he was cornered, he knew his instinct to fight was wrong.

"I can get it for you fast if you let me go," said Rat. "Ten minutes, fifteen. You look like you need it."

"What are you talking about?" The fed's bravado started to crumble, and Rat knew he had the man. The fed wanted the dust for himself. He was one of the dead.

"Don't make it hard on yourself," said Rat. "There's a terminal in my nest. By the crack. Ten minutes." He started to pull himself toward the nest. He knew the fed would not dare stop him; the man was already deep into withdrawal. "Only ten minutes and you can have all the dust you want." The poor fool could not hope to fight the flood of neuroregulators pumping crazily across his synapses. He might break any minute, let his weapon slip from trembling hands. Rat reached the crack and scrambled through into comforting darkness.

The nest was built around a century-old shopping cart and a stripped subway bench. Rat had filled the gaps in with pieces of synthetic rubber, a hubcap, plastic greeting cards, barbed wire, disk casings, Baggies, a NO PARKING sign, and an assortment of bones. Rat climbed in and lowered himself onto the soft bed of shredded thousand-dollar bills. The profits of six years of deals and betrayals, a few dozen murders, and several thousand dusty deaths.

The fed sniffled as Rat powered up his terminal to notify Security. "Someone set me up some vicious bastard slipped it to me I don't know when I think it was Barcelona . . . it would kill Sarah to see . . ." He began to weep. "I wanted to turn myself in . . . they keep working on new treatments you know but it's not fair damn it! The success rate is less than . . . I made my first buy two weeks only two God it seems . . . killed a man to get some lousy dust . . . but they're right it's, it's, I can't begin to describe what it's like. . . ."

Rat's fingers flew over the glowing keyboard, describing his situation, the layout of the rooms, a strategy for the assault. He had overridden the smart door's recognition sequence. It would be tricky, but Security could take the fed out if they were quick and careful. Better to risk a surprise attack than to dicker with an armed and unraveling dead man.

"I really ought to kill myself . . . would be best but it's not only me . . . I've seen ten-year-olds . . . what kind of animal sells dust to kids . . . I should kill myself and you." Something changed in the fed's voice as Rat signed off. "And you." He stooped and reached through the crack.

"It's coming," said Rat quickly. "By messenger. Ten doses. By the time you get to the door, it should be here." He could see the fed's hand and burrowed into the rotting pile of money. "You wait by the door, you hear? It's coming any minute."

"I don't want it." The hand was so large it blocked the light. Rat's fur went erect and he arched his spine. "Keep your fucking dust."

Rat could hear the guards fighting their way through the clutter. Shelves crashed. So clumsy, these men.

"It's you I want." The hand sifted through the shredded bills, searching for Rat. He had no doubt that the fed could crush the life from him—the hand was huge now. In the darkness he could count the lines on the palm, follow the whorls on the fingertips. They seemed to spin in Rat's brain—he was losing control. He realized then that one of the capsules must have broken, spilling a megadose of first-quality Algerian Yellow dust into his gut. With a hallucinatory clarity, he imagined sparks streaming through his blood, igniting neurons like tinder. Suddenly the guards did not matter. Nothing mattered except that he was cornered. When he could no longer fight the instinct to strike, the fed's hand closed around him. The man was stronger than Rat could have imagined. As the fed hauled him—clawing and biting—back into the light, Rat's only thought was of how terrifyingly large a man was. So much larger than a rat.

the first law of thermodynamics

He had dropped acid maybe a dozen times, but had never forgotten his name before. He remembered the others—Cassie, Lance, Van—even though he'd left them waiting in the parking lot—when? A couple, ten minutes ago? An hour? Up until then, the farthest out he'd ever been was in high school, when he stared through the white on a sixty-watt bulb and saw the filament vibrating to a solo on Cream's "Sitting on Top of the World." It called to him in guitarese and he shrieked back. The filament said all life vibrated with a common energy, that we would exist only as long as our hearts beat to that indestructible rhythm. *Brang-brangeddy-brong, brang-brangeddy-brong!* Or something like. Actually, he might have been on mescaline the time the light bulb had played him the secret of the universe, or maybe it was Clapton, who was wailing back then like the patron saint of hallucinogens. But tonight his mind was well and truly blown by the blotter acid his new friends had called blue magic.

He wasn't particularly worried that he couldn't remember his straight name. He didn't feel at all attached to that chump at the moment, or to his dreary future. A name was nothing but a fence, closing him in. He was much happier now that the blue magic had transformed him into the wizard *Space Cowboy,* whose power was to leap all fences and zigzag through Day-Glo infinities at the speed of methamphetamine. Remembering the name on his student ID card was about as important as remembering the first law of thermodynamics. His secret identity was flunking physics and probably freshman comp, too, which meant he wasn't going to last much longer at Notre Dame. And since his number in the draft lottery was fourteen, he was northbound just as soon as they booted him out of college—no way Nixon was sending *him* to Cambodia! So long, Amerika, hello Toronto. Or maybe Vancouver. New episodes in the *Adventures of Space Cowboy,* although he wasn't all that excited about picking snot icicles from his mustache. Lance said Canada would be a more happening country if it had beachfront on the Gulf of Mexico.

He realized he had forgotten something else. Why had he come back to his room? Nineteen years old and his mind was already Swiss fucking cheese! He laughed at himself and then admired all the twisty little holes that were busy drilling themselves into the floor. The dull reality of the dorm emptied into them like soapy water swirling down a drain. The room reeked of Aqua Velva and Brylcreem, Balsinger's familiar weekend stink. *That's it.* Something to do with Balls, he thought. But his roommate was long since gone, no doubt sucking down quarts of Stroh's while he told some Barbie doll his dream of becoming the world's most polyester dentist. Balls was the enemy; their room was divided territory, the North and South Vietnam of Walsh Hall. Even when they were out, their stuff remained on alert. His pointy-toed boots were aimed at Balls's chukkas. Pete Townshend swung a guitar at Glen Campbell's head, and *Zap Comix* blew cartoon smoke through the steamy windows of *Penthouse.* Now he remembered, sort of. He was supposed to borrow something—except the paint was melting off the walls. He picked the black cowboy hat off a pile of his dirty clothes, uncrumpled it, and plunked it on. Sometimes the hat helped him think.

There was a knock. "Space?" Cassie peeked in and saw him idling at the desk. "Space, we're leaving."

It was Lance who had abridged his freak name—Lance, the

wizard of words. Space didn't care; if someone he didn't like called him Space, he just played a few bars of Steve Miller's "Space Cowboy" in his head. Cassie he liked; she could call him whatever she wanted. In his opinion, Cassandra Demaras was the coolest chick who had ever gotten high. She stood almost six foxy feet tall and was wearing a man's pin-striped vest from Goodwill over a green T-shirt. Her hair was black as sin. Space lusted to see it spread across his pillow, only he knew it would never happen. She was a senior and artsy and Lance's. Not his future.

"Did you find it?" she asked.

"Ah . . . not yet," said Space cautiously. At least *someone* knew why he was here.

She stepped into the room. "Lance is going to split without you, man." Space had only joined the tribe last month and had already been left behind twice for stoned incompetence. "What's the problem?"

Her question was an itch behind his ear, so he scratched. She stared at him as if his skull were made of glass, and he felt the familiar tingle of acid telepathy. She used her wizardly powers to read his mind—what there was of it—and sighed. "The key, Space. You're supposed to be looking for what's-his-face's key."

"Balls." Suddenly he was buried in a memory landslide. They had been sitting around waiting for the first rush, and Lance had been laying down this rap about how they should do something about Cambodia and how some yippies at Butler had liberated the ROTC building with balloons and duct tape, and then Space had started in about how Balsinger was at school on a work-study grant and had to put in twelve hours a week pushing a broom through O'Shaughnessy Hall, the liberal arts building, *for which he had the key,* and then everybody had gotten psyched, so to impress them all Space had volunteered to lift the key, except in the stairwell he had been blown away by a rush so powerful that he'd forgotten who he was and what the hell he was supposed to be doing, despite which his body had continued on to the room anyway and had been waiting here patiently for his mind to show up.

Space giggled and said, "He keeps it in the top drawer."

Cassie went to Balls's desk, opened it, and then froze as if she was peering over the edge of reality.

"What's he got in there now?" he asked. "Squid?"

As he came up behind her, he caught a telepathic burst that was like chewing aluminum foil. She was freaking out, and he knew exactly why. This was where Balls kept his school supplies: a stack of blank three-by-five file cards held together with a red rubber band, Scotch tape, a box of paper clips, six Number 2 pencils with pristine erasers, six Bic ballpoints, a slide rule, an unopened bottle of Liquid Paper, and behind, loose-leaf, graph, and onionskin paper in perfect stacks. But it wasn't just Balls's stuff that had disturbed her. It was the way he had arranged everything, fitted it together with jigsaw-puzzle precision. In a world burning with love and napalm, this pinhead had taken the time to align pencils and pens, neaten stacks of paper—Space wouldn't have been surprised if he had reorganized the paper clips in their box. All this brutal order was proof that aliens from Planet Middle America had landed and were trying to pass for human! Space was used to Balsinger, but imagining the straightitude of his roommate's mind had filled Cassie with psychedelic dread.

"Space, are you as wasted as I think I am?" Her eyes had gone flat as tattoos.

"I don't know. What's the date?"

She frowned. "May 2, 1970."

"Who's president of the United States?"

"That's the problem."

He held up a fist. "How many fingers?"

She shook her head and was recaptured by the drawer.

The key to O'Shaughnessy Hall was next to the slide rule. Space picked it up and juggled it from one hand to another. It flickered through the air like a goldfish. This time when she glanced up, he bumped the drawer shut with his thigh. "Hey, remember what the dormouse said."

"No, I'm serious." She shook her head and her hair danced. "It's like time is breaking down. You know what I mean? One second doesn't connect to the next."

"Right on!" He caught the key and closed his fist around it.

"Listen! I've got to know where the peak is, or else I can't maintain. What if I just keep going up and up and up?"

"You'll have a hell of a view."

Maybe it was the wrong time for jokes. Space could see panic wisping off her like smoke. When he breathed it in, he got even higher. "Okay," he said, "so the first wave is a mother. But I'm here and you're with me, so we'll just ride it together, okay?" He surfed an open hand toward her. "Then we groove."

"You don't understand." She licked her lower lip with a strawberry tongue. "Lance has decided he wants to score again, so we can trip all weekend. He's weirding me out, Space. My brains are already oozing from my fucking ears, and he's looking for the next hit.''

The blue magic was giving him a squirrelly vibe; he thought he could feel a bad moon rising over this trip. Space had seen a bummer just once, back in high school, when a kid claimed he had a tiny Hitler stuck in his throat and thrashed around and drank twenty-seven glasses of water until he puked. Space had been paranoid that whatever monsters were chewing on the kid's brain would have him for dessert. But this kid—Space remembered him now—Lester Something, Lester was a pinched nobody who couldn't even tie his shoes when he was buzzed, not a wizard like Cassie or Lance or Space, with powers and abilities far beyond those of mortal men.

''Am I okay, Space?'' She had never asked him for help before, put herself in his power. ''What's going to happen to us?''

''We're going to have an adventure.'' Although he was worried about her, he was also turned on. He wanted to kiss his way through her hair to the pale skin on her neck. Instead he tugged at the brim of his hat. He was *Space Cowboy.* His power was that nothing could stop him, nothing could touch him. And so what if things were spinning out of control? That was the fun in doing drugs, wasn't it?

''Ready to cruise?'' He beamed at her and was relieved to see his smile reflected palely on her face.

Somewhere in the future, a van honked.

''Say 'wonderful.' '' Lance was giving Cassie orders.

The spooky moonlight spilled across the cornfields. Space glanced up from the floor of the van occasionally to see if the psychic ambience had improved any, but the lunar seas still looked like mold on a slice of electric bread.

''Wonderful,'' she said absently.

''No, mean it.''

''Won . . . der . . . ful.'' Cassie's voice was a chickadee fluttering against her chest. Space knew this because she was wedged between him and Lance and they had their arms around her, crossing behind her back and over her chest, protecting her from lysergic acid diethylamide demons. He could feel her blood booming; her shallow breathing fondled his ribs. The Econoline's tires drummed over seams in the pavement as its headlights unzipped the highway at sixty-five miles an hour.

He found himself listening to the world with his shoulders and toes.

"Full of wonder." Lance was smooth as an apple as he talked her down; his wizard power was making words dance. "I know, that can be scary, because you don't know where you're going or what you're going to find. Strangeness probably, but so what? Life is strange, people are strange. Don't fight it, groove on it." He squeezed her and Space took his cue to do the same. "Say you're a little girl at the circus at night and a clown comes up in the dark, and it's like, *holy shit,* where's mommy? But throw some light on him and you're laughing." He reached to flick on the overhead light. "See?"

It was the right thing to say because she blinked in the light and smiled, sending them flashes of pink cotton candy and dancing elephants and an acrobat hanging from a trapeze by his teeth. Space could feel her come spinning down toward them like a leaf. "Wonderful," she said, focusing. "I'll try."

Space was suddenly aware that his elbow was flattening her left breast and he was clutching Lance's shoulder. He shivered, let his arm slip down, and wiped his sweaty palm on his jeans.

"Heavy, man," said Van. "You want to turn the light off before I miss the turn?" Van was at the wheel of his 1962 Ford Econoline van. It had a 144-cubic-inch six-cylinder engine and a three-speed manual shift on the steering column, and its name was Bozo. Van had lifted all Bozo's seats except his and replaced them with orange shag carpeting and a mattress fitted with a tie-dyed sheet. He had the Jefferson Airplane on the eight-track; Grace Slick wondered if he needed somebody to love. The answer was yes, thought Space. Yes, damn it! Lance was holding Cassie's hand. Van checked the rearview mirror, then braked, pulled off the highway, and drove along the shoulder, craning his head to the right. Finally he spotted an unmarked dirt track that divided a vast and unpromising nothingness in two.

"Where the fuck are we?" said Space.

"We're either making a brief incursion into Cambodia," said Van, "or we're at the ass-end of Mishawaka, Indiana." Van had the power of mobility. He and Bozo were one, a machine with a human brain. No matter how stoned the world turned, Van could navigate through it. No one demanded poetry or cosmic truths from Van; all they expected of him was to deliver.

"Looks like nowhere to me."

"To the unenlightened eye, yes," said Lance. "But check it out and you'll see another frontier of human knowledge. Tripping is like doing science, Space. You can't just lounge around your room anymore listening to Joni Mitchell and dreaming up laws of nature. You have to go out into the field and gather data in order to grok the universe. Study the stars and ponds, turn rocks over, taste the mushrooms, smoke some foliage."

"Would someone take my boots off?" said Cassie.

"It's freezing, man," said Van. "Your feet will get cold." As Bozo bumped down the track, the steering wheel kept squirming in his hands like a snake.

"I've got cold feet already."

"Science is bullshit!" said Space. "Nothing but a government conspiracy to bring us down." He slid across the shag carpet and rolled the right leg of Cassie's jeans over an ankle-length black boot. "Like, if they hadn't passed the law of gravity, we could all fly."

Van laughed. "Maybe we could get Dicky Trick to repeal it."

"Somebody should repeal that asshole," said Cassie.

"Science is napalm," said Space. "Science is plastic. It's Tang." He eased her boot off. She was wearing cotton socks, soft and nubbly.

"It's the bomb," said Lance.

"Are we going to the farm?" Cassie wiggled her toes in Space's hand. "This is the way to the farm, isn't it?"

Her foot reminded him of the baby rabbit that Katie McCauley had brought for show-and-tell in the sixth grade; he hadn't wanted to put it down either. He pressed his thumb gently against her instep.

"You've never been to the farm, have you, Space?" said Lance. The road spat stones at Bozo's undercarriage.

"He's home," said Van. "I can see lights, man."

"Who?" Space said.

"Do you follow baseball?" Lance started to laugh.

The farm buildings sprawled across the land like a moonbathing giant. The barrel-chested body was a Quonset hut; a red silo arm saluted the stars. The weather-bitten face of the house was turned toward them; its narrow porch pouted. There were lights in the eyes, and much more light streaming from the open slider of the Quonset. Van parked next to a '59 Studebaker Lark that had been driven to Mars and back. He opened his door, took a deep breath of the night, and disappeared.

"Oh, wow!" They could hear him scrabbling on the ground. "I forget how to walk," he said.

Space was the first to reach him. Van was doing a slow backstroke across the lawn toward the house. "For a moment there, man," he said, "I could've sworn I had wheels."

"Come on, you." Lance motioned Space to grab Van's shoulders, and together they tried to lift him. "Get up." It was like stacking Jell-O.

"No, no, *no.*" Van giggled. "I'm too wasted."

"I'm so glad you waited until now to tell us," said Lance. "How the hell do we get back to campus?"

"Oh, I'm cool to drive, man. I just can't stand up."

They managed to fold him back into the driver's seat, and Cassie slapped Big Brother into the eight-track. Space glanced over to the Quonset and saw a silhouette on the canvas of light framed by the huge open doorway. For a moment a man watched—no, *sensed* him. When he sniffed the air, something feathered against Space's cheek. Then the man ghosted back into the barn.

"Old Rog doesn't seem very glad to see us," said Lance.

The barn was fiercely lit—north of supermarket bright, just south of noon at the beach. The wildly colored equipment seemed to shimmer in the hard light. A golden reaper, a pink cultivator, and a lobster-red baler were lined up beside a John Deere that looked like it had been painted in a tornado. The man had poked his head under its hood.

"Evening, Rog," said Lance. "Space, this is Roger Maris."

The man turned toward them; Space blinked. Roger Maris was wearing a pair of black jeans with a hole in the left knee and a greasy Yankees jersey over a gray sweatshirt. He stood maybe six feet tall and weighed a paunchy two hundred and change. He had that flattop crewcut, all right, and the nose like a thumb, but Space wasn't buying that he was Roger Maris. At least not *the* Roger Maris.

He'd been ten years old when Maris hit sixty-one home runs to break Babe Ruth's record, but in 1961 Space and his parents had been National League fans. They lived in Sheboygan and followed the Milwaukee Braves. Space's imagination had been more than filled by the heroics of Hank Aaron and Eddie Mathews; there was no room for damn Yankees. But then the Braves moved south in 1966 and Space had to accept the harsh reality that not only was God dead, but Warren Spahn was retired. After that, he'd lost interest in baseball. He had no clue what had become of *the* Roger Maris since.

"Space?" Maris waved a socket wrench at him. "What the hell kind of name is Space?"

"Short for Space Cowboy," said Cassie.

Maris considered this, then put the wrench down, wiped his left hand on the pin-striped jersey, and offered it to Space. "A hat don't make no cowboy," he said.

They shook. "A shirt don't make no ballplayer," said Space.

Maris's smile bandaged irritation. "What can I do you folks out of?" He gave Space a parting grip strong enough to crush stone.

"You got any more blue magic in your bag of tricks?" said Lance. "We're thinking of going away for the weekend."

"To where, Oz?" Maris shut his eyes; his lids were the color of the last olive in the jar. "Cowboy here ever done magic before?"

Now Space was annoyed; he was proud of his dope résumé. "I've dropped Owsley, wedding bells, and some two-way brown dot."

"Practically Ken Kesey." Cassie laughed. "And only a freshman."

"That shit's just acid," said Maris. "Magic goes deeper."

"He handled the first rush all right," said Lance. "We all did."

"You driving around with a head full of blue magic?" Maris frowned.

"Actually," said Lance, "Van's driving."

But Maris wasn't listening. He had closed his eyes again and kept them closed, his head cocked to one side as he received secret instructions from outer space. "It's your funeral," he said abruptly, and strode from the barn as if he'd just remembered he'd left the bathwater running.

"I guess we scored." Lance shrugged. "Hey, Rog, wait up!" He paused at the door of the Quonset, glanced uncertainly at Cassie and Space, and then plunged after Maris.

"What does he mean, our funeral?" Cassie had turned the color of a saltine.

"Don't ask me; I'm the rookie. Can't you see these training wheels on my head?"

"Deeper? Deeper than what?"

Space put his arm around her shoulder and led her from the Quonset into the baleful night.

Pacing Roger Maris's front parlor, Space remembered what Cassie had said about things getting disconnected. How could anyone deal acid and live in a place as square as a doctor's waiting room? The wallpaper was Midwestern Hideous: golden flag-bearing eagles flapped between Civil War cannons on a cream field. If he stared long enough, the blue magic animated the pattern for him. Madness, *madness*—and Norman Mailer wondered why we were in Vietnam! Lance and Cassie waited for Maris on a long, low brown couch in front of an oval rug braided in harvest colors. Cassie watched the brick fireplace in which four dusty birch logs were stacked. Nearby, a television the size of a Shetland pony was tethered to the wall socket.

Space couldn't stand still. "Where did you dig this loon up?"

"He found us." Lance shot a quizzical look at Cassie. "After the Santana concert?"

She bit her lip and said, "Don't talk to me. I'm not here."

"Okay." Lance was teeth-grindingly patient. "That's cool."

By the door, a heavy brass pot was filled by a man's black umbrella and three baseball bats. "I mean, check this room," said Space.

Lance laughed. "I keep expecting Wally Cleaver to materialize and ask if I want to sniff some glue."

On waist-high shelves beside a rocking chair were stacked a build-it-yourself Heathkit tuner, amp, and turntable. Next to them was a rack of LPs. Space worried through them; they contradicted everything in the room. Maris had the rare nude version of John and Yoko's *Two Virgins, Weasels Ripped My Flesh* by the Mothers of Invention, Moby Grape, everything by Quicksilver Messenger Service, Dylan's *Blonde on Blonde,* the Airplane's *Surrealistic Pillow.*

"Look at this!" Space waved a copy of *Workingman's Dead* at Lance. "This is *not* Roger Maris—he's not anyone. His pieces don't fit together."

Lance pointed silently at a framed Western Union telegram that hung beside a painting of Guernseys.

> MY HEARTIEST CONGRATULATIONS TO YOU ON HITTING YOUR SIXTY-FIRST HOME RUN. THE AMERICAN PEOPLE WILL ALWAYS ADMIRE A MAN WHO OVERCOMES GREAT PRESSURE TO ACHIEVE AN OUTSTANDING GOAL.
>
> JOHN F. KENNEDY.

"So?" Space didn't know why it had become so important to him that this clyde wasn't the famous ballplayer. "He could've got this anywhere—could've sent it to himself." Everything seemed so slippery all of a sudden; he felt a familiar twinge of dread. Just when he'd finally figured the world out, he was afraid he might have to stop believing in something. Again. This was exactly how it had felt when he had given up on baseball, Catholicism, America, love, *Star Trek*, college. What was it this time? The only illusions he had left were that nothing mattered, that acid was wisdom, and that he was a wizard.

He heard Maris on the stairs and skittered back to the couch next to Cassie, who was still elsewhere.

"A dozen hits of magic." Maris offered them a plastic baggie with a scatter of confetti clinging to the inside. Space took it. Each blotter was the size of a fingernail and was labeled with a blue ∞. "Sixty," said Maris.

Lance pulled two twenties and a joint from his T-shirt pocket. "Want to smoke?" He liked to close deals with some ceremonial pot. He said it was the Indian way, and also helped detect narcs. While he lit up, Space counted out a ten, a five, and five ones, and put an empty wallet back in his jeans.

Lance passed the joint to Maris, who took an impatient toke.

"You said this is deeper than acid." Space jiggled the baggie. "What's that supposed to mean, anyway?"

Cassie twitched and returned from the dark side of the moon.

"You take a trip, you come back, nothing really changes." The smoky words curled out of his mouth. "This shit makes you become yourself faster, kind of hurries things along."

"Something wrong with that?" said Cassie.

"Depends on who you're supposed to be." Maris tucked the wad of money into his jeans. "But if I was you kids, I'd take the long way to the future." He offered Cassie the joint; she waved it over to Space.

"Sounds like Timothy Leary bullshit to me." Space took a deep, disgusted pull and immediately regretted it. Lance's pot tasted like electrical fire; it was probably laced with Mr. Clean.

" 'Timothy Leary's dead,' " sang Lance. "So if I'm not myself, who am I? Marshall McLuhan? Abbie Hoffman?"

"You're faking it, that's what being young is all about. When you're young, there ain't all that much of you, so you pretend there's more."

"Hell, you're the one preten—" Space couldn't hold it in anymore; he was racked by a fit of coughing.

"Space," said Cassie.

"You never hit sixty-one homers." Space gasped; his head felt like it was filling with helium. "I bet you've never even been to Yankee Stadium."

Maris's face was hard as the Bible. "You want to see my license, Cowboy?" In the uneasy silence, he fetched an ashtray from the hi-fi shelf. "Me, I stayed young a long time, mostly because I never did nothing but play ball. Growing up ain't something they really encourage in the bigs. When I got traded to the Yankees, I was just the kid who was going to play right field next to Mantle. I was MVP that season. 'Sixty." Talking about baseball seemed to calm him. He took another drag, ashed the joint, and then offered it again to Cassie.

"Mantle?" This time she puffed politely.

"Mickey Mantle played center field," said Lance. "Tell them about the home run." Space wasn't sure whether Lance really believed or was egging Maris on for a goof.

"That was the next year, when me and Mick hit all the homers. Only he got sick and I still didn't have the record on the last day of the season. We were playing the Red Sox at the Stadium. By then a lot of people had given up, probably thought I didn't have sixty-one in me. I remember it was a cool day but real bright, the sun beating down on all the empty seats. The fans who showed were jammed into the right-field stands, just in case. The Sox started Tracy Stallard, a righty, fastball pitcher. I flied out to Yaz in the first, but when I came up in the fourth. . . ."

The contours of his body changed, as if the weight of the last nine years had fallen away.

"He started me with two balls away. Then the third pitch, he made a mistake, got too much of the plate. I was always a mistake hitter. I got a real good cut at it and then . . . I just stood and watched. It landed near the bullpen, about ten rows into the stands, people scrambling after it. There was a fog of noise; it was like I couldn't find my way around the bases. When I got back to the dugout, Blanchard and Skowron and Lopez wouldn't let me in, they were blocking the top step, making me go back out into the noise. That was the problem, I couldn't never find my way out of that goddamned noise."

"Is that why you left baseball?" asked Cassie.

"Nah." Maris closed his eyes again; he was definitely listening to *something*. "Nah, it's 'cause I ain't a kid anymore." Suddenly he looked spent; Space could see a looseness under the chin. "I'm thirty-six years old."

"That's still pretty young," said Cassie.

"Well then, there's this." He rolled up the gray sweatshirt, uncovering his left forearm. A scar, smooth and white as the belly of a snake, sliced from the ball of his thumb up toward the elbow. "The VC likes to rig these homemade mines, see. Couple of fragmentation grenades with the spoons attached to a tripwire. Me and Luther Nesson were walking point outside of Da Lat, and the poor bastard stepped into one. Died in a splatter and left me a souvenir. A chunk of shrapnel chewed on my *palmaris longus* muscle and severed a couple of tendons."

Space contemplated the wound with vast relief; for a moment back there, Maris had almost convinced him. Now he felt a grudging admiration for Maris's creativity, his devotion to detail, the weight of his portrayal—the man had elevated lunacy to an art. And of course the 'Nam angle made it all the more poignant. Space imagined that, if he had seen what Maris had seen, he might well be strumming a ukulele and warbling like Tiny Tim.

"Bummer." Lance stubbed the roach out and took the baggie. "Hey, we better go check on Van, make sure he didn't float away." He stood. "So anyway, thanks, man." He reached for Cassie's hand.

"What's happening?" Cassie scooted away from him and bumped into Space. "We're going already? What about the rest of the story?"

Maris waved at the parlor. "Sister, you're looking at it."

Outside, Van was amusing himself by flashing a light show against the side of the farmhouse while he sang along to *Sgt. Pepper.* High beam-low beam-right blinker-off-low beam-left blinker . . . "—the *girl* with ka*lei*doscope *eyes.*" He had a voice like a loose fan belt.

Maris followed them onto the porch and watched, flickering in the headlights. As Cassie ducked into Bozo, Maris called out. "Cowboy! How much you want for the hat?"

"Huh?"

"Pay no attention," Lance hissed. "Just get in."

"It's not for sale." Space stepped away from Bozo.

"Sixty bucks says it is."

Space tugged at the brim; he had almost forgotten he was wearing it. He started back toward Maris. It wasn't much of a hat—Space had stepped on it many times, spilled Boone's Farm Apple Wine on it, watched as one of Lenny Kemmer's Winstons had burned a hole in the black felt crown. "Is this some kind of joke?"

Van killed the lights and Beatles. Lance and Cassie deployed on either side of Bozo.

Maris came to the top of the porch steps. ''You got doubts,'' he said. ''You think I've been shitting you all night.''

When Space tried to deny it, his tongue turned to peanut butter.

''Hell, Cowboy, you don't believe in nothing.''

''So?''

''So I want to buy the hat.'' Maris came down the first step. ''For an experiment.'' Second step. ''And you gotta help.'' Bottom step. ''Sixty.'' He unfolded the wad of bills and thrust them at Space.

''Hey, Rog,'' said Lance. ''He's just a kid. Leave him alone.''

Abraham Lincoln gazed up at Space, appraising the quality of his courage.

''What kind of experiment?'' said Cassie.

''Scientific. Cowboy and me are going to measure something.''

Space nipped the money without speaking and offered Maris the hat.

Maris clapped him on the shoulder. ''You just hold on to that for now.'' He turned Space toward the Quonset. ''See that barn? How far would you say it is?''

As Space peered into night, the Quonset receded and then flowed back toward him. ''I don't know. Fifty, sixty feet?''

''More like a hundred, but that's okay. Now you're gonna stand in that doorway and get a good tight grip on the brim.'' He raised Space's arm. ''Hold it to one side, just like that. Arm's length.''

''Space.'' Cassie slipped between them. ''Give him back his money and let's get out of here.''

Maris brushed past her and surveyed the shrubbery along the porch. He poked by a couple of crewcut yews, a rhododendron in bud, a forsythia already gone by.

Cassie kept insisting. ''Time to *go,* man.'' Like she was his mother.

The edge of the garden was defined by a row of smooth beach stones, painted white. Maris knelt with a grunt and hefted one the size of a peach, only flatter and more egg-shaped.

''Everyone remembers me for the homers, but I could play the field too.'' He brushed dirt off the stone. ''Won a Gold Glove, you know. Didn't nobody stretch a single on Roger Maris.''

''Jesus God,'' said Cassie, ''what are you morons trying to

prove? That your balls are bigger than your brains?''

That summed it up nicely, thought Space. Maris was playing a testosterone game with his head. Space was at once a creature of the game and a spectator. A poor nervous physics major sat in the stands, watching in horror, while Space Cowboy was grooving on a Grade A adrenaline high. And why not? He was a nineteen-year-old wizard whose power was that nothing could touch him, nothing could stop him. He looked over at Lance, who was pale as the moon. ''Right *on!*'' Space said.

He counted the paces off: thirty-nine, forty, forty-one. Forty-two to the Quonset's open doorway—figure three feet to a pace, so let's see, three times two was six and three times four was twelve—was that right? He had won his high school's Math Medal back in the Pleistocene. A hundred and twenty-six feet was just about the distance from third base to first. He bowed, flourished the hat to Cassie, and then held it up in his moist, outstretched hand.

Maris turned at a right angle to the Quonset; he held the stone behind him, just off the hip. He scowled at the hat over his front shoulder and then paused. He shut his eyes and listened to the howl of the Dog Star long enough for a bead of sweat to dribble from Space's armpit. Then Maris nodded, reared back, and strode quickly forward—*Open your eyes, goddamnit!* His arm snapped past his ear, and the stone came screaming at Space like the headlamp of God's own Harley—or maybe it was Space who screamed, he couldn't tell, he couldn't move, his entire future had collapsed into an egg-shaped stone and time stopped and for an eternity he thought, *What a fucking waste,* and then time resumed with a sneeze and the hat spun him halfway around but he held on to it and something *thwocked* against the concrete floor of the Quonset and again, *thwocka-thwocka-thwok!* For a moment there was utter silence, which drummed in his ears like the finale of the *1812 Overture.* Space whispered, ''Out of sight,'' and giggled. Then he shouted so the others could hear. ''OUT OF SIGHT!''

Space was surprised that the stone hadn't ripped off the top of the hat but instead had come through the pinch on the front side, leaving a hole big enough for Lance to put his fist through. Lance handed it to Van who offered it to Cassie who wanted no part of it. ''Are you boys about through?'' Her voice was a fistful of nails.

''Yeah,'' said Lance. ''Time to cruise.''

Van brought the hat to Maris, who was kneading his biceps. Maris stared right through him. "See what magic can do, Cowboy?" His smile had no teeth in it. "You can make yourself into a star, if that's who you're supposed to be."

"Mr. Maris," said Space, opening his wallet. "How much for that hat?"

Van, Space, and Lance staggered out of Kresge's and across the parking lot, laughing. The cashier had rung up the eight cans of Rust-Oleum—two each of red, yellow, green, and black—the one-pound bag of Fritos, the four Almond Joys, the six packages of Fun Tyme Balloons, the dozen rolls of crepe ribbon, the two packs of Teaberry gum, and then, as the register stuck out its paper tongue at her, she had asked them who the party was for. When Lance had said, "President Nixon, ma'am," she was so transparently croggled that it was all Space could do to keep from dropping to his belly and barking like a seal.

Cassie, who had been waiting for them in Bozo, didn't see what was so funny, but then she hadn't eaten that second blotter of blue magic, either. Ken Kesey and the Merry Pranksters had a saying: You were either on the bus or off. Space was no telepath, but it occurred to him that Cassie might be about to stand up and pull the signal cord for her stop.

"She's probably calling the cops on us right now," Cassie said.

"For what, indecent composure?" said Lance. "Chortling in a No Humor Zone?"

"How about possession? You've got Space here mooning around in a cowboy hat with a frontal lobotomy and you two are so wasted you're tripping over gum spots on the parking lot." She shook her head. "You guys are dangerous, you know that?"

"Only to ourselves." Van swerved Bozo around an oncoming Vega and roared onto the highway, headed back toward campus. "Break out the chips."

They crunched to themselves for a few moments. Space was glad that Cassie was no longer freaking out, only now she had turned so fucking sensible that she was stretching his nerves. They were tripping, *ferchrissakes;* this was no time to be responsible. "How about some tunes?" he said.

Van turned on the radio.

"—of student protests continued today in the wake of President

Nixon's decision to send troops into Cambodia. In Maryland, Governor Marvin Mandel has put the National Guard on alert after two days of unrest on the campus . . ."

"I said tunes!" Space leaned forward to punch a selector button.

"Ssh, listen." Lance yanked him back.

"And at Kent State University in Ohio, a fire of undetermined origin swept through the ROTC building this evening. Firemen responding to the blaze were hampered by students throwing rocks and cutting hoses."

"Hey, man," said Van. "Maybe we should go after ROTC too."

"Earlier today, a group of two thousand students marched through downtown Kent, prompting local officials to order a dawn-to-dusk . . ."

"No," Lance said. "That's where they'll be expecting trouble. Besides, we've got the key to O'Shag."

"This whole gig is bogus." Cassie nudged the paper Kresge's sack with her boot. "It's not going to accomplish anything, except maybe get us arrested."

"Hey, we're going to wake up this fucking campus," Space said.

"Fucking A!" said Van.

"Shake the jocks out of their beds."

"Right on, man, right on!" Van pumped his fist.

"Light a fire under old Hesburgh."

"Tell it, brother!" Van leaned on the horn.

"Lay off, you guys," said Lance. "Cassie, you heard the radio. People all over the country are protesting. We've got a chance to make a statement here."

"With balloons and spray paint?"

"Better than guns and bombs." Lance rested his hand on her knee. "You thought it was cool before."

"That wasn't me, that was the acid."

"Turning to sports, Dust Commander has won the Kentucky Derby. A fifteen-to-one shot . . ."

She rested her cheek against the window. "Look, I'm going to graduate in a couple of weeks. I'm too old to be playing Wendy to your Lost Boys. Maybe I should just go back to the dorm and crash."

"And in the American League, the Angels beat the Red Sox, eight–four, it was the Yankees seven, the Brewers six . . ."

Space fingered the hole in his hat and wondered if he had it in him to be a star.

Van sauntered toward the main entrance to O'Shaughnessy Hall. The liberal arts building was one of the largest and ugliest on campus, a stack of four Gothic Revival ice cube trays with a yellow brick veneer. Cassie, Space, and Lance watched from the chill shadows as Van waltzed innocently up to the door, tried it as if he'd expected O'Shag to be open at 11:34 on a Saturday night, shrugged and cruised on.

"Of course, if it wasn't locked, we wouldn't be breaking and entering." Cassie made no effort to keep her voice down. "Jerry Rubin would have to take points off."

Lance had used his wizard power to talk Cassie into sticking with them, but Space wasn't sure it had been his swiftest move of the evening. Doubt was contagious, especially when your feet were wet. They had left Bozo in student parking and stolen across the tidy greens of the campus, weighting their shoes with spring dew. The night was getting colder; Space could see his breath plume. He ground his teeth to keep them from chattering. It took Van forever to circle back to them.

They slunk around to O'Shag's smaller north entrance, checking for any signs of activity inside. The classrooms were all dark, but that didn't mean some English professor might not be late-nighting in one of the windowless offices, slugging Jim Beam and writing poems about English professors for the *Dead Tree Review.* This time the others stayed behind while Space approached the door, clutching Balls's key. It wasn't until he was fitting it into the lock that he realized there might be an alarm. He looked back at the others in a panic, but they were no help. Neither were the stars, some of which were flashing blue like the cherry on a cop car. He could almost hear the Pleiades shrilling at him as he tried to turn the key to the right. It wouldn't budge. He thought the moon's alarm would sound deeper and more reproachful, like a foghorn. He turned the key left and the deadbolt clicked. *Moon, spoon, you fucking loon.* He pushed against the door and it swung open, dumping him into O'Shaughnessy Hall.

He went through a dimly lit stairwell to the long, dark hall of the first floor. The block walls on either side were pierced by wooden doors. Space could not make out the far end. Although he had passed this way every Monday, Wednesday, and Friday for eight months, Space felt lost. The place he knew and hated teemed with sound and light and bodies. This one was empty, silent as a dream and all the doors were closed, creating an odd pressure in the hall, as if the building were holding its breath.

He heard a door tick open, a squeak of sneakers against the rubber mat in the stairwell, the whisper of corduroy pants. Lance said that the reason Van always wore corduroys was that he needed more texture in his life.

"In here," said Space.

"No lights?" Van peered.

"No."

They joined Lance and Cassie in the stairwell. Lance knelt in a corner of the stairwell and handed out supplies from the Kresge's bag. "We'll each take a floor," he said. "Fifteen minutes and out."

"But what should we say, man?" asked Van.

"Like I said, just make a statement," said Lance. "It's your life and their war."

Cassie waved off a package of balloons. "Keep the party favors." She went up the stairs with a can of Rust-Oleum in each hand.

"Bring the empties back, and no fingerprints, okay?" said Lance. "Fifteen minutes—let's do it!" He and Van took the stairs two at a time.

Space sprayed a blue peace sign on the door to Room 160 but was strangely unconvinced by it. Then what kind of statement did he have in him? He immediately regretted the *Fuck Nixon;* it was obvious as air. *Hell No, We Won't Go* sprawled the entire length of Room 149 and came to a disappointing conclusion on 147. Room 141 read *Out Now.* He took a balloon from his pocket, blew it up, and almost fainted but managed to hold it pinched between thumb and forefinger. Out of where? Cambodia? Vietnam? Notre Dame? Instead of tying the balloon, Space let it go and it leapt, hissing, from his hand. He wrote *Revolution* on the east wall, *Make Love Not War* on the west, then left them to futile debate. He was now deep into the hall; the visibility was less than a classroom in either direction. He could feel the future watching as he wrote *Acid Test* on Room 133. Pale secondhand moonlight glimmered through the tall wire-reinforced glass slits in each door. One twenty-five said, *God Is Dead.* Long red runs dribbled from the *o* in *God,* like blood from the crown of thorns. Was proclaiming the demise of the deity a political statement? *Maris 61/61* on 117. That would leave the campus fuzz scratching their balls, even though Old Rog had proved that it was cool to *talk the talk,* man, just as long as you can *walk the walk.* But Space still couldn't see the end of the fucking hall.

At that moment, something splatted on his cheek. Space

swiped at it, thinking it might be his own sweat. The finger came away dry; he could feel his skin tighten in fear. *Pa-chuk.*

"Hey!"

Pa-chuk, pa-chuk. The two drops hit his left arm like marbles on a snare drum, and he spun wildly away. *Pa-chuk.* Space moaned and started to run. A phantom storm in the middle of O'Shaugnessy Hall was hairy enough, but these weren't just polite raindrops. They were big and cold and rude as eggs. *Pa-chuk.*

And this was it, he realized: the bummer he had helped Cassie dodge was seething all around him and he knew he had to get out—get *out*—that he had been wandering blindly and without purpose down this hallway ever since he had come to Notre Dame *papa-chuk* but he could no longer go back to his parents and Sheboygan and Cathy, that lying bitch *pa-chuk,* but there was no sense in going any farther because the hallway stretched on to some distant and unknowable infinity and besides, he had to get the hell out, which was when the doors began to vibrate and the light of insight came knifing through the long, thin windows and he saw the hall with the same acid clarity with which he had heard the filament of a sixty-watt bulb riffing about the mysterious energy that abided in all life, only now he could sense a new secret *papa-chuk:* that there was no future in wandering down an empty hall, that in order to find his life he would have to choose where to expend his energy. Pick a door, *damn* it. Room 110 was right in front of him, but it was even and Space knew he had to be odd. He about-faced; nothing could stop him. The doorknob of 109 was warm as a kiss.

Space put a hand to his forehead to shield his eyes. Sunlight poured through windows that framed snow-covered mountains. The sky was the blue of heaven; the snow on the ground glistened. He had entered a classroom all right, but it obviously wasn't in the same corner of reality as South Bend, Indiana.

A balding man stood behind the head desk and typed with two fingers—the teacher, Space assumed. He was wearing suede cowboy boots, black pants, a denim work shirt buttoned to the neck, and—*holy shit,* the dude had a gold earring!

He did not seem to notice Space.

Neither did the students now filing in behind him. They seemed too young to be in college; they had that stunned glaze of high-school seniors—except that some of them had tattoos. The sides of one girl's head had been shaved to a gunmetal shadow. A boy in a flannel shirt had on the flimsiest headphones Space had ever seen; they were attached to a transistor radio hooked to the kid's belt. *Walkman*—the word sprang unbidden to his mind. *Walk the walk,* man.

Space's first instinct was to bolt from the room, or at least slouch like a student behind a desk in the back, but instead he approached the teacher. As he got closer he saw that the squashed typewriter had no paper in it, that it wasn't any kind of machine Space had ever seen before, but then there was another strange word melting on his tongue like a Life Saver—*laptop.* It was a funny word and he might have laughed, except that he had by now come too close to the teacher, close enough so that he could wiggle his toes inside the man's boots, so close that he could jingle the keys to an '88 Dodge Caravan in his front pants pocket and, in the back pocket, feel the bulk of a wallet not quite filled with thirty-eight dollars and a NatWest Visa card with an unpaid balance of $3,734.80 on which he was paying a 9.9 percent APR and a California driver's license and a picture of a pretty little blonde girl named Kaitlin, so impossibly close that he could feel the weight of a single gold band around the fourth finger of his left hand and remember Judy's breath feathering against his neck after she kissed him good-bye that morning.

The bell rang, and the class came to what passed for attention at Memorial High.

"Good morning, people." He turned to the board and scrawled, *1st law of thermodynamics* in handwriting that was almost as legible as an EKG scan. He faced the class again. "Can anyone tell me what this is?"

He was astonished to see Ben Strock with his hand up. Most days the kid sat looking as if he had just been hit in the head with a shovel, even though he *was* pulling down a B-plus. "Yes, Ben?"

"Uh . . . bathroom pass, Mr. Casten."

Jack Casten waved him from the room. "Anyone else?"

Of course, Feodor Papachuk raised his hand. *Fucking suck-up,* thought the part of Jack Casten that was still Space Cowboy and always would be. "Go ahead, Feodor."

"The first law of thermodynamics," said Feodor Papachuk, "is that energy can neither be created or destroyed, but may be changed from one form to another."

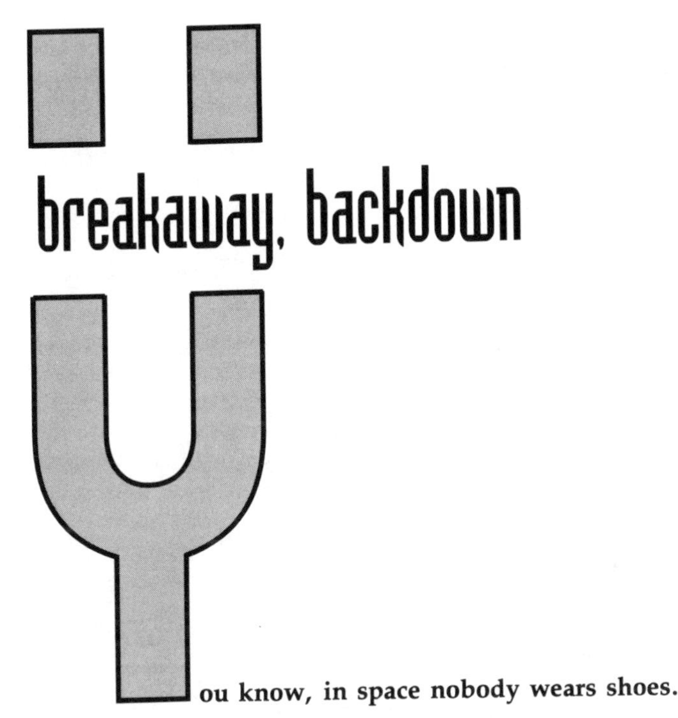

breakaway, backdown

You know, in space nobody wears shoes.

Well, new temps wear slippers. They make the soles out of that adhesive polymer, griprite or griptite. Sounds like paper ripping when you lift your feet. Temps who've been up a while wear this glove thing that snugs around the toes. The breakaways, they go barefoot. You can't really walk much in space, so they've reinvented their feet so they can pick up screwdrivers and spoons and stuff. It's hard because you lose fine motor control in micro gee. I had . . . have this friend, Elena, who could make a krill and tomato sandwich with her feet, but she had that operation that changes your big toe into a thumb. I used to kid her that maybe breakaways were climbing down the evolutionary ladder, not jumping off it. Are we people or chimps? She'd scratch her armpits and hoot.

Sure, breakaways have a sense of humor. They're people, after all; it's just that they're like no people you know. The thing was, Elena was so limber that she could bite her toenails. So can you fix my shoe?

How long is that going to take? Why not just glue the heel back on?

I know they're Donya Durands, but I've got a party in half an hour, okay?

What, you think I'm going to walk around town barefoot? I'll wait—except what's with all these lights? It's two in the morning, and you've got this place bright as noon in Khartoum. How about a little respect for the night?

Thanks. What did you say your name was? I'm Cleo.

You are, are you? Jane honey, lots of people *think* about going to space, but you'd be surprised at how few actually apply —much less break away. So how old are you?

Oh no, they like them young, just as long as you're over nineteen. No kids in space. So the stats don't scare you?

Not shoe repair, that's for sure. But if you can convince them you're serious, they'll find something for you to do. They trained me and I was nobody, a business major. I temped for almost fifteen months on *Victor Foxtrot,* and I never could decide whether I loved or hated it. Still can't, so how could I even think about becoming a breakaway? Everything is loose up there, okay? It makes you come unstuck. The first thing that happens is you get spacesick. For a week your insides are so scrambled that you're trying to digest lunch with your cerebellum and write memos with your large intestine. Meanwhile your face puffs up so that you can't find yourself in the mirror anymore and your sinuses fill with cotton candy and you're fighting a daily hair mutiny. I might've backed down right off if it hadn't been for Elena—you know, the one with the clever toes? Then when you're totally miserable and empty and disoriented, your brain sorts things out again and you realize it's all magic. Some astrofairy has enchanted you. Your body is as light as a whisper, free as air. I'll tell you the most amazing thing about weightlessness. It doesn't go away. You keep falling: down, up, sideways, whatever. You might bump into something once in a while, but you never, ever slam into the ground. Extremely sexy, but it does take some getting used to. I kept having dreams about gravity. Down here you have a whole planet hugging you. But in space, it's not only you that's enchanted, it's all your stuff too. For instance, if *you* put that brush down, it stays. It doesn't decide to drift across the room and out the window and go visit Elena over on B deck. I had this pin that had been my mother's—a silver dove with a diamond eye—and somehow it escaped from a locked jewelry box. Turned up two months later in a dish of butterscotch pudding, almost broke Jack Pitzer's tooth. You get a lot of pudding in space. Oatmeal. Stews. Sticky food is easier to eat, and you can't taste much of anything but salt and sweet anyway.

Why, do you think I'm babbling? God, I *am* babbling. It must be the Zentadone. The woman at the persona store said it was just supposed to be an icebreaker with a flirty edge to it, like Panital only more sincere. You wouldn't have any reset, would you?

Hey, spare me the lecture, honey. I know they don't allow personas in space. Anyway, imprinting is just a bunch of probrain propaganda. Personas are temporary—*period.* When you stop taking the pills, the personas go away and you're your plain old vanilla self again; there's bushels of studies that say so. I'm just taking a little vacation from Cleo. Maybe I'll go away for a weekend, or a week or a month, but eventually I'll come home. Always have, always will.

I don't care *what* your Jesus puppet says; you can't trust godware, okay? Look, I'm not going to convince you and you're not going to convince me. Truce?

The shoes? Four, five years. Let's see, I bought them in '36. Five years. I had to store them while I was up.

You get used to walking in spike heels, actually. I mean, I'm not going to run a marathon or climb the Matterhorn. Elena has all these theories of why men think spikes are sexy. Okay, they're kind of a short-term body mod. They stress the leg muscles, which makes you look tense, which leads most men to assume you could use a serious screwing. And they push your fanny out like you're making the world an offer. But most important is that, when you're teetering around in heels, it tells a man that if he chases you, you're not going to get very far. Not only do spike heels say you're vulnerable, they say you've *chosen* to be vulnerable. Of course, it's not quite the same in micro gee. She was my mentor, Elena. Assigned to teach me how to live in space.

I was an ag tech. Worked as a germ wrangler in the edens.

Microorganisms. Okay, you probably think that if you stick a seed in some dirt, add some water and sunlight, and wait a couple of months, mother nature hands you a head of lettuce. Doesn't work that way, especially not in space. The edens are synergistic, symbiotic ecologies. Your carbo crops, your protein crops, your vitamin crops—they're all fussy about the neighborhood germs. If you don't keep your *clostridia* and *rhizobia* in balance, your eden will rot to compost. Stinky, slimy compost. It's important work—and duller than accounting. It wouldn't have been so bad if we could've talked on the job, but CO_2 in the edens runs 6 percent, which is great for plants but will kill you if you're not wearing a breather. Elena painted an enormous smile on mine, with about eight hundred teeth in it. She had lips on hers, puckered so that they looked like she was ready to be kissed. Alpha Ralpha the chicken man had this plastic beak. Only sometimes we switched—confused the hell out of the nature lovers. I'll tell you, the job would've been a lot easier if we could've kept the rest of the crew out, but the edens are designed for recreation as much as food production. On *Victor Foxtrot* we had to have sign-ups between 8:00 and 16:00. See, the edens have lots of open space and we keep them eight degrees over crew deck nominal and they're lit twenty hours a day by grolights and solar mirrors and they have big windows. Crew floats around sucking up the view, soaking up photons, communing with the life force, shredding foliage, and in general getting in our way. Breakaways are the worst; they actually adopt plants like they were pets. Is that crazy or what? I mean, a tomato has a life span of three, maybe four months before it gets too leggy and stops bearing. I've seen grown men cry because Elena pulled up their favorite marigold.

No, all my plants now are silk. When I backed down, I realized that I didn't want anything to do with the day. My family was a bunch of poor nobodies; we moved to the night when I was seven. So nightshifting was like coming home. The fact is, I got too much sun while I was up. The sun is not my friend. Haven't seen real daylight in over a year; I make a point of it. I have a day-night timeshare at Lincoln Street Under. While the sun is shining I'm asleep or safely cocooned. At dusk, my roomie comes home and I go out to work and play. Hey, being a mommy to legumes is *not* what I miss about space. How about you? What turned you into an owl?

Well, well, maybe you *are* serious about breaking away. Sure, they prefer recruits who've nightshifted. Shows them you've got circadian discipline.

Elena said something like that once. She said that it's hard to scare someone to death in broad daylight. It isn't just that the daytime is too crowded, it's too tame. The night is edgier, scarier. Sexier. You say and do things that wouldn't occur to you at lunchtime. It's because we don't really belong in the night. In order to survive here, we have to fight all the old instincts warning us not to wander around in the dark because we might fall off a cliff or get eaten by a saber-toothed tiger. Living in the night gives you a kind of extra . . . I don't know. . . .

Right. And it's the same with space; it's even scarier and sexier. Well, maybe *sexy* isn't exactly the right word, but you know what I mean. Actually, I think that's what I miss most about it. I was more alive then than I ever was before. Maybe too alive. People live fast up there. They know the stats; they *have* to. You know, you sort of remind me of Elena. Must be the eyes—it sure as hell isn't the body. If you ever get up, give her a shout. You'd like her, even though she doesn't wear shoes anymore.

Almost a year. I wish we could talk more, but it's hard. She transferred to the *Marathon;* they're out surveying Saturn's moons. There's like a three-hour lag; it's impossible to have real-time conversation. She sent a few vids, but it hurt too much to watch them. They were all happy chat, you know? Nothing important in them. I didn't plan on missing her so much. So, you have any college credits?

No real difference between Harvard and a net school, unless you're some kind of snob about bricks.

Now that's a hell of a thing to be asking a perfect stranger. What do I look like, some three-star slut? Don't make assumptions just because I'm wearing spike heels. For all you know, honey, I could be dating a basketball player. Maybe I'm tired of staring at his navel when we dance. If you're going to judge people by appearances, hey, *you're* the one with the machine stigmata. What's that supposed to be, rust or dried blood?

Well, you ought to be. Though actually, that's what everyone wants to know. That, and how do you go to the bathroom. Truth is, Jane, sex is complicated, like everything about space. First of all, forget all that stuff you've heard about doing it while you're floating free. It's dangerous, hard work and no fun. You want to have sex in space, one or both of you have to be tied down. Most hetero temps use some kind of a joystrap. It's this wide circular elastic that fits around you and your partner. Helps you stay coupled, okay? But even with all the gear, sex can be kind of subtle. As in disappointing. You don't realize how erotic weight is until there isn't any. You want to make love to a balloon? Some people do nothing but oral—keeps the vectors down. Of course the breakaways, they've reinvented love, just like everything else. They have this kind of sex where they don't move. If there's penetration they just float in place, staring into one another's eyes or some such until they tell one another that it's time to have an orgasm and then they do. If they're homo, they just touch each other. Elena tried to show me how, once. I don't know why, but it didn't happen for me. Maybe I was too embarrassed because I was the only one naked. She said I'd learn eventually, that it was part of breaking away.

No, I thought I was going to break away, I really did. I stuck it out until the very last possible day. It's hard to explain. I mean, when nobodies on earth look up at night—no offense, Jane, I was one too—what calls them is the romance of it all. The high frontier, okay? Sheena Steele and Captain Kirk, cowboys and asteroids. Kid stuff, except they don't let kids in space because of the cancer. Then you go up and once you're done puking, you realize that it was all propaganda. Space is boring and it's indescribably magic at the same time—how can that be? Sometimes I'd be working in an eden and I'd look out the windows and I'd see earth, blue as a dream, and I'd think of all the people down there, twelve billion ants, looking up into the night and wondering what it was like to be me. I swear I could feel their envy, as sure as I can feel your floor beneath me now. It's part of what holds you up when you're in space. You know you're not an ant; there are fewer than twenty thousand breakaways. You're brave and you're doomed and you're different from everyone else who has ever lived. Only then your shift ends, and it's time to go to the gym and spend three hours pumping the ergorack in a squeeze suit to fight muscle loss in case you decide to back down. I'll tell you, being a temp is hell. The rack is hard work; if you're not exhausted afterward, you haven't done it right. And you sweat, *God.* See, the sweat doesn't run off. It pools in the small of your back and the crook of your arm and under your chin and clings there, shivering like an amoeba. And while you're slaving on the rack, Elena is getting work done or reading or sleeping or talking about you with her breakaway pals. They have three more hours in their day, see, and they don't ever have to worry about backing down. Then every nine weeks you have to leave what you're doing and visit one of the wheel habitats and readjust to your weight for a week so that when you come back to *Victor Foxtrot,* you get spacesick all over again. But you tell yourself it's all worth it because it's not only space that you're exploring; it's yourself. How many people can say that? You have to find out who you are so that you decide what to hold on to and what to let go of. . . . Excuse me, I can't talk about this anymore right now.

No, I'll be all right. Only . . . okay, so you don't have any reset. You must have some kind of flash?

That'll have to do. Tell you what, I'll buy the whole liter from you.

Ahh, ethanol with a pedigree. But a real backdown kind of drug, Jane—weighs way too much to bring out of the gravity well. And besides, the flash is about the same as hitting yourself over the head with the bottle. Want a slug?

Come on, it's two-thirty. Time to start the party. You're making me late, you know.

Do me a favor, would you? Pass me those shoes on the shelf there . . . no, no the blue ones. Yes. Beautiful. Real leather, right? I love leather shoes. They're like faces. I mean, you can polish them but once they get wrinkles, you're stuck with them. Look at my face, okay? See these wrinkles here, right at the corner of my eyes? Got them working in the edens. Too much sun. How old do you think I am?

Twenty-nine, but that's okay. I was up fifteen months and it only aged me four years. Still, my permanent bone loss is less than 8 percent and I've built my muscles back up and I only picked up eighteen rads and I'm not half as crazy as I used to be. Hey, I'm a walking advertisement for backing down. So have I talked you out of it yet? I don't mean to, okay? I'd probably go up again, if they'd have me.

Don't plan on it; the wheel habitats are strictly for tourists. They cost ten times as much to build as a micro gee can, and once you're in one you're pretty much stuck to the rim. And you're still getting zapped by cosmic rays and solar X-rays and energetic neutrons. If you're going to risk living in space, you might as well enjoy it. Besides, all the important work gets done by breakaways.

See, that's where you're wrong. It's like Elena used to say. We didn't conquer space, it conquered us. Break away and you're giving up forty, maybe fifty years of life, okay? The stats don't lie. Fifty-six is the *average.* That means some breakaways die even younger.

You don't? Well, good for you. Hey, it looks great—better than new. How much?

Does that include the vodka?

Well, thanks. Listen, Jane, I'm going to tell you something, a secret they ought to tell everybody before they go up.

No, I'm not. Promise. So anyway, on my breakaway day Elena calls me to her room and tells me that she doesn't think I should do it, that I won't be happy living in space. I'm so stunned that I start crying, which is a very backdown thing to do. I try to argue, but she's been mentoring for years and knows what she's talking about. Only about a third break away—but, of course, you know that. Anyway, it gets strange then. She says to me, "I have something to show you," and then she starts to strip. See, the time she'd made love to me, she wouldn't let me do anything to her. And like I said, she'd kept her clothes on; breakaways have this thing about showing themselves to temps. I mean, I'd seen her hands before, her feet. They looked like spiders. And I'd seen her face. Kissed it, even. But now I'm looking at her naked body for the first time. She's fifty-one years old. I think she must've been taller than me once, but it's hard to be sure because she has the deep micro-gee slouch. Her muscles have atrophied so her papery skin looks as if it's been sprayed onto her bones. She's had both breasts prophylactically removed. "I've got 40 percent bonerot," she says, "and I mass thirty-eight kilos." She shows the scars from the operations to remove her thyroid and ovaries, the tap on her hip where they take the monthly biopsy to test for leukemia. "Look at me," she says. "What do you see?" I start to tell her that I've read the literature and watched all the vids and I'm prepared for what's going to happen, but she shushes me. "Do you think I'm beautiful?" she says. All I can do is stare. "*I* think I am," she says. "So do the others. It's our nature, Cleo. This is how space makes us over. Can you tell me you *want* this to happen to you?" And I couldn't. See, she knew me better than I knew myself. What I wanted was to float forever, to feel I was special, to stay with her. Maybe I was in love with her. I don't know if that's possible. But loving someone isn't a reason to break away, especially if the stats say that someone will be dead in five years. So I told her she was right and thanked her for everything she'd done and got on the shuttle that same day and backed down and became just another nobody. And she gave up mentoring and went to Saturn, and as soon as we forget all about each other we can start living happily ever after.

No, here's the secret, honey. The heart is a muscle, okay? That means it shrinks in space. All breakaways know it, now you do too. Anyway, it's been nice talking to you.

Sure. Good night.

standing in line with mister jimmy

So I'm walking down Hope Street on my way to the parole office and Mister Jimmy's playing my favorite, "Brain Sausage" by the Barking Fish, and I see this line. At first I think I'm having another flashback because it's mostly suits, in all the colors of gray. Silver ghosts in ash gray, mouse gray women, smog gray, sidewalk gray—maybe a couple of real misfits in navy blue. You know, the kind of yawnboys who sit at desks all day and talk to computers in Tokyo. So why should I care, except that I recognize a scattering of ralphs from Southie? One old grope of mine, Tweezer, is near the end and she's got on a white shirt and that stupid little ribbon tie she has to wear when she flips nineteen-cent McKrillwiches and over it is this sport jacket the color of a recycling sack with sleeves down to her knees. I guess it must have been dark when she stole it.

Mister Jimmy goes, "She's the one who wanted to be a

dancer,'' but I remember. I'm not as stupid as he thinks I am. ''Check it out, Chip,'' he goes and because he's my ThinkMate, I do.

''Hey, Tweeze, where's the party?''

She looks too tired to flirt, like she's been sleeping in somebody's closet again because she doesn't go, ''Hi, Chip,'' or ''I'm the party,'' or anything. She just stares through me like I'm made of glass.

Then there's a hand tapping my shoulder and the suit behind me goes, ''No cutting, Mister. End of the line is way back.''

I brush the hand off without bothering to look. ''Snap off, jack. My sister here is saving my place. Right, Tweeze?''

She goes, ''You ain't my brother,'' and her face is like a wall and I realize something has happened to her. Maybe it's the clothes, or the company she's been keeping.

The suit in front of us is giving me the hard eye, as if he's remembering me to describe to the cops. And the hand comes back. It's heavier this time. I think about biting it, but Mister Jimmy goes, ''Better not, Chip, or we'll be late. Let me look into this,'' and he starts playing my favorite, ''Double-Parked on Trouble Street'' by 54321 and the music walks me out of there. But I'm still putting Tweeze down for payback.

Anyway, the line is a lot longer than I thought. It ripples down Hope Street, a wool-blend snake with a couple of hundred heads and no personality. When it takes a right on Chelsea Avenue, it changes. As I walk alongside I can't help but sense an edge to it that's sharp enough to draw blood. For beautiful people they're in an ugly mood. Maybe they're not used to lines. This one stretches three blocks down Chelsea until it passes an Infomart and turns down an alley that I never knew was there before. I've got to see this—there's a handful of other ralphs wandering down the alley who feel the same way. After all, you don't usually find that many suits so far from downtown. So we scope the front of the line, which stops at a white-painted steel door hung on a steel frame built into the brick wall. No sign, no buzzer, no handle, no keyhole. Could be the back door to the Infomart, but Mister Jimmy thinks no.

Now this door bothers me—did I say it was white? I mean spotless, whiter than the Pope's sheets. That kind of clean is hard to find in the city. Still, Mister Jimmy is telling me this is probably a whole bunch of nothing and I might believe him except that the pigeon-gray suit at the head of the line is watching this door like it's going to have his baby right there on the pavement. And the woman behind him is sweating even though it's a cool spring day and the alley is in deep shade. And the people behind her are practically vibrating. Then the door opens and everyone who's not in line crowds over for a peek.

You know how, when you get a headful of glitter, you can stare at something ordinary and it gets like more and more real until it pulses into that weird, sparkly hyperreality that means you're flashing? I see a long hallway lit by a single naked bulb. There's another white door at the far end. The cement floor has just been hosed down because there are still puddles around the drain. Someone has painted the words *Live* and *Free* on either wall. The building's breath is moist and warm and it smells like the corners of basements. The lucky leader mumbles as he steps through and I pull Mister Jimmy out of one ear so I can hear, ". . . full of grace, the Lord is with thee. Blessed art thou among women and blessed is the fruit . . ." The suit takes the plugs of his own ThinkMate out and slips them into his pocket as he walks down the hall and just before the door shuts behind him, I think I see the puddles start to sparkle like I'm having a flashback.

The woman next in line pulls out a limp handkerchief and wipes her forehead.

"Hey, Jackie!" One of us innocent bystanders goes up to her. "What are you waiting for?"

She glances at him and tightens her grip on her attaché case like she wants to hit him with it but thinks twice because she's got better things to do—like worry about the door opening.

Someone next to me goes, "They don't say. They won't answer questions." A guy in a croaker goes, "New drug, maybe?" and a couple of people nod but then someone else goes, "Nah, you don't stand in line in broad daylight waiting for drugs," and the first guy goes, "Maybe it's so new, it's still legal."

A suit farther back in line calls out, "Leave her alone."

"Hey, jack, I was just asking. . . ."

"Line up and find out for yourself."

A couple of newcomers come snooping down the alley. "What is this anyway?"

So I go, "Mass hallucination—watch out, it's catching." I laugh when they pull up short. The woman twists her handkerchief as she waits her turn.

Now I really do want to find out what's happening here but,

like Mister Jimmy says, the clock is ticking so I head back to the street. I mean, there are all kinds of lines. Food lines, job lines, ticket lines, tram lines at rush hour, lines in front of stores whenever there's something you can afford, which isn't often. Line up to get your check from the state and again to get it cashed. They say when you're on maintenance, you should get on every line you can find. Maybe that works for the good citizens but I haven't got the patience. Still, I've never seen two hundred yards of jacksuits before, homeowners with leather shoes and credit cards. Whatever's behind the door, it's worth something to people who already have a lot—and to ralphs like poor Tweezer, who's wearing a man's sport coat. I keep waiting for Mister Jimmy to break in with the answer or advice or a song or something but he's quiet. A line with a secret. Yeah, sure I'm interested.

The Department of Corrections is in a building as ugly as Cleveland but not quite as big. Check-in sprawls across the entire seventeenth floor and it's the usual uproar. You have to take turns breathing as all the prolees squeeze toward the wall of receivers while their moms and lovers and accomplices try to look invisible as the cops thump by in their immense blue body armor, dragging handcuffed prisoners behind them like yellow duckies. I spot some ralphs I know, but I'm not here to party. I've made good time. I got the page at 9:00 and it's only 10:37. The parole office gives you two hours on a random check, so I'm not really worried as I place my palm flat on the reader and fit my concuff into the receiver. Then the little green screen flashes. Ved Chiplunkar, 1102298, report to Room 1841. Damn, I don't want to chat up some case hack, I just want to get verified and get out. Anyway, Mister Jimmy plays the Screws' "Meat Sins" while I search for Room 1841 and that helps a little.

In a previous life, Room 1841 might have been a toilet, but now it's a windowless pus-yellow cubby that is almost big enough for a desk, two folding chairs, a terminal, and a skinny woman whose plastic ID says she's Angela Sternwood. She isn't much older than me, but she's already got a job and a whiskey-colored suit and a string of fake pearls. She's easy enough on the eyes, although she is a little beaky and I hate scented earrings.

"Tell me about yourself, Ved."

"Read the file—or are they hiring illiterates now?"

"I want to hear it in your own words."

It's a dumb line but I'll forgive a redhead almost anything so

I go, "Name's Chip. I'm twenty-four and I've got two convictions, one for possession of glitter, one for mugging a suit so I could score some glitter. My cuff says I'm clean. I wish it was wrong."

"You graduated from South High and were accepted at War Martyrs Junior College, but you never went. Why?"

"Didn't like the school colors."

"And you've been cashing maintenance checks since, let's see, '22?"

I ignore that because Mister Jimmy finally tracks down her public file. "DOB is 4/11/06—younger than you, Chip! She's a citizen, lives at 2381 Green Street up in the Heights and she's been working here less than a month, probably still in training."

She goes, "Would you please take your plugs out, Chip?"

I ignore her some more.

"Says here you haven't even tried for a job since your last check-in."

"I'm allergic to clocks." When I laugh, she looks nervous. "You're new at this job, aren't you?"

"Why do you say that?" She chews her lip. "Anyway, we're here to talk about you."

Mister Jimmy goes, "Keep on her, Chip. She's so raw they're probably still evaluating her on closed circuit. Who knows, maybe if she doesn't sell you a suit, they'll fire her."

She goes, "So you like taking maintenance? You live well on eighty-seven dollars a month?"

So I give her my best hope-to-grope smile. See, I don't really want to argue with Angela Sternwood. I want to take her out dancing and put my hands on her ass and later take her back to my place. Or better, her place—she probably has hot water.

She goes, "I said pull the damn ThinkMate so I can talk to you!" I've got her squirming now.

Mister Jimmy goes, "Better humor her, Chip," so I do.

I drop the plugs onto the desk and reach inside my shirt. "Want the system unit too?" It's in a pouch that hangs from a chain around my neck.

"No." She pulls a tissue from a drawer, picks a plug up with it, rubs the ear wax off, and reads the label. Mister Jimmy is a genuine Matsushita. I can tell she's impressed because she goes, "Pricey tech for someone on maintenance." She pushes the plug back toward me. "Where'd you get it?"

"My pa left it to me instead of a ranch."

"Any idiot can make jokes, Chip." She checks the screen of

her terminal. "Okay, what gang are you running with these days?"

"No gang—just me and Mister Jimmy against the world."

"Mister Jimmy?"

I nod at the plugs on her desk and she goes, "You know an Elvis Malloy?"

"Uh-uh."

"Elvis Malloy was arrested at twelve forty-eight last Tuesday night. Seems he's working this puppet house on Harmony Street in Southie, slipping into booths while the johns are busy slamming their robots through the orgies. He lifts at least six wallets, maybe more—not everyone reports, of course. Then somebody spots him. He flies out the front door with this naked guy after him, and it just so happens there are two cops having coffee across the street. Malloy runs twelve blocks, flinging the swag into the crowds he passes. The cops catch him eventually, but there's no evidence on him and nobody turns anything in, which isn't surprising considering the neighborhood."

"So Malloy wins the Nobel prize for stupidity. So?"

Her mouth twists as she thinks this over. I can tell she's getting wrinkled at me. I don't think she's happy in her new job. "I'm sorry you're playing it this way, Chip, but it's your choice." She swivels the monitor around so I can see. "One of the cops who gave chase was rigged for vid. It's new tech, a pilot program. The computer enhancement takes time, but we get some really cute pictures." I'm highlighted on the screen, framed between a floating ad window for Coors and a weather gypsy wearing three hats and seven coats. I'm staring at a brown wallet on the sidewalk in the foreground, also highlighted. "What do you think, Chip? Like it for the yearbook?"

I need Mister Jimmy's advice but I don't dare let her know that. "So I'm there. So's he." I point at the gypsy. "Talked to him yet? And probably others off camera. Where's your case? I never touched that wallet."

So then she loses her temper. "I don't need a case, Mister. There's a time stamp on this vid that puts you on Harmony Street at twelve thirty-two A.M."

"What? You're calling me on a curfew violation?"

"That's right. Maybe if I thought you were trying to turn yourself around, we could work something out." She raps the keyboard and the terminal mutters and suddenly a pink slip is sticking out of the printer slot like a paper tongue. "But you're not and you've got an attitude." She tears the slip out. "I take it you don't follow the news? Too bad. The feds are gearing up to build that new Friendship Highway through Mexico to keep our troops supplied. They've set manpower quotas for each state, which we're supposed to meet from our maintenance rolls. The governor says to sweep the streets, and you're just the kind of trash voters tend to notice." She hands me the slip. "Report to the Reed Armory on National Unity Square before noon tomorrow. Don't forget your sunblock."

"Wait a minute." I jam Mister Jimmy back in and together we read the pink work order that says I'll be getting my mail at Jaltipan Work Camp in the Provisional State of Veracruz for the next six months. Mister Jimmy goes, "That's the steamiest part of the jungle, Chip. They get a hundred inches of rain a year. I won't last two minutes in that kind of weather."

"This isn't fair," I go. "I'll appeal. You call this justice?"

"You want justice?" she goes. "Get a job." She stands up and brushes right past me and out the door with her big nose puckered like I'm a bad smell. I think about punching it for her but, as Mister Jimmy points out, that will only make the trouble I'm already in seem like a week at a disney.

So I hit the street again, feeling like I've just been force-fed a brick. I wander into the business district, the only living ralph in a desert of suits, and I'm headed nowhere with a scheduled layover in Mexico where the rain is a blunt instrument. Every so often I whang my concuff against one of the pipes set along the curb that used to have parking meters back when gas cost less than vodka. Doesn't hurt the cuff—that's indestructible—but it makes my hand sting, which reminds me of what's coming if I don't think of something fast.

So why should I follow the news when it's always the same? "In Washington today the suits announced that taxes are too high and the President called on the poor ralphs of America to bend over one more time." *Whang.* Besides, I can tell that bitch would've been a frozen turkey in bed anyway. I gave her my best lines and she never even smiled. *Whang.* No question I have to show up at the Armory or else the alarm on my concuff will start shrieking and probably turn my brains to soup even before the cops come to haul me away. *Whang.* No, the only way to dodge Mexico is to get off maintenance and the only way to get off maintenance is to get enough money to live and the way to get that kind of money is to get a job but jobs are scarcer than ninth-grade virgins even if you do own a suit. Which I don't.

Whang. Yeah, good advice, Mister Jimmy. Keep on her. She's new, see if you can push her around.

He goes, "We're in trouble, Chip. That climate rots electronics. You can't take me down there; I'm not designed for it."

"So I'll stash you somewhere. Hey, I'm pissed too."

"For six months, Chip? Six months of no input and I'll go crazy. And what if you don't come back? It's possible."

"Then I won't care, will I?" Problem is, you can't just turn a ThinkMate off like some stupid computer. I don't know why, exactly—Mister Jimmy is in charge of understanding all that tech stuff.

"You can lend me to someone, Chip."

"Who do I know would give you back?"

I'm so busy arguing with Mister Jimmy that I almost crash into this jack in a tuxedo except he sees me first. He puts his hands together like he's praying and then spreads them apart and somehow in the space between them he's projecting this window that says:

Desperate?
Now you know Bad Times can ruin Good People.
You can't Achieve Success until you admit Failure.
If you're ready to Give Up
We Can Help.
Proper Dress Required.
Wednesdays only.
No homeless Please.

"Snap off, I'm broke." I try to go around but he stays in my way. "You hear me? Maybe Jesus saves, but I don't."

But he won't let me pass until I notice him. Okay, so he looks like some groom who took a wrong turn at the wedding. He's wearing a high-necked white shirt and a cummerbund. His tux is black and there's a white carnation in the silk lapel. He's a little newt of a man with a peaceful, almost goofy expression you don't see much in the city. Maybe his bow tie is too tight and he's not getting enough oxygen.

So I'm thinking here's another flashback, which is okay because at this point I could use a little free hallucination and then it occurs to me. "Hey, this have anything to do with the line on Chelsea Avenue?"

He claps his hands again and between them are the words:

He shows me a smile that has about eight teeth too many. He says nothing.

"I was down there this morning. No one would tell what they were waiting for."

Still giving me his headlight smile, he claps his hands one last time and the window closes. He says nothing.

"So what's this all about?"

He turns the smile off and shrugs.

"I'm asking you a question, man. What's behind the damn door?"

Mister Jimmy realizes I'm getting wrinkled at this jack so he tries to smooth me out with "Vegetable Kingdom" by Round Woman Square Men. But I don't want violins, I want answers. When I grab his lapels and shake him, his flower falls out and he makes this weird gurgling sound.

"Talk to me, you stupid jack."

So he opens his mouth and shows me all those perfect teeth again except there's nothing behind them but a pink hole. He's trying his best to say something but it sounds like he's swallowing a snake. I let him go. I tell him to shut his mouth but he won't. It's as if he wants to be sure I see his glistening stump waggle, as if he's *happy* someone cut his tongue out, as if it's the secret of his success and he wants to share it with me.

I spin away but he keeps after me, *"Ah-ahh-er-ah!"* and shoves an envelope into my pocket and then maybe he realizes I'm about to hit him because he pulls back.

I take a few steps before I turn again but by then he's disappeared. It's like the street has swallowed him. Suits bump by me on their way to lunch as ad windows glide over our heads. Business as usual in skyscraper land, so why am I shaking? Because what I really need now is about ten cc's of glitter. Yeah,

I'm that desperate—my brain feels like it's swelling up inside my head from too much thinking, and I've been on the verge of a flashback all morning. But I know Mister Jimmy is right when he reminds me that if my cuff shows positive for flash, they'll ruin me at the Armory tomorrow. I laugh because I guess I just qualified for the line on Chelsea Avenue. This is the worst day of the worst life ever lived and since I can't get anything I want, maybe I *should* give up. So I take out the envelope and open it and there's Ben Franklin giving me the green eye and on the flip side the words "In God We Trust" have been circled in red. Maybe the reason I can't feel my feet touching the sidewalk is that I've never held a hundred-dollar bill in my hand before. It's not as intense a high as glitter, but it'll do.

Expose that much money to the air in Southie and the ralphs will smell it and come swarming, but maybe this happens all the time downtown because the suits pay no attention as I slide the money into the pouch next to Mister Jimmy's system unit. I start home with the clock running down and the score Questions 32, Answers 0. The obvious play is to forget what just happened and spend the little time I have left pissing this miracle down all my favorite toilets in the city. I'm really tempted but Mister Jimmy goes, "Chip, if you've got to pick between a suit and a shovel, there's a Salvation Army over on April Eleventh Street," which is not the advice I'm hoping for, even if it makes sense.

"But what the hell am I lining up for?"

"Maybe a chance to get out of Mexico. So far all I know is that a Live Free Foundation was established as a tax-exempt charitable trust in New Hampshire four years ago. There's no annual report and somebody got the IRS to seal the returns, but at least we know they file so they're probably legitimate. I say we have to check it out."

Now I'm worried because *probably* is a luck word and my luck is usually bad. What I really want is a sure thing except the only one I've got is six months of laying blacktop in green hell. I guess Mister Jimmy has a point: when you're desperate, you take chances.

So an hour later a new Chip trick-or-treats down Chelsea Avenue, disguised in a gray woolet suit and a blue shirt and plastic loafers. I've shortened the pants and fixed the ripped lining with Kmart fashion tape but there was nothing I could do about the shoulders. The whole outfit cost only twenty-three bucks and they even threw in a tie the color of dead pizza. So

I'm properly dressed and I've got seventy-seven bucks left from the angel in the tux and nine from the wallet Elvis Malloy threw away on Harmony Street together with my life savings of twelve and I'm wondering how much luck ninety-eight dollars will buy. Mister Jimmy is finishing "Contents under Pressure" by Vinnie's Ear as I come up to the line.

I watch for Tweeze but she must have already gone through the door. The line is shorter—the end is near the corner of Hope and Chelsea, in front of Tibawi's Discount Flooring Outlet. I almost don't get on because of the old lady carrying the dog. I hate dogs, especially rich people's greedy, stupid, useless dogs. This one is losing patches of its wiry fur and it smells like an old couch someone left out in the rain.

The lady turns and scopes me and I scope her and I guess neither of us likes what we see. She probably doesn't approve of browns—or blacks or spanics or asians. She's wearing a cement-colored jacket over a matching skirt and there's a silk scarf around her neck held together with a fat gold ring that I bet I could get fifty bucks for, if it's real. She has gray hair so fine you can see her pale scalp. There's a glaze of dried dog slobber on her sleeve.

I go, "Hi." She says nothing. She doesn't seem very desperate. Maybe she couldn't get tickets to the opera.

She nods at me, shifts the dog into a more comfortable position and faces forward again. The dog scrabbles up and watches me over her shoulder.

The line creeps forward. Business is terrible at Tibawi's Discount Flooring Outlet. The price tags for the oriental rugs draped in the display window have faded in the sunlight. Up ahead the lawn and lowlight moss carpets are turning yellow around the edges. A wide-bearded man with all the charm of a hammer stands behind the door and scopes us like he's thinking of closing up and getting in line too. He'd better hurry and make up his mind because now there's a fidgety guy in a charcoal three-piece behind me. Two more men are arguing about palladium futures on the Mercantile Exchange as they settle in behind him. Then a ralph in a silver and black Raiders jacket comes up and asks what we're waiting for and the old lady goes rigid. When I see the glitter in the ralph's eyes, I decide I'm not talking to this flashface about my troubles. They're none of his damn business and besides, thinking about them only makes me crazy. I'm not admitting to him or anyone that I don't exactly know why I'm here. Hey, I don't exactly know why I was born or where my mom went to or why shit stinks, okay? I'm not happy about being ignorant but there it is. So I tell him to snap off except it takes a while for him to understand what with all the beautiful sparks flashing inside his head. As he leaves, I scope the suits in line behind me and even though they glance away, I'm sure they're glad I got rid of the ralph because they didn't want to answer questions either. You don't admit to strangers that you're desperate—it's hard enough admitting it to yourself. But I can smell their fear, or maybe it's my own stink I smell. I wonder if this is what happened to Tweezer. The line has a grip on me. I'm not sure I can get away anymore.

Anyway, we're all the way up to the corner when Angela Sternwood stalks by without noticing me. Maybe it's my new suit but I doubt she's seeing much at all. She's so angry that her knees don't bend when she walks and her face is all wrinkled like she's thinking of things she wished she had said to someone. Not me, I hope. I almost fall into the street when she gets in line.

"Sternwood!" I lean way out and wave, trying to get her attention. "Hey, Angela!" She's too busy drilling holes into the sidewalk with her eyes and then the line swings me around the corner onto Chelsea. The dog sneezes and the old lady coos and kisses it. Maybe she feels safer with me now because she goes, "He's sick, poor baby, but I know they can cure him," but I don't want to talk to her. I want Angela. It takes maybe thirty seconds before I overdose on curiosity and walk back. Mister Jimmy's shriek is like a nail in my ear so I yank him out. Hey, the line's moving along and I'm only losing nine places.

I go, "Shouldn't you be downtown taking milk money away from orphans?"

She gives me a look that's about as friendly as a fist—then she recognizes me. "Oh, *no.* What the hell are you doing here?"

"I was in line up ahead. I came back to keep you company."

Her eyes get shiny. "Jesus. I don't deserve this." A tear trickles down her face. "Leave me alone."

I like the way she cries. Some people gush, others sniff and try to hold off, but most of them are just crying for the crowd. Angela's tears are her own. She's not ashamed of them, she's not proud—they're something that happens sometimes when the world smacks you in the face and there's no one you can hit back.

"Hey, you'll never get to know me if you keep sending me away." I don't tell her I'm attracted to women who ask me to leave them alone.

"Listen, ralph, I don't like you in a suit any better than I liked you in a T-shirt."

"Seems to me we're standing in the same line."

She doesn't have to answer because the line gathers itself and we press forward. When I pop Mister Jimmy back in, he has calmed down. We shuffle around the corner and down Chelsea maybe ten yards before everything bunches up again and stops. People mutter and groan and straddle their briefcases and glance at their watches and go up on tiptoes to see ahead. The suit in back of me starts whistling like he's on his way to the circus. He's bald but he's got a gray beard so thick it looks like his head is on upside down. The guy in front of Angela opens a readman and cups his hand so that only he can see the screen.

Meanwhile I scope Angela from behind. She has the long slender fingers of a guitar god—no rings—and the kind of leg muscles you don't get sitting on a couch in front of sitcoms. Her red hair is cut to a silky brush. I decide I could find my way past her nose. Sure, I'd grope her, if only she wasn't who she was.

Eventually she gets tired of pretending I'm not staring. "Where'd you get those clothes? The Salvation Army?" Her tears have dried up.

"I found them on the sidewalk on Harmony Street."

"You shouldn't make so many jokes, Chad. People who are really smart don't try so hard to prove it. You know, if you had played straight with me, I wouldn't have sent you to Mexico."

"Maybe I'm not going. Maybe that's why I'm on line here."

"You think they'll take you?" She shakes her head. "Well, maybe they will. You want to hear what kind of trouble jokes can get you into? I made a joke today, because you made me angry." She frowns. "No, it wasn't only you; it was the hundred prolees I saw before you. None of you wanted anything to do with me. You wouldn't let me help, you insulted me. But of all of them, Chad, you were especially irritating, because you have a brain and you're wasting it."

Mister Jimmy goes, "Want to know why she's here? I checked her public files. Congratulations, Chip, I think you just got your new case hack fired."

"They didn't care that I gave you the pink slip, you know. I've got quotas to meet; that's what they hired me to do. But they said I got too involved with the interview. I made this joke, you see. I told you to remember your sunblock, and so Friday is my last day. They said that I wasn't professional enough. They want case officers who can maintain proper distance."

She's the one who hurt me, right? So I should enjoy watching her fall into a hole—but I can't. Maybe it's because people all around us are eavesdropping. The jack behind me is practically resting his beard on my shoulder. I'm sure they've already decided that we're both losers. I go, "Seems like they make it awfully easy for a ralph to fuck up in this city."

"I'm no ralph." I should've known she'd be insulted. "I went to junior college, I passed the civil service exam. These people aren't ralphs."

"What are they doing here, then?"

"The same thing you're doing."

"Trying not to go to Mexico?"

That shuts her up for a while. The line drags us past the Chelsea Drugstore and Superior Public Showers—*Our Water Guaranteed 100 Percent Non-Toxic.* The fragrance of hot oil as we go by Felipe's Fish Fry reminds me that I haven't eaten yet today. I'm hungry enough to pick onion rings out of a dumpster.

"I'm sorry, Chad." Angela slumps with her hands in her pockets and her head down, not giving me much of a target. "I'm more sorry that I got fired, but I guess I'm sorry for what happened to you too."

"Sure, except it's Chip."

"What?"

"Name's Chip, not Chad. What's wrong with taking maintenance like the rest of the world? At least until you find another job."

"You don't understand." She shook her head. "Once there's a maintenance flag in your files, personnel assumes you're probably employment-impaired. I'd be lucky to find something at minimum wage. Maybe if I had some savings I could live off while I searched on JobLink . . . but I don't and I've got rent, food, net, transcard. I owe five more years on my student loan."

So that's why the only work they ever offered me was scraping gum off bus seats. Mister Jimmy is trying to distract me with "My Career (in Air Conditioning)" by Cheap Wine, which normally makes me laugh, except he should've told me I never had a chance for a real job. But just when I'm ready to call him on this, the suit in front of us gets careless and tips his readman so that I can see. One screen has my angel's message about Bad

Times and Giving Up, the other has the same words, but arranged in different order like they're in some kind of code. I nudge Angela. "Seen that?" I whisper.

"So?" She shrugs. "It's all over JobLink." She speaks loud enough for the suit to hear and he slaps the readman shut. "Come to think of it, where did you see it? You're on maintenance, you can't afford to subscribe to the net."

"A guy walks up to me in the street and opens a pocket window. I get a peek and that's all. He doesn't say a word and then he's gone." I leave the $100 out because I've got more audience than I want, even if they are all rich suits. "I'm still waiting for someone to tell me what it means."

"*Space,* my friend." When the jack with the beard leans forward, I can smell all the bars on DuPont Street. "We're bound for the new L5 colony, *Freedom Station.*"

Angela rolls her eyes toward the corner of the sky where lunatics play house. She goes, "All I know is that some foundation with more secrets than the CIA started running the ad about a week ago. A guy from the sixteenth floor answered it last Wednesday, and he must've gotten some offer because he never even bothered to come back and clean out his desk."

"Isn't it *obvious?*" The spaceman butts back into our conversation. "Live *Free?* If we're going to survive as a species we have to *free* ourselves from the gravity well. Break the chains of Earth. The Department of Space needs the *best,* the brightest, and the bravest. The new *pioneers.*" What's obvious is that he's one of those ravers who have everything figured out—wrong.

"That's not what I heard." The suit behind him spoke up. "My cousin lives in New Hampshire, and she says that the Liberty Party is building a new co-op up in the White Mountains and they're supposedly recruiting business people to help run it."

"I've been watching since nine this morning," someone else goes. "I've circled the block I don't know how many times. So far a couple of thousand have gone in—at least that many—but nobody's come out. Don't they reject *anyone?*"

"I heard it was the Charismatics. They'll take anyone they can get."

"You think *God* is waiting behind that door?" The spaceman sniffs. "Sure it's not the Blue Elves? Listen, *Freedom Station* opens in just three years. . . ."

I go to Angela, "Maybe they can't leave."

"What?"

"Maybe they're rounding up warm bodies for the army. Or

wasting everyone who steps through the door? *Boom.*" I shoot the spaceman with my finger. "Instant population control." I don't necessarily believe it, I'm just saying it to get a reaction. They're quiet for about three seconds and then they all turn on me, their voices sharp with fear.

"The cops wouldn't just stand by . . ."

". . . such a thing as the Constitution."

"Things are bad, but not *that* bad."

". . . the brain drain," goes the spaceman. "Maybe if all they wanted were people on *maintenance* . . ."

Mister Jimmy goes, "Easy, Chip, these are suits. They're not built for trouble; scare them, and they might do something stupid."

"Okay," I go, "okay, you're right," and I hold up my hands to surrender but they're too nervous to take any prisoners. What saves me is a couple of asian ralphs in mirrorshirts who are swaggering down the street like they're trying to decide which one of us to mug first. As they approach, everyone stops arguing and gives them the hard eye, including me. I'm surprised at my reaction, but it's like I have no choice. I'm in line too, aren't I? We've come this far together and we've all got our places to protect and no ignorant street trash is going to stop any of us from getting where we're going.

One ralph asks the other, "What these jacks waiting for, man? Personality transplants?" The other snickers.

Nobody says anything after they pass. We scuff along for a few minutes in silence and the line loosens its grip on me. There's nothing to do but think, which is a pain. Mister Jimmy tries to help by playing my favorite, "Go Away Please Stay" by Lezbeth. It doesn't work. When I look back there's at least fifty suits lined up behind me but I feel like they're standing on my chest. What we need is a theme song. "Get in line, everything's fine here in the line with a mind of its own." I ought to write that down and send it to Lezbeth except that's not something suits do. I don't belong here. Mister Jimmy reminds me of Mexico and tells me we're getting close to the end but then I think about a drain on a cement floor and those puddles. I know I just made that stuff up about shooting all of us. Still, it sure looked as if they had just cleaned up a mess, didn't it?

Mister Jimmy goes, "They're not killing anyone. This is America, Chip, and these are taxpayers. Cash cows—they can't afford to slaughter the herd. Besides, we haven't got any choice."

"So why should I trust you? You never explained about how

taking maintenance meant I couldn't get a real job. You're supposed to tell me this stuff but no, I have to hear it from Angela."

He goes, "Your dad was taking maintenance when you were born, Chip, and you started taking on your own long before you got me. I didn't want to discourage you. Besides, it's not true that you can't get a job; it's just harder."

"You should've told me."

Angela glances over her shoulder. "You talking to me?"

"Nah, I'm arguing with Mister Jimmy."

"Who's winning?"

It's no contest, I'd much rather talk to her than Mister Jimmy. When her earring catches the sunlight, it leaks perfume that must be laced with pheromones because it's all I can do to keep from putting my arms around her and nibbling. "What I don't understand," I go, "is why you're here. You could hit a friend for a loan to hold you over."

She pauses, inviting me to slide up beside her. "I graduated last month," she goes. "I only just moved here."

"Someone with your looks and you haven't got an old grope you could call?"

"It's been a rough month." She gives me a lemon smile. "I don't want to talk about it."

"Okay, how come you don't wear a ThinkMate?"

"I like to make my own decisions."

"Well, maybe you're smarter than me."

"Or you're lazier than me. You ever take that thing off?"

"Why?" The idea surprises me. "Like when?"

"When you watch vid—I don't know. At night, before you go to bed."

I bump gently against her. "Want to find out for yourself?"

She flushes and moves ahead of me again.

I can't decide whether she's teasing me or not. Mister Jimmy plays "Burning the Snow" by Penile Colony, which I decide I don't like as much as I used to. I tell him I don't want to hear any more music for a while. It's getting colder now as the sun touches the skyline. Whirlwinds of trash stir in the street. The line can't make up its mind anymore. It moves in spasms. Sometimes it surges, then it'll stop and catch its breath before crawling forward again. Probably some of the suits ahead are giving up and going home to meat loaf and clean sheets. They're not desperate enough. Angela doesn't seem that desperate. I wonder if I am.

One big push carries us across Martyrs Street and we're

almost there. Up ahead the yellow Infomart window floats over the sidewalk and the come-on scrolls across in letters tall enough to start for the Celtics. *Infomart . . . more than just facts . . . knowledge.* The rest of the block is taken up by a used robot store called Machine Age. You can buy robot vacuums and lawnmowers, mobile video and smartcarts that will follow you anywhere, three-wheelers and food processors that'll turn a dollar's worth of soy paste into a meal for seven—if none of them are very hungry. There's a window full of ThinkMate clones and next to it are the puppets, lean sport models in bright uniforms and leering sex machines with big lips and glossy stain-resistant skin.

Just ahead three suits peel off the line and scuttle back toward us like cockroaches someone is trying to squash. After they clear out I see that what scared them was a couple of cops in full riot armor. There's a patrol wagon with intimate seating for twenty parked in the alley. I guess even suits get arrested once in a while. These cops look strange to me, although I'm not sure why exactly until Mister Jimmy points out the two bulges on their helmets, one for the spotlight, the other for the lens. They're IDing people at random. Looking for criminals in a line full of desperate people—it's such a good idea that I'm surprised the cops thought of it. "Be smooth, Chip," Mister Jimmy goes. "You're legal until noon tomorrow."

I touch Angela's arm. "That the rig they got me with?"

One of the cops clunks down the sidewalk, stops about ten feet from us, and asks a suit to say his name.

Angela goes, "Yeah, only they use infrared at night. When they cross-reference your voice print with your picture, they can access all your G3 files right down to the dailies in under ten seconds."

Maybe I'd be worried if I'd understood what she said but information tech is Mister Jimmy's responsibility. Besides, the suit with the readman is frightened enough for both us. He's pale as bread as he turns to Angela. "They can read *dailies?*" He's practically hissing.

She nods.

He tries to lunge past me but as long as I'm wearing a suit, I decide to play good citizen. I manage to stay in the way just long enough.

"Excuse me, sir." This cop could arm-wrestle a backhoe. "Were you going somewhere?" He doesn't have any problem holding on to a limp suit.

The cop IDs the jack as Lawrence Prendergast, DOB 7/9/88, an employee of Atlantic Trust wanted for questioning on a charge of unauthorized use of a credit instrument. When the cop pats him down, he finds that Larry's paunch is actually a money belt stuffed with enough cash to buy a round of drinks for the entire city. Three minutes later, Larry's been cuffed, read his rights, and loaded into the wagon. From the way the suits around me are staring, I doubt any of them have ever seen justice up this close.

"He's lucky they caught him here," goes the spaceman, "because on *Freedom Station* there's no *jail*. The budget was too tight."

Nobody says anything. We don't want to encourage him.

"You break the law up there, and you'd better be able to breathe *space*." He laughs at his own joke. Somebody has to.

We finally reach the top of the alley. Colors are washing out in the twilight and it's hard to tell people from shadows. Soon the city will be gray enough to hide us all but by then it'll be too late. The white door has turned the color of bone. We're about fifteen yards away—twenty, maybe thirty people are ahead of us. Each step I take is a battle and I'm not sure anymore this is a war I want to win.

Mister Jimmy goes, "Steady, Chip, I can't do this without you. We're almost home."

I focus on the back of Angela's neck and follow her fragrance through the gloom. I must be losing it because I'm standing in line to jump off a cliff with a bunch of strangers and instead of panicking like any normal person, I'm hallucinating about how I'd feel if her head was on a green pillow and her eyelids were fluttering shut and her lips had parted for me. She's a jack suit and I'm a lazy ralph, but suddenly it's the most important thing in the world that she's a thrill I'll never have as long as I stand in this line. I touch her arm and she turns and now I have to speak even though Mister Jimmy tells me to keep quiet and I can't think, except words take me by surprise and I listen in amazement to what I'm saying.

"You lied when you said you didn't have any savings. Maybe it's not enough but you have something. You're not the type to let yourself go broke. How much, Angela?"

"Why should I tell you?"

I laugh because a snub from her steadies me more than all of Mister Jimmy's cheerleading.

"I'm not worth ripping off," she goes, "if that's what you're thinking.'' She waits for me to answer but I don't. It's up to her to decide if she trusts me. ''Almost thirty dollars. Why, Chip?''

I'm thinking now and Mister Jimmy doesn't like that because that's not my job. ''Chip, Chip! What is this?''

Up ahead the ugly little dog starts to howl. Maybe it's afraid of the dark. I unbutton my new blue shirt, draw out the pouch, pull my money from next to Mister Jimmy's system unit. I show it to her. ''Thirty and ninety-eight is a hundred and twenty-eight. You could stay in my apartment for six weeks on that, easy. The rent's paid through May. So you live in a dive and you eat slop and you blow off your loan and spend the rest searching for a job on the net. The worst that can happen is that a couple of Wednesdays from now you line up again, only this time you go through the door broke. So what? Thirty bucks doesn't buy first class on the shuttle, believe me.''

''*Excuse* me, ma'am,'' goes the spaceman, ''but I hope you're not going to listen to this man. Are you *seriously* suggesting . . .''

I whip around and backhand him across the mouth. ''Say one more word, jack, and I'll rip that beard off and stuff it down your throat.'' I glare at him and I know he's going to take it. Like all suits, he's got the backbone of a banana. The suits behind him mutter and disapprove but they're too busy thinking line thoughts to cause trouble now.

The dog's frantic yelping is cut off when the door shuts. I doubt it was appropriately dressed. The silence echoes in the cold. Angela hasn't budged and there's a gap between her and the suit in front of us.

''Move up,'' someone yells.

''Let's *go.*'' The line is impatient.

''I don't know what to say,'' she goes.

''Make sense? Not bad for a lazy ralph?''

''You're not joking?'' I'm close enough to see her breath. I think about what it would be like to taste it. ''You'd do that for me?''

''Sure, and I'd do it for me too. I've got a life here. Maybe it stinks, but it's mine. You said Friday's your last day. What if you show up for work tomorrow and take me off the work roster and put me back on maintenance?''

''Brilliant, Chip,'' Mister Jimmy goes. ''I didn't think you had it in you.''

''I can't do that,'' she goes.

''Angela, the street price for deferral is two hundred, so

don't tell me it can't be done. Now I haven't got that much so I'm asking a favor—from a friend. What are they going to do, fire you?''

She considers. ''Where are you going to live?''

''Where the hell do you think? In my apartment with you.''

I couldn't tell at first what she thought of the idea.

''Yes,'' goes Mister Jimmy, ''and after Friday you can dump her whenever you want.''

It's not his fault that he doesn't understand. He's like the line, he doesn't have an imagination. Still, I have to pull his plugs out and curl my hand around them.

There's only one suit between Angela and the door. She glances at him and then back at me. ''I'm not sleeping with you.''

''No?'' I don't think she can see me smile. It doesn't matter. ''Well, you'd better decide in a hurry because you're next and I'm sure as hell not charging through that door to rescue you.''

She hesitates and I realize I'm losing her. Maybe Mister Jimmy is a better judge of character than I gave him credit for. I can feel his tinny scream buzzing in my fist.

''This is il*legal,*'' goes the spaceman. ''I'm calling the police. Don't do it, young lady. You're turning down the *chance* of a lifetime.'' When I turn around to snap him off I realize I've made another mistake. He's backed out of reach and even in the dark I can see that he's holding a gun, or at least something that looks real enough to freeze me. ''I'm not going to let *either* of you do this to yourselves. You're young. You've got your whole *future* in front of you.''

I back away from the gun but it follows me. ''Go ahead and shoot, you jack. Like you say, the cops are right around the corner. They like desperate people, desperate people are some of their best customers. The door is open, spaceman, but we're getting out of line. That makes you next. Better hurry or the shuttle will leave without you.''

He looks at the open door, the naked bulb, the long cement hallway. There are more puddles than there were in the morning and they're *all* glittery. The line yells at us. ''Move, *move.*'' The spaceman marches to the doorway like a war hero accepting his medal, turns and levels the gun at me.

In the light from the hall the gun looks even more real. When I stare at the barrel, it *sparkles* with reality because the flashback I've felt coming all day has finally arrived. The gun starts singing to me, ''Come with us, Chip, come with us now. We've got everything you want and all you need to know.'' And the music walks me toward the white door that I finally realize opens onto the flash that never ends. ''Can't let you go,'' sings the gun. ''We love you so.'' And it sounds just like Mister Jimmy so I have to, I have to except that Angela kicks the door shut.

There's a sound like a gunshot that shatters my flashback. I stagger and Angela catches me and I put my arm around her. Maybe it's only the other door slamming.

I watch as everybody in line moves up one, and then I peel Mister Jimmy's contact lens from my right eye and drop it into the pouch with the plugs and the system unit.

Angela steers me toward the street. ''Anyone want to buy a ThinkMate?'' I go to the suits still waiting in line. ''Hey, genuine Matsushita!''

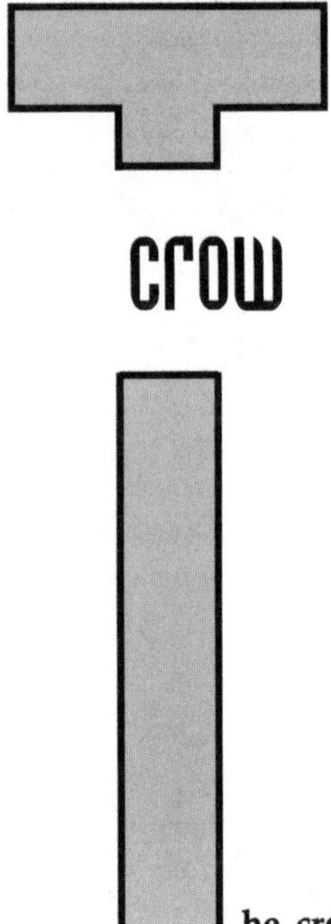

crow

The crow came first. It glided around the rocket on the village green and then landed on the dead oak nearby. Lucy was sitting on the front porch when she saw it, and she ran through the house to tell Juan. It was the first bird either of them had seen that summer.

Juan was in the backyard tending his crop. He farmed by instinct; there was no one to teach him. The little plot did not produce much: some bitter lettuce, chard, a few puny tomatoes. Most seeds he found were too old. Once, in another town, Juan had planted a huge plot of Burpee's Silver Queen corn. They had both been excited when the seedlings sprouted, but then a midsummer frost had nipped the entire crop. Juan had cried when he knew they were dying. He told her that he was giving up, that they would never grow enough to feed themselves. Still, he liked to plant a little garden wherever he lived.

Juan said that crows were bad for the garden. They sat in rocking chairs on the front porch and watched it.

"Scarecrow," said Lucy. She had been six when it happened and could remember more things. She could print capital and small letters and could read most labels. She was twenty-two now.

"Shoot it." Juan had only been three; he did not remember anything.

"No," she said. The bird, any bird, was a good sign. Lucy was a believer in signs.

When they got hungry they walked over to the grocery store. She knew that they would have to move to a new town in the fall; they had eaten all the Dinty Moore Beef Stew and the Campbell's Chunky Chicken Soup and the B&M Baked Beans. Lucy got some spaghetti and Progresso Tomato Sauce. Juan carried another case of Sterno home from the hardware store. They sometimes cooked on wood fires, but Sterno gave a more even heat. She worried about Juan and wood fires. He tended to get careless, especially when it was time to move on. He had burned down most of the places they had lived.

Lucy did not want to leave the rocket on the village green. She thought it was magic. She said that was why the town around it was so untouched by what had happened. They had found a few piles of bones and rotted clothes, but none of the devastation they had seen in other places. Both of them loved to sit on the porch and dream about the rocket. They had seen trains and boats and even weather-beaten airplanes tethered on small town runways. But there was only one rocket.

Everything they needed was within walking distance of their house on the village green: the grocery, the hardware store, the drugstore, the library. The library had a wonderful children's section, full of picture books about fairies and magical kingdoms. Juan liked the art books with their color plates of fat naked women and landscapes full of live trees and animals and crowded cities where nobody was ever lonely. Lucy had already set aside some books she wanted to bring with them when they moved. She knew Juan would not approve. He never brought anything along.

They had supper on the porch. The crow had not moved. When they were done Lucy had an idea. She scraped the leftovers onto a paper plate and left them by the rocket. They watched the crow flutter out of the tree and peck at the garbage.

"A pet." Lucy was delighted.

She let him touch her that night. Before, when there had been no touching, Juan used to tease her with the magazines from the drugstores. He wanted to know why she did not look like the women with big tits and tiny asses. She told him that she was alive and they were dead. Now she did not try to keep him away with angry words. She liked to feel him growing in her hand. When he felt her, the blood pounded in her head and almost made her forget how the Bad Daddy had hurt her. Almost—she still would not let Juan do the thing that the Bad Daddy had done.

The stranger came the next day. She drove a flatbed truck with some kind of digging machine on it. She was wearing blue jeans, work boots, and a flannel shirt with the sleeves rolled up. Her hair was very thin, and it was streaked with gray. Lucy had never seen anyone with gray hair before. Maybe that was how she knew the stranger was crazy. The stranger did not roll her eyes or twitch or talk to ghosts. She parked next to the village green and walked around the rocket three times. She stared up at the crow. Then she sat down on the weeds and began to write on yellow paper.

Juan and Lucy watched her all morning from behind the curtains of the front parlor. For years they had made believe that they were the last people in the world. They had tangled with a few other survivors—none recently. The roads were full of potholes now, the winters lasted ten months this far north.

"If she has a gun. . . ." Lucy closed her hand around the knife she had brought from the kitchen. The Bad Daddy had carried a gun and had locked them up after it had happened and had beat them when he was drunk. She pretended for Juan's sake that she was not scared.

In time the stranger got up and walked over to the grocery store.

"Let's go," said Lucy.

They crossed the green to the stranger's truck. The cab smelled of old sweat and oil. There was a cardboard box of books and a tool chest with four drawers. The steering column was rusty, and the driver's side door was held shut with wire. There was no gun.

"Crazy." Lucy was no longer afraid. The stranger was old and alone. Lucy sat at the picnic table under the dead oak and waited for her to come back.

The stranger was snacking from a can of La Choy Chow Mein Noodles when she stepped onto the broken street. She did not seem surprised to see them. She walked slowly toward the picnic table.

"This your town?"

"We live here." Since she was the elder, Lucy had always spoken for them.

"I mean you no harm. All I want is the missile."

"Why?"

She shook her head. "I know all about you, you know. Two seconds after I walked into the store. You live in the dead places, and you've never made a damn thing in your lives. You drink out of ponds and squat in the woods. When you get sick, you suffer until you get too sick and die. You're scavengers and you want me to explain what a rocket is for?" She laughed and offered Lucy some chow mein noodles.

Lucy thought she looked too small to drive such a big truck. Juan grabbed a handful of noodles.

"You're going up," said Lucy.

The woman laughed until she started to cough. "Up." She spat into the weeds and licked blood from her lips. "Yes."

"We'll watch," said Juan. He sat down at the table. Lucy was angry, but she would not cross him in front of the stranger. She sat too.

"Not here, damn it." There was no anger in the stranger's voice; she sounded like the Bad Daddy often had when he was drunk and did not want them bothering him. The stranger showed them the sketches she had made on the yellow pad. "I'm going to load it on the truck and take it away."

The crow cawed and hopped to a higher branch. Lucy and the stranger looked up. Juan gazed at the sketches as if they were magic spells. He nodded. "We'll come."

The stranger's name was Hannah.

Her yellow backhoe awed Juan. It moved on two treads that chewed earth and stone and wood alike. With its flat blade at one end it could push down a house; with its bucket shovel at the other it could bury the remains. Hannah used it to dig a hole beside the rocket. She made a ramp leading to the hole and backed her truck down it so that the flatbed was level with the tail of the rocket. Then she ran a steel cable from the nose cone to a hook on the tractor's bucket. She hacksawed the bolts that held the rocket on its concrete base and slowly lowered it onto the truck. The job took three days. It would have taken Juan and Lucy a year, had they been able to do it at all.

The stranger's craziness made Lucy nervous. At night Hannah would bring beer from the grocery store and sit on the porch and drink. The beer made her sick. Sometimes a fit of coughing would take her and she would stagger to the edge of the porch and hang over the rail, heaving and cursing between heaves. Then she would sit and drink another beer. Lucy wondered if Hannah was cooked. The Bad Daddy had told them after it happened that everyone who was cooked would die—some sooner than others. Throwing up was one of the signs of being cooked.

Hannah talked about things that they did not understand, about nuclear winter and solid-fuel rockets and why it had happened. Sometimes she did not talk. Silence worried Lucy most of all. It was when the Bad Daddy was drunk and had stopped talking that he was most dangerous. She was not afraid that Hannah would hurt them. Lucy would kill her if she tried. But her silence made Lucy want to cry. There was a sadness to it that knifed into Lucy and would not be moved. Lucy did not want to feel sad. She was alive. She had Juan.

The backhoe's roar scared the crow, and it flew around the back of the house on the village green. It found Juan's garden. She watched as it pecked the tomatoes; she made no effort to stop it. Juan would not miss them now.

When the crow had finished the garden, she scattered food for it on the back porch. It liked Planter's Dry Roasted Cashews and Spam and Pringles. When it cawed, she would caw back at it. Then it would cock its head to one side and stare at her. It seemed more a person than a bird. She gazed into its tiny black searching eyes and wondered if it was magic, like in the storybooks.

She had not expected it to be so friendly. It hopped right up to her once and took a cashew out of her hand. On an impulse, she swiped at it and seized it by the legs. The swiftness of her attack must have taken the crow by surprise. She realized that it had never suspected that a human being could be a wild thing like itself. The crow screeched and fluttered and jabbed at her with its beak. It opened a gash on her arm before she caught it by the head with her free hand. With a quick twist she could have broken its neck.

"We're going." She smiled at the helpless bird. "You too."

Hannah lived alone at the Snowflake Lodge, near a partially burned-out ski town. Most of the ski area had escaped the fire.

She drove them to a barn that looked like a giant red can sliced lengthwise. Outside were the remains of snowmakers and groomers and snowmobiles. Inside were Hannah's treasures: two jeeps, a dump truck, an oil tanker semi, a yellow pumper fire truck, dusty stacks of boxes filled with parts, and a vast workshop with hundreds of tools. Out back was a gas-powered generator that had been used to run the lifts in case of power failure. Hannah turned it on when she worked in the barn or when she wanted to pump gas or diesel fuel from the underground tanks.

Juan climbed over the trucks. He took the tools down from their hooks and fiddled with them. He watched while Hannah worked over the generator. When the lights flickered on overhead, he dropped to his knees and shouted. It was a cry of wonder and joy and recognition, as if he had looked into a mirror for the first time. Hannah watched with a lopsided grin on her face. Lucy realized then that what Hannah wanted was to change their lives.

"Come here," said Hannah. "Here's the real prize." She led them to the far corner of the barn. "A space capsule. From the Gemini program of the sixties. I found it in a museum basement."

The hatch was off. Juan ducked in. Lucy hesitated.

"Does it work?"

"Lucy, I'd give two fingers and a toe to find out." Hannah shrugged. "The batteries need replacement, but I can get some systems to power up. There're lots of things I haven't been able to figure out. It didn't come with an owner's manual."

Lucy thought she understood then. It was in Hannah's voice, the angle of her shoulders, the way her hands moved. She loved the space capsule—and she hated it for not loving her back. She was a foolish, lonely, cooked woman.

"Small." Juan wriggled back out. "Can it go up?"

"I was just telling Lucy, I don't know. I hope so, but we won't know for a long time. It's not just the capsule; I have to find a way to boost it high enough. I'm working on a couple of angles. Then maybe we can jury-rig a coupling with the missile. And then we'll have to find some way to reset the guidance systems."

Lucy heard her say the word. *We.* But she knew that Juan had not heard. He never seemed to hear what Hannah was really saying. "When?" said Juan.

"Not soon." Hannah's face twisted. "There's lots to do."

Juan nodded. He still did not understand. Lucy wanted to take him out and shake some sense into him like she used to do when they were children. But those times were gone.

Hannah was watching her. Lucy knew they must be enemies. "Come out," she said. She had left her lucky crow in a basket in the cab of the truck. It was time to set it free.

She would not let Juan live at the lodge with Hannah. Instead they explored the ruins for a place to stay. The town was farther north than they had ever been before, but Lucy did not mind. Despite the fires that had devoured its heart, the town was still alive. She spotted more different kinds of birds than she had seen since it happened. At night they could hear peepers, and in the day they saw chipmunks and squirrels. The mountains around the town were covered with a thick stand of pine and hemlock.

On the far side of town, a shallow river with a sandy bottom had stopped the fires. The buildings on the opposite side were scorched but intact. She picked out a blue motel called Ray's Riverside with a view across the water. A rusting bridge was a block away. It was a half-hour walk to the ski area.

Hannah had an answer for her. She gave them a jeep.

"Cher . . . ok . . . ee." Lucy sounded out the name on the back. "Cherokee?"

"A kind of Indian," said Hannah.

"What's a Indian?" said Juan.

Hannah laughed. "You are."

Lucy had never seen him so happy. For a while he stopped going to the red can barn. They spent the last days of summer racing down the old roads, exploring the abandoned towns, swimming naked in the cold mountain streams. Sometimes when she looked at Juan, Lucy felt a tightness within her, as if her body was too small to contain her own unexpected joy. Then she would reach for his hand or slip her arm around him. When they touched each other at night, the past no longer seemed to matter. It was as if it had never happened, as if the Bad Daddy had never caught them. One night she helped him enter her for the first time. "It's all right," she said. She laughed and grasped his hips and knew it was the truth.

For a few weeks the world seemed newly made. Only one thing marred her contentment: she had not seen her crow since the day she had released it. Still, she believed that she remained under its lucky spell.

Slowly, though, Juan changed. It began with his fierce pride in the Cherokee. There had been other cars, years ago, but they had run out of gas or broken down. In time none of the cars would even start. But the jeep was different. It worked and it was *his.* When it stalled one day, he wept and slammed his hands against the steering wheel. He shouted at it as if the machine had betrayed him. Lucy recognized Hannah's madness in his rage. They walked back to the barn. He and Hannah brought the Cherokee back on the flatbed. They opened the hood, and he listened while Hannah explained how they were going to fix it.

They.

Lucy walked alone to Ray's Riverside. Juan did not come home that night. The next day the Cherokee roared into the motel's parking lot. Juan honked the horn until Lucy came out. He slapped the passenger seat. "Get in, get in," he said. "We fixed it!" She tried to scold him, but he was too happy to pay attention. He drove her straight back to the barn.

Juan still took her for rides, but it was not the same. The first frosts came; summer had lasted but six weeks. Juan started to spend too much time at the barn, listening to Hannah. Soon he was taking care of the jeep by himself and boring Lucy with talk of dwell meters and compression ratios. Hannah gave him his own set of tools. He began to learn about diesel engines. He even borrowed a greasy do-it-yourself book from Hannah and would sit up at night looking at the pictures and sounding out words until she called him to bed. His studies worried her. She had never known him to pay attention to anything but her for more than a few days at a time.

She thought they did not want her at the barn, so she stayed away. Instead she hiked up and down the ski trails, searching for her crow. It still had not come back. She was sorry now that she had not respected its wildness. She knew what it was like to be captured and helpless. A bird was not a toy, like a storybook or a jeep. Sometimes she left piles of cashews out in the parking lot of Ray's Riverside and around the barn. She never saw what ate them. As she walked, she thought it must be watching her from some hidden perch, its tiny eyes filled with hatred and fear. This thought began to haunt her, feeding on her loneliness. The luck of the crow was turning.

She stopped by the barn to see Juan. He was sitting in the sun on the Cherokee's rear bumper, eating StarKist tuna out of a can and drinking a Budweiser. Lucy felt the hollowness inside her filling with rage.

"Is this what she teaches you?" Lucy grabbed the bottle and shattered it on the side of the jeep. "You little shit," she said. It was what the Bad Daddy used to call them. They had never before spoken like that to each other.

"Lucy, I didn't . . ."

"Shut up, shut up!"

Hannah came running. "What's going on here?"

Lucy emptied Juan's toolbox onto the blacktop and began kicking the tools. She sent a spark plug wrench skittering toward Hannah, who charged her. She caught Lucy's arms and tried to pin her against the jeep. "Calm down for a minute, would you? What's the matter? Tell me."

Juan jerked Hannah away. "Leave her."

Lucy spun around and kicked Juan in the balls. He dropped to the pavement, writhing in pain. Hannah started toward her again. Lucy stooped and picked up a tire iron. Hannah froze. All of a sudden she looked very old. Lucy swiped at her and she fell backward.

"No, Lucy." Juan could barely talk. "No."

They had made a pledge to each other on a dark night eleven years ago. They had dipped their hands into the Bad Daddy's blood and smeared their faces and promised that they would stay together always and protect each other from the craziness that came out of a bottle. "We don't drink beer, you old shit." She threw the iron. It gouged a hole in the blacktop two inches from Hannah's head. "We don't drink."

She and Juan argued all night. They did not know how to argue, and they did it badly. She wanted them to go away. He would not leave. She blamed Hannah for the beer, but Juan would not hear it. Hannah had told him there was no harm in a bottle or two. She called Hannah a liar. Juan said that there were many things he wanted to try and that he was not going to live like a child anymore.

Lucy wanted to hurt Juan then. Words were not sharp enough. She slapped him. Juan struck her with his fist, and she stumbled backward against the wall.

"Go ahead, Juan." She looked up at him, and all she felt was sadness. She was losing him to a crazy woman. "You're the Bad Daddy now. Go ahead and beat me."

"Lucy." He shuddered; she could see the anger leave him.

"No." She remembered the nightmares he had when he was a boy and the look on his face as the last scream died in his throat.

"Something bad is happening to us," she said.

He nodded. His eyes were bright with tears.

"What can we do?"

"Don't know."

She held out her arms to him, but he did not come. She wanted to hold up a mirror so he could see Hannah's crazy sadness on his face.

"Don't know."

Lucy felt sick the next morning. At first she thought it was because of the fight. Juan went to the barn as if nothing had happened. Lucy did not ask him to stay. She knew that if he refused her, she would have to leave him. She was not yet ready to make Juan choose between Hannah and her.

After he had gone she walked along the river road, kicking stones into the water. There was a chill in the morning air. The trees were splashed with color. Soon they would have to move out of Ray's Riverside to a place with heat. She felt a rush of dizziness at the thought, shivered and threw up. After she had finished, she took a few steps and sat abruptly in the middle of the broken road. She had never been so sick before. She wondered if she was cooked.

Caw-caaw.

Lucy looked up and saw the crow wheeling in the sky just above her. She clapped and called out to it. "Crow, crow! Here I am." She raised her arms as if she were inviting Juan to bed. The crow swooped down and landed on the branch of a nearby tree. She did not move. The crow fluttered to a new branch. And another. Always downward. Closer. She stopped breathing. It glided to the ground about twenty feet away. It cocked its head.

"Crow." Nothing moved but her mouth. "I won't hurt you."

It hopped toward her. She thought she could make it come to her if she held out her hand, but then it would expect something to eat. "I haven't got anything," she said. "I'm still glad to see you."

She heard the crunch of gravel beneath wheels, the mutter of an idling engine. The crow flapped its black wings and leapt into the air. Lucy watched as if remembering a dream. That is our way, she thought. The way of wild things. Fly away. She did not move. Fly.

A jeep swerved around the corner. Its horn honked. Hannah pulled up next to her and opened the door. Lucy could see a half-empty fifth of Jack Daniel's Tennessee Sour Mash Whiskey on the passenger seat.

"Lucy. You all right?" Hannah stood over her, swaying. Her face was slack and she reeked of alcohol. "What you doing, sitting out here like this?"

"I threw up."

"Where?"

Lucy pointed. "I think I might be cooked."

"Cooked?" Hannah bent to sniff the vomit. "Stinks. No blood in it though. What did you eat last night?"

"Didn't. I fought with Juan." She gathered herself to stand. Her bones seemed to ache. "You're drunk."

She nodded as if Lucy had said something profound. "When was your last period?"

Lucy did not understand the question. "I feel better now."

"The bleeding." Hannah grasped her arm. "Comes every month."

"You're crazy. Who keeps track of *that?*" Lucy shook free.

"Lovers do. Juan said . . ." For a moment her eyes were very bright and Lucy thought the old drunk might cry. "Been talking to Juan." Hannah steadied. "You got him pretty upset. Talking nonsense. He says you're going to make him go away. You can't do that to me, Lucy. Can't do that to yourself. Look, I want to be your friend. I just don't know what you want from me. I never intended to come between you and Juan, Lucy. Never crossed my mind. I just wanted some company. Someone to talk to. Maybe someone to believe in what I'm doing. Lucy, you listening to me?"

She smiled. She wondered what the crow would say if it could talk. Maybe it would ask for a cashew.

"You think I'm crazy. Maybe I am crazy to think that old rocket will ever boost again. But I'm not crazy to think that people can fly. That you and I . . . I'm not crazy to hope that someday someone will climb into a rocket and. . . ." She sounded desperate. There was a glitter in her eye, as if the more she talked about not being crazy the crazier she became. "All I want," she said, "is a chance to convince you. One last chance. Come back to the barn with me. I'll show you something you'll never forget. Juan's waiting. Will you come?"

She saw then how fragile Hannah had become. She was like a picture of a woman in a rotting magazine. She was brown and dry and as dead as the world that had made her. Only she did not know it yet. When she did, she would curl up and blow away. Lucy laughed at her. "Yes."

It was big, big enough to shake Lucy's confidence. The thing could have swallowed a house. It was red and green and had pictures of winged giants on the outside. On the ground beneath it was a large wicker basket. In the basket was Juan. He gaped up into the mouth of the balloon like a madman.

"The ski area needed summer income," said Hannah. Lucy had made her throw the bottle away. She seemed more sober now. "So they started a ballooning center. Were two in the barn when I got here, but one of the bags was pretty badly torn up. Never had the patience to sew it." She parked the jeep beside the basket. Lucy looked but did not get out. Supported by pipes between the basket and the balloon, a coil of metal tubing made an angry sound. She thought of an animal's snarl, the hiss of a grease fire. The thing was hot.

"Must seem a little frightening to you," said Hannah. "But don't worry, it's safe. I've taken it up many times. Float for an hour, land in a field, and walk back. Juan's not worried."

"Up, Lucy." Juan grasped the edge of the basket and shook it like he had once shaken his playpen. "Up!"

Hannah stumbled around the jeep and offered Lucy a hand to help her down. "Don't be afraid. It's just a bag filled with hot air. Hot air rises. The thing at the top of the basket is a burner. Makes a noise and shoots a flame, but it can't hurt you. I just want you to see, Lucy. To understand."

Lucy pushed Hannah's hand away and climbed out herself.

"I'm going to have Juan turn the burner up now," Hannah said, "so that you can hear how it sounds."

Juan pulled a lever, and a tongue of blue flame leapt out of the burner. Lucy covered her ears and turned away, but she did not cry out. The basket tugged at its tether lines. Juan pushed the lever back.

"You ready, Lucy?" said Hannah.

Lucy could feel her blood pounding. The thing was so big, so loud.

"Lucy," said Juan. He laughed and waved at the sky. She could see the whites of his eyes as he looked up. Hannah was wrong. He was frightened. "We'll be like birds, Lucy. Like your crow."

Hannah swayed and grasped the edge of the basket.

Crow. Lucy steadied. The word named some part of her and in that naming tapped a wild strength that had kept her alive all these years. This balloon was part of the old craziness that was killing Hannah. Now Juan was sliding into it. Lucy knew he would go up with or without her. No matter how drunk Hannah was. The crow in her said to fly away. But she could not leave Juan. She would have to fight the craziness to keep him. One last time and she would win.

She climbed into the basket beside him. He put an arm around her and squeezed.

"Turn on the burner." Hannah cast off the last tether, dove at the basket, and tumbled aboard. Juan helped her up. They sailed across the parking lot, inches above the pavement. Then the balloon climbed. Hannah turned the burner off, waited a few minutes, then gave another short blast. The ground fell away. "We'll stabilize at a thousand feet. Take you higher, but I have to watch out for the wind. Sometimes you catch a gust swirling around the mountain."

They cleared the treetops and drifted over the burned-out town. The balloon moved like a cloud. Lucy picked out the roof of Ray's Riverside and felt dizzy. It was not just the height. It was the way of seeing. She had climbed mountains before and looked down. But even at the top of the highest mountain she was still on the ground. In a place. Now she passed over the familiar buildings like a mind without a body. She was afraid.

Juan pointed out things that she could see for herself. His face was flushed with the heat and excitement. He chattered like a little boy who was afraid to stop talking. As they went higher and the land spread out below them, he said less. The view demanded silence. The evergreen forest that rolled over the northern mountains was already filling with snow. The hills to the south were mottled with patches of brown and scummy green.

Hannah did not waste her time looking down. She gazed up into the clear autumn sky. "I was fourteen when it happened," she said. "My parents were survivalists. They saw it coming, but they didn't see it all. The germ bombs. The winter. They died in our shelter. I buried them and waited to die myself." Her laugh was short and bitter. "Still waiting. There were books. I educated myself. A lot of guns. And a radio. That's what kept me going." She pointed up at the white crescent of the moon. "You two have spent your whole lives looking at the sky and never knew. There are people up there. Our people.

They live the way we used to, by the rules we believed in. *Kennedy Base.* Two orbiting factories. A handful of spacelabs. I used to talk to them on the radio. I begged them to come and get me. They never would, afraid of contamination. One night I got so mad I shot the radio. Just set it up on the table and emptied a few dozen rounds into it. Crying like a baby. Waste of good ammunition."

She shut off the burner. "This high enough for you?" She patted Juan on the back. "That's it, get a good look, Juan. Next time you can take her up yourself. How about you, Lucy? Not quite what you expected, eh? Still think I'm crazy?"

"You can't have Juan."

"Don't talk, Lucy." Juan glared at her. "Not now. Not up here."

Hannah slumped. "Maybe we'll start down." As she stared up at the moon, Lucy could imagine a lonely girl crying. Lucy shut her eyes.

"NASA used balloons all the time in atmospheric research," said Hannah. "Not this kind; zero-pressure gas jobs, enormous things. Some in combination with rockets went up sixty miles. Sixty miles high, that's almost halfway to low orbit. Now if we could get a hold of one of them, we'd really have something. Of course in the old days no one ever used balloons as boosters. But then the old days are gone, aren't they?"

The treetops loomed. They were coming down fast.

"What I really need is a booster rocket. A Saturn or even an old Titan. But a Titan weighs three hundred thousand pounds. I'm just one woman. I'm all alone."

Juan reached over Hannah and turned on the burner. Too late. The balloon did not immediately react. They dropped still lower and hemlock branches whipped at them. "Damn it!" Hannah's face was gray. "Hold on." They hit a trunk and the basket lurched. "Come on, baby. Lift, lift!" Juan moaned and reached for Lucy's hand. They began to twist, and Hannah shut the burner down to keep from scorching the cables and the skirt of the balloon. Then they came free. The basket spun back and forth.

"Sorry." Hannah's eyes were out of focus. "Too busy talking, got careless." She took a deep breath that ended in coughing. "Turn the . . . burner . . ." She covered her mouth with a handkerchief and doubled over.

Juan gave the bag a short blast. The wind was picking up. The ground rushed by beneath them. Juan and Lucy looked at each other. They shared their fear without speaking. Hannah was trying to kill herself—and them as well.

Hannah stood and grasped the edge of the basket. "We'll land. The first field." There were flecks of pink foam at the corners of her mouth. "Any open place. Watch out for old power lines."

There were no fields. They skimmed the treetops. Hannah shut her eyes for minutes at a time.

Lucy thought she heard a voice calling her. It was not a human voice. She looked back and picked out a shadow against the sky. It seemed to shimmer like a mirage. "Crow! It's me." The mirage solidified into a bird. The crow swooped down on them. Lucy waved. Her confidence returned. Lucky crow. Magic crow. It circled the balloon, its outspread wings knifing through the air. Then it flew on ahead and dropped into a hole in the forest.

"Looks like a pond." Hannah shook herself and peered at the fuel gauge on the propane tank attached to the burner. "Down to five percent. We'll have to chance a water landing. Can you swim?"

Lucy and Juan shook their heads.

"Damn." Hannah craned for a better view. "It's not very big. I'll try to drop her near shore. Even if the basket floods, the empty propane tank should keep it afloat. I'll swim to shore with a line and try to haul you in."

They swooped down into the trees. Some high branches caught at the basket. "That's okay." Hannah was talking to herself. "Moving fast but we're okay." She did not sound convinced. The basket tilted. The bag was ahead of it, dragging it through the treetops. "Hold on now." The basket tipped and then pulled free. Below them was the pond. "Here we go." Hannah tugged on the red strap that hung from the top of the bag down to the basket. A large panel of fabric at the top of the balloon pulled free. The bag shriveled and they fell.

The force of the landing knocked them sprawling. The bag collapsed into the pond downwind, pulling the basket onto its side.

Lucy thrashed through icy water in a panic. Her hand closed around the edge of the basket. She clung there for a second, stretching for the bottom. Too deep. She climbed up the side of the basket that was still above water. Hannah straddled the burner supports and clung there with eyes closed.

"Juan!" Lucy scrambled around her bobbing perch. "Juan,

where are you?'' There was no sign of him in the dark pond.

Hannah shivered and opened her eyes. She stared at Lucy for a moment with that crazy glitter in her eyes. She took a deep breath and slipped into the water.

Lucy screamed.

She was answered by the crow's harsh cry. She had startled it. The bird flapped out of a pine tree and skimmed low across the pond.

''Crow, help! Crow.''

The crow climbed past her, its black wings beating faster. It cleared the treetops, banked south.

''Crow!''

She watched it disappear into the blue sky. No sign, no magic: a bird. She realized that her crow and Hannah's rocket were the same kind of lies.

Hannah surfaced behind her and started coughing blood. Lucy reached out and grasped her outstretched hand. When she tried to haul Hannah to the basket, Lucy nearly tumbled back into the pond. It was impossible. The old woman was not that heavy.

A pale shadow floated toward the surface of the brown water beside Hannah. Lucy lowered herself into the water, clinging with one hand to the basket. She clutched at the shadow and caught it. Juan's head broke the surface.

First she pushed Juan onto the basket, then Hannah. It tipped when she climbed up. Water lapped at their knees. Juan was not breathing.

''Mouth. Blow into . . .'' Hannah was racked by a spasm of coughing. ''Make him . . . breathe.''

Lucy covered Juan's mouth with hers and breathed several times. Juan did not respond. She knew he was dead. She raised her head and glared. Hannah had killed him.

''Don't stop!'' Hannah's voice was a croak. ''Harder . . . deep breaths.'' Hannah caught Lucy's shirt in her trembling hand. ''Save him!''

She thought Hannah had finally gone mad. The old woman would not let go until Lucy continued. Only then did Hannah fall back onto the basket. She licked the blood from her lips and panted.

Lucy worked over Juan until she was dizzy. She did not notice the first whisper of breath in his lungs. Suddenly he was breathing on his own and she did not know what to do. She looked to Hannah. Hannah glared at the moon. She was crying.

Juan moaned and Lucy pulled back. "C-cold," he said.

"Juan! Are you all right?"

His eyelids flickered. He rolled to the edge of the basket and gagged.

"Juan." Hannah was panting like the Bad Daddy on the night Lucy killed him.

"He can't hear you." Lucy crouched over her. "I think he's all right."

"Go." Her eyes stared right through Lucy. "Burn it and go. Crazy, yes. Lucy's right. It's over. Her world now."

She took two days to die. They buried her at the top of the ski lift. They had never buried anyone before, not even the Bad Daddy. But she had made Juan promise.

When they finished, they walked down the slope in silence. A light snow had begun to fall. Lucy had filled the Cherokee with gas and packed enough food for a week. It was parked in front of the rocket on the flatbed.

"She said to burn it."

Juan shook his head.

"Let's go then." Lucy jingled the keys nervously.

"You heard her. You can't go." There was a crazy glitter in Juan's eyes that chilled Lucy. "She said you're having a baby."

Lucy did not believe in babies. They were the same as the crow: lies that fools made themselves believe. The old woman had been cooked. Crazy with her pain. There were no babies anymore.

"We'll stay." He nodded at the rocket and the barn behind it. "It's ours now."

Lucy had been very tired lately. She could not find the strength to argue. In a few months Juan would realize that nothing was going to happen and then they would go. She could wait.

Juan held out his hand. She gave him the keys.

monsters

When Henry looked in his dad's old mirror, he couldn't see the monster. He touched his reflection. Nothing. No shock, no secret thrill, not even a tingle. Usually his nipples tightened or the insides of his knees would get crinkly, and if he were in a certain mood he'd crawl back under the covers and think very hard about women in black strapless bras. But this morning—zero. He stared at a fattish naked white man with thinning hair and yellow teeth. A face as interesting as lint. He wished for a long purple tongue or a disfiguring scar that forked down his cheek, except he didn't want any pain. Not for himself, anyway. Henry hated looking so vanilla. There was nothing terrifying about him except the bad thoughts, which he told no one, not even God. But this morning the monster was cagey. It wanted to get loose, and he was tired of holding it back. Something was going to happen. He decided not to shave.

The gray Dacron shirt and shiny blue polyester pants hanging on the line over the bathtub had dripped dry overnight. His nylon underwear was dry too, but the Orlon socks were still damp, so he draped them over the towel bar. Henry wore synthetics because they wouldn't shrink or wrinkle and he could wash them in the sink. Some days, after wallowing in other people's mung, he boiled his clothes. He liked his showers hot too; he stood in the rusty old claw-footed tub for almost half an hour until his skin bloomed like a rose. The shower beat all the thoughts out of his head; nothing wormy had ever happened in the tub. He opened his mouth, let it fill with hot water, and spat at the wall.

He owned just five shirts: gray, white, beige, blue, and blue-striped; and three pairs of pants: blue, gray, and black. As he tried to decide what to wear to work, he had a bad thought. Not a thought, exactly—he flashed an image of himself bending toward a TV minicam, hands locked behind him as he was pushed into a police car. Blue or blue-striped would show up best on the six o'clock news.

He petted the shirts. Maybe he was already crazy, but it seemed to him that if he wore blue today, it might set off the chain reaction of choices the creature was always trying to start. He pulled the white shirt from its hanger.

Henry ate only two kinds of breakfast cereal, Cheerios and Rice Chex. Over the years he had tried to simplify his life; routines were a defense against bad thoughts. That's why he always watched the Weather Channel when he ate Cheerios. He liked the satellite pictures of storms sweeping across the country because he thought that was what weather must look like to God. He didn't understand how people could think weather was boring; obviously they hadn't seen it get loose.

After breakfast he tried to slip past the shrine and out the front door, but he couldn't. The monster was stirring even though he had chosen the white shirt. He dug the key out of his pocket, opened the shrine, and turned on the light. He was in the apartment's only closet, seven feet by four. Henry bolted the door behind him.

The walls were shaggy with pictures he'd ripped out of magazines, but he didn't look at them. Not yet. He pressed the Play button on the boombox, and the Rolling Stones bongoed into "Sympathy for the Devil." He knelt at the oak chest that served as the altar. Inside was a plastic box. Inside the box, cradled in pink velvet, was the Beretta.

He had bought the 92SB because of its honest lines. A little bulky in the grip, the salesman had said, but only because inside was a fifteen-shot double-column magazine. It was cool as a snake to the touch, thirty-five hard ounces of steel, anodized aluminum, and black plastic. He wrapped his right hand around the grip and felt the gentle bite of the serrations on the front and rear of the frame. He stood, supported his right hand with his left, extended his arms, and howled along with Jagger. "Ow!"

Schwarzenegger trembled in his sights; even cyborgs feared the thing lurking inside Henry West. "Now!" The pistol had a thrilling heft; it was more real than he was. "*Wham!*" he cried, then let his arms drop. Manson gave him a shaggy grimace of approval. Madonna shook her tits. The monster was stretching; its claw slid up his throat.

He spun then and ruined Robert Englund, *wham,* David Duke, *wham,* and Mike Tyson, *wham, wham, wham.* Metallica gave him sweaty glares. Imelda Marcos simpered. Henry let a black rain of bad thoughts drench him. He'd give in and let it loose on the Market Street bus or in the First Savings where that twisty young teller never looked at him when she cashed his paycheck. He'd blaze into Rudy's Lunch Bucket like that guy in Texas and keep slapping magazines into the Beretta until he had the mass murder record. Only not when Stefan was behind the counter. Stefan always gave him an extra pickle. Or else he'd just suck on the gun himself, take a huge bloody gulp of death. He sagged against Jim Jones, laughing so he wouldn't scream.

"Why me, God?" he said, rubbing the barrel along the stubble on his chin. "Let me pass on this, okay?" But He wasn't listening. Just because He could be everywhere, didn't mean He'd want to be. He wouldn't stoop to this place, not while Henry was celebrating slaughter.

When the music ended, he fit the pistol back into its velvet cradle. He felt split into two different Henrys, both of them moist and expended. Part of him suspected this was nothing more than a bughouse riff, like old Jagger prancing across some stage playing Lucifer. The Beretta wasn't even loaded; he'd hidden the ammo under the sink behind the paper towels. But if this were nothing but pretend, why did it give him more pleasure than a mushroom pizza and a jug of Carlo Rossi Pink Chablis and a new stroke flick? It may have started as a game, but it felt real now. Under the influence of the gun, he was solid as a brick. The rest of his life was smog.

He locked the shrine behind him and went back to the mirror, the only thing he'd kept when he closed Dad's house. The creature leered at him. He stuck out his thumb and smudged his reflected eye. The hair on the back of his neck prickled. He thought then he knew what was going to happen. It wanted to touch someone else, and he was going to let it.

The new bus driver was a plush moon-faced woman. She didn't even bother to look at him as he slid a dollar onto her outstretched hand, brushing fingertips quickly across the ridges of her skin. He was nobody to her, another zero. The monster's looping murderous rage was building like an electric charge as she jabbed at the coin dispenser for his change. Notice me, pay attention. She dropped the quarter into his palm and he curled his fingers suddenly, grazing her palm. The unholy spark of madness crackled between them. She yipped, jerked her hand away, and stared at him. "Oops," he said. "Sorry." She gave him an uneasy laugh, like someone who has just suffered through a sick joke she didn't want to hear. She'd think it was just static—what else could it be? She couldn't know how good it felt to give away pain. He was still grinning when he swung into an empty seat and saw her watching him in the rearview mirror.

Another monster worked at Kaplan's Cleaners. Celeste Sloboda pressed and folded shirts across the room. Only she didn't count. She hadn't made the choice; she'd been born a hunchback. Besides, she wore her thick black hair down to her belt when she wasn't working, trying to cover her deformity. She would've had better luck hiding a chain saw in her purse. What made it worse was that Celeste was tiny, barely five feet; she looked like a twelve-year-old going on forty, complete with sags and wrinkles and a hump the size of a turkey. She smiled too much and hummed to herself and yattered about her cats as if they were smarter than she was. Jerry said she was kind of cute if you pretended she wasn't lopsided, but Henry didn't have that kind of imagination.

He knew that the reason Celeste kept honeying up to him was that she wanted to switch over to the cleaning side. Kaplan kept crabbing that there was no money in shirts, that he only took them so that shirt customers would bring in cleaning business. If Kaplan axed shirts, he'd have to ax Celeste too—or else move her over to Henry's side. But Henry already had a helper, and even though Jerry was a jack-around, at least he left Henry alone.

Celeste perched on a stool, steaming shirts on the form press they called the susie. The laundry had delivered just three mesh bags; usually there were between five and eight. "Guess what I had for breakfast today?" she said.

Henry, at the spotting bench, did not reply. In the six months Celeste had been at Kaplan's, he'd learned to pretend that he couldn't hear her over the rumble of the cleaning drum.

"Broccoli in Velveeta sauce. I know you think that's weird, but then you think everything I do is weird. Besides, I like leftovers for breakfast. Meat loaf, potatoes, lasagna, I don't care. When I was a kid I knew this girl poured root beer on her cornflakes, so I guess broccoli for breakfast isn't so bad."

Henry followed a trail of coffee splatters up the placket of a silk blouse, sponging them with wet spotter. He blotted the blouse and set it aside for a few moments.

"What if our bodies don't wake up all at once? I mean, the eyes are always last, right? Ears wake up before. I swear I can smell coffee brewing even though I'm asleep. So maybe my taste buds have insomnia or something. Say they're up at two in the morning. By six-thirty, it's lunchtime. I can't remember the last time I ate bacon and eggs. What did you have for breakfast, Henry?"

He scraped the splotch on the lapel of a charcoal suit jacket with his fingernail. Some kind of wax—a candlelight dinner gone sour? The cleaning machine buzzed and the drum creaked to a stop.

Celeste cupped a hand over her mouth. "I said, what did you have for breakfast?"

"You talking to me?" He flushed the wax away with the steam gun. "Cheerios." He tossed the jacket into a basket filled with darks "With milk." There were enough clothes in it to make a new load. "Jerry," he called. "Yo, Jerry!"

"He's pretending he can't hear you." Celeste giggled. "Probably trying to get into Maggie's pants."

That was his squawk with Jerry. When something needed doing, Jerry was either at the front counter flirting with the cashier or in the bathroom. Henry ducked around the coat hanging beside the spotting bench, grabbed an empty basket, and wheeled it to the cleaning machine. As he gathered the warm clothes from the drum, he breathed in harsh perchloroethylene fumes. He pushed the basket over to the empty rail next to the presses. Perk nauseated some people, but Henry liked the smell. It filled his head like "Stairway to Heaven."

"How do you clean a syrup stain, anyway?" said Celeste.

"I thought you didn't eat breakfast stuff." He started pulling the clothes onto hangers and setting them on the rail. "You want my job, is that it?"

"Your job?" She buttoned a white spread-collar shirt onto the susie and stepped on the compressed air pedal. With a hiss, steam ballooned the shirt away from the form and jetted from the neck and sleeves. "Don't be paranoid, Henry—you're the best. Just trying for a little friendly chitchat, is all." She pulled at her hair net. "Hey, I like pancakes for supper. Syrup's an accident I'll probably have someday."

He grunted and hung the last of the load on the rail. "Sponge it with water, then use wet spotter with a couple drops of vinegar. When it's loose, you blot."

"Now was that so hard? Shit, how come getting you to say anything is like moving a refrigerator?" She wiped her forehead. Her work smock, already limp with moisture, clung to her child's body. Pressing shirts on the susie was hot, dreary work. At least on his side, every garment was different. Henry didn't blame her for being bored; he just didn't want to entertain her.

Henry was pitching darks into the machine when Kaplan elbowed the back door open. He was carrying a bag filled with takeout from Rudy's.

"Gonna rain." Louis Kaplan was a pink little man who wore a short-sleeved shirt and a paisley tie that some customer had neglected to pick up—probably on purpose. He set the bag on a shelf next to a jug of acetone. "What're you doing?" he said to Henry. Without waiting for an answer, he turned to Celeste. "What's he doing?"

"Getting ready to run a load?" she said.

"I can see that. But I'm not paying him to do the idiot work. Where's Jerry?"

"I didn't know it was my turn to watch him." She pulled a damp shirt from the blue mesh laundry bag beside her and snapped it out. Kaplan scuttled toward the front of the store.

"If that's what being boss does to you, I'm sure as hell glad it's him in charge and not me." She draped the shirt over the susie. "Well, I'm ready for a break."

While Henry finished emptying the basket into the drum, she pulled an assortment of Styrofoam coffee cups and cardboard sandwich boxes from the bag and sorted through them. "Want yours now?"

"Not yet." He didn't want her near him. Touching the bus driver hadn't satisfied the thing inside him. Maybe she hadn't felt enough pain. All morning long the monster's need had been swelling like a balloon. If Celeste accidently touched him, he wasn't sure he could keep it from striking out at her. He had never let it touch anyone at work before.

"You get time off for good behavior, Henry."

"I said, in a minute."

She shrugged and went back to her stool, unwrapped an egg bagel with cream cheese and lox. Only when she was settled did he pick out his tea with extra milk and the English muffin. Coffee break could be the longest fifteen minutes of the day. He needed Jerry right now to shield him from Celeste. That was about all the kid was good for. What were they doing up there?

"Don't you ever get bored eating the same damn muffin over and over again?" she said.

"It's a new muffin every day."

He was dunking the tea bag when he heard someone up front shouting; the racks of clean clothes muffled the sound. "Shush!" As he strained to hear, he felt a twinge of dread. He hadn't worn the blue, but still, something was happening. The noise got closer; he recognized Jerry's whine.

"What do you want me to say? No, *really,* tell me what I'm supposed to say. I mean, I'm sorry and all and it won't happen again."

Kaplan was the first through the door; his pink face had flushed a meaty red.

"Why won't you *listen* to me?" Jerry tagged behind like a bad dog on a short leash. "Nobody saw, really. How could they? We were way, way back, behind the *W* rack."

Kaplan hesitated, trapped by his own machines. If he wanted to keep walking away from Jerry, he'd have to leave the store. He glanced blindly around before deciding his only escape was to dive into a cup of Rudy's coffee.

"*Please,* Louis."

Jerry tried to come around to face him, but Kaplan veered away. He clutched the Styrofoam cup close to him and fixed on it as if it were telling him secrets.

"Nobody could've seen us back there," said Jerry. "Go look for yourself. Besides, there *weren't* any customers. Maggie was listening for the door chime. Mr. Kaplan, please say something."

The creature squirmed in delight at Kaplan's distress, watching as he worried at the drink tab on the lid. "You had your hand in her pants."

Celeste used both hands to smother a giggle, and Jerry realized he had an audience. Since Kaplan's back was turned, he let a grin slink across his face.

"No, no," he said. "You don't understand. Yes, we were kissing. That's what you saw and I'm sorry, but it's not what you think."

Kaplan tore the plastic lid off, and hot coffee slopped onto his hand and down his trousers. "Shit!" When he tried to dance out of the way, he bumped into Jerry and half the cup splatted onto his shoes. Celeste laughed out loud.

"Okay, okay, so I was playing with the elastic a little." Jerry's smirk curdled what little sincerity he had left. "But that was as far as we were going. I mean, this is a public place. We're not *stupid* or anything."

"You're right, Jerry. You're not stupid." Kaplan put the dripping coffee cup back on the shelf as if it were a weight he was glad to set down. "I'm the stupid." He finally turned to confront Jerry. "You've worked here for two whole months and done nothing but screw up. I guess that makes me dumb as a box of rocks. But I've learned my lesson, kid. Get your stuff and go. You're finished."

"You're firing me?" Jerry seemed to shrink six inches. "What is this, a joke?"

"I'll give you a week's severance. The check will be ready by closing. You can come back then."

"Oh, come on, Mr. Kaplan. Give me a break."

His voice was hard as the sidewalk. "Take your lunch, you can even take your coffee, if you want. But go."

"*Henry.*" Jerry spun toward him in desperation. "You can't let this happen. He'll make you do both our jobs, Henry. Tell him you need help."

Henry was certain that if he opened his mouth the monster would leap out and strangle them all. Jerry plucked a vest from the basket and shook it at Henry. "Who do you think is going to clean this? Miss Dumpty Humpty?"

"He already does most of your work," said Celeste. "Asshole."

"Celeste," said Kaplan. "Enough."

"*No.*" Jerry threw the vest to the floor. "I'm not going anywhere unless you ask Henry. He runs this place, but you're all afraid of him. I'm the only one he ever talks to."

A sound like the squealing of brakes filled Henry's head. He knew it wasn't real but held his breath, waiting for the crash.

"Celeste," said Kaplan, "I think you should call the police. Tell them we're having a little problem here."

"See, Henry?" Jerry was full of scorn. "They don't even trust you with the phone."

"Get the hell out of my store!" Kaplan stepped toward Jerry.

Celeste edged off her stool. Henry tried to think of a way to stop her. He knew Jerry and Kaplan were very close to fighting; she was going to keep them from hurting each other. When he closed his eyes, Henry saw broken teeth and dark blood beading on the floor tiles. His fists clenched. This was so much better than the shrine. He had never been this close to real violence before.

"Aww, fuck all of you." Jerry snatched his coat. "I never liked working here anyway. The pay sucks, and you're nothing but a bunch of loonies and losers." He retreated toward the back door. "Just make sure my check is ready." He stalked out, not even bothering to slam the door behind him.

Kaplan slumped against the spotting bench. "I'm sorry you had to listen to that." Henry guessed he meant both of them, even though he was speaking to Celeste. "I should've taken care of him after work, but I. . . . Listen, we're going to have to pull together for a couple of days." He looked about as together as dust. "I'll get an ad in the paper right away. I—I should stay up front today, keep an eye on Maggie. What I think we need to do is keep pushing the cleaning out on schedule, which means you'll have to help Henry. If there's time left, we'll worry about the shirts. No money in goddamn shirts, anyway." He considered for a moment, then gathered himself. "That little weasel." He pushed away from the bench and clapped his hands. "So, then, can we handle this?"

Henry had been flashing Kaplan firing Jerry after work, when there'd be no witnesses. Jerry coldcocked the brittle old man, then straddled him and grasped the pink head between his hands. When he pounded it against the floor, it exploded like a light bulb. The monster was frustrated that nothing had happened. "It stinks," Henry said.

"I'm sorry, Henry. Just give me a couple of days."

"Don't worry, Louis," said Celeste. "We'll handle it."

Kaplan shot her a grateful look and hurried off to keep Maggie from ransacking the till. Henry bent to snare the vest Jerry had thrown. He dropped it in the hamper.

"Look at you." Celeste chuckled. "He's gone and you're still picking up after him."

"It's your fault." He snapped at her. "You laughed, you got him fired."

"That's bullshit, Henry, and you know it. Jerry blew this job off long ago. If you ask me, he got what he deserved. I'm sorry if that bothers you. I'm sorry if you hate my guts. But other people don't make you do bad things. You do them yourself."

Even though she was wrong, he didn't reply; she'd only chew his ear some more. He folded his untouched muffin and rammed it into the cup still half full of lukewarm tea. Of course other people could make you do wrong. Henry was proof of that. And he didn't really hate her. Yes, the grotesque hump repelled him and she had the personality of Brillo, but he was also a little sorry for her.

It was the monster who hated her.

"So what do you want me to do?" she said.

Henry figured that the reason it was always dark in church was because God didn't like bright places. His God tended to lurk in the shadows and not say much, like a stranger at a wedding. When He spoke in His midnight whisper, it always took Henry by surprise. God certainly wasn't a rattletongue like Celeste or a smartmouth like Jerry. Henry believed that He preferred the dark because, like Henry, He was shy.

Even though Our Lady of Mercy was only two blocks from Kaplan's, Henry's midday routine was to bring his lunch to St. Sebastian's because the light there was so bad that it was hard for anyone to see him eating. Also, Sebastian was the martyr that some Roman emperor had shot full of arrows; his painting was in the side chapel. Henry liked to sit in the third pew from the back with his regular tuna sandwich, pickle, and chocolate milk. The priests usually left him alone because he never made a mess, but sometimes parishioners would crab at him.

The rain had come earlier than predicted, chasing at least a dozen other people into the church, so he had to be cagey about eating. And the clouds had dulled his favorite stained glass; the reds had gone to mud, the blues almost black. Each of the fourteen narrow windows of St. Sebastian's depicted one of the Stations of the Cross. Henry liked to pray to the sixth: Veronica wiping the face of Jesus. Once, years ago, he had wondered whether the impression of His face that Jesus had left on Veronica's handkerchief could be removed with wet spotter, or maybe a hydrogen peroxide soak. It was as close as he had ever come to having a bad thought in church.

After he finished the pickle, he slid forward onto the kneeler to say a Hail Mary. The monster snuffed the prayer by ramming a fist up Henry's windpipe. He rocked back onto the pew, choking. People turned to stare; Henry put a hand to his mouth and pretended to cough into it. It took a moment before he could breathe again. He sat very still, closed his eyes, and tried not to panic. *Our Father,* he thought, *Who art in . . .* His head snapped back as veins of fire pulsed across his lids; it felt as if someone were squashing his eyes into his skull. He couldn't speak, couldn't even think to Him. Henry had never needed God's help more. Why couldn't he ask for it? Nothing else had changed: up at the altar, votive candles still flickered like angels and the tabernacle glittered with the gold of heaven. But Henry could not pray. He covered his face with his hands.

"Hey, you. *Bum.*"

Henry turned and blinked at a pale twitchy man in a rain-spattered blue jacket stitched with the name Phil.

"This is a church, scumbag." Phil's voice swelled with outrage, snapping through the gloom like a sermon. "Not some flop where you can sleep off a drunk. You understand? And look at all this garbage. Go on, get out of here!"

Henry crumbled the sandwich box and the wax paper into a ball. The last place he wanted something to happen was in God's house. He sensed the creature plugging into the man's anger, feeding off it into a frenzy. If Phil tried to hurt him, it would hurt him back. *Oh God.* He had to get away before it was too late. As he gathered in the milk carton, Phil decided he wasn't hurrying fast enough.

"Now, bum! Or I'm calling the cops." He grabbed at Henry to haul him out of the pew.

He tried to twist away, but Phil's hand closed on his shoulder. Henry moaned with dread and pleasure as he yielded to the madness. The spark surged down his arm; muscles spasmed in an explosion of awful strength. He snapped his attacker back as easily as a wet shirt. Phil hit the wall of the church with a sharp *crack.* He sagged to the floor, face slack, eyes like eggs.

Someone screamed. The shock of monstrous pleasure had

left Henry momentarily limp; now he shuddered and flung himself out of the pew past the body. The touch had never been this good before, this vicious. He sprinted through the baptistry out the side door into the rain. He ran five blocks before he realized no one was paying attention to him. Everyone was hunkered down against the weather.

He slowed to a walk. His cheeks were hot; he was in no hurry to get out of the rain. The monster was spent and he was back in control. He hadn't felt this relaxed in weeks. What harm had been done, really? Phil would wake up with a headache and a story he'd exaggerate down at the corner bar for years. So Henry would have lunch at Our Lady of Mercy for a while. Or find an even darker church.

"Hail Mary, full of grace," he said to a parking meter. "The Lord is with thee." He fished a dime from his pocket, cranked it into the slot, and the violation flag clicked down. "Deliver us from evil." He laughed. "Amen."

By the time he got back to Kaplan's, he had convinced himself that for today, at least, he'd left the nightmare behind.

It rained that afternoon on everyone but Henry; he was still shining hours after lunch. Even Celeste's yattering failed to rile him, perhaps because she talked mostly about dry cleaning instead of her cats and rice pudding and the world's tallest woman. And she worked much harder than Jerry; he was secretly impressed. She may have been a rattletongue, but when Celeste started something, it got done.

He was pressing pants and she was hanging whites. "How long ago did you start in cleaning anyway?" she said. "Ten years, twenty?"

"Before your time."

"Really?" She brightened. "How old do you think I am?"

He didn't understand why she was still honeying up to him, now that she had what she wanted. Henry pulled a pair of gray pinstripes off the rail and ignored her.

"Don't be such a gentleman. The answer is thirty-six, same age as you. Or at least that's how old Jerry said you were. Unless he was making it up."

"No."

"So how come you never opened a store of your own?"

He stepped on the compressor pedal; steam billowed through the pants. His own shop? That's what his dad used to say. But the thought had never appealed to Henry; he had enough to worry about.

"After all," said Celeste, "you know the business."

"Twenty-five pounder is the smallest rig they make." He nodded at the dry-cleaning machine. "Cost Kaplan thirty grand." He took his foot off the steam pedal and the pants deflated. "You've got to be smart to play for those stakes."

"So? You're smart. All you need is a rich uncle. Or else hit the lottery. I play my birthday and Madonna's every week. 7/28/56 and 8/16/58. Tell you what: when I win, I'll stake you. Only you have to name the store after me. Sloboda's Cleaners."

Brown gabardines were next on the rail. He said nothing.

"Because it's nice work," she said, "dry cleaning. I mean, it's fun because there's progress. You can see what you've done at the end of the day, not like bagging groceries or stitching shoes. You start with something ugly and it ends up pretty. How many jobs are there where you try to make the world a more beautiful place?"

Henry had no idea; he cared zero for the world. He liked the iron tang of steam hissing from the presses, the furriness of wet wool, the backbeat of the spinning drum, the way silk clung like caterpillars to his rough skin, the perfect chemical luster of nylon, the attic smell of shirt cardboards, leather jackets as heavy as raw steak, the airiness of rayon, the delicate crinkling of plastic bags fresh off the roll, and especially the intoxicating palette of chemicals at the spotting table. He liked sweating through his tank top in the numbing heat of July and basking in the cozy humidity of the back room at Christmas. What mattered to Henry was that the job filled his senses and kept away the bad thoughts. Mostly.

"Yeah," she was saying, "I like it here just fine, even though it's not exactly what I want to do for the rest of my life." She waved her finger at him. "Don't you dare tell Kaplan I said that. I'm trusting you."

A pair of tan suit pants.

"No, what I really want to be someday is a travel agent. That way I'll get to go all over so I can tell people where the best times are. You know, like a librarian has to read all those books? Because I'd love to see the pyramids and China and San Francisco and the Disneys—all the Disneys. I read where they have one in France now. And learn to ski. And I'm going to try all those warm places where you just lay around on the beach in your bikini and waiters bring you drinks with cherries in them."

The idea of Celeste in a bikini made him laugh. She'd need to buy a third piece to cover her hump.

"Yeah, what's so funny?" She was suddenly brittle, as if a

cruel word might shatter her. "You don't think I could do it?"

He had never seen her fold up like this; maybe she had never told him anything that mattered before. He sensed that if he said what he really thought, she might never speak to him again. A couple hours ago he would've killed for this chance. Now he let it pass. "Don't you have to go to school for that?" He waved vaguely toward downtown.

"Probably. I don't know. Never mind." She picked an armful off the rail of hanging clothes and carried them over to the big press. "It's just something I've been thinking about."

She didn't speak, sing, or hum for fifteen minutes. She just hurled clothes around like curses: yanked them onto the press, jerked down the cover, threw them onto hangers when they were done. Kaplan wheeled in a basket filled with dirty clothes from up front and parked it by the spotting bench. He beamed when he saw the long line of finished orders ready for bagging.

"I should've gotten you two together weeks ago." He rubbed his hands. "This is great; I really mean it. Look, it's been a tough day. Go ahead and finish up the shirts, and you can knock off a half hour early."

Olive twills.

"Thanks, Louis," said Celeste. She watched him go with a lemon expression on her face. "Half an hour early? Shit, we should go home now. We've already done a hell of a day's work." Then she chuckled; Celeste wasn't built to pout. "Well, if you'll bag up the cleaning, I'll move over to shirts."

"Sure."

"You're an odd one, you know that, Henry? At first I thought that you didn't like me. Then Jerry said you didn't like anyone. But we talked today and you survived. My guess is that you're just shy."

He hung the last pair of pants.

"Mind if I ask you a question?"

He sighed.

"What are you doing after work?"

It had been three years since Henry had last ridden in a car—not since he first started having bad thoughts. Now he remembered why. The bus might be crowded and slow, but it was safe as the living-room couch. Cars were vicious. The streets seethed with tense, drunk, angry, worried, impatient drivers. They were lost, late, stuck in traffic, and their windshields kept fogging up. There was no place to park, some scut had just cut them off, so they screamed back at their radios. He could see them jittering behind the steering wheels of their weapons, feel the darkness inside him feasting on their anger.

He should have known better than to disrupt the routines. The monster was back.

"It's because they think I'm their mother," said Celeste, who drove as if she were alone on the road. "For a cat, leaving a dead mouse in the middle of the kitchen floor is the best way to say 'I love you.' They can't understand why I'm not grateful. Probably think I'm crazy."

Her junker '82 Escort would have lost a collision with a lunchbox. He grasped the shoulder belt with his left arm; his right hand crushed the armrest on the door. Something was happening.

"My mom used to say that there are two kinds of people in the world, cat people and dog people. But come to find out there're all kinds of people. Bird people, fish people, snake people, plant people, even petless people. Bet that's you. You don't strike me as the pet type."

He shook his head.

"See? So what does that mean? That you're not human?"

Riding a tuna wagon down the mean streets was bad enough, but what really spooked him was Celeste's driving. She was barely tall enough to see over the dashboard. He had never realized how big her hump was until he had watched her wiggle it into the tiny car. It forced her forward so that she seemed to be looking through the steering wheel at the road. Except she wasn't. She kept trying to make eye contact with him while she babbled about cats.

"Of course, Slippers leaves most of the little prizes, these days. Figaro isn't quite the mouser he used to be since the operation. They cut a tumor off his chest. Cost me two hundred dollars. So what about your dad? You didn't say whether he's covered by insurance or not."

"We're okay." Henry should never have told her that he always visited his dad on the way home from work. And then he should've realized what would happen when she'd asked what hospital he was in. And then he should've lied about the forty-minute bus ride that got him there fifteen minutes before visiting hours ended. He and his dad did not have that much to say to one another anyway.

"Pick a lane, Grandma!" She swerved around a LeBaron with Alabama plates. "That's good, because a hospital bill can kill you faster than any peckerhead doctor. Believe me, it'd be cheaper for him to stay in the presidential suite at the Sheraton. Probably more fun. How is he taking it anyway? My mother died of lung cancer, which isn't surprising seeing as how she smoked like Pittsburgh. She was an okay mom, better than I deserved. But I'll tell you, she was a bitch at the end. It was really hard."

"He's drugged," said Henry. "Doesn't talk much."

She signaled for a left turn, and the Escort rattled up the ramp onto the interstate. "See," she said. "Almost there. Dad will have a nice surprise." As the speedometer skulked toward seventy, Henry braced against the floorboards hard enough to leave footprints. "I think the worst of it was when she decided she had to find God before she died. She hadn't been within spitting distance of a church for forty years, and the next thing I know she's a born-again Baptist. Three weeks later I buried her. Only I have to put up with this douche bag in a collar who throws dirt on her and talks about how she's eating bonbons with Jesus in the Kingdom of God. And charging me fifty bucks for the privilege. You're not a believer, are you, Henry?"

Henry hesitated, fighting a bad thought. If he touched her now, she'd faint. He could whip the wheel over, and they'd jump the median into the oncoming traffic. "I go to church every day," he said.

"Oh." She turned pale, as if he'd said his hobby was drowning kittens. "Me and my big mouth." She signaled for Exit 7. "Sorry. I guess I fucked up." At the bottom of the ramp, Memorial loomed like a giant's headstone. She pulled up to the main entrance. "See you tomorrow then. Sorry."

"Yeah." Henry bolted from the car before the monster ripped her hump off and stuffed it down her throat.

"You look like a bum." Roger West had been cranked into a semiupright position and propped in his hospital bed with pillows. "You come in here again, you shave." Cancer had chewed on him until there was only the wrinkled brown pit of a man left. "Why're you here?" His eyes were bright with pain.

"I came to visit, Dad. I always come."

"Not before the pill, you don't. Time is it?"

Henry glanced at his watch. "Four-eleven."

"Jesus God, nineteen years until four-thirty. Go find the nurse, tell her I can't wait. Service stinks in this lousy hospital you stuck me in, kid. I keep begging them for the pill, but they don't bring me nothing.'' His fingers curled and scrabbled at the sheet. ''Why am I here? I hate this.''

''You're sick, Dad. The doctor brought you here to take care of you.''

''That's right.'' He licked his lips. ''Okay.''

''The reason I'm early today is I didn't take the bus. I got a ride over.''

His dad closed his eyes. He sounded like he was breathing through a straw; the arms that used to hold Henry were limp as wet cardboard. Henry sat beside the bed and gazed out the window. At least his dad had the view. The middle bed was empty. The privacy curtain was drawn around Mr. DeCredico's bed near the door.

''What she say?'' His dad didn't open his eyes.

''Who?''

''The nurse. My son's coming, don't you understand? I need my pill.''

The room got very small then, so Henry went to the hall. He leaned against the doorway and listened to the fluorescents hum. Down the hall someone was watching *Jeopardy.* The PA system chimed. He scuffed the carpet. It was gun-barrel gray. The wallpaper was beige and shiny and easy to wash. Henry rubbed a hand through the stubble along his jaw. It wasn't a bad thought to want to kill Dad. He could do it with a pillow; he wouldn't even need the Beretta. Dad would be grateful for the favor. It'd be payback for everything he had done for Henry, bringing him up all by himself. But this was the only murder the monster didn't lust for, and Henry didn't have the spunk to do it by himself. He went back in.

''You're early,'' his dad said. ''You didn't get fired, did you?''

''No, Dad, I told you, I got a ride with someone.''

''A ride? With someone?''

The monster hated Celeste and, for the moment, so did Henry. She had done this to them by disrupting the routine. He should've taken the bus and his dad would've scarfed the pill and none of this mung would've happened.

''Time is it?''

''Almost four-thirty.''

His dad's laugh sounded like a cough. There was a plant with long shiny leaves like swords that he had bought for his dad by the window. Snake plant, the florist had said. Nothing could kill it. Henry could see the interstate, the bridges, and the river glittering like the road to heaven. His dad had a room with a view on the twelfth floor. All the fabric snobs in the worsted wool suits he cleaned would kill for the chance to sit behind a desk with a view like this.

"Know why I can't get a pill? I can't pay. If I still had a credit card, I could charge all the pills I need." He swallowed painfully. "I know what they're trying to do. They're hoping I'll get sick of the lousy service and leave. I should. Just go home."

"You're sick, Dad."

"Don't tell me that. You don't know what sick is. You get a runny nose, you take a day off. But I'm empty. Nothing inside me. At least the pills fill me up." His mouth hung open as he gasped for breath. "But they're not giving me mine because you sold the house. That's why I can't go home, isn't it? I get sick and you let them take everything. I built that house. Where's my furniture, Henry?"

"Take it easy, Dad. It's safe in the warehouse."

"You think I can live in some damn warehouse?"

"Don't swear. When you get out, we'll rent an apartment."

"I'm not getting out. You're just like the nurses. Here I'm dying and you want to wait until four-thirty. I don't know why I had you, you useless bum. We would've been better off buying a dog."

"Why, Mr. West, good afternoon." The nurse carried a tray with a clear plastic cup of apple juice and a tiny paper cup with the pill. "You're early today." Her acrylic uniform dress was whiter than anything Henry had ever cleaned. There was so much pain in the room, it was hard not to touch her. He flashed on the monster hurling her through the window. There'd be stains on her uniform that would never come out.

"He wants his pill," he said.

"Of course he does, it's four-thirty."

"Don't mind him." Roger West lifted his head off the pillow. "He's having a rough day." He opened his mouth for the pill as if he were taking the sacrament.

Henry was dancing with the boombox. No more routines; it was finally happening. Guns N' Roses was cranked to the bughouse level. He cradled the noise to his chest, balanced it across his shoulders like an electronic hump, swung it in a straight-arm loop over his head. Someone was out to get Axl Rose, but he wasn't going to take it. Neither was Henry, not as long as Slash was allowed to perform brain surgery with a guitar. Henry's underwear was not as white as a nurse's uniform. He had pulled one sock halfway off. The bathtub was filling up.

He whirled into the bedroom, set the boombox on the nightstand, and hurled himself at the unmade bed. He bounced up and sprang again. Again, three, five times, as if the mattress were the plane of sanity that he might crash through, if only he tried hard enough. The song ended, the next one was about drugs. Henry didn't need drugs; he was high on death. He punched the Eject button, flung the tape across the room, and carried the boombox to the shrine. The door was wide open.

He slapped the Talking Heads into the player and snatched the Beretta off the altar. *Wham!* No more Louis Farrakhan. *Wham!* Die, Robert De Niro. But pretending wasn't enough anymore. He wanted to flash like he had when Phil had put a hand on him. He wanted to feel the gun kick when he pulled the trigger. While David Byrne was quavering about psycho killers, Henry decided to show the Beretta the rest of their nasty little apartment. The boombox came along for the ride. They turned off the water in the bathtub and changed channels on the TV and straightened the picture of Henry and Dad at the lake. They were on their way to the kitchen to look behind the paper towels under the sink when the phone rang. *Qu'est-ce que c'est?*

As soon as he turned off the music, he knew it was the hospital calling to tell him Dad had died. Henry had let him down, hadn't given him what he wanted. It rang five times, six. A hand he wasn't quite in control of trembled over the phone but did not pick up. *Ring.* He was crying. *Ring.*

"Hello," he said.

"Henry? This is Celeste."

Hail Mary, he thought, full of grace. "Yeah?"

"Hey look, I'm sorry for what I said this afternoon. You know, about religion and all. It's my problem, okay? It has nothing to do with you."

He dabbed at a tear running down his cheek. "Uh-huh."

"Anyway, I've been driving around ever since then, thinking about what a jerk I was and I just looked at my watch and saw that it was six-thirty and realized I was hungry and I'm just around the block from Angelina's and I was wondering . . . I was wondering if you liked pizza? Because I was thinking I'd spring for a large with pepperoni or mushroom or extra cheese or whatever you want and bring it over and we could split it and then maybe I could convince you to forgive me for being such an idiot. I mean, it's okay if you're busy but . . ."

"Mushroom," said the monster.

Her squeal of delight made the speaker buzz. "Mushroom? All right! How about something to drink? Beer? Wine?"

"Carlo Rossi Pink Chablis."

"No problem. This is great, Henry. I knew you'd understand. This shouldn't take long; what if we say I'll be there around seven-fifteen. I mean if that's too soon, I can come later."

"Seven-fifteen," it said. "You know where I live?"

"Sure, One-seventeen Queensberry, apartment twenty-two. Jerry told me. See you then."

The monster hung up the phone and glanced around. The apartment needed some straightening up. Things needed to be put in their places. It stuck the gun in its belt and went out to the kitchen to check behind the paper towels.

The bed was made, the breakfast dishes were washed and put away, the living-room floor was vacuumed, the door to the shrine was locked, and the Beretta was loaded and stashed under a cushion of the couch. The sound of Henry's mewling for it to stop came as if from a great distance, as it opened the door for its guest.

"Pouring out there." The rain had flattened Celeste's hair but hadn't washed away her smile. "It's a good night to stay home."

"Thanks for coming." It took the pizza box from her. "Come in." The top was soaked, but the bottom was still hot.

"Ta-da!" She pulled a squat jug of wine from a paper bag. "Took me three stores to find it."

It hung her slicker over the bathtub and saw that she'd changed her clothes. She'd been wearing a red pocket tee and acid-washed jeans under her work smock. Now she had on a ramie skirt that hung just above the knee and a fake batik polyester blouse—a smart choice of fabrics. You could get bloodstains out of ramie, as long as they were fresh.

It had already decided not to rush. Now that it was in charge, there was no need to lunge; it could enjoy the moment. Besides, even monsters liked mushroom pizza and it hadn't eaten since lunch.

They sat at the kitchen table and tucked away all but a slice and drank sweet wine out of coffee cups while she babbled about crusts and exotic toppings and *Roseanne* and the high cost of mufflers and kitty litter. She asked what kind of movies it liked, and it told her comedies but that its VCR was broken. She confessed to staying up too many late nights with horror flicks. Her favorite was the *Nightmare on Elm Street* series.

"Too violent for me." The monster couldn't help but notice that she was watching it like a movie. Her eyes never left its face. She was lit with an expression of fascinated suspense that got brighter and brighter with each cup of wine.

"The problem is," she was saying, "they're running out of ideas. You can watch just so many decapitations before you stop taking them seriously. Half the horror flicks these days play for laughs. The other half are about as scary as Count Chocula."

It offered the jug for a refill. She laughed and waved it away. "I've still got plenty left. You trying to get rid of it or what?"

"Maybe we should move to the couch?" It was excited now. "More comfortable there."

She stumbled coming out of her chair and it caught her, exercising so much restraint it thought it might burst.

" 'Scuse me," she said, her voice suddenly husky. "Hell of a lot drunker up here than I thought." She steadied herself with an arm around its waist and let it lead her down the hall. Her body was firm under her clothes; it could feel her heart pumping. "Where'd you say we were going?"

It steered her through the door. "You remember the living room?"

"Ah, yes. We were introduced earlier. Miss Lamp." She bowed. "Mr. TV. Mr. Table." She giggled and twisted around in a deft way that took it by surprise. She pressed closer and closer, arching up on tiptoes, stretching until their lips touched. Her tongue nipped against his teeth and she was kissing Henry, not the monster. When he realized he was back in control, he began to tremble.

"I know." She moaned softly and pushed him toward the couch. "Me too," she said. "But sit down first."

He slid as far away from the gun as he could and gaped as she unbuttoned her blouse.

"You probably think I do this all the time." She was wearing more underwear than he had expected. Her bra was white lace, sheer enough that he could see her nipples. Above it was a wide elastic harness made of ace bandages stitched together. He remembered the three-piece bathing suit, but he didn't laugh. Her skin frightened him. "Well, you're wrong," she said. "I don't get many requests, and the ones that do ask are always perverts." She released three metal clips, and the harness unwrapped itself and fell to the floor.

The hump on her back unfolded with a sound like hands rubbing together. Celeste grunted and twisted her head back and forth as if she had a crick. "No, it's all right," she said. "They just get a little stiff after being cooped up all day." She shook herself, and two pointed masses of flesh dropped low behind her back and then slowly rose up past her shoulders.

She smiled shyly at him and beat her wings; he could feel air on his face. They were double-jointed; he could see outlines of bones that reminded him of posters of starving children.

"Oh, my God," he said.

The skin stretched between the needle digits was the same color as her face, flushed an embarrassed red. He could see a filigree of arteries. She had a span of about four feet.

"Can you fly?"

She shook her head. "I'm afraid they're pretty useless." She giggled. "Except maybe as fans."

"I don't . . . this is . . . my God, Celeste." He shivered. "Can I touch them?"

"Mister, you can touch anything you want."

It was as if he was swimming across the room toward her. The wine burned in his belly like a pool of fire. She turned her back to him and held her wings still. They were covered with downy black hair and were hot as her lips. "Hey, you, I'm standing here in my underwear and you're still dressed." She faced him. "Time to catch up." Her fingers tickled his chest as she took off his white shirt. She laughed drunkenly as she fumbled at his belt.

His legs went out beneath him and he sank to his knees. "Thank you, God." Now he knew he could beat the monster. "You've sent me an angel."

She grabbed a fistful of his hair and hauled him up.

"Listen, Henry." He had never seen her angry before. "I walked in here on my own two feet because you're the only man who never stared at me. Nobody pushed me in here, especially not God. There is no fucking God! Or if there is, He's got to be the most heartless asshole in the universe." Her wings were flapping like pennants. "You look at me. Go ahead. I'm a freak, a monster. I didn't ask to be one, and I had to learn to live with these damn things. And nobody helped—my mother gave me this dumb name—I still haven't got any goddamn help. So if you want to thank somebody, you can thank Celeste Sloboda for staying sane despite the way most everyone stares." She was crying. "So that's the way it is, okay? I've pissed you off, you pissed me off, and now we can go home and hate each other."

"Celeste." She could think whatever she wanted. He knew God's work when he saw it. She was full of a kind of pain the monster couldn't use. Only he could. He knew that as long as he believed in this miracle, nobody, nothing could stop him from being himself. "Let go of my hair?"

She released him and immediately stroked the back of his head. "I didn't mean to hurt you." Her gaze softened. "I'm sorry. I didn't want it like this."

He could feel the monster slipping away. "I want you," he said. Her face kept getting bigger until it was the only thing Henry could see. They kissed forever and amen. Henry wasn't sure how he got naked. As he led her to the bedroom, he couldn't remember if any woman had ever seen him naked before.

She paused by the bathroom, traced the line of his chin, and smiled. "Henry," she said, "do you think you might shave?"

Much later, he eased out from under the covers so as not to wake her. He realized where the monster had gone when it left him. He pulled on his jeans, padded into the living room, and felt under the cushion. It was in the Beretta. His first thought was to lose it in the dumpster behind his apartment, but he was barefoot and it had set him back $538. Tomorrow after work he could pawn it and buy some nice woman thing for Celeste.

He stripped the magazine, picked the shells out, and wrapped everything in a green garbage bag. Or maybe he should keep the gun for protection. God knows there were monsters loose in the city. He hid it under the sink and snuck back to bed with his angel.

itsy bitsy spider

hen I found out that my father was still alive after all these years and living at Strawberry Fields, I thought he'd gotten just what he deserved. Retroburbs are where the old, scared people go to hide. I'd always pictured the people in them as deranged losers. Visiting some fantasy world like the disneys or Carlucci's Carthage is one thing, moving to one is another. Sure, 2038 is messy, but it's a hell of a lot better than nineteen-sixty-whatever.

Now that I'd arrived at 144 Bluejay Way, I realized the place was worse than I had imagined. Strawberry Fields was pretending to be some long, lost suburb of the late twentieth century, except that it had the sterile monotony of cheap VR. It was clean, all right, and neat, but it was everywhere the same. And the scale was wrong. The lots were squeezed together and all the houses had shrunk—like the dreams of their owners. They were about the size of a one-car garage, modular units tarted up at the factory to look like ranches, with old double-hung storm windows and hardened siding of harvest gold, barn red, forest green. Of course, there were no real garages; faux Mustangs and VW buses cruised the quiet streets. Their carbrains were listening for a summons from Barbara Chesley next door at 142, or the Goltzes across the street, who might be headed to Penny Lanes to bowl a few frames, or the hospital to die.

There was a beach chair with blue nylon webbing on the front stoop of 144 Bluejay Way. A brick walk led to it, dividing two patches of carpet moss, green as a dream. There were names and addresses printed in huge lightstick letters on all the doors in the neighborhood; no doubt many Strawberry Fielders were easily confused. The owner of this one was Peter Fancy. He had been born Peter Fanelli, but had legally taken his stage name not long after his first success as Prince Hal in *Henry IV, Part I.* I was a Fancy too; the name was one of the few things of my father's I had kept.

I stopped at the door and let it look me over. "You're Jen," it said.

"Yes." I waited in vain for it to open or to say something else. "I'd like to see Mr. Fancy, please." The old man's house had worse manners than he did. "He knows I'm coming," I said. "I sent him several messages." Which he had never answered, but I didn't mention that.

"Just a minute," said the door. "She'll be right with you."

She? The idea that he might be with another woman now hadn't occurred to me. I'd lost track of my father a long time ago—on purpose. The last time we'd actually visited overnight was when I was twenty. Mom gave me a ticket to Port Gemini, where he was doing the Shakespeare in Space program. The orbital was great, but staying with him was like being underwater. I think I must have held my breath for the entire week. After that there were a few sporadic calls, a couple of awkward dinners—all at his instigation. Then twenty-three years of nothing.

I never hated him, exactly. When he left, I just decided to show solidarity with Mom and be done with him. If acting was more important than his family, then to hell with Peter Fancy. Mom was horrified when I told her how I felt. She cried and claimed the divorce was as much her fault as his. It was too much for me to handle; I was only eleven years old when they separated. I needed to be on *someone's* side, and so I had chosen her. She never did stop trying to talk me into finding him again, even though after a while it only made me mad at her. For the past few years, she'd been warning me that I'd developed a warped view of men.

But she was a smart woman, my mom—a winner. Sure, she'd had troubles, but she'd founded three companies, was a millionaire by twenty-five. I missed her.

A lock clicked and the door opened. Standing in the dim interior was a little girl in a gold-and-white checked dress. Her dark curly hair was tied in a ribbon. She was wearing white ankle socks and black Mary Jane shoes that were so shiny they had to be plastic. There was a Band-Aid on her left knee.

"Hello, Jen. I was hoping you'd really come." Her voice surprised me. It was resonant, impossibly mature. At first glance I'd guessed she was three, maybe four; I'm not much good at guessing kids' ages. Now I realized that this must be a bot—a made person.

"You look just like I thought you would." She smiled, stood on tiptoe, and raised a delicate little hand over her head. I had to bend to shake it. The hand was warm, slightly moist, and very realistic. She had to belong to Strawberry Fields; there was no way my father could afford a bot with skin this real.

"Please come in." She waved on the lights. "We're so happy you're here." The door closed behind me.

The playroom took up almost half of the little house. Against one wall was a miniature kitchen. Toy dishes were drying in a rack next to the sink; the pink refrigerator barely came up to my waist. The table was full-sized; it had two normal chairs and a booster chair. Opposite this was a bed with a ruffled Pumpkin Patty bedspread. About a dozen dolls and stuffed animals were arranged along the far edge of the mattress. I recognized most of them: Pooh, Mr. Moon, Baby Rollypolly, the Sleepums, Big Bird. And the wallpaper was familiar too: Oz figures like Toto and the Wizard and the Cowardly Lion on a field of Munchkin blue.

"We had to make a few changes," said the bot. "Do you like it?"

The room seemed to tilt then. I took a small unsteady step, and everything righted itself. My dolls, my wallpaper, the chest of drawers from Grandma Fanelli's cottage in Hyannis. I stared at the bot and recognized her for the first time.

She was me.

"What is this," I said, "some kind of sick joke?" I felt like I'd just been slapped in the face.

"Is something wrong?" the bot said. "Tell me. Maybe we can fix it."

I swiped at her and she danced out of reach. I don't know what I would have done if I had caught her. Maybe smashed her through the picture window onto the patch of front lawn or shaken her until pieces started falling off. But the bot wasn't responsible, my father was. Mom would never have defended him if she'd known about *this.* The old bastard. I couldn't believe it. Here I was, shuddering with anger, after years of feeling nothing for him.

There was an interior door just beyond some shelves filled with old-fashioned paper books. I didn't take time to look as I went past, but I knew that Dr. Seuss and A. A. Milne and L. Frank Baum would be on those shelves. The door had no knob.

"Open up," I shouted. It ignored me, so I kicked it. "Hey!"

"Jennifer." The bot tugged at the back of my jacket. "I must ask you. . . ."

"You can't have me!" I pressed my ear to the door. Silence. "I'm not this thing you made." I kicked it again. "You hear?"

Suddenly an announcer was shouting in the next room. "*. . . Into the post to Russell, who kicks it out to Havlicek all alone at the top of the key, he shoots . . . and Baylor with the strong rebound.*" The asshole was trying to drown me out.

"If you don't come away from that door right now," said the bot, "I'm calling Security."

"What are they going to do?" I said. "I'm the long-lost daughter, here for a visit. And who the hell are you, anyway?"

"I'm bonded to him, Jen. Your father is no longer competent to handle his own affairs. I'm his legal guardian."

"Shit." I kicked the door one last time, but my heart wasn't in it. I shouldn't have been surprised that he had slipped over the edge. He was almost ninety.

"If you want to sit and talk, I'd like that very much." The bot gestured toward a banana-yellow beanbag chair. "Otherwise, I'm going to have to ask you to leave."

It was the shock of seeing the bot, I told myself—I'd reacted like a hurt little girl. But I was a grown woman and it was time to start behaving like one. I wasn't here to let Peter Fancy worm his way back into my feelings. I had come because of Mom.

"Actually," I said, "I'm here on business." I opened my purse. "If you're running his life now, I guess this is for you." I passed her the envelope and settled back, tucking my legs beneath me. There is no way for an adult to sit gracefully in a beanbag chair.

She slipped the check out. "It's from Mother." She paused, then corrected herself, "Her estate." She didn't seem surprised.

"Yes."

"It's too generous."

"That's what I thought."

"She must've taken care of you too?"

"I'm fine." I wasn't about to discuss the terms of Mom's will with my father's toy daughter.

"I would've liked to have known her," said the bot. She slid the check back into the envelope and set it aside. "I've spent a lot of time imagining Mother."

I had to work hard not to snap at her. Sure, this bot had at least a human-equivalent intelligence and would be a free citizen someday, assuming she didn't break down first. But she had a cognizor for a brain and a heart fabricated in a vat. How could she possibly imagine my mom, especially when all she had to go on was whatever lies *he* had told her?

"So how bad is he?"

She gave me a sad smile and shook her head. "Some days are better than others. He has no clue who President Huong is or about the quake, but he can still recite the dagger scene from *Macbeth*. I haven't told him that Mother died. He'd just forget it ten minutes later."

"Does he know what you are?"

"I am many things, Jen."

"Including me."

"You're a role I'm playing, not who I am." She stood. "Would you like some tea?"

"Okay." I still wanted to know why Mom had left my father $438,000 in her will. If he couldn't tell me, maybe the bot could.

She went to her kitchen, opened a cupboard, and took out a regular-sized cup. It looked like a bucket in her little hand. "I don't suppose you still drink Constant Comment?"

His favorite. I had long since switched to rafallo. "That's fine." I remembered when I was a kid, my father used to brew cups for the two of us from the same bag because Constant Comment was so expensive. "I thought they went out of business long ago."

"I mix my own. I'd be interested to hear how accurate you think the recipe is."

"I suppose you know how I like it?"

She chuckled.

"So does he need the money?"

The microwave dinged. "Very few actors get rich," said the bot. I didn't think there had been microwaves in the sixties, but then strict historical accuracy wasn't really the point of Strawberry Fields. "Especially when they have a weakness for Shakespeare."

"Then how come he lives here and not in some flop? And how did he afford you?"

She pinched sugar between her index finger and thumb, then rubbed them together over the cup. It was something I still did, but only when I was by myself. A nasty habit; Mom used to yell at him for teaching it to me. "I was a gift." She shook a teabag loose from a canister shaped like an acorn and plunged it into the boiling water. "From Mother."

The bot offered the cup to me; I accepted it nervelessly. "That's not true." I could feel the blood draining from my face.

"I can lie if you'd prefer, but I'd rather not." She pulled the booster chair away from the table and turned it to face me. "There are many things about themselves that they never told us, Jen. I've always wondered why that was."

I felt logy and a little stupid, as if I had just woken from a thirty-year nap. "She just gave you to him?"

"And bought him this house, paid all his bills, yes."

"But why?"

"*You* knew her," said the bot. "I was hoping you could tell me."

I couldn't think of what to say or do. Since there was a cup in my hand, I took a sip. For an instant, the scent of tea and dried oranges carried me back to when I was a little girl and I was sitting in Grandma Fanelli's kitchen in a wet bathing suit, drinking Constant Comment that my father had made to keep my teeth from chattering. There were knots like brown eyes in the pine walls, and the green linoleum was slick where I had dripped on it.

"Well?"

"It's good," I said absently and raised the cup to her. "No, really, just like I remember."

She clapped her hands in excitement. "So," said the bot. "What was Mother like?"

It was an impossible question, so I tried to let it bounce off me. But then neither of us said anything; we just stared at each other across a yawning gulf of time and experience. In the silence, the question stuck. Mom had died three months ago, and this was the first time since the funeral that I'd thought of her as she really had been—not the papery ghost in the hospital room. I remembered how, after the divorce, she always took my calls when she was at the office, even if it was late, and how she used to step on imaginary brakes whenever I drove her anywhere and how grateful I was that she didn't cry when I told her that Rob and I were getting divorced. I thought about Easter eggs and raspberry Pop-Tarts and when she sent me to Antibes for a year when I was fourteen and that perfume she wore on my father's opening nights and the way they used to waltz on the patio at the house in Waltham.

"West is walking the ball up court, setting his offense with fifteen seconds to go on the shot clock, nineteen in the half . . ."

The beanbag chair that I was in faced the picture window. Behind me, I could hear the door next to the bookcase open.

"Jones and Goodrich are in each other's jerseys down low, and now Chamberlain swings over and calls for the ball on the weak side . . ."

I twisted around to look over my shoulder. The great Peter Fancy was making his entrance.

Mom once told me that when she met my father, he was typecast playing men that women fall hopelessly in love with. He'd had great successes as Stanley Kowalski in *Streetcar* and Sky Masterson in *Guys and Dolls* and the Vicomte de Valmont in *Les Liaisons Dangereuses.* The years had eroded his good looks but had not obliterated them; from a distance he was still a handsome man. He had a shock of close-cropped white hair. The beautiful cheekbones were still there; the chin was as sharply defined as it had been in his first head shot. His gray eyes were distant and a little dreamy, as if he were preoccupied with the War of the Roses or the problem of evil.

"Jen," he said, "what's going on out here?" He still had the big voice that could reach into the second balcony without a mike. I thought for a moment he was talking to me.

"We have company, Daddy," said the bot, in a four-year-old trill that took me by surprise. "A lady."

"I can see that it's a lady, sweetheart." He took a hand from the pocket of his jeans, stroked the touchpad on his belt, and his exolegs walked him stiffly across the room. "I'm Peter Fancy," he said.

"The lady is from Strawberry Fields." The bot swung around behind my father. She shot me a look that made the terms and conditions of my continued presence clear: if I broke the illusion, I was out. "She came by to see if everything is all right with our house." The bot disturbed me even more, now that she sounded like young Jen Fancy.

As I heaved myself out of the beanbag chair, my father gave me one of those lopsided flirting grins I knew so well. "Does the lady have a name?" He must have shaved just for the company, because now that he had come close I could see that he had a couple of fresh nicks. There was a button-sized patch of gray whiskers by his ear that he had missed altogether.

"Her name is Ms. Johnson," said the bot. It was my ex, Rob's, last name. I had never been Jennifer Johnson.

"Well, Ms. Johnson," he said, hooking thumbs in his pants pockets. "The water in my toilet is brown."

"I'll . . . um . . . see that it's taken care of." I was at a loss for what to say next, then inspiration struck. "Actually, I had another reason for coming." I could see the bot stiffen. "I don't know if you've seen *Yesterday,* our little newsletter? Anyway, I was talking to Mrs. Chesley next door and she told me that you were an actor once. I was wondering if I might interview you. Just a few questions, if you have the time. I think your neighbors might . . ."

"Were?" he said, drawing himself up. "*Once?* Madam, I am now an actor and will always be."

"My daddy's famous," said the bot.

I cringed at that; it was something I used to say. My father squinted at me. "What did you say your name was?"

"Johnson," I said. "Jane Johnson."

"And you're a reporter? You're sure you're not a critic?"

"Positive."

He seemed satisfied. "I'm Peter Fancy." He extended his right hand to shake. The hand was spotted and bony and it trembled like a reflection in a lake. Clearly whatever magic—or surgeon's skill—it was that had preserved my father's face had not extended to his extremities. I was so disturbed by his infirmity that I took his cold hand in mine and pumped it three, four times. It was dry as a page of one of the bot's dead books. When I let go, the hand seemed steadier. He gestured at the beanbag.

"Sit," he said. "Please."

After I had settled in, he tapped the touchpad and stumped over to the picture window. "Barbara Chesley is a broken and bitter old woman,'' he said, ''and I will not have dinner with her under any circumstances, do you understand?'' He peered up Bluejay Way and down.

''Yes, Daddy,'' said the bot.

''I believe she voted for Nixon, so she has no reason to complain now.'' Apparently satisfied that the neighbor wasn't sneaking up on us, he leaned against the windowsill, facing me. ''Mrs. Thompson, I think today may well be a happy one for both of us. I have an announcement.'' He paused for effect. ''I've been thinking of Lear again.''

The bot settled onto one of her little chairs. ''Oh, Daddy, that's wonderful.''

''It's the only one of the big four I haven't done,'' said my father. ''I was set for a production in Stratford, Ontario, back in '99; Polly Matthews was to play Cordelia. Now there was an actor; she could bring tears to a stone. But then my wife Hannah had one of her bad times and I had to withdraw so I could take care of Jen. The two of us stayed down at my mother's cottage on the Cape; I wasted the entire season tending bar. And when Hannah came out of rehab, she decided that she didn't want to be married to an underemployed actor anymore, so things were tight for a while. She had all the money, so I had to scramble—spent almost two years on the road. But I think it might have been for the best. I was only forty-eight. Too old for Hamlet, too young for Lear. My Hamlet was very well received, you know. There were overtures from PBS about a taping, but that was when the BBC decided to do the Shakespeare series with that doctor, what was his name? Jonathan Miller. So instead of Peter Fancy, we had Derek Jacobi, whose brilliant idea it was to roll across the stage, frothing his lines like a rabid raccoon. You'd think he'd seen an alien, not his father's ghost. Well, that was another missed opportunity, except, of course, that I was too young. Ripeness is all, eh? So I still have Lear to do. Unfinished business. My comeback.''

He bowed, then pivoted solemnly so that I saw him in profile, framed by the picture window. ''Where have I been? Where am I? Fair daylight?'' He held up a trembling hand and blinked at it uncomprehendingly. ''I know not what to say. I swear these are not my hands.''

Suddenly the bot was at his feet. ''O look upon me, sir,'' she said, in her childish voice, ''and hold your hand in benediction o'er me.''

''Pray, do not mock me.'' My father gathered himself in the

flood of morning light. "I am a very foolish, fond old man, fourscore and upward, not an hour more or less; and to deal plainly, I fear I am not in my perfect mind."

He stole a look in my direction, as if to gauge my reaction to his impromptu performance. A frown might have stopped him, a word would have crushed him. Maybe I should have, but I was afraid he'd start talking about Mom again, telling me things I didn't want to know. So I watched instead, transfixed.

"Methinks I should know you"—he rested his hand briefly on the bot's head—"and know this stranger." He fumbled at the controls, and the exolegs carried him across the room toward me. As he drew nearer, he seemed to sluff off the years. "Yet I am mainly ignorant what place this is; and all the skill I have remembers not these garments, nor I know not where I did lodge last night." It was Peter Fancy who stopped before me; his face a mere kiss away from mine. "Do not laugh at me; for, as I am a man, I think this lady to be my child, Cordelia."

He was staring right at me, into me, knifing through make-believe indifference to the wound I'd nursed all these years, the one that had never healed. He seemed to expect a reply, only I didn't have the line. A tiny, sad squeaky voice within me was whimpering, *You left me and you got exactly what you deserve.* But my throat tightened and choked it off.

The bot cried, "And so I am! I am!"

But she had distracted him. I could see confusion begin to deflate him. "Be your tears wet? Yes, faith. I pray . . . weep not. If you have poison for me, I will drink it. I know you do not love me . . ."

He stopped and his brow wrinkled. "It's something about the sisters," he muttered.

"Yes," said the bot, " 'for your sisters have done me wrong . . .' "

"Don't feed me the fucking lines!" he shouted at her. "I'm Peter Fancy, goddamn it!"

After she calmed him down, we had lunch. She let him make the peanut butter and banana sandwiches while she heated up some Campbell's tomato and rice soup, which she poured from a can made of actual metal. The sandwiches were lumpy because he had hacked the bananas into chunks the size of walnuts. She tried to get him to tell me about the daylilies blooming in the backyard and the old Boston Garden and the time he and Mom had had breakfast with Bobby Kennedy. She asked whether he wanted TV dinner or potpie for dinner. He refused all her conversational gambits. He only ate half a bowl of soup.

He pushed back from the table and announced that it was her nap time. The bot put up a perfunctory fuss, although it was clear that it was my father who was tired out. However, the act seemed to perk him up. Another role for his résumé: the doting father. "I'll tell you what," he said. "We'll play your game, sweetheart. But just once—otherwise you'll be cranky tonight."

The two of them perched on the edge of the bot's bed next to Big Bird and the Sleepums. My father started to sing, and the bot immediately joined in.

"The itsy bitsy spider went up the water spout."

Their gestures were almost mirror images, except that his ruined hands actually looked like spiders as they climbed into the air.

"Down came the rain, and washed the spider out."

The bot beamed at him as if he were the only person in the world.

"Out came the sun, and dried up all the rain.

"And the itsy bitsy spider went up the spout again."

When his arms were once again raised over his head, she giggled and hugged him. He let them fall around her, returning her embrace. "That's a good girl," he said. "That's my Jenny."

The look on his face told me that I had been wrong: this was no act. It was as real to him as it was to me. I had tried hard not to, but I still remembered how the two of us always used to play together, Daddy and Jenny, Jen and Dad.

Waiting for Mommy to come home.

He kissed her and she snuggled under the blankets. I felt my eyes stinging.

"But if you do the play," she said, "when will you be back?"

"What play?"

"That one you were telling me. The king and his daughters."

"There's no such play, Jenny." He sifted her black curls through his hands. "I'll never leave you, don't worry now. Never again." He rose unsteadily and caught himself on the chest of drawers.

"Nighty noodle," said the bot.

"Pleasant dreams, sweetheart," said my father. "I love you."

"I love you too."

I expected him to say something to me, but he didn't even

seem to realize that I was still in the room. He shambled across the playroom, opened the door to his bedroom, and went in.

"I'm sorry about that," said the bot, speaking again as an adult.

"Don't be," I said. I coughed—something in my throat. "It was fine. I was very . . . touched."

"He's usually a lot happier. Sometimes he works in the garden." The bot pulled the blankets aside and swung her legs out of the bed. "He likes to vacuum."

"Yes."

"I take good care of him."

I nodded and reached for my purse. "I can see that." I had to go. "Is it enough?"

She shrugged. "He's my daddy."

"I meant the money. Because if it's not, I'd like to help."

"Thank you. He'd appreciate that."

The front door opened for me, but I paused before stepping out into Strawberry Fields. "What about . . . after?"

"When he dies? My bond terminates. He said he'd leave the house to me. I know you could contest that, but I'll need to sell in order to pay for my twenty-year maintenance."

"No, no. That's fine. You deserve it."

She came to the door and looked up at me, little Jen Fancy and the woman she would never become.

"You know, it's you he loves," she said. "I'm just a stand-in."

"He loves his little girl," I said. "Doesn't do me any good—I'm forty-seven."

"It could if you let it." She frowned. "I wonder if that's why Mother did all this. So you'd find out."

"Or maybe she was just plain sorry." I shook my head. She was a smart woman, my mom. I would've liked to have known her.

"So, Ms. Fancy, maybe you can visit us again sometime." The bot grinned and shook my hand. "Daddy's usually in a good mood after his nap. He sits out front on his beach chair and waits for the ice cream truck. He always buys us some. Our favorite is Yellow Submarine. It's vanilla with fat butterscotch swirls, dipped in white chocolate. I know it sounds kind of odd, but it's good."

"Yes," I said absently, thinking about all the things Mom had told me about my father. I was hearing them now for the first time. "That might be nice."

mr. boy

I **was already twitching by the time they strapped me** down. Nasty pleasure and beautiful pain crackled through me, branching and rebranching like lightning. Extreme feelings are hard to tell apart when you have endorphins spilling across your brain. Another spasm shot down my legs and curled my toes. I moaned. The stiffs wore surgical masks that hid their mouths, but I knew they were smiling. They hated me because my mom could afford to have me stunted. When I really was just a kid I did not understand that. Now I hated them back; it helped me get through the therapy. We had a very clean transaction going here. No secrets between us.

Even though it hurts, getting stunted is still the ultimate flash. As I unlived my life, I overdosed on dying feelings and experiences. My body was not big enough to hold them all; I thought I was going to explode. I must have screamed because

I could see the laugh lines crinkling around the stiffs' eyes. You do not have to worry about laugh lines after they twank your genes and reset your mitotic limits. My face was smooth and I was going to be twelve years old forever, or at least as long as Mom kept paying for my rejuvenation.

I giggled as the short one leaned over me and pricked her catheter into my neck. Even through the mask, I could smell her breath. She reeked of dead meat.

Getting stunted always left me wobbly and thick, but this time I felt like last Tuesday's pizza. One of the stiffs had to roll me out of recovery in a wheelchair.

The lobby looked like a furniture showroom. Even the plants had been newly waxed. There was nothing to remind the clients that they were bags of blood and piss. You are all biological machines now, said the lobby, clean as space-station lettuce. A scattering of people sat on the hard chairs. Stennie and Comrade were fidgeting by the elevators. They looked as if they were thinking of rearranging the furniture—like maybe into a pile in the middle of the room. Even before they waved, the stiff seemed to know that they were waiting for me.

Comrade smiled. *"Zdrast'ye."*

"You okay, Mr. Boy?" said Stennie. Stennie was a grapefruit-yellow stenonychosaurus with a brown underbelly. His razor-clawed toes clicked against the slate floor as he walked.

"He's still a little weak," said the stiff, as he set the chair's parking brake. He strained to act nonchalant, not realizing that Stennie enjoys being stared at. "He needs rest. Are you his brother?" he said to Comrade.

Comrade appeared to be a teenaged spike neck with a head of silky black hair that hung to his waist. He wore a window coat on which twenty-three different talking heads chattered. He could pass for human, even though he was really a Panasonic. *"Nyet,"* said Comrade. "I'm just another one of his hallucinations."

The poor stiff gave him a dry nervous cough that might have been meant as a chuckle. He was probably wondering whether Stennie wanted to take me home or eat me for lunch. I always thought that the way Stennie got reshaped was more funny-looking than fierce—a python that had rear-ended an ostrich. But even though he was a head shorter than me, he did have enormous eyes and a mouthful of serrated teeth. He stopped next to the wheelchair and rose up to his full height. "I appreciate everything you've done.'' Stennie offered the stiff his spindly three-fingered hand to shake. ''Sorry if he caused any trouble.''

The stiff took it gingerly, then shrieked and flew backward. I mean, he jumped almost a meter off the floor. Everyone in the lobby turned, and Stennie opened his hand and waved the joy buzzer. He slapped his tail against the slate in triumph. Stennie's sense of humor was extreme, but then he was only thirteen years old.

Stennie's parents had given him the Nissan Alpha for his twelfth birthday, and we had been customizing it ever since. We installed blue mirror glass, and Stennie painted scenes from the Late Cretaceous on the exterior body armor. We ripped out all the seats, put in a wall-to-wall gel mat and a fridge and a microwave and a screen and a minidish. Comrade had even done an illegal operation on the carbrain so that we could override in an emergency and actually steer the Alpha ourselves with a joystick. It would have been cramped, but we would have lived in Stennie's car if our parents had let us.

''You okay there, Mr. Boy?'' said Stennie.

''Mmm.'' As I watched the trees whoosh past in the rain, I pretended that the car was standing still and the world was passing me by.

''Think of something to do, okay?'' Stennie had the car and all and he was fun to play with, but ideas were not his specialty. He was probably smart for a dinosaur. ''I'm bored.''

''Leave him alone, will you?'' Comrade said.

''He hasn't said anything yet.'' Stennie stretched and nudged me with his foot. ''Say something.'' He had legs like a horse: yellow skin stretched tight over long bones and stringy muscle.

''*Prosrees!* He just had his genes twanked, you jack.'' Comrade always took good care of me. Or tried to. ''Remember what that's like? He's in damage control.''

''Maybe I should go to socialization,'' Stennie said. ''Aren't they having a dance this afternoon?''

''You're talking to me?'' said the Alpha. ''You haven't earned enough learning credits to socialize. You're a quiz behind and forty-five minutes short of E-class. You haven't linked since . . .''

''Just shut up and drive me over.'' Stennie and the Alpha did not get along. He thought the car was too strict. ''I'll make up the plugging quiz, okay?'' He probed a mess of empty juice boxes and snack wrappers with his foot. ''Anyone see my comm anywhere?''

Stennie's schoolcomm was wedged behind my cushion. ''You know,'' I said, ''I can't take much more of this.'' I leaned forward, wriggled it free, and handed it over.

''Of what, *poputchik?*'' said Comrade. ''Joyriding? Listening to the lizard here?''

''Being stunted.''

Stennie flipped up the screen of his comm and went on-line with the school's computer. ''You guys help me, okay?'' He retracted his claws and tapped at the oversized keyboard.

''It's extreme while you're on the table,'' I said, ''but now I feel empty. Like I've lost myself.''

''You'll get over it,'' said Stennie. ''First question: Brand name of the first wiseguys sold for home use?''

''NEC-Bots, of course,'' said Comrade.

''Geneva? It got nuked, right?''

''*Da.*''

''Haile Selassie was that king of Ethiopia who the Marleys claim is god, right? Name the Cold Wars: Nicaragua, Angola . . . Korea was the first.'' Typing was hard work for Stennie; he did not have enough fingers for it. ''One was something like Venezuela. Or something.''

''Sure it wasn't Venice?''

''Or Venus?'' I said, but Stennie was not paying attention.

''All right, I know that one. And that. The Sovs built the first space station. Ronald Reagan—he was the president who dropped the bomb?''

Comrade reached inside of his coat and pulled out an envelope. ''I got you something, Mr. Boy. A get-well present for your collection.''

I opened it and scoped a picture of a naked dead fat man on a stainless-steel table. The print had a DI verification grid on it, which meant this was the real thing, not a composite. Just above the corpse's left eye there was a neat hole. It was rimmed with purple that had faded to bruise blue. He had curly gray hair on his head and chest, skin the color of dried mayonnaise, and a wonderfully complicated penis graft. He looked relieved to be dead. ''Who was he?'' I liked Comrade's present. It was extreme.

''CEO of Infoline. He had the wife, you know, the one who stole all the money so she could download herself into a computer.''

I shivered as I stared at the dead man. I could hear myself

breathing and feel the blood squirting through my arteries. "Didn't they turn her off?" I said. This was the kind of stuff we were not even supposed to imagine, much less look at. Too bad they had cleaned him up. "How much did this cost me?"

"You don't want to know."

"Hey!" Stennie thumped his tail against the side of the car. "I'm taking a quiz here, and you guys are drooling over porn. When was the First World Depression?"

"Who cares?" I slipped the picture back into the envelope and grinned at Comrade.

"Well, let me see then." Stennie snatched the envelope. "You know what I think, Mr. Boy? I think this corpse jag you're on is kind of sick. Besides, you're going to get in trouble if you let Comrade keep breaking laws. Isn't this picture private?"

"Privacy is twentieth-century thinking. It's all information, Stennie, and information should be accessible." I held out my hand. "But if *glasnost* bothers you, give it up." I wiggled my fingers.

Comrade snickered. Stennie pulled out the picture, glanced at it, and hissed. "You're scaring me, Mr. Boy."

His schoolcomm beeped as it posted his score on the quiz, and he sailed the envelope back across the car at me. "Not Venezuela, Vietnam. Hey, *Truman* dropped the plugging bomb. Reagan was the one who spent all the money. What's wrong with you dumbscuts? Now I owe school another fifteen minutes."

"Hey, if you don't make it look good, they'll know you had help." Comrade laughed.

"What's with this dance anyway? You don't dance." I picked Comrade's present up and tucked it into my shirt pocket. "You find yourself a cush or something, lizard boy?"

"Maybe." Stennie could not blush, but sometimes when he was embarrassed the loose skin under his jaw quivered. Even though he had been reshaped into a dinosaur, he was still growing up. "Maybe I am getting a little. What's it to you?"

"If you're getting it," I said, "it's got to be microscopic." This was a bad sign. I was losing him to his dick, just like all the other pals. No way I wanted to start over with someone new. I had been alive for twenty-five years now. I was running out of things to say to thirteen-year-olds.

As the Alpha pulled up to the school, I scoped the crowd waiting for the doors to open for third shift. Although there was a handful of stunted kids, a pair of gorilla brothers who were football stars and Freddy the Teddy—a bear who had furry hands instead of real paws—the majority of students at New Canaan High looked more or less normal. Most working stiffs thought that people who had their genes twanked were freaks.

"Come get me at five-fifteen," Stennie told the Alpha. "In the meantime, take these guys wherever they want to go." He opened the door. "You rest up, Mr. Boy, okay?"

"What?" I was not paying attention. "Sure." I had just seen the most beautiful girl in the world.

She leaned against one of the concrete columns of the portico, chatting with a couple other kids. Her hair was long and nut-colored and the ends twinkled. She was wearing a loose black robe over mirror skintights. Her schoolcomm dangled from a strap around her wrist. She appeared to be seventeen, maybe eighteen. But of course, appearances could be deceiving.

Girls had never interested me much, but I could not help but admire this one. "Wait, Stennie! Who's that?" She saw me point at her. "With the hair?"

"She's new—has one of those names you can't pronounce." He showed me his teeth as he got out. "Hey, Mr. Boy, you're *stunted.* You haven't got what she wants."

He kicked the door shut, lowered his head, and crossed in front of the car. When he walked, he looked like he was trying to squash a bug with each step. His snaky tail curled high behind him for balance, his twiggy little arms dangled. When the new girl saw him, she pointed and smiled. Or maybe she was pointing at me.

"Where to?" said the car.

"I don't know." I sank low into my seat and pulled out Comrade's present again. "Home, I guess."

I was not the only one in my family with twanked genes. My mom was a three-quarter-scale replica of the Statue of Liberty. Originally she wanted to be full-sized, but then she would have been the tallest thing in New Canaan, Connecticut. The town turned her down when she applied for a zoning variance. Her lawyers and their lawyers sued and countersued for almost two years. Mom's claim was that since she was born human, her freedom of form was protected by the Thirtieth Amendment. However, the form she wanted was a curtain of reshaped cells that would hang on a forty-two-meter-high ferroplastic skeleton. Her structure, said the planning board, was clearly subject to building codes and zoning laws. Eventually they reached an out-of-court settlement, which was why Mom was only as tall as an eleven-story building.

She complied with the town's request for a setback of five hundred meters from Route 123. As Stennie's Alpha drove us down the long driveway, Comrade broadcast the recognition code that told the robot sentries that we were okay. One thing Mom and the town agreed on from the start: no tourists. Sure, she loved publicity, but she was also very fragile. In some places her skin was only a centimeter thick. Chunks of ice falling from her crown could punch holes in her.

The end of our driveway cut straight across the lawn to Mom's granite-paved foundation pad. To the west of the plaza, directly behind her, was a utility building faced in ashlar that housed her support systems. Mom had been bioengineered to be pretty much self-sufficient. She was green not only to match the real Statue of Liberty but also because she was photosynthetic. All she needed was a yearly truckload of fertilizer, water from the well, and 150 kilowatts of electricity a day. Except for emergency surgery, the only time she required maintenance was in the fall, when her outer cells tended to flake off and had to be swept up and carted away.

Stennie's Alpha dropped us off by the doorbone in the right heel and then drove off to do whatever cars do when nobody is using them. Mom's greeter was waiting in the reception area inside the foot.

"Peter." She tried to hug me, but I dodged out of her grasp. "How are you, Peter?"

"Tired." Even though Mom knew I did not like to be called that, I kissed the air near her cheek. Peter Cage was her name for me; I had given it up years ago.

"You poor boy. Here, let me see you." She held me at arm's length and brushed her fingers against my cheek. "You don't look a day over twelve. Oh, they do such good work—don't you think?" She squeezed my shoulder. "Are you happy with it?"

I think my mom meant well, but she never did understand me. Especially when she talked to me with her greeter remote. I wormed out of her grip and fell back onto one of the couches. "What's to eat?"

"Doboys, noodles, fries—whatever you want." She beamed at me and then bent over impulsively and gave me a kiss that

I did not want. I never paid much attention to the greeter; she was lighter than air. She was always smiling and asking five questions in a row without waiting for an answer and flitting around the room. It wore me out just watching her. Naturally, everything I said or did was cute, even if I was trying to be obnoxious. It was no fun being cute. Today Mom had her greeter wearing a dark blue dress and a very dumb white apron. The greeter's umbilical was too short to stretch up to the kitchen. So why was she wearing an apron? "I'm really, really glad you're home," she said.

"I'll take some cinnamon doboys." I kicked off my shoes and rubbed my bare feet through the dense black hair on the floor. "And a beer."

All of Mom's remotes had different personalities. I liked Nanny all right; she was simple, but at least she listened. The lovers were a challenge because they were usually too busy looking into mirrors to notice me. Cook was as pretentious as a four-star menu; the housekeeper had all the charm of a vacuum cleaner. I had always wondered what it would be like to talk directly to Mom's main brain up in the head, because then she would not be filtered through a remote. She would be herself.

"Cook is making you some nice broth to go with your doboys," said the greeter. "Nanny says you shouldn't be eating dessert all the time."

"Hey, did I ask for broth?"

At first Comrade had hung back while the greeter was fussing over me. Then he slid along the wrinkled pink walls of the reception room toward the plug where the greeter's umbilical was attached. When she started in about the broth, I saw him lean against the plug. Carelessly, you know? At the same time he stepped on the greeter's umbilical, crimping the furry black cord. She gasped and the smile flattened horribly on her face, as if her lips were two ropes someone had suddenly yanked taut. Her head jerked toward the umbilical plug.

"E-Excuse me." She was twitching.

"What?" Comrade glanced down at his foot as if it belonged to a stranger. "Oh, sorry." He pushed away from the wall and strolled across the room toward us. Although he seemed apologetic, about half the heads on his window coat were laughing.

The greeter flexed her cheek muscles. "You'd better watch out for your toy, Peter," she said. "It's going to get you in trouble someday."

Mom did not like Comrade much, even though she had given him to me when I was first stunted. She got mad when I snuck him down to Manhattan a couple of years ago to have a chop job done on his behavioral regulators. For a while after the operation, he used to ask me before he broke the law. Now he was on his own. He got caught once, and she warned me he was out of control. But she still threw money at the people until they went away.

"Trouble?" I said. "Sounds like fun." I thought we were too rich for trouble. I was the trust baby of a trust baby; we had vintage money and lots of it. I stood and Comrade picked up my shoes for me. "And he's not a toy; he's my best friend." I put my arms around his shoulder. "Tell Cook I'll eat in my rooms."

I was tired after the long climb up the circular stairs to Mom's chest. When the roombrain sensed I had come in, it turned on all the electronic windows and blinked my message indicator. One reason I still lived in my mom was that she kept out of my rooms. She had promised me total security, and I believed her. Actually I doubted that she cared enough to pry, although she could easily have tapped my windows. I was safe from her remotes up here, even the housekeeper. Comrade did everything for me.

I sent him for supper, perched on the edge of the bed, and cleared the nearest window of army ants foraging for meat through some Angolan jungle. The first message in the queue was from a gray-haired stiff wearing a navy blue corporate uniform. "Hello, Mr. Cage. My name is Weldon Montross and I'm with Datasafe. I'd like to arrange a meeting with you at your convenience. Call my DI number, 408-966-3286. I hope to hear from you soon."

"What the hell is Datasafe?"

The roombrain ran a search. "Datasafe offers services in encryption and information security. It was incorporated in the state of Delaware in 2013. Estimated billings last year were three hundred and forty million dollars. Headquarters are in San Jose, California, with branch offices in White Plains, New York, and Chevy Chase, Maryland. Foreign offices . . ."

"Are they trying to sell me something or what?"

The room did not offer an answer. "Delete," I said. "Next?"

Weldon Montross was back again, looking exactly as he had before. I wondered if he were using a virtual image. "Hello, Mr.

Cage. I've just discovered that you've been admitted to the Thayer Clinic for rejuvenation therapy. Believe me when I say that I very much regret having to bother you during your convalescence, and I would not do so if this were not a matter of importance. Would you please contact Department of Identification number 408-966-3286 as soon as you're able?"

"You're a pro, Weldon, I'll say that for you." Prying client information out of the Thayer Clinic was not easy, but then the guy was no doubt some kind of op. He was way too polite to be a salesman. What did Datasafe want with me? "Any more messages from him?"

"No," said the roombrain.

"Well, delete this one too, and if he calls back tell him I'm too busy unless he wants to tell me what he's after." I stretched out on my bed. "Next?" The gel mattress shivered as it took my weight.

Happy Lurdane was having a smash party on the twentieth, but Happy was a boring cush and there was a bill from the pet store for the iguanas that I paid and a warning from the SPCA that I deleted and a special offer for preferred customers from my favorite fireworks company that I saved to look at later and my dad was about to ask for another loan when I paused him and deleted and last of all there was a message from Stennie, time-stamped ten minutes ago.

"Hey, Mr. Boy, if you're feeling better I've lined up a VE party for tonight." He did not quite fit into the school's telelink booth; all I could see was his toothy face and the long yellow curve of his neck. "Bunch of us have reserved some time on Playroom. Come in disguise. That new kid said she'd link, so scope her yourself if you're so hot. I found out her name, but it's kind of unpronounceable. Tree-something Joplin. Anyway, it's at seven, meet on channel seventeen, password is *warhead*. Hey, did you send my car back yet? Later." He faded.

"Sounds like fun." Comrade kicked the doorbone open and backed through, balancing a tray loaded with soup and fresh doboys and a mug of cold beer. "Are we going?" He set it onto the nightstand next to my bed.

"Maybe." I yawned. It felt good to be in my own bed. "Flush the damn soup, would you?" I reached over for a doboy and felt something crinkle in my jacket pocket. I pulled out the picture of the dead CEO. About the only thing I did not like about it was that the eyes were shut. You feel dirtier when the corpse stares back. "This is one sweet hunk of meat, Comrade." I propped the picture beside the tray. "How did you get it, anyway? Must have taken some operating."

"Three days' worth. Encryption wasn't all that tough, but there was lots of it." Comrade admired the picture with me as he picked up the bowl of soup. "I ended up buying about ten hours from IBM to crack the file. Kind of pricey, but since you were getting stunted, I had nothing else to do."

"You see the messages from that security op?" I bit into a doboy. "Maybe you were a little sloppy." The hot cinnamon scent tickled my nose.

"Ya v'rot ego ebal!" He laughed. "So some stiff is cranky? Plug him if he can't take a joke."

I said nothing. Comrade could be a pain sometimes. Of course I loved the picture, but he really should have been more careful. He had made a mess and left it for me to clean up. Just what I needed. I knew I would only get mad if I thought about it, so I changed the subject. "Well, do you think she's cute?"

"What's-her-face Joplin?" Comrade turned abruptly toward the bathroom. "Sure, for a *perdunya,*" he said over his shoulder. "Why not?" Talking about girls made him snippy. I think he was afraid of them.

I brought my army ants back onto the window; they were swarming over a lump with brown fur. Thinking about him hanging on my elbow when I met this Tree-something Joplin made me feel weird. I listened as he poured the soup down the toilet. I was not myself at all. Getting stunted changes you; no one can predict how. I chugged the beer and rolled over to take a nap. It was the first time I had ever thought of leaving Comrade behind.

"VE party, Mr. Boy." Comrade nudged me awake. "Are we going or not?"

"Huh?" My gut still ached from the rejuvenation, and I woke up mean enough to chew glass. "What do you mean *we?*"

"Nothing." Comrade had that blank look he always put on so I would not know what he was thinking. Still, I could tell he was disappointed. "Are you going then?" he said.

I stretched—*ouch!* "Yeah, sure, get my joysuit." My bones felt brittle as candy. "And stop acting sorry for yourself." This nasty mood had momentum; it swept me past any regrets. "No way I'm going to lie here all night watching you pretend you have feelings to hurt."

"Tak tochno." He saluted and went straight to the closet. I got out of bed and hobbled to the bathroom.

"This is a costume party, remember," Comrade called. "What are you wearing?"

"Whatever." Even his efficiency irked me; sometimes he did too much. "You decide." I needed to get away from him for a while.

Playroom was a new virtual-environment service on our local net. If you wanted to throw an electronic party at Versailles or Monticello or San Simeon, all you had to do was link—if you could get a reservation.

I came back to the bedroom and Comrade stepped up behind me, holding the joysuit. I shrugged into it, velcroed the front seam, and eyed myself in the nearest window. He had synthesized some kid-sized armor in the German Gothic style. My favorite. It was made of polished silver, with great fluting and scalloping. He had even programmed a little glow into the image so that on the window I looked like a walking night-light. There was an armet helmet with a red ostrich plume; the visor was tipped up so I could see my face. I raised my arm, and the joysuit translated the movement to the window so that my armored image waved back.

"Try a few steps," he said.

Although I could move easily in the lightweight joysuit, the motion interpreter made walking in the video armor seem realistically awkward. Comrade had scored the sound effects, too. Metal hinges rasped, chain mail rattled softly, and there was a satisfying *clunk* whenever my foot hit the floor.

"Great." I clenched my fist in approval. I was awake now and in control of my temper. I wanted to make up, but Comrade was not taking the hint. I could never quite figure out whether he was just acting like a machine or whether he really did not care how I treated him.

"They're starting." All the windows in the room lit up with Playroom's welcome screen. "You want privacy, so I'm leaving. No one will bother you."

"Hey, Comrade, you don't have to go . . ."

But he had already left the room. Playroom prompted me to identify myself. "Mr. Boy," I said, "Department of Identification number 203-966-2445. I'm looking for channel seventeen; the password is *warhead.*"

A brass band started playing "Hail to the Chief" as the title screen lit the windows:

The White House
1600 Pennsylvania Avenue
Washington, DC, USA
© 2096, Playroom Presentations
REPRODUCTION OR REUSE STRICTLY PROHIBITED

and then I was looking at a wraparound view of a VE ballroom. A caption bar opened at the top of the windows and a message scrolled across. *This is the famous East Room, the largest room in the main house. It is used for press conferences, public receptions, and entertainments.* I lowered my visor and entered the simulation.

The East Room was decorated in bone white and gold; three chandeliers hung like cut-glass mushrooms above the huge parquet floor. A band played skitter at one end of the room, but no one was dancing yet. The band was Warhead, according to thelr drum set. I had never heard of them. Someone's disguise? I turned, and the joysuit changed the view on the windows. Just ahead Satan was chatting with a forklift and a rhinoceros. Beyond, some blue cartoons were teasing Johnny America. There was not much furniture in the room, a couple of benches, an ugly piano, and some life-sized paintings of George and Martha. George looked like he had just been peeled off a cash card. I stared at him too long, and the closed-caption bar informed me that the painting had been painted by Gilbert Stuart and was the only White House object dating from the mansion's first occupancy in 1800.

"Hey," I said to a girl who was on fire. "How do I get rid of the plugging tour guide?"

"Can't," she said. "When Playroom found out we were kids, they turned on all their educational crap and there's no override. I kind of don't think they want us back."

"Dumbscuts." I scoped the room for something that might be Stennie. No luck. "I like the way your hair is burning." Now that it was too late, I was sorry I had to make idle party chat.

"Thanks." When she tossed her head, sparks flared and crackled. "My mom helped me program it."

"So, I've never been to the White House. Is there more than this?"

"Sure," she said. "We're supposed to have pretty much the whole first floor. Unless they shorted us. You wouldn't be Stone Kinkaid in there, would you?"

"No, not really." Even though the voice was disguised, I could tell this was Happy Lurdane. I edged away from her. "I'm going to check the other rooms now. Later."

"If you run into Stone, tell him I'm looking for him."

I left the East Room and found myself in a long marble passageway with a red carpet. A dog skeleton trotted toward me. Or maybe it was supposed to be a sheep. I waved and went through a door on the other side.

Everyone in the Red Room was standing on the ceiling; I knew I had found Stennie. Even though what they see is only a simulation, most people lock into the perceptual field of a VE as if it were real. Stand on your head long enough—even if only in your imagination—and you get airsick. It took kilohours of practice to learn to compensate. Upside down was one of Stennie's trademark ways of showing off.

The Red Room is an intimate parlor in the American Empire style of 1815–20 . . .

"Hi," I said. I hopped over the wainscoting and walked up the silk-covered wall to join the three of them.

"You're wearing German armor." When the boy in blue grinned at me, his cheeks dimpled. He was wearing shorts and white knee socks, a navy sweater over a white shirt. "Augsburg?" said Little Boy Blue. Fine blond hair drooped from beneath his tweed cap.

"Try Wolf of Landshut," I said. Stennie and I had spent a lot of time fighting VE wars in full armor. "Nice shorts." Stennie's costume reminded me of Christopher Robin. Terminally cute.

"It's not fair," said the snowman, who I did not recognize. "He says this is what he actually looks like." The snowman was standing in a puddle that was dripping onto the rug below us. Great effect.

"No," said Stennie, "what I said was I *would* look like this if I hadn't done something about it, okay?"

I had not known Stennie before he was a dinosaur. "No wonder you got twanked." I wished I could have saved this image, but Playroom was copy-protected.

"You've been twanked? No joke?" The great horned owl ruffled in alarm. She had a girl's voice. "I know it's none of my business, but I don't understand why anyone would do it. Especially a kid. I mean, what's wrong with good old-fashioned surgery? And you can be whoever you want in a VE.'' She paused, waiting for someone to agree with her. No help. ''Okay, so I don't understand. But when you mess with your genes, you change who you are. I mean, don't you like who you are? *I* do.''

''We're so happy for you.'' Stennie scowled. ''What is this, mental health week?''

''We're rich,'' I said. ''We can afford to hate ourselves.''

''This may sound rude''—the owl's big blunt head swiveled from Stennie to me—''but I think that's sad.''

''Yeah well, we'll try to work up some tears for you, birdie,'' Stennie said.

Silence. In the East Room, the band turned the volume up.

''Anyway, I've got to be going.'' The owl shook herself. ''Hanging upside down is fine for bats, but not for me. Later.'' She let go of her perch and swooped out into the hall. The snowman turned to watch her go.

''You're driving them off, young man.'' I patted Stennie on the head. ''Come on now, be nice.''

''Nice makes me puke.''

''You *do* have a bit of an edge tonight.'' I had trouble imagining this dainty little brat as my best friend. ''Better watch out you don't cut someone.''

The dog skeleton came to the doorway and called up to us. ''We're supposed to dance now.''

''About time.'' Stennie fell off the ceiling like a drop of water and splashed headfirst onto the beige Persian rug. His image went all muddy for a moment and then he re-formed, upright and unharmed. ''Going to skitter, tin man?''

''I need to talk to you for a moment,'' the snowman murmured.

''You *need* to?'' I said.

''Dance, dance, dance,'' sang Stennie. ''Later.'' He swerved after the skeleton out of the room.

The snowman said, ''It's about a possible theft of information.''

Right then was when I should have slammed it into reverse. Caught up with Stennie or maybe faded from Playroom altogether. But all I did was raise my hands over my head. ''You got me, snowman; I confess. But society is to blame, too, isn't it? You will tell the judge to go easy on me? I've had a tough life.''

''This is serious.''

''You're Weldon—what's your name?'' Down the hall, I could hear the thud of Warhead's bass line. ''Montross.''

''I'll come to the point, Peter.'' The only acknowledgment he made was to drop the kid voice. ''The firm I represent provides information security services. Last week someone operated on the protected database of one of our clients. We have reason to believe that a certified photograph was accessed and copied. What can you tell me about this?''

''Not bad, Mr. Montross, sir. But if you were as good as you think you are, you'd know my name isn't Peter. It's Mr. Boy. And since nobody invited you to this party, maybe you'd better tell me now why I shouldn't just go ahead and have you deleted?''

''I know that you were undergoing genetic therapy at the time of the theft, so you could not have been directly responsible. That's in your favor. However, I also know that you can help me clear this matter up. And you need to do that, son, just as quickly as you can. Otherwise there's big trouble coming.''

''What are you going to do, tell my mommy?'' My blood started to pump; I was coming back to life.

''This is my offer. It's not negotiable. You let me sweep your files for this image. You turn over any hardcopies you've made and you instruct your wiseguy to let me do a spot reprogramming, during which I will erase his memory of this incident. After that, we'll consider the matter closed.''

''Why don't I just drop my pants and bend over while I'm at it?''

''Look, you can pretend if you want, but you're not a kid anymore. You're twenty-five years old. I don't believe for a minute that you're as thick as your friends out there. If you think about it, you'll realize that you can't fight us. The fact that I'm here and I know what I know means that all your personal information systems are already tapped. I'm an op, son. I could wipe your files clean any time and I will, if it comes to that. However, my orders are to be thorough. The only way I can be sure I have everything is if you cooperate.''

''You're not even real, are you, Montross? I'll bet you're nothing but cheesy old code. I've talked to elevators with more personality.''

''The offer is on the table.''

''Stick it!''

The owl flew back into the room, braked with outstretched wings, and caught onto the armrest of the Dolley Madison sofa. ''Oh, you're still here,'' she said, noticing us. ''I didn't mean to interrupt. . . .''

''Wait there,'' I said. ''I'm coming right down.''

"I'll be in touch," said the snowman. "Let me know just as soon as you change your mind." He faded.

I flipped backward off the ceiling and landed in front of her; my video armor rang from the impact. "Owl, you just saved the evening." I knew I was showing off, but just then I was willing to forgive myself. "Thanks."

"You're welcome, I guess." She edged away from me, moving with precise little birdlike steps toward the top of the couch. "But all I was trying to do was escape the band."

"Bad?"

"And loud." Her ear tufts flattened. "Do you think shutting the door would help?"

"Sure. Follow me. We can shut lots of doors." When she hesitated, I flapped my arms like silver wings. Actually, Montross had done me a favor; when he threatened me, some inner clock had begun an adrenaline tick. If this was trouble, I wanted more. I felt twisted and dangerous and I did not care what happened next. Maybe that was why the owl flitted after me as I walked into the next room.

The sumptuous State Dining Room can seat about 130 for formal dinners. The white-and-gold decor dates from the administration of Theodore Roosevelt.

The owl glided over to the banquet table. I shut the door behind me. "Better?" Warhead still pounded on the walls.

"A little." She settled on a huge bronze doré centerpiece with a mirrored surface. "I'm going soon anyway."

"Why?"

"The band stinks, I don't know anyone, and I hate these stupid disguises."

"I'm Mr. Boy." I raised my visor and grinned at her. "All right? Now you know someone."

She tucked her wings into place and fixed me with her owlish stare. "I don't like VEs much."

"They take some getting used to."

"Why bother?" she said. "I mean, if anything can happen in a simulation, nothing matters. And I feel dumb standing in a room all alone jumping up and down and flapping my arms. Besides, this joysuit is hot and I'm renting it by the hour."

"The trick is not to look at yourself," I said. "Just watch the screens and use your imagination."

"Reality is less work. You look like a little kid."

"Is that a problem?"

"Mr. Boy? What kind of name is that anyway?"

I wished she would blink. "A made-up name. But then all names are made up, aren't they?"

"Didn't I see you at school Wednesday? You were the one who dropped off the dinosaur."

"My friend Stennie." I pulled out a chair and sat facing her. "Who you probably hate because he's twanked."

"That was him on the ceiling, wasn't it? Listen, I'm sorry about what I said. I'm new here. I'd never met anyone like him before I came to New Canaan. I mean, I'd heard of reshaping and all—getting twanked. But where I used to live, everybody was pretty much the same."

"Where was that, Squirrel Crossing, Nebraska?"

"Close." She laughed. "Elkhart; it's in Indiana."

The reckless ticking in my head slowed. Talking to her made it easy to forget about Montross. "You want to leave the party?" I said. "We could go into discreet."

"Just us?" She sounded doubtful. "Right now?"

"Why not? You said you weren't staying. We could get rid of these disguises. And the music."

She was silent for a moment. Maybe people in Elkhart, Indiana, did not ask one another into discreet unless they had met in Sunday school or the 4-H Club.

"Okay," she said finally, "but I'll enable. What's your DI?"

I gave her my number.

"Be back in a minute."

I cleared Playroom from my screens. The message Enabling discreet mode flashed. I decided not to change out of the joysuit; instead I called up my wardrobe menu and chose an image of myself wearing black baggies. The loose folds and padded shoulders helped hide the scrawny little boy's body.

The message changed. Discreet mode enabled. Do you accept, yes/no?

"Sure," I said.

She was sitting naked in the middle of a room filled with tropical plants. Her skin was the color of cinnamon. She had freckles on her shoulders and across her breasts. Her hair tumbled down the curve of her spine; the ends glowed like embers in a breeze. She clutched her legs close to her and gave me a curious smile. Teenage still life. We were alone and secure. No one could tap us while we were in discreet. We could say anything we wanted. I was too croggled to speak.

"You *are* a little kid," she said.

I did not tell her that what she was watching was an enhanced image, a virtual me. "Uh . . . well, not really." I was glad Stennie could not see me. Mr. Boy at a loss—a first. "Sometimes I'm not sure what I am. I guess you're not going to like me either. I've been stunted a couple of times. I'm really twenty-five years old."

She frowned. "You keep deciding I won't like people. Why?"

"Most people are against genetic surgery. Probably because they haven't got the money."

"Myself, I wouldn't do it. Still, just because you did doesn't mean I hate you." She gestured for me to sit. "But my parents would probably be horrified. They're realists, you know."

"No fooling?" I could not help but chuckle. "That explains a lot." Like why she had an attitude about twanking. And why she thought VEs were dumb. And why she was naked and did not seem to care. According to hard-core realists, first came clothes, then jewelry, fashion, makeup, plastic surgery, skin tints, and hey jack! here we are up to our eyeballs in the delusions of 2096. Gene twanking, VE addicts, people downloading themselves into computers—better never to have started. They wanted to turn back to worn-out twentieth-century modes. "But you're no realist," I said. "Look at your hair."

She shook her head and the ends twinkled. "You like it?"

"It's extreme. But realists don't decorate!"

"Then maybe I'm not a realist. My parents let me try lots of stuff they wouldn't do themselves, like buying hairworks or linking to VEs. They're afraid I'd leave otherwise."

"Would you?"

She shrugged. "So what's it like to get stunted? I've heard it hurts."

I told her how sometimes I felt as if there were broken glass in my joints and how my bones ached and—more showing off—about the blood I would find on the toilet paper. Then I mentioned something about Mom. She had heard of Mom, of course. She asked about my dad, and I explained how Mom paid him to stay away but that he kept running out of money. She wanted to know if I was working or still going to school, and I made up some stuff about courses in history I was taking from Yale. Actually I had faded after my first semester. Couple of years ago. I did not have time to link to some boring college; I was too busy playing with Comrade and Stennie. But I still had an account at Yale.

"So that's who I am." I was amazed at how little I had lied. "Who are you?"

She told me that her name was Treemonisha but her friends called her Tree. It was an old family name; her great-great-grandsomething-or-other had been a composer named Scott Joplin. *Treemonisha* was the name of his opera.

I had to force myself not to stare at her breasts when she talked. "You like *opera?*" I said.

"My dad says I'll grow into it." She made a face. "I hope not."

The Joplins were a franchise family; her mom and dad had just been transferred to the Green Dream, a plant shop in the Elm Street Mall. To hear her talk, you would think she had ordered them from the Good Fairy. They had been married for twenty-two years and were still together. She had a brother, Fidel, who was twelve. They all lived in the greenhouse next to the shop where they grew most of their food and where flowers were always in bloom and where everybody loved everyone else. Nice life for a bunch of mall drones. So why was she thinking of leaving?

"You should stop by sometime," she said.

"Sometime," I said. "Sure."

For hours after we faded, I kept remembering things about her I had not realized I had noticed. The fine hair on her legs. The curve of her eyebrows. The way her hands moved when she was excited.

It was Stennie's fault: after the Playroom party he started going to school almost every day. Not just linking to E-class with his comm, but actually showing up. We knew he had more than remedial reading on his mind, but no matter how much we teased, he would not talk about his mysterious new cush. Before he fell in love we used to joyride in his Alpha afternoons. Now Comrade and I had the car all to ourselves. Not as much fun.

We had already dropped Stennie off when I spotted Treemonisha waiting for the bus. I waved, she came over. The next thing I knew we had another passenger on the road to nowhere. Comrade stared vacantly out the window as we pulled onto South Street; he did not seem pleased with the company.

"Have you been out to the reservoir?" I said. "There are some extreme houses out there. Or we could drive over to Greenwich and look at yachts."

"I haven't been anywhere yet, so I don't care," she said. "By the way, you don't go to college." She was not accusing me or even asking—merely stating a fact.

"Why do you say that?" I said.

"Fidel told me."

I wondered how her twelve-year-old brother could know anything at all about me. Rumors maybe, or just guessing. Since she did not seem mad, I decided to tell the truth.

"He's right," I said, "I lied. I have an account at Yale, but I haven't linked for months. Hey, you can't live without telling a few lies. At least I don't discriminate. I'll lie to anyone, even myself."

"You're bad." A smile twitched at the corners of her mouth. "So what *do* you do then?"

"I drive around a lot." I waved at the interior of Stennie's car. "Let's see . . . I go to parties. I buy stuff and use it."

"Fidel says you're rich."

"I'm going to have to meet this Fidel. Does money make a difference?"

When she nodded, her hairworks twinkled. Comrade gave me a knowing glance, but I paid no attention. I was trying to figure out how she could make insults sound like compliments when I realized we were flirting. The idea took me by surprise. *Flirting.*

"Do you have any music?" Treemonisha said.

The Alpha asked what groups she liked, and so we listened to some mindless dance hits as we took the circle route around the Laurel Reservoir. Treemonisha told me about how she was sick of her parents' store and rude customers and especially the dumb Green Dream uniform. "Back in Elkhart, Daddy used to make me wear it to school. Can you believe that? He said it was good advertising. When we moved, I told him either the khakis went or I did."

She had a yellow-and-orange dashiki over midnight-blue skintights. "I like your clothes," I said. "You have taste."

"Thanks." She bobbed her head in time to the music. "I can't afford much because I can't get an outside job because I have to work for my parents. It makes me mad, sometimes. I mean, franchise life is fine for Mom and Dad; they're happy being tucked in every night by GD, Inc. But I want more. Thrills, chills—you know, adventure. No one has adventures in the mall."

As we drove, I showed her the log castle, the pyramids, the private train that pulled sleeping cars endlessly around a two-mile track, and the marble bunker where Sullivan, the assassinated president, still lived on in computer memory. Comrade kept busy acting bored.

"Can we go see your mom?" said Treemonisha. "All the kids at school tell me she's awesome."

Suddenly Comrade was interested in the conversation. I was not sure what the kids at school were talking about. Probably they wished they had seen Mom, but I had never asked any of them over—except for Stennie.

"Not a good idea." I shook my head. "She's more flimsy than she looks, you know, and she gets real nervous if strangers just drop by. Or even friends."

"I just want to look. I won't get out of the car."

"Well," said Comrade, "if she doesn't get out of the car, who could she hurt?"

I scowled at him. He knew how paranoid Mom was. She was not going to like Treemonisha anyway, but certainly not if I brought her home without warning. "Let me work on her, okay?" I said to Treemonisha. "One of these days. I promise."

She pouted for about five seconds and then laughed at my expression. When I saw Comrade's smirk, I got angry. He was just sitting there watching us. Looking to cause trouble. Later there would be wisecracks. I had had about enough of him and his attitude.

By that time the Alpha was heading up High Ridge Road toward Stamford. "I'm hungry," I said. "Stop at the 7-Eleven up ahead." I pulled a cash card out and flipped it at him. "Go buy us some doboys."

I waited until he disappeared into the store and then ordered Stennie's car to drive on.

"Hey!" Treemonisha twisted in her seat and looked back at the store. "What are you doing?"

"Ditching him."

"Why? Won't he be mad?"

"He's got my card; he'll call a cab."

"But that's mean."

"So?"

Treemonisha thought about it. "He doesn't say much, does he?" She did not seem to know what to make of me—which I suppose was what I wanted. "At first I thought he was kind of like your teddy bear. Have you seen those big ones that keep little kids out of trouble?"

"He's just a wiseguy."

"Have you had him long?"

"Maybe too long."

I could not think of anything to say after that, so we sat

quietly listening to the music. Even though he was gone, Comrade was still aggravating me.

"Were you really hungry?" Treemonisha said finally. "Because I was. Think there's something in the fridge?"

I waited for the Alpha to tell us, but it said nothing. I slid across the seat and opened the refrigerator door. Inside was a sheet of paper. "Dear Mr. Boy," it said. "If this was a bomb, you and Comrade would be dead and the problem would be solved. Let's talk soon. Weldon Montross."

"What's that?"

I felt the warm flush that I always got from good corpse porn, and for a moment I could not speak. "Practical joke," I said, crumpling the paper. "Too bad he doesn't have a sense of humor."

Push-ups. *Ten, eleven.*

"Uh-oh. Look at this," said Comrade.

"I'm busy!" *Twelve, thirteen, fourteen, fifteen . . . sixteen . . . seven. . . .* Dizzy, I slumped and rested my cheek against the warm floor. I could feel Mom's pulse beneath the tough skin. It was no good. I would never get muscles this way. There was only one fix for my skinny arms and bony shoulders. Grow up, Mr. Boy.

"*Ya yebou!* You really should scope this," said Comrade. "Very spooky."

I pulled myself onto the bed to see why he was bothering me; he had been pretty tame since I had stranded him at the 7-Eleven. Most of the windows showed the usual: army ants next to old war movies next to feeding time from the Bronx Zoo's reptile house. But Firenet, which provided twenty-four-hour coverage of killer fires from around the world, had been replaced with a picture of a morgue. There were three naked bodies, shrouds pulled back for identification: a fat gray-haired CEO with a purple hole over his left eye, Comrade, and me.

"You look kind of dead," said Comrade.

My tongue felt thick. "Where's it coming from?"

"Viruses all over the system," he said. "Probably Montross."

"You know about him?" The image on the window changed back to a *barrida* fire in Lima.

"He's been in touch." Comrade shrugged. "Made his offer."

Crying women watched as the straw walls of their huts peeled into flame and floated away.

"Oh." I did not know what to say. I wanted to reassure him, but this was serious. Montross was invading my life, and I had no idea how to fight back. "Well, don't talk to him anymore."

"Okay." Comrade grinned. "He's dull as a spoon anyway."

"I bet he's a simulation. What else would a company like Datasafe use? You can't trust real people." I was still thinking about what I would look like dead. "Whatever, he's kind of scary." I shivered, worried and aroused at the same time. "He's slick enough to operate on Playroom. And now he's hijacking windows right here in my own mom." I should probably have told Comrade then about the note in the fridge, but we were still not talking about that day.

"He tapped into Playroom?" Comrade fitted input clips to the spikes on his neck, linked and played back the house files. "*Zayebees.* He was already here then. He piggybacked on with you." Comrade slapped his leg. "I can't understand how he beat my security so easily."

The roombrain flicked the message indicator. "Stennie's calling," it said.

"Pick up," I said.

"Hi, it's that time again." Stennie was alone in his car. "I'm on my way over to give you jacks a thrill." He pushed his triangular snout up to the camera and licked at the lens. "Doing anything?"

"Not really. Sitting around."

"I'll fix that. Five minutes." He faded.

Comrade was staring at nothing.

"Look, Comrade, you did your best," I said. "I'm not mad at you."

"Too plugging easy." He shook his head as if I had missed the point.

"What I don't understand is why Montross is so cranky anyway. It's just a picture of meat."

"Maybe he's not really dead."

"Sure he is," I said. "You can't fake a verification grid."

"No, but you can fake a corpse."

"You know something?"

"If I did I wouldn't tell you," said Comrade. "You have enough problems already. Like how do we explain this to your mom?"

"We don't. Not yet. Let's wait him out. Sooner or later he's got to realize that we're not going to use his picture for anything. I mean, if he's that nervous, I'll even give it back. I don't care anymore. You hear that, Montross, you dumbscut? We're harmless. Get out of our lives!"

"It's more than the picture now," said Comrade. "It's me. I found the way in." He was careful to keep his expression blank.

I did not know what to say to him. No way Montross would be satisfied erasing only the memory of the operation. He would probably reconnect Comrade's regulators to bring him back under control. Turn him to pudding. He would be just another wiseguy, like anyone else could own. I was surprised that Comrade did not ask me to promise not to hand him over. Maybe he just assumed I would stand by him.

We did not hear Stennie coming until he sprang into the room.

"Have fun or die!" He was clutching a plastic gun in his spindly hand, which he aimed at my head.

"Stennie, *no.*"

He fired as I rolled across the bed. The jellybee buzzed by me and squished against one of the windows. It was a purple, and immediately I smelled the tang of artificial grape flavor. The splatter on the wrinkled wall pulsed and split in two, emitting a second burst of grapeness. The two halves oozed in opposite directions, shivered, and divided again.

"Fun extremist!" He shot Comrade with a cherry as he dove for the closet. "Dance!"

I bounced up and down on the bed, timing my move. He fired a green at me that missed. Comrade, meanwhile, gathered himself up as zits of red jellybee squirmed across his window coat. He barreled out of the closet into Stennie, knocking him sideways. I sprang on top of them and wrestled the gun away. Stennie was paralyzed with laughter. I had to giggle too, in part because now I could put off talking to Comrade about Montross.

By the time we untangled ourselves, the jellybees had faded. "Set for twelve generations before they all die out," Stennie said as he settled himself on the bed. "So what's this my car tells me, you've been giving free rides? Is this the cush with the name?"

"None of your business. You never tell me about your cush."

"Okay. Her name is Janet Hoyt."

"Is it?" He caught me off-guard again. Twice in one day, a record. "Comrade, let's see this prize."

Comrade linked to the roombrain and ran a search. "Got her." He called Janet Hoyt's DI file to screen, and her face ballooned across an entire window.

She was a tanned blue-eyed blonde with the kind of off-the-shelf looks that med students slapped onto rabbits in genoplasty courses. Nothing on her face said she was different from any other ornamental moron fresh from the OR—not a dimple or a mole, not even a freckle. "You're ditching me for her?" It took all the imagination of a potato chip to be as pretty as Janet Hoyt. "Stennie, she's generic."

"Now wait a minute," said Stennie. "If we're going to play critic, let's scope your cush, too."

Without asking, Comrade put Tree's DI photo next to Janet's. I realized he was still mad at me because of her; he was only pretending not to care. "She's not my cush," I said, but no one was listening.

Stennie leered at her for a moment. "She's a stiff, isn't she?" he said. "She has that hungry look."

Seeing him standing there in front of the two huge faces on the wall, I felt like I was peeping on a stranger—that I was a stranger, too. I could not imagine how the two of us had come to this: Stennie and Mr. Boy with cushes. We were growing up. A frightening thought. Maybe next Stennie would get himself untwanked and really look like he had on Playroom. Then where would I be?

"Janet wants me to plug her," Stennie said.

"Right, and I'm the queen of Brooklyn."

"I'm old enough, you know." He thumped his tail against the floor.

"You're a dinosaur!"

"Hey, just because I got twanked doesn't mean my dick fell off."

"So do it then."

"I'm going to. I will, okay? But . . . this is no good." Stennie waved impatiently at Comrade. "I can't think with them watching me." He nodded at the windows. "Turn them off already."

"N'ye pizdi!" Comrade wiped the two faces from the windows, cleared all the screens in the room to blood red, yanked the input clips from his neck spikes, and left them dangling from the roombrain's terminal. His expression empty, he walked from the room without asking permission or saying anything at all.

"What's his problem?" Stennie said.

"Who knows?" Comrade had left the door open; I shut it. "Maybe he doesn't like girls."

"Look, I want to ask a favor." I could tell Stennie was nervous; his head kept swaying. "This is kind of embarrassing, but . . . okay, do you think maybe your mom would maybe let me practice on her lovers? I don't want Janet to know I've never done it before, and there's some stuff I've got to figure out."

"I don't know," I said. "Ask her."

But I did know. She would be amused.

People claimed my mom did not have a sense of humor. Lovey was huge, an ocean of a woman. Her umbilical was as big around as my thigh. When she walked, waves of flesh heaved and rolled. She had beautiful skin, flawless and moist. It did not take much to make her sweat. Peeling a banana would do it. Lovey was as oral as a baby; she would put anything into her mouth. And when she did not have a mouthful, she would babble on about whatever came into Mom's head. Dear hardly ever talked, although he could moan and growl and laugh. He touched Lovey whenever he could and shot her long smoldering looks. He was not furry, exactly, but he was covered with fine silver hair. Dear was a little guy, about my size. Although he had one of Upjohn's finest penises, elastic and overloaded with neurons, he was one of the least convincing males I had ever met. I doubt Mom herself believed in him all that much.

Big chatty woman, squirrelly tongue-tied little man. It *was* funny in a bent sort of way to watch the two of them go at each other. Kind of like a tug churning against a supertanker. They did not get the chance that often. It was dangerous; Dear had to worry about getting crushed, and poor Lovey's heart had stopped two or three times. Besides, I think Mom liked building up the pressure. Sometimes, as the days without sex stretched, you could almost feel lust sparkling off them like static electricity.

That was how they were when I brought Stennie up. Their suite took up the entire floor at the hips, Mom's widest part. Lovey was lolling in a tub of warm oil. She liked it flowery and laced with pheromones. Dear was prowling around her with a desperate expression, like he might jam his plug into a wall socket if he did not get taken care of soon. Stennie's timing was perfect.

"Look who's come to visit, Dear," said Lovey. "Peter and Stennie. How nice of you boys to stop by." She let Dear mop her forehead with a towel. "What can we do for you?"

The skin under Stennie's jaw quivered. He glanced at me, then at Dear, and then at the thick red lips that served as the bathroom door. Never even looked at her. He was losing his nerve.

"Oh my, isn't this exciting, Dear? There's something going on." She sank into the bath until her chin touched the water. "It's a secret, isn't it, Peter? Share it with Lovey."

"No secret," I said. "He wants to ask a favor." And then I told her.

She giggled and sat up. "I love it." Honey-colored oil ran from her hair and slopped between her breasts. "Were you thinking of both of us, Stennie? Or just me?"

"Well, I . . ." Stennie's tail switched. "Maybe we just ought to forget it."

"No, no." She waved a hand at him "Come here, Stennie. Come close, my pretty little monster."

He hesitated, then approached the tub. She reached for his right leg and touched him just above the heelknob. "You know, I've always wondered what scales would feel like." Her hand climbed; the oil made his yellow hide glisten. His eyes were the size of eggs.

The bedroom was all mattress. Beneath the transparent skin was a screen implant, so that Mom could project images not only on the walls but on the surface of the bed itself. Under the window was a layer of heavily vascular flesh, which could be stiffened with blood or drained until it was as soft as raw steak. A window dome arched over everything and could show slo-mo or thermographic fx across its span. The air was warm and wet and smelled like a chemical engineer's idea of a rose garden.

I settled by the lips. Dear ghosted along the edges of the room, dragging his umbilical like a chain, never coming quite near enough to touch anyone. I heard him humming as he passed me, a low moaning singsong, as if to block out what was happening. Stennie and Lovey were too busy with each other to care. As Lovey knelt in front of Stennie, Dear gave a mocking laugh. I did not understand how he could be jealous. He was with her, part of it. Lovey and Dear were Mom's remotes, two nodes of her nervous system. Yet his pain was as obvious as her pleasure. At last he squatted and rocked back and forth on his heels. I glanced up at the fx dome; yellow scales slid across oily rolls of flushed skin.

I yawned. I had always found sex kind of dull. Besides, this was all on the record. I could have Comrade replay it for me anytime. Lovey stopped breathing—then came four or five shuddering gasps in a row. I wondered where Comrade had gone. I felt sorry for him. Stennie said something to her about rolling over. "Okay?" Feathery skin sounds. A grunt. The soft wet slap of flesh against flesh. I thought of my mother's brain, up there in the head where no one ever went. I had no idea how much attention she was paying. Was she quivering with Lovey and at the same time calculating insolation rates on her chloroplasts? Investing in soy futures on the Chicago Board of Trade? Fending off Weldon Montross's latest attack? *Plug Montross.* I needed to think about something fun. My collection. I started piling bodies up in my mind. The hangings and the open-casket funerals and the stacks of dead at the camps and all those muddy soldiers. I shivered as I remembered the empty rigid faces. I liked it when their teeth showed. "Oh, oh, *oh!*" My greatest hits dated from the late twentieth century. The dead were everywhere back then, in vids and the news and even on T-shirts. They were not shy. That was what made Comrade's photo worth having; it was hard to find modern stuff that dirty. Dear brushed by me, his erection bobbing in front of him. It was as big around as my wrist. As he passed, I could see Stennie's leg scratch across the mattress skin, which glowed with blood-blue light. Lovey giggled beneath him and her umbilical twitched and suddenly I found myself wondering whether Tree was a virgin.

I came into the mall through the Main Street entrance and hopped the westbound slidewalk headed up Elm Street toward the train station. If I caught the 3:36 to Grand Central, I could eat dinner in Manhattan, far from my problems with Montross and Comrade. Running away had always worked for me before. Let someone else clean up the mess while I was gone.

The slidewalk carried me past a real-estate agency, a flash bar, a jewelry store, and a Baskin-Robbins. I thought about where I wanted to go after New York. San Francisco? Montreal? Maybe I should try Elkhart, Indiana—no one would think to look for me there. Just ahead, between a drugstore and a take-out Russian restaurant, was the wiseguy dealership where Mom had bought Comrade.

I did not want to think about Comrade waiting for me to come home, so I stepped into the drugstore and bought a dose of Carefree for $4.29. Normally I did not bother with drugs. I had been stunted; no over-the-counter flash could compare to that. But the propyl dicarbamates were all right. I fished the cash card out of my pocket and handed it to the stiff behind the counter. He did a double take when he saw the denomination, then carefully inserted the card into the reader to deduct the cost of the Carefree. It had my mom's name on it; he must have expected it would trip some alarm for counterfeit plastic or stolen credit. He stared at me for a moment, as if trying to remember my face so he could describe me to a cop, and then gave the cash card back. The denomination readout said it was still good for $16,381.18.

I picked out a bench in front of a specialty shop called The Happy Hippo, hiked up my shorts, and poked Carefree into the widest part of my thigh. I took a short dreamy swim in the sea of tranquillity and when I came back to myself, my guilt had been washed away. But so had my energy. I sat for a while and scoped the display of glass hippos and plastic hippos and fuzzy stuffed hippos, hippo vids and sheets and candles. Down the bench from me a homeless woman dozed. It was still pretty early in the season for a weather gypsy to have come this far north. She wore red shorts and droopy red socks with plastic sandals and four long-sleeved shirts, all unbuttoned, over a Funny Honey halter top. Her hair needed vacuuming and she smelled old. All grown-ups smelled that way to me; it was something I had never gotten used to. No perfume or deodorant could cover up the leathery stink of adulthood. Kids could smell bad too, but usually from something they got on them. It did not come from a rotting body. I rubbed a finger in the dampness under my arm, slicked it, and sniffed. There was a sweetness to kid sweat. I touched the drying finger to my tongue. You could even taste it. If I gave up getting stunted, stopped being Mr. Boy, I would smell like the woman at the end of the bench. I would start to die. I had never understood how grown-ups could live with that.

The gypsy woke up, stretched, and smiled at me with gummy teeth. "You left Comrade behind?" she said.

I was startled. "What did you say?"

"You know what this is?" She twitched her sleeve, and a penlight appeared in her hand.

My throat tightened. "I know what it looks like."

She gave me a wicked smile, aimed the penlight, and burned a pinhole through the bench a few centimeters from my leg. "Maybe I could interest you in some free laser surgery?"

I could smell scorched plastic. "You're going to needle me here, in the middle of the Elm Street Mall?" I thought she was bluffing. Probably. I hoped.

"If that's the way you want it. Mr. Montross wants to know when you're delivering the wiseguy to us."

"Get away from me."

"Not until you do what needs to be done."

When I saw Happy Lurdane come out of The Happy Hippo, I waved. A desperation move, but then it was easy to be brave with a head full of Carefree.

"Mr. Boy." She veered over to us. "Hi!"

I scooted farther down the bench to make room for her between me and the gypsy. I knew she would stay to chat. Happy Lurdane was one of those chirpy lightweights who seemed to want lots of friends but did not really try to be one. We tolerated her because she did not mind being snubbed and she threw great parties.

"Where have you been?" She settled beside me. "Haven't seen you in ages." The penlight disappeared, and the gypsy fell back into drowsy character.

"Around."

"Want to see what I just bought?"

I nodded. My heart was hammering.

She opened the bag and took out a fist-sized bundle covered with shipping plastic. She unwrapped a statue of a blue hippopotamus. "Be careful." She handed it to me.

"Cute." The hippo had crude flower designs drawn on its body; it was chipped and cracked.

"Ancient Egyptian. That means it's even *before* antique." She pulled a slip from the bag and read. "Twelfth Dynasty, 1991–1786 B.C. Can you believe you can just buy something like that here in the mall? I mean, it must be like a thousand years old or something."

"Try four thousand."

"No wonder it cost so much. He wasn't going to sell it to me, so I had to spend some of next month's allowance." She took it from me and rewrapped it. "It's for the smash party tomorrow. You're coming, aren't you?"

"Maybe."

"Is something wrong?"

I ignored that.

"Hey, where's Comrade? I don't think I've ever seen you two apart before."

I decided to take a chance. "Want to get some doboys?"

"Sure." She glanced at me with delighted astonishment. "Are you sure you're all right?"

I took her arm, maneuvering to keep her between me and the gypsy. If Happy got needled, it would be no great loss to Western Civilization. She babbled on about her party as we stepped onto the westbound slidewalk. I turned to look back. The gypsy waved as she hopped the eastbound.

"Look, Happy," I said, "I'm sorry, but I changed my mind. Later, okay?"

"But . . ."

I did not stop for an argument. I darted off the slidewalk and sprinted through the mall to the station. I went straight to a ticket window, shoved the cash card under the grill, and asked the agent for a one-way to Grand Central. Forty thousand people lived in New Canaan; most of them had heard of me because of my mom. Nine million strangers jammed New York City; it was a good place to disappear. The agent had my ticket in her hand when the reader beeped and spat the card out.

"No!" I slammed my fist on the counter. "Try it again." The cash card was guaranteed by AmEx to be secure. And it had just worked at the drugstore.

She glanced at the card, then slid it back under the grill. "No use." The denomination readout flashed alternating messages: Voided and Bank recall. "You've got trouble, son."

She was right. As I left the station, I felt the Carefree struggle one last time with my dread—and lose. I did not even have the money to call home. I wandered around for a while, dazed, and then I was standing in front of the flower shop in the Elm Street Mall.

GREEN DREAM
CONTEMPORARY AND CONVENTIONAL PLANTS

I had telelinked with Tree every day since our drive, and every day she had asked me over. But I was not ready to meet her family; I suppose I was still trying to pretend she was not a stiff. I wavered at the door now, breathing the cool scent of damp soil in clay pots. The gypsy could come after me again; I might be putting these people in danger. Using Happy as a shield was one thing, but I liked Tree. A lot. I backed away and peered through a window fringed with sweat and teeming with bizarre plants with flame-colored tongues. Someone wearing khaki moved. I could not tell if it was Tree or not. I thought of what she had said about no one having adventures in the mall.

The front of the showroom was a green cave, darker than I had expected. Baskets dripping with bright flowers hung like stalactites; leathery-leaved understory plants formed stalagmites. As I threaded my way toward the back, I came upon the kid I had seen wearing the Green Dream uniform, a khaki nightmare of pleats and flaps and brass buttons and about six too many pockets. He was misting leaves with a pump bottle filled with blue liquid. I decided he must be the brother.

"Hi," I said. "I'm looking for Treemonisha."

Fidel was shorter than me and darker than his sister. He had a wiry plush of beautiful black hair that I was immediately tempted to touch.

"Are you?" He eyed me as if deciding how hard I would be to beat up, then he smiled. He had crooked teeth. "You don't look like yourself."

"No?"

"What are you, scared? You're whiter than rice, cashman. Don't worry, the stiffs won't hurt you." Laughing, he feinted a punch at my arm; I was not reassured.

"You're Fidel."

"I've seen your DI files," he said. "I asked around, I know about you. So don't be telling my sister any more lies, understand?" He snapped his fingers in my face. "Behave yourself, cashman, and we'll be fine." He still had the boyish excitability I had lost after the first stunting. "She's out back, so first you have to get by the old man."

The rear of the store was brighter; sunlight streamed through the clear krylac roof. There was a counter and behind it a glass-doored refrigerator filled with cut flowers. A side entrance opened to the greenhouse. Mrs. Schlieman, one of Mom's lawyers who had an office in the mall, was deciding what to buy. She was shopping with her wiseguy secretary, who looked like he had just stepped out of a vodka ad.

"Wait." Fidel rested a hand on my shoulder. "I'll tell her you're here."

"But how long will they last?" Mrs. Schlieman sniffed a frilly yellow flower. "I should probably get the duraroses."

"Whatever you want, Mrs. Schlieman. Duraroses are a good product, I sell them by the truckload," said Mr. Joplin with a chuckle. "But these carnations are real flowers, raised here in my greenhouse. So maybe you can't stick them in your dishwasher, but put some where people can touch and smell them and I guarantee you'll get compliments."

"Why, Peter Cage," said Mrs. Schlieman. "Is that you? I haven't seen you since the picnic. How's your mother?" She did not introduce her wiseguy.

"Extreme," I said.

She nodded absently. "That's nice. All right then, Mr. Joplin, give me a dozen of your carnations—and two dozen yellow duraroses."

Mrs. Schlieman chatted politely at me while Tree's father wrapped the order. He was a short, rumpled, balding man who smiled too much. He seemed to like wearing the corporate uniform. Anyone else would have fixed the hair and the wrinkles. Not Mr. Joplin; he was a museum-quality throwback. As he took Mrs. Schlieman's cash card from the wiseguy, he beamed at me over his glasses. Glasses!

When Mrs. Schlieman left, so did the smile. "Peter Cage?" he said. "Is that your name?"

"Mr. Boy is my name, sir."

"You're Tree's new friend." He nodded. "She's told us about you. She's doing chores just now. You know, we have to work for a living here."

Sure, and I knew what he left unsaid: *unlike you, you spoiled little freak.* It was always the same with these stiffs. I walked in the door and already they hated me. At least he was not pretending, like Mrs. Schlieman. I gave him two points for honesty and kept my mouth shut.

"What is it you want here, Peter?"

"Nothing, sir." If he was going to "Peter" me, I was going to "sir" him right back. "I just stopped by to say hello. Treemonisha did invite me, sir, but if you'd rather I left. . . ."

"No, no. Tree warned us you might come."

She and Fidel raced into the room as if they were afraid their father and I would already be at each other's throats. "Oh, hi, Mr. Boy," she said.

Her father snorted at the sound of my name.

"Hi." I grinned at her. It was the easiest thing I had done that day.

She was wearing her uniform. When she saw that I had noticed, she blushed. "Well, you asked for it." She tugged self-consciously at the waist of her fatigues. "You want to come in?"

"Just a minute." Mr. Joplin stepped in front of the door, blocking our escape. "You finished E-class?"

"Yes."

"Checked the flats?"

"I'm almost done."

"After that you'd better pick some dinner and get it started. Your mama called and said she wouldn't be home until six-fifteen."

"Sure."

"And you'll take orders for me on line two?"

She leaned against the counter and sighed. "Do I have a choice?"

He backed away and waved us through. "Sorry, sweetheart. I don't know how we would get along without you." He caught her brother by the shirt. "Not you, Fidel. You're misting, remember?"

A short tunnel ran from their mall storefront to the rehabbed furniture warehouse built over the Amtrak rails. Green Dream had installed a krylac roof and fans and a grolighting system; the Joplins squeezed themselves into the leftover spaces not filled with inventory. The air in the greenhouse was heavy and warm and it smelled like rain. No walls, no privacy other than that provided by the plants.

"Here's where I sleep." Tree sat on her unmade bed. Her space was formed by a cinder-block wall painted yellow and a screen of palms. "Chinese fan, bamboo, lady, date, kentia," she said, naming them for me like they were her pets. "I grow them myself for spending money." Her schoolcomm was on top of her dresser. Several drawers hung open; pink skintights trailed from one. Clothes were scattered like piles of leaves across the floor. "I guess I'm kind of a slob," she said as she stripped off the uniform, wadded it, and then banked it off the dresser into the top drawer. I could see her bare back in the mirror plastic taped to the wall. "Take your things off if you want."

I hesitated.

"Or not. But it's kind of muggy to stay dressed. You'll sweat."

I unvelcroed my shirt. I did not mind at all seeing Tree without clothes. But I did not undress for anyone except the stiffs at the clinic. I stepped out of my pants. Being naked somehow had got connected with being helpless. I had this puckery feeling in my dick, like it was going to curl up and die. I could imagine the gypsy popping out from behind a palm and laughing at me. No, I was not going to think about *that*. Not here.

"Comfortable?" said Tree.

"Sure." My voice was turning to dust in my throat. "Do all Green Dream employees run around the back room in the nude?"

''I doubt it.'' She smiled as if the thought tickled her. ''We're not exactly your average mall drones. Come help me finish the chores.''

I was glad to let her lead so that she was not looking at me, although I could still watch her. I was fascinated by the sweep of her buttocks, the curve of her spine. She strolled, flat-footed and at ease, through her private jungle. At first I scuttled along on the balls of my feet, ready to dart behind a plant if anyone came. But after a while I decided to stop being so skittish. I realized I would probably survive being naked.

Tree stopped in front of a workbench covered with potted seedlings in plastic trays and picked up a hose from the floor.

''What's this stuff?'' I kept to the opposite side of the bench, using it to cover myself.

''Greens.'' She lifted a seedling to check the water level in the tray beneath.

''What are greens?''

''It's too boring.'' She squirted some water in and replaced the seedling.

''Tell me, I'm interested.''

''In greens? You liar.'' She glanced at me and shook her head. ''Okay.'' She pointed as she said the names. ''Lettuce, spinach, pak choi, chard, kale, rocket—got that? And a few tomatoes over there. Peppers, too. GD is trying to break into the food business. They think people will grow more of their own if they find out how easy it is.''

''Is it?''

''Greens are.'' She inspected the next tray. ''Just add water.''

''Yeah, sure.''

''It's because they've been photosynthetically enhanced. Bigger leaves arranged better, low respiration rates. They teach us this stuff at GD Family Camp. It's what we do instead of vacation.'' She squashed something between her thumb and forefinger. ''They mix all these bacteria that make their own fertilizer into the soil—fix nitrogen right out of the air. And then there's this other stuff that sticks to the roots, rhizobacteria and mycorrhizae.'' She finished the last tray and coiled the hose. ''These flats will produce under candlelight in a closet. Bored yet?''

''How do they taste?''

''Pretty bland, most of them. Some stink, like kale and rocket. But we have to eat them for the good of the corporation.'' She stuck her tongue out. ''You want to stay for dinner?''

Mrs. Joplin made me call home before she would feed me; she refused to understand that my mom did not care. So I linked, asked Mom to send a car to the back door at 8:30, and faded. No time to discuss the missing sixteen thousand.

Dinner was from the cookbook Tree had been issued at camp: a bowl of cold bean soup, fresh corn bread, and chard and cheese loaf. She let me help her make it, even though I had never cooked before. I was amazed at how simple corn bread was. Six ingredients: flour, cornmeal, baking powder, milk, oil, and ovobinder. Mix and pour into a greased pan. Bake twenty minutes at 220°C and serve! There is nothing magic or even very mysterious about homemade corn bread, except for the way its smell held me spellbound.

Supper was the Joplins' daily meal together. They ate in front of security windows near the tunnel to the store; when a customer came, someone ran out front. According to contract, they had to stay open twenty-four hours a day. Many of the suburban malls had gone to all-night operation; the competition from New York City was deadly. Mr. Joplin stood duty most of the time, but since they were a franchise family everybody took turns. Even Mrs. Joplin, who also worked part-time as a factfinder at the mall's DataStop.

Tree's mother was plump and graying, and she had a smile that was almost bright enough to distract me from her naked body. She seemed harmless, except that she knew how to ask questions. After all, her job was finding out stuff for DataStop customers. She had this way of locking onto you as you talked; the longer the conversation, the greater her intensity. It was hard to lie to her. Normally that kind of aggressiveness in grown-ups made me jumpy.

No doubt she had run a search on me; I wondered just what she had turned up. Factfinders had to obey the law, so they only accessed public-domain information—unlike Comrade, who would cheerfully operate on whatever I set him to. The Joplins' bank records, for instance. I knew that Mrs. Joplin had made about $11,000 last year at the Infomat in the Elkhart Mall, that the family borrowed $135,000 at 9.78 percent interest to move to their new franchise, and that they lost $213 in their first two months in New Canaan.

I kept my research a secret, of course, and they acted innocent too. I let them pump me about Mom as we ate. I was used to being asked; after all, Mom was famous. Fidel wanted to know how much it had cost her to get twanked, how big she was, what she looked like on the inside and what she ate, if she got cold in the winter. Stuff like that. The others asked more personal questions. Tree wondered if Mom ever got lonely and whether she was going to be the Statue of Liberty for the rest of her life. Mrs. Joplin was interested in Mom's remotes, of all things. Which ones I got along with, which ones I could not stand, whether I thought any of them was really her. Mr. Joplin asked if she liked being what she was. How was I supposed to know?

After dinner, I helped Fidel clear the table. While we were alone in the kitchen, he complained. ''You think they eat this shit at GD headquarters?'' He scraped his untouched chard loaf into the composter.

''I kind of liked the corn bread.''

''If only he'd buy meat once in a while, but he's too cheap. Or doboys. Tree says you bought her doboys.''

I told him to skip school sometime and we would go out for lunch; he thought that was a great idea.

When we came back out, Mr. Joplin actually smiled at me. He had been losing his edge all during dinner. Maybe chard agreed with him. He pulled a pipe from his pocket, began stuffing something into it, and asked me if I followed baseball. I told him no. Paintball? No. Basketball? I said I watched dino fights sometimes.

''His pal is the dinosaur that goes to our school,'' said Fidel.

''He may look like a dinosaur, but he's really a boy,'' said Mr. Joplin, as if making an important distinction. ''The dinosaurs died out millions of years ago.''

''Humans aren't allowed in dino fights,'' I said, just to keep the conversation going. ''Only twanked dogs and horses and elephants.''

Silence. Mr. Joplin puffed on his pipe and then passed it to his wife. She watched the glow in the bowl through half-lidded eyes as she inhaled. Fidel caught me staring.

''What's the matter? Don't you get twisted?'' He took the pipe in his turn.

I was so croggled I did not know what to say. Even the Marleys had switched to THC inhalers. ''But smoking is bad for you.'' It smelled like a dirty sock had caught fire.

''Hemp is ancient. Natural.'' Mr. Joplin spoke in a clipped voice as if swallowing his words. ''Opens the mind to what's real.'' When he sighed, smoke poured out of his nose. ''We grow it ourselves, you know.''

I took the pipe when Tree offered it. Even before I brought the stem to my mouth, the world tilted and I watched myself slide into what seemed very much like an hallucination. Here I was sitting around naked, in the mall, with a bunch of stiffs, smoking antique drugs. And I was enjoying myself. Incredible. I inhaled and immediately the flash hit me; it was as if my brain were an enormous bud, blooming inside my head.

''Good stuff.'' I laughed smoke and then began coughing.

Fidel refilled my glass with ice water. ''Have a sip, cash-man.''

''Customer.'' Tree pointed at the window.

''Leave!'' Mr. Joplin waved impatiently at him. ''Go away.'' The man on the screen knelt and turned over the price tag on a fern. ''Damn.'' He jerked his uniform from the hook by the door, pulled on the khaki pants, and was slithering into the shirt as he disappeared down the tunnel.

''So is Green Dream trying to break into the flash market too?'' I handed the pipe to Mrs. Joplin. There was a fleck of ash on her left breast.

''What we do back here is our business,'' she said. ''We work hard so we can live the way we want.'' Tree was studying her fingerprints. I realized I had said the wrong thing, so I shut up. Obviously, the Joplins were drifting from the lifestyle taught at Green Dream Family Camp.

Fidel announced he was going to school tomorrow, and Mrs. Joplin told him no, he could link to E-class as usual, and Fidel claimed he could not concentrate at home, and Mrs. Joplin said he was trying to get out of his chores. While they were arguing, Tree nudged my leg and shot me a *let's leave* look. I nodded.

''Excuse us.'' She pushed back her chair. ''Mr. Boy has got to go home soon.''

Mrs. Joplin pointed for her to stay. ''You wait until your father gets back,'' she said. ''Tell me, Mr. Boy, have you lived in New Canaan long?''

''All my life,'' I said.

''How old did you say you were?''

''Mama, he's twenty-five,'' said Tree. ''I told you.''

''And what do you do for a living?''

''*Mama,* you promised.''

''Nothing,'' I said. ''I'm lucky, I guess. I don't need to worry about money. If you didn't need to work, would you?''

''Everybody needs work to do,'' Mrs. Joplin said. ''Work makes us real. Unless you have work to do and people who love you, you don't exist.''

Talk about twentieth-century humanist goop! At another time in another place, I probably would have snapped, but now the words would not come. My brain had turned into a flower; all I could think were daisy thoughts. The Joplins were such a strange combination of fast-forward and rewind. I could not tell what they wanted from me.

"Seventeen dollars and ninety-nine cents," said Mr. Joplin, returning from the storefront. "What's going on in here?" He glanced at his wife, and some signal that I did not catch passed between them. He circled the table, came up behind me, and laid his heavy hands on my shoulders. I shuddered; I thought for a moment he meant to strangle me.

"I'm not going to hurt you, Peter," he said. "Before you go, I have something to say."

"*Daddy.*" Tree squirmed in her chair. Fidel looked uncomfortable too, as if he guessed what was coming.

"Sure." I did not have much choice.

The weight on my shoulders eased but did not entirely go away. "You should feel the ache in this boy, Ladonna."

"I know," said Mrs. Joplin.

"Hard as plastic." Mr. Joplin touched the muscles corded along my neck. "You get too hard, you snap." He set his thumbs at the base of my skull and kneaded with an easy circular motion. "Your body isn't some machine that you've downloaded into. It's alive. Real. You have to learn to listen to it. That's why we smoke. Hear these muscles? They're screaming." He let his hand slide down my shoulders. "Now listen." His fingertips probed along my upper spine. "Hear that? Your muscles stay tense because you don't trust anyone. You always have to be ready to take a hit, and you can't tell where it's coming from. You're rigid and angry and scared. Reality . . . your body is speaking to you."

His voice was as big and warm as his hands. Tree was giving him a look that could boil water, but the way he touched me made too much sense to resist.

"We don't mind helping you ease the strain. That's the way Mrs. Joplin and I are. That's the way we brought the kids up. But first you have to admit you're hurting. And then you have to respect us enough to take what we have to give. I don't feel that in you, Peter. You're not ready to give up your pain. You just want us poor stiffs to admire how hard it's made you. We haven't got time for that kind of shit, okay? You learn to listen to yourself and you'll be welcome around here. We'll even call you Mr. Boy, even though it's a damn stupid name."

No one spoke for a moment.

"Sorry, Tree," he said. "We've embarrassed you again. But we love you, so you're stuck with us." I could feel it in his hands when he chuckled. "I suppose I do get carried away sometimes."

"Sometimes?" said Fidel. Tree just smoldered.

"It's late," said Mrs. Joplin. "Let him go now, Jamaal. His mama's sending a car over."

Mr. Joplin stepped back, and I almost fell off my chair from leaning against him. I stood, shakily. "Thanks for dinner."

Tree stalked through the greenhouse to the rear exit, her hairworks glittering against her bare back. I had to trot to keep up with her. There was no car in sight, so we waited at the doorway and I put on my clothes.

"I can't take much more of this." She stared through the little wire-glass window in the door, like a prisoner plotting her escape. "I mean, he's not a psychologist or a great philosopher or whatever the hell he thinks he is. He's just a pompous mall drone."

"He's not that bad." Actually, I understood what her father had said to me; it was scary. "I like your family."

"You don't have to live with them!" She kept watching at the door. "They promised they'd behave with you; I should have known better. This happens every time I bring someone home." She puffed an imaginary pipe, imitating her father. "Think what you're doing to yourself, you poor fool, and say, isn't it just too bad about modern life? Love, love, love—*fuck!*" She turned to me. "I'm sick of it. People are going to think I'm as sappy and thickheaded as my parents."

"I don't."

"You're lucky. You're rich and your mom leaves you alone. You're New Canaan. My folks are Elkhart, Indiana."

"Being New Canaan is nothing to brag about. So what are you?"

"Not a Joplin." She shook her head. "Not much longer, anyway; I'm eighteen in February. I think your car's here." She held out her arms and hugged me good-bye. "Sorry you had to sit through that. Don't drop me, okay? I like you, Mr. Boy." She did not let go for a while.

Dropping her had never occurred to me; I was not thinking of anything at all except the silkiness of her skin, the warmth of her body. Her breath whispered through my hair and her nipples brushed my ribs and then she kissed me. Just on the cheek, but the damage was done. I was stunted. I was not supposed to feel this way about anyone.

Comrade was waiting in the backseat. We rode home in silence; I had nothing to say to him. He would not understand—none of my friends would. They would warn me that all she wanted was to spend some of my money. Or they would make bad jokes about the nudity or the Joplins' mushy realism. No way I could explain the innocence of the way they touched one another. *The old man did what to you?* Yeah, and if I wanted a hug at home who was I supposed to ask? Comrade? Lovey? The greeter? Was I supposed to climb up to the head and fall asleep against Mom's doorbone, waiting for it to open, like I used to do when I was really a kid?

The greeter was her usual nonstick self when I got home. She was so glad to see me and she wanted to know where I had been and if I had a good time and if I wanted Cook to make me a snack? Around. Yes. No.

She said the bank had called about some problem with one of the cash cards she had given me, a security glitch that they had taken care of and were very sorry about. Did I know about it and did I need a new card and would twenty thousand be enough? Yes. Please. Thanks.

And that was it. I found myself resenting Mom because she did not have to care about losing sixteen or twenty or fifty thousand dollars. And she had reminded me of my problems when all I wanted to think of was Tree. She was no help to me, never had been. I had things so twisted around that I almost told her about Montross myself, just to get a reaction. Here some guy had tapped our files and threatened my life, and she asked if I wanted a snack. Why keep me around if she was going to pay so little attention? I wanted to shock her, to make her take me seriously.

But I did not know how.

The roombrain woke me. "Stennie's calling."

"Mmm."

"Talk to me, Mr. Party Boy." A window opened; he was in his car. "You dead or alive?"

"Asleep." I rolled over. "Time is it?"

"Ten-thirty and I'm bored. Want me to come get you now, or should I meet you there?"

"Wha . . . ?"

"Happy's. Don't tell me you forgot. They're doing a *piano.*"

"Who cares?" I crawled out of bed and slouched into the bathroom.

"She says she's asking Tree Joplin," Stennie called after me.

"Asking her what?" I came out.

"To the party."

"Is she going?"

"She's your cush." He gave me a toothy smile. "Call back when you're ready. Later." He faded.

"She left a message," said the roombrain. "Half hour ago."

"Tree? You got me up for Stennie and not for her?"

"He's on the list, she's not. Happy called, too."

"Comrade should've told you. Where is he?" Now I was grouchy. "She's on the list, okay? Give me playback."

Tree seemed pleased with herself. "Hi, this is me. I got myself invited to a smash party this afternoon. You want to go?" She faded.

"That's all? Call her!"

"Both her numbers are busy; I'll set redial. I found Comrade; he's on another line. You want Happy's message?"

"No. Yes."

"You promised, Mr. Boy." Happy giggled. "Look, you really, really don't want to miss this. Stennie's coming, and he said I should ask Joplin if I wanted you here. So you've got no excuse."

Someone tugged at her. "Stop that! Sorry, I'm being molested by a thick . . ." She batted at her assailant. "Mr. Boy, did I tell you that this Japanese reporter is coming to shoot a vid? What?" She turned off camera. "Sure, just like on the nature channel. Wildlife of America. We're all going to be famous. In Japan! This is history, Mr. Boy. And you're . . ."

Her face froze as the redial program finally linked to the Green Dream. The roombrain brought Tree up in a new window. "Oh, hi," she said. "You rich boys sleep late."

"What's this about Happy's?"

"She invited me." Tree was recharging her hairworks with a red brush. "I said yes. Something wrong?"

Comrade slipped into the room; I shushed him. "You sure you want to go to a smash party? Sometimes they get a little crazy."

She aimed the brush at me. "You've been to smash parties before. You survived."

"Sure, but . . ."

"Well, I haven't. All I know is that everybody at school is talking about this one, and I want to see what it's about."

"You tell your parents you're going?"

"Are you kidding? They'd just say it was too dangerous. What's the matter, Mr. Boy, are you scared? Come on, it'll be extreme."

"She's right. You *should* go," said Comrade.

"Is that Comrade?" Tree said. "You tell him, Comrade!"

I glared at him. "Okay, okay, I guess I'm outnumbered. Stennie said he'd drive. You want us to pick you up?"

She did.

I flew at Comrade as soon as Tree faded. "Don't you ever do that again!" I shoved him, and he bumped up against the wall. "I ought to throw you to Montross."

"You know, I just finished chatting with him." Comrade stayed calm and made no move to defend himself. "He wants to meet—the three of us, face to face. He suggested Happy's."

"He suggested . . . I told you not to talk to him."

"I know." He shrugged. "Anyway, I think we should do it."

"Who gave you permission to think?"

"You did. What if we give him the picture back and open our files and then I grovel, say I'm sorry, it'll never happen again, *blah, blah, blah.* Maybe we can even buy him off. What have we got to lose?"

"You can't bribe software. And what if he decides to snatch us?" I told Comrade about the gypsy with the penlight. "You want Tree mixed up in this?"

All the expression drained from his face. He did not say anything at first, but I had watched his subroutines long enough to know that when he looked this blank, he was shaken. "So we take a risk, maybe we can get it over with," he said. "He's not interested in Tree, and I won't let anything happen to you. Why do you think your mom bought me?"

Happy Lurdane lived on the former estate of Philip Johnson, a notorious twentieth-century architect. In his will Johnson had arranged to turn his compound into the Philip Johnson Memorial Museum, but after he died his work went out of fashion. The glass skyscrapers in the cities did not age well; they started to fall apart or were torn down because they wasted energy. Nobody visited the museum, and it went bankrupt. The Lurdanes had bought the property and made some changes.

Johnson had designed all the odd little buildings on the estate himself. The main house was a shoebox of glass with no inside walls; near it stood a windowless brick guest house. On a pond below was a dock that looked like a Greek temple. Past the circular swimming pool near the houses were two galleries that had once held Johnson's art collection, long since sold off. In Johnson's day, the scattered buildings had been connected only by paths, which made the compound impossible in the frosty Connecticut winters. The Lurdanes had enclosed the paths in clear tubes and commuted in a golf cart.

Stennie told his Alpha not to wait, since the lot was already full and cars were parked well down the driveway. Five of us squeezed out of the car: me, Tree, Comrade, Stennie, and Janet Hoyt. Janet wore a Yankees jersey over pin-striped shorts, Tree was a little overdressed in her silver jaunts, I had on baggies padded to make me seem bigger, and Comrade wore his usual window coat. Stennie lugged a box with his swag for the party.

Freddy the Teddy let us in. "Stennie and Mr. Boy!" He reared back on his hindquarters and roared. "Glad I'm not going to be the only beastie here. Hi, Janet. Hi, I'm Freddy," he said to Tree. His pink tongue lolled. "Come in, this way. Fun starts right here. Some kids are swimming, and there's sex in the guest house. Everybody else is with Happy having lunch in the sculpture gallery."

The interior of the Glass House was bright and hard. Dark wood-block floor, some unfriendly furniture, huge panes of glass framed in black-painted steel. The few kids in the kitchen were passing an inhaler around and watching a microwave fill up with popcorn.

"I'm hot." Janet stuck the inhaler into her face and pressed. "Anybody want to swim? Tree?"

"Okay." Tree breathed in a polite dose and breathed out a giggle. "You?" she asked me.

"I don't think so." I was too nervous: I kept expecting someone to jump out and throw a net over me. "I'll watch."

"I'd swim with you," said Stennie, "but I promised Happy I'd bring her these party favors as soon as I arrived." He nudged the box with his foot. "Can you wait a few minutes?"

"Comrade and I will take them over." I grabbed the box and headed for the door, glad for the excuse to leave Tree behind while I went to find Montross. "Meet you at the pool."

The golf cart was gone, so we walked through the tube toward the sculpture gallery. "You have the picture?" I said.

Comrade patted the pocket of his window coat.

The tube was not air-conditioned, and the afternoon sun pounded us through the optical plastic. There was no sound inside; even our footsteps were swallowed by the astroturf. The box got heavier. We passed the entrance to the old painting gallery, which looked like a bomb shelter. Finally I had to break the silence. ''I feel strange, being here,'' I said. ''Not just because of the thing with Montross. I really think I lost myself last time I got stunted. Not sure who I am anymore, but I don't think I belong with these kids.''

''People change, *tovarisch,*'' said Comrade. ''Even you.''

''Have I changed?''

He smiled. ''Now that you've got a cush, your own mother wouldn't recognize you.''

''You know what your problem is?'' I grinned and bumped up against him on purpose. ''You're jealous of Tree.''

''Shouldn't I be?''

''Oh, I don't know. I can't tell if Tree likes who I was or who I might be. She's changing, too. She's so hot to break away from her parents, become part of this town. Except that what she's headed for probably isn't worth the trip. I feel like I should protect her, but that means guarding her from people like me, except I don't think I'm Mom's Mr. Boy anymore. Does that make sense?''

''Sure.'' He gazed straight ahead, but all the heads on his window coat were scoping me. ''Maybe when you're finished changing, you won't need me.''

The thought had occurred to me. For years he had been the only one I could talk to, but as we closed on the gallery, I did not know what to say. I shook my head. ''I just feel strange.''

And then we arrived. The sculpture gallery was designed for show-offs: short flights of steps and a series of stagy balconies descended around the white-brick exterior walls to the central exhibition area. The space was open so you could chat with your little knot of friends and, at the same time, spy on everyone else. About thirty kids were eating pizza and Crispix off paper plates. At the bottom of the stairs, as advertised, was a black upright piano. Piled beside it was the rest of the swag. A Boston rocker, a case of green Coke bottles, a Virgin Mary in half a blue bathtub, a huge conch shell, china and crystal and assorted smaller treasures, including a four-thousand-year-old ceramic hippo. There were real animals too, in cages near the gun rack: a turkey, some stray dogs and cats, turtles, frogs, assorted rodents.

I was threading my way across the first balcony when I was stopped by the Japanese reporter, who was wearing microcam eyes.

''Excuse me, please,'' he said, ''I am Matsuo Shikibu, and I will be recording this event today for Nippon Hoso Kyokai. Public telelink of Japan." He smiled and bowed. When his head came up, the red light between his lenses was on. "You are . . . ?"

"Raskolnikov," said Comrade, edging between me and the camera. "Rodeo Raskolnikov." He took Shikibu's hand and pumped it. "And my associate here, Mr. Peter Pan." He turned as if to introduce me, but we had long since choreographed this dodge. As I sidestepped past, he kept shielding me from the reporter with his body. "We're friends of the bride," Comrade said, "and we're really excited to be making new friends in your country. Banzai, Nippon!"

I slipped by them and scooted downstairs. Happy was basking by the piano; she spotted me as I reached the middle landing.

"Mr. Boy!" It was not so much a greeting as an announcement. She was wearing a body mike, and her voice boomed over the sound system. "You made it."

The stream of conversation rippled momentarily, a few heads turned, and then the party flowed on. Shikibu rushed to the edge of the upper balcony and caught me with a long shot.

I set the box on the Steinway. "Stennie brought this."

She opened it eagerly. "Look, everyone!" She held up a stack of square cardboard albums, about thirty centimeters on a side. There were pictures of musicians on the front, words on the back. "What are they?" she asked me.

"Phonograph records," said the kid next to Happy. "It's how they used to play music before digital."

"Erroll Garner, *Soliloquy,*" she read aloud. "What's this? D-j-a-n-g-o Reinhardt and the American Jazz Giants. Sounds scary." She giggled as she pawed quickly through the other albums. Handy, Ellington, Hawkins, Parker, three Armstrongs. One was *Piano Rags by Scott Joplin.* Stennie's bent idea of a joke? Maybe the lizard was smarter than he looked. Happy pulled a black plastic record out of one sleeve and scratched a fingernail across little ridges. "Oh, a nonslip surface."

The party had a limited attention span. When she realized she had lost her audience, she shut off the mike and put the box with the rest of the swag. "We have to start at four, no matter what. There's so much stuff." The kid who knew about records wormed into our conversation; Happy put her hand on his shoulder. "Mr. Boy, do you know my friend Weldon?" she said. "He's new."

Montross grinned. "We met on Playroom."

"Where *is* Stennie, anyway?" said Happy.

"Swimming," I said. Montross appeared to be in his late teens. Bigger than me—everyone was bigger than me. He wore green shorts and a window shirt of surfers at Waimea. He looked like everybody; there was nothing about him to remember. I considered bashing the smirk off his face, but it was a bad idea. If he was software, he could not feel anything and I would probably break my hand on his temporary chassis. "Got to go. I promised Stennie I'd meet him back at the pool. Hey, Weldon, want to tag along?"

"You come right back," said Happy. "We're starting at four. Tell everyone."

We avoided the tube and cut across the lawn for privacy. Comrade handed Montross the envelope. He slid the photograph out, and I had one last glimpse. This time the dead man left me cold. In fact, I was embarrassed. Although he kept a straight face, I knew what Montross was thinking about me. Maybe he was right. I wished he would put the picture away. He was not one of us; he could not understand. I wondered if Tree had come far enough yet to appreciate corpse porn.

"It's the only copy," Comrade said.

"All right." Finally Montross crammed it into the pocket of his shorts.

"You tapped our files; you know it's true."

"So?"

"So enough!" I said. "You have what you wanted."

"I've already explained." Montross was being patient. "Getting this back doesn't close the case. I have to take preventive measures."

"Meaning you turn Comrade into a carrot."

"Meaning I repair him. You're the one who took him to the chop shop. Deregulated wiseguys are dangerous. Maybe not to you, but certainly to property and probably to other people. It's a straightforward procedure. He'll be fully functional afterward."

"Plug your procedure, jack. We're leaving."

Both wiseguys stopped. "I thought you agreed," said Montross.

"Let's go, Comrade." I grabbed his arm, but he shook me off.

"Where?" he said.

"Anywhere! Just so I never have to listen to this again." I pulled again, angry at Comrade for stalling. Your wiseguy is supposed to anticipate your needs, do whatever you want.

"But we haven't even tried to . . ."

"Forget it then. I give up." I pushed him toward Montross. "You want to chat, fine, go right ahead. Let him rip the top of your head off while you're at it, but I'm not sticking around to watch."

I checked the pool, but Tree, Stennie, and Janet had already gone. I went through the Glass House and caught up with them in the tube to the sculpture gallery.

"Can I talk to you?" I put my arm around Tree's waist, just like I had seen grown-ups do. "In private." I could tell she was annoyed to be separated from Janet. "We'll catch up." I waved Stennie on. "See you over there."

She waited until they were gone. "What?" Her hair, slick from swimming, left dark spots where it brushed her silver jaunts.

"I want to leave. We'll call my mom's car." She did not look happy. "I'll take you anywhere you want to go."

"But we just got here. Give it a chance."

"I've been to too many of these things."

"Then you shouldn't have come."

Silence. I wanted to tell her about Montross—everything—but not here. Anyone could come along and the tube was so hot. I was desperate to get her away, so I lied. "Believe me, you're not going to like this. I know." I tugged at her waist. "Sometimes even I think smash parties are too much."

"We've had this discussion before," she said. "Obviously you weren't listening. I don't need you to decide for me whether I'm going to like something, Mr. Boy. I have two parents too many; I don't need another." She stepped away from me. "Hey, I'm sorry if you're having a bad time. But do you really need to spoil it for me?" She turned and strode down the tube toward the gallery, her beautiful hair slapping against her back. I watched her go.

"But I'm in trouble," I muttered to the empty tube—and then was disgusted with myself because I did not have the guts to say it to Tree. I was too scared she would not care. I stood there, sweating. For a moment the stink of doubt filled my nostrils. Then I followed her in. I could not abandon her to the extremists.

The gallery was jammed now; maybe a hundred kids

swarmed across the balconies and down the stairs. Some perched along the edges, their feet scuffing the white brick. Happy had turned up the volume.

". . . according to *Guinness,* was set at the University of Oklahoma in Norman, Oklahoma, in 2012. Three minutes and fourteen seconds." The crowd rumbled in disbelief. "The challenge states each piece must be small enough to pass through a hole thirty centimeters in diameter."

I worked my way to an opening beside a rubber tree. Happy posed on the keyboard of the piano. Freddy the Teddy and the gorilla brothers, Mike and Bubba, lined up beside her. "No mechanical tools are allowed." She gestured at an armory of axes, sledgehammers, spikes, and crowbars laid out on the floor. A paper plate spun across the room. I could not see Tree.

"This piano is over two hundred years old," Happy continued, "which means the white keys are ivory." She plunked a note. "Dead elephants!" Everybody heaved a sympathetic *awww.* "The blacks are ebony, hacked from the rain forest." Another note, less reaction. "It deserves to die."

Applause. Comrade and I spotted each other at almost the same time. He and Montross stood toward the rear of the lower balcony. He gestured for me to come down; I ignored him.

"Do you boys have anything to say?" Happy said.

"Yeah." Freddy hefted an ax. "Let's make landfill."

I ducked around the rubber tree and heard the *crack* of splitting wood, the iron groan of a piano frame yielding its last music. The spectators hooted approval. As I bumped past kids, searching for Tree, the instrument's death cry made me think of taking a hammer to Montross. If fights broke out, no one would care if Comrade and I dragged him outside. I wanted to beat him until he shuddered and came unstrung and his works glinted in the thudding August light. It would make me feel extreme again. *Crunch!* Kids shrieked, "Go, go, go!" The party was lifting off and taking me with it.

"You are Mr. Boy Cage." Abruptly Shikibu's microcam eyes were in my face. "We know your famous mother." He had to shout to be heard. "I have a question."

"Go away."

"Thirty seconds." A girl's voice boomed over the speakers.

"U.S. and Japan are very different, yes?" He pressed closer. "We honor ancestors, our past. You seem to hate so much." He gestured at the gallery. "Why?"

"Maybe we're spoiled." I barged past him.

I saw Freddy swing a sledgehammer at the exposed frame. *Clang!* A chunk of twisted iron clattered across the brick floor, trailing broken strings. Happy scooped the mess up and shoved it through a thirty-centimeter hole drilled in an upright sheet of particle board.

The timekeeper called out again. *"One minute."* I had come far enough around the curve of the stairs to see her.

"Treemonisha!"

She glanced up, her face alight with pleasure, and waved. I was frightened for her. She was climbing into the same box I needed to break out of. So I rushed down the stairs to rescue her—little boy knight in shining armor—and ran right into Comrade's arms.

"I've decided," he said. *"Mnye vcyaw ostoyeblo."*

"Great." I had to get to Tree. "Later, okay?" When I tried to go by, he picked me up. I started thrashing. It was the first fight of the afternoon and I lost. He carried me over to Montross. The gallery was in an uproar.

"All set," said Montross. "I'll have to borrow him for a while. I'll drop him off tonight at your mom. Then we're done."

"Done?" I kept trying to get free, but Comrade crushed me against him.

"It's what you want." His body was so hard. "And what your mom wants."

"Mom? She doesn't even know."

"She knows everything," Comrade said. "She watches you constantly. What else does she have to do all day?" He let me go. "Remember you said I was sloppy getting the picture? I wasn't; it was a clean operation. Only someone tipped Datasafe off."

"But she promised. Besides, that makes no . . ."

"Two minutes," Tree called.

". . . but he threatened me," I said. "He was going to blow me up. Needle me in the mall."

"We wouldn't do that." Montross spread his hands innocently. "It's against the law."

"Yeah? Well, then, drop dead, jack." I poked a finger at him. "Deal's off."

"No, it's not," said Comrade. "It's too late. This isn't about the picture anymore, Mr. Boy; it's about you. You weren't supposed to change, but you did. Maybe they botched the last stunting, maybe it's Treemonisha. Whatever, you've outgrown me, the way I am now. So I have to change too, or else I'll keep getting in your way."

He always had everything under control; it made me crazy. He was too good at running my life. "You should have told me Mom turned you in." *Crash!* I felt like the crowd was inside my head, screaming.

"You could've figured it out, if you wanted to. Besides, if I had said anything, your mom wouldn't have bothered to be subtle. She would've squashed me. She still might, even though I'm being fixed. Only by then I won't care. *Rosproyebi tvayou mat!*"

I heard Tree finishing the count. ". . . *twelve, thirteen, fourteen!*" No record today. Some kids began to boo, others laughed. "Time's up, you losers!"

I glared at the two wiseguys. Montross was busy emulating sincerity. Comrade found a way to grin for me, the same smirk he always wore when he tortured the greeter. "It's easier this way."

Easier. My life was too plugging easy. I had never done anything important by myself. Not even grow up. I wanted to smash something.

"Okay," I said. "You asked for it."

Comrade turned to Montross and they shook hands. I thought next they might clap one another on the shoulder and whistle as they strolled off into the sunset together. I felt like puking. "Have fun," said Comrade. "*Da svedanya.*"

"Sure." Betraying Comrade, my best friend, brought me both pain and pleasure at once—but not enough to satisfy the shrieking wildness within me. The party was just starting.

Happy stood beaming beside the ruins of the Steinway. Although nothing of what was left was more than half a meter tall, Freddy, Mike, and Bubba had given up now that the challenge was lost. Kids were already surging down the stairs to claim their share of the swag. I went along with them.

"Don't worry," announced Happy. "Plenty for everyone. Come take what you like. Remember, guns and animals outside, if you want to hunt. The safeties won't release unless you go through the door. Watch out for one another, people, we don't want anyone shot."

A bunch of kids were wrestling over the turkey cage; one of them staggered backward and knocked into me. "Gobble, gobble," she said. I shoved her back.

"Mr. Boy! Over here." Tree, Stennie, and Janet were waiting on the far side of the gallery. As I crossed to them, Happy gave the sign and Stone Kinkaid hurled the four-thousand-year-old ceramic hippo against the wall. It shattered. Everybody cheered.

In the upper balconies, they were playing catch with a frog.

"You see who kept time?" said Janet.

"Didn't need to see," I said. "I could hear. They probably heard in Elkhart. So you like it, Tree?"

"It's about what I expected: dumb but fun. I don't think they. . . ." The frog sailed from the top balcony and splatted at our feet. Its legs twitched and guts spilled from its open mouth. I watched Tree's smile turn brittle. She seemed slightly embarrassed, as if she had just been told the price of something she could not afford.

"This is going to be a war zone soon," Stennie said.

"Yeah, let's fade." Janet towed Stennie to the stairs, swerving around the three boys lugging Our Lady of the Bathtub out to the firing range.

"Wait." I blocked Tree. "You're here, so you have to destroy something. Get with the program."

"I have to?" She seemed doubtful. "Oh, all right—but no animals."

A hail of antique Coke bottles crashed around Happy as she directed traffic at the dwindling swag heap. "Hey, people, please be very careful where you throw things." Her amplified voice blasted us as we approached. The first floor was a graveyard of broken glass and piano bones and bloody feathers. Most of the good stuff was already gone.

"Any records left?" I said.

Happy wobbled closer to me. "What?" She seemed punchy, as if stunned by the success of her own party.

"The box I gave you. From Stennie." She pointed; I spotted it under some cages and grabbed it. Tree and the others were on the stairs. Outside I could hear the crackle of small-arms fire. I caught up.

"Sir! Mr. Dinosaur, please." The press still lurked on the upper balcony. "Matsuo Shikibu, Japanese telelink NHK. Could I speak with you for a moment?"

"Excuse me, but this jack and I have some unfinished business." I handed Stennie the records and cut in front. He swayed and lashed his tail upward to counterbalance their weight.

"Remember me?" I bowed to Shikibu.

"My apologies if I offended . . ."

"Hey, Matsuo—can I call you Matsuo? This is your first smash party, right? Please, eyes on me. I want to explain why I was rude before. Help you understand the local customs. You see, we're kind of self-conscious here in the U.S. We don't like it when someone just watches while we play. You either join in or you're not one of us."

My little speech drew a crowd. "What's he talking about?" said Janet. She was shushed.

"So if you drop by our party and don't have fun, people resent you," I told him. "No one came here today to put on a show. This is who we are. What we believe in."

"Yeah!" Stennie was cheerleading for the extreme Mr. Boy of old. "Tell him." Too bad he did not realize it was his final appearance. What was Mr. Boy without his Comrade? "Make him feel some pain."

I snatched an album from the top of the stack, slipped the record out, and held it close to Shikibu's microcam eyes. "What does this say?"

He craned his neck to read the label. "John Coltrane, *Giant Steps.*"

"Very good." I grasped the record with both hands and raised it over my head for all to see. "We're not picky, Matsuo. We welcome everyone. Therefore today it is my honor to initiate you—and the home audience back on NHK. If you're still watching, you're part of this too." I broke the record over his head.

He yelped and staggered backward and almost tripped over a dead cat. Stone Kinkaid caught him and propped him up. "Congratulations," said Stennie, as he waved his claws at Japan. "You're all extremists now."

Shikibu gaped at me, his microcam eyes askew. A couple of kids clapped.

"There's someone else here who has not yet joined us." I turned on Tree. "Another spectator." Her smile faded.

"You leave her alone," said Janet. "What are you, crazy?"

"I'm not going to touch her." I held up empty hands. "No, I just want her to ruin something. That's why you came, isn't it, Tree? To get a taste?" I rifled through the box until I found what I wanted. "How about this?" I thrust it at her.

"Oh yeah," said Stennie, "I meant to tell you. . . ."

She took the record and scoped it briefly. When she glanced up at me, I almost lost my nerve.

"Matsuo Shikibu, meet Treemonisha Joplin." I clasped my hands behind my back so no one could see me tremble. "The great-great-great-granddaughter of the famous American composer, Scott Joplin. Yes, Japan, we're all celebrities here in New Canaan. Now please observe." I read the record for him. "*Piano*

Rags by Scott Joplin, Volume III. Who knows, this might be the last copy. We can only hope. So, what are you waiting for, Tree? You don't want to be a Joplin anymore? Just wait until your folks get a peek at this. We'll even send GD a copy. Go ahead, enjoy."

"Smash it!" The kids around us took up the chant. "Smash it!" Shikibu adjusted his lenses.

"You think I won't?" Tree pulled out the disk and threw the sleeve off the balcony. "This is a piece of junk, Mr. Boy." She laughed and then shattered the album against the wall. She held on to a shard. "It doesn't mean anything to me."

I heard Janet whisper. "What's going on?"

"I think they're having an argument."

"You want me to be your little dream cush." Tree tucked the piece of broken plastic into the pocket of my baggies. "The stiff from nowhere who knows nobody and does nothing without Mr. Boy. So you try to scare me off. You tell me you're so rich, you can afford to hate yourself. Stay home, you say, it's too dangerous, we're all crazy. Well, if you're so sure this is poison, how come you've still got your wiseguy and your cash cards? Are you going to move out of your mom, leave town, stop getting stunted? You're not giving it up, Mr. Boy, so why should I?"

Shikibu turned his camera eyes on me. No one spoke.

"You're right," I said. "She's right." I could not save anyone until I saved myself. I felt the wildness lifting me to it. I leapt onto the balcony wall and shouted for everyone to hear. "Shut up and listen, everybody! You're all invited to my place, okay?"

There was one last thing to smash.

"Stop this, Peter." The greeter no longer thought I was cute. "What're you doing?" She trembled as if the kids spilling into her were an infection.

"I thought you'd like to meet my friends," I said. A few had stayed behind with Happy, who had decided to sulk after I hijacked her guests. The rest had followed me home in a caravan so I could warn off the sentry robots. It was already a hall-of-fame bash. "Treemonisha Joplin, this is my mom. Sort of."

"Hi," Tree held out her hand uncertainly.

The greeter was no longer the human doormat. "Get them out of me." She was too jumpy to be polite. "Right now!"

Someone turned up a boombox. Skitter music filled the room

like a siren. Tree said something I could not hear. When I put a hand to my ear, she leaned close and said, "Don't be so mean, Mr. Boy. I think she's really frightened."

I grinned and nodded. "I'll tell Cook to make us some snacks."

Bubba and Mike carried boxes filled with the last of the swag and set them on the coffee table. Kids fanned out, running their hands along her wrinkled blood-hot walls, bouncing on the furniture. Stennie waved at me as he led a bunch upstairs for a tour. A leftover cat had gotten loose and was hissing and scratching underfoot. Some twisted kids had already stripped and were rolling in the floor hair, getting ready to have sex.

"Get dressed, you." The greeter kicked at them as she coiled her umbilical to keep it from being trampled. She retreated to her wall plug. "You're *hurting* me." Although her voice rose to a scream, only half a dozen kids heard her. She went limp and sagged to the floor.

The whole room seemed to throb, as if to some great heartbeat, and the lights went out. It took a while for someone to kill the sound on the boombox. "What's wrong?" Voices called out. "Mr. Boy? Lights."

Both doorbones swung open, and I saw a bughead silhouetted against the twilit sky. Shikibu in his microcams. "Party's over," Mom said over her speaker system. There was nervous laughter. "Leave before I call the cops. Peter, go to your room right now. I want to speak to you."

As the stampede began, I found Tree's hand. "Wait for me?" I pulled her close. "I'll only be a minute."

"What are you going to do?" She sounded frightened. It felt good to be taken so seriously.

"I'm moving out, chucking all this. I'm going to be a working stiff." I chuckled. "Think your dad would give me a job?"

"Look out, dumbscut! Hey, *hey*. Don't push!"

Tree dragged me out of the way. "You're crazy."

"I know. That's why I have to get out of Mom."

"Listen," she said, "you've never been poor, you have no idea. . . . Only a rich kid would think it's easy being a stiff. Just go up, apologize, tell her it won't happen again. Then change things later on, if you want. Believe me, life will be a lot simpler if you hang on to the money."

"I can't. Will you wait?"

"You want me to tell you it's okay to be stupid, is that it? Well, I've *been* poor, Mr. Boy, and still am, and I don't recommend it. So don't expect me to stand around and clap while you throw away something I've always wanted.'' She spun away from me, and I lost her in the darkness. I wanted to catch up with her, but I knew I had to do Mom now or I would lose my nerve.

As I was fumbling my way upstairs, I heard stragglers coming down. ''On your right,'' I called. Bodies nudged by me.

''Mr. Boy, is that you?'' I recognized Stennie's voice.

''He's gone,'' I said.

Seven flights up, the lights were on. Nanny waited on the landing outside my rooms, her umbilical stretched nearly to its limit. She was the only remote that was physically able to get to my floor, and this was as close as she could come.

It had been a while since I had seen her; Mom did not use her much anymore and I rarely visited, even though the nursery was only one flight down. But this was the remote who used to pick me up when I cried and who had changed my diapers and who taught me how to turn on my roombrain. She had skin so pale you could almost see veins and long black hair piled high on her head. I never thought of her as having a body because she always wore dark turtlenecks and long woolen skirts and silky panty hose. Nanny was a smile and warm hands and the smell of fresh pillowcases. Once upon a time, I thought her the most beautiful creature in the world. Back then I would have done anything she said.

She was not smiling now. ''I don't know how you expect me to trust you anymore, Peter.'' Nanny had never been a very good scold. ''Those brats were out of control. I can't let you put me in danger this way.''

''If you wanted someone to trust, maybe you shouldn't have had me stunted. You got exactly what you ordered, the never-ending kid. Well, kids don't have to be responsible.''

''What do you mean, what I ordered? It's what you wanted, too.''

''Is it? Did you ever ask? I was only ten, the first time, too young to know better. For a long time I did it to please you. Getting stunted was the only thing I did that seemed important to you. But *you* never explained. You never sat me down and said, 'This is the life you'll have and this is what you'll miss and this is how you'll feel about it.' ''

''You want to grow up, is that it?'' She was trying to threaten me. ''You want to work and worry and get old and die someday?'' She had no idea what we were talking about.

"I can't live this way anymore, Nanny."

At first she acted stunned, as if I had spoken in Albanian. Then her expression hardened when she realized she had lost her hold on me. She was ugly when she was angry. "They put you up to this." Her gaze narrowed in accusation. "That little black cush you've been seeing. Those realists!"

I had always managed to hide my anger from Mom. Right up until then. "How do you know about her?" I had never told her about Tree.

"Peter, they live in a mall!"

Comrade was right. "You've been spying on me." When she did not deny it, I went berserk. "You liar." I slammed my fist into her belly. "You said you wouldn't watch." She staggered and fell onto her umbilical, crimping it. As she twitched on the floor, I pounced. "You promised." I slapped her face. "Promised." I hit her again. Her hair had come undone and her eyes rolled back in their sockets and her face was slack. She made no effort to protect herself. Mom was retreating from this remote too, but I was not going to let her get away.

"Mom!" I rolled off Nanny. "I'm coming up, Mom! You hear? Get ready." I was crying; it had been a long time since I had cried. Not something Mr. Boy did.

I scrambled up to the long landing at the shoulders. At one end another circular stairway wound up into the torch; in the middle, four steps led into the neck. It was the only doorbone I had never seen open; I had no idea how to get through.

"Mom, I'm here." I pounded. "Mom! You hear me?"

Silence.

"Let me in, Mom." I smashed myself against the doorbone. Pain branched through my shoulder like lightning, but it felt great because Mom shuddered from the impact. I backed up and, in a frenzy, hurled myself again. Something warm dripped on my cheek. She was bleeding from the hinges. I aimed a vicious kick at the doorbone, and it banged open. I went through.

For years I had imagined that if only I could get into the head I could meet my real mother. Touch her. I had always wondered what she looked like; she got reshaped just after I was born. When I was little I used to think of her as a magic princess glowing with fairy light. Later I pictured her as one or another of my friends' moms, only better dressed. After I had started getting twanked, I was afraid she might be just a brain floating in nutrient solution, like in some pricey memory bank. All wrong.

The interior of the head was dark and absolutely freezing.

There was no sound except for the hum of refrigeration units. "Mom?" My voice echoed in the empty space. I stumbled and caught myself against a smooth wall. Not skin, like everywhere else in Mom—metal. The tears froze on my face.

"There's nothing for you here," she said. "This is a clean room. You're compromising it. You must leave immediately."

Sterile environment, metal walls, the bitter cold that superconductors needed. I did not need to see. No one lived here. It had never occurred to me that there was no Mom to touch. She had downloaded, become an electron ghost tripping icy logic gates. "How long have you been dead?"

"This isn't where you belong," she said.

I shivered. "How long?"

"Go away," she said.

So I did. I had to. I could not stay very long in her secret place, or I would die of the cold.

As I reeled down the stairs, Mom herself seemed to shift beneath my feet and I saw her as if she were a stranger. Dead—and I had been living in a tomb. I ran past Nanny; she still sprawled where I had left her. All those years I had loved her, I had been in love with death. Mom had been sucking life from me the way her refrigerators stole the warmth from my body.

Now I knew there was no way I could stay, no matter what anyone said. I knew it was not going to be easy leaving, and not just because of the money. For a long time Mom had been my entire world. But I could not let her use me to pretend she was alive, or I would end up like her.

I realized now that the door had always stayed locked because Mom had to hide what she had become. If I wanted, I could have destroyed her. Downloaded intelligences have no more rights than cars or wiseguys. Mom was legally dead and I was her only heir. I could have had her shut off, her body razed. But somehow it was enough to go, to walk away from my inheritance. I was scared, and yet with every step I felt lighter. Happier. Extremely free.

I had not expected to find Tree waiting at the doorbone, chatting with Comrade as if nothing had happened. "I just had to see if you were really the biggest fool in the world," she said.

"Out." I pulled her through the door. "Before I change my mind."

Comrade started to follow us. "No, not you." I turned and stared back at the heads on his window coat. I had not intended to see him again; I had wanted to be gone before Montross returned him. "Look, I'm giving you back to Mom. She needs you more than I do."

If he had argued, I might have given in. The old unregulated Comrade would have said something. But he just slumped a little and nodded and I knew that he was dead, too. The thing in front of me was another ghost. He and Mom were two of a kind. "Pretend you're her kid, maybe she'll like that." I patted his shoulder.

"Prekrassnaya ideya," he said. *"Spaceba."*

"You're welcome," I said.

Tree and I trotted together down the long driveway. Robot sentries crossed the lawn and turned their spotlights on us. I wanted to tell her she was right. I had probably just done the single most irresponsible thing of my life—and I had high standards. Still, I could not imagine how being poor could be worse than being rich and hating yourself. I had seen enough of what it was like to be dead. It was time to try living.

"Are we going someplace, Mr. Boy?" Tree squeezed my hand. "Or are we just wandering around in the dark?"

"Mr. Boy is a damn stupid name, don't you think?" I laughed. "Call me Pete." I felt like a kid again.